A reporter witnesses a legendary Ranger in action and gets the story of a lifetime, in **L. J. Washburn's** "Top o' The Hill."

Elizabeth Fackler follows a young Ranger on a personal quest for justice—one that leads him to a mysterious beauty and a deadly showdown in the dusty Mexican village of "Corazón."

Brendan DuBois's "To Kill a Ranger" finds two cocky outlaws ready to go up against a retired Texas Ranger, only to end up facing something even greater than the lawman—his legend.

Read these stories and much more in . . .

Texas Rangers

Texas Rangers

Edited by
Ed Gorman
and Martin H. Greenberg

BERKLEY BOOKS, NEW YORK

THE BERKLEY PUBLISHING GROUP
Published by the Penguin Group
Penguin Group (USA) Inc.
375 Hudson Street, New York, New York 10014, USA
Penguin Group (Canada), 10 Alcorn Avenue, Toronto, Ontario M4V 3B2, Canada
(a division of Pearson Penguin Canada Inc.)
Penguin Books Ltd., 80 Strand, London WC2R 0RL, England
Penguin Group Ireland, 25 St. Stephen's Green, Dublin 2, Ireland (a division of Penguin Books
Ltd.)
Penguin Group (Australia), 250 Camberwell Road, Camberwell, Victoria 3124, Australia
(a division of Pearson Australia Group Pty. Ltd.)
Penguin Books India Pvt. Ltd., 11 Community Centre, Panchsheel Park, New Delhi–110 017,
India
Penguin Group (NZ), Cnr. Airborne and Rosedale Roads, Albany, Auckland 1310, New Zealand
(a division of Pearson New Zealand Ltd.)
Penguin Books (South Africa) (Pty.) Ltd., 24 Sturdee Avenue, Rosebank, Johannesburg 2196,
South Africa

Penguin Books Ltd., Registered Offices: 80 Strand, London WC2R 0RL, England

TEXAS RANGERS

A Berkley Book / published by arrangement with the editors

PRINTING HISTORY
Berkley edition / September 2004

Copyright © 2004 by Tekno Books and Ed Gorman.
A complete listing of the individual copyrights and permissions can be found on pages 307–308.

ISBN: 0-425-19680-1

BERKLEY®
Berkley Books are published by The Berkley Publishing Group,
a division of Penguin Group (USA) Inc.,
375 Hudson Street, New York, New York 10014.
BERKLEY is a registered trademark of Penguin Group (USA) Inc.
The "B" design is a trademark belonging to Penguin Group (USA) Inc.

PRINTED IN THE UNITED STATES OF AMERICA

10 9 8 7 6 5 4 3 2 1

Contents

Introduction

～◦◦◦～

THE LONE RANGER. Zorro. Matt Dillon. Exciting Western legends.

Well, not legends exactly. Because they never existed. Except in our imaginations.

What loyalty they inspired. I'm told I always insisted on eating a bowl of Cheerios when the Lone Ranger came on the radio. And I'll never forget my box-top pair of Tom Mix glow-in-the-dark spurs. Just like the real cowhands wore.

I guess what makes the Texas Rangers so much fun to read about is that they actually existed. And exist today.

It was one thing for the Lone Ranger and Tonto to clear out a gang of bank robbers in the dusty streets of radio and television. It was quite another—in the baking sun; and often outgunned—to do it in reality.

When you read even the briefest history of the Texas Rangers, you'll see why the mists of myth surround them. They did things not even pulp-fiction heroes dreamed of doing. And some of them died doing it. That's the big difference, of course, between fiction and reality. In reality, people get killed.

In this book you'll find a collection of short stories that deal with virtually every aspect and era of the Texas Rangers. A lot of action, a bit of humor, even a bit of romance—but more than anything else, roughneck history. Taming a land as varied and violent as historical Texas sure wasn't for lily-livers.

So ease back that Stetson; put those spur-jingling boots up for a spell; and prepare yourself for a wild ride through some of the most exciting Western stories you've ever read.

—Ed Gorman

Down Sonora Way

by Louis L'Amour

Louis L'Amour (1908–1988) was the most successful Western writer of all time, selling 15,000–20,000 books a day at the height of his popularity. He wrote the kind of action fiction beloved by so many generations of Americans, with strong heroes, evil villains, proud, energetic heroines, and all of the excitement and danger that the West represented. His novels include such masterpieces as *Hondo*, *Shalako*, *Down the Long Hills*, *The Cherokee Trail*, and *Last of the Breed*. His most famous series was the Sacketts saga, later made into several excellent television movies.

DOWN ON HIS stomach in the sand behind his dead horse, Chick Bowdrie waited for the sun to go down. It was a hot Sonora sun and the nearest shade was sixty yards away in a notch of the Sierra de Espuelas, where Tensleep Mooney waited with a Winchester.

Bowdrie had scooped out sand to dig himself a few inches deeper below the surface, but a bullet burn across the top of his shoulder and two double holes in his black flat-crowned hat demonstrated both the accuracy and the intent behind Tensleep's shooting.

Five hundred miles behind them in Texas were two dead men, the seventh and eighth on the list of Mooney's killings, and Bowdrie was showing an understandable reluctance to become number nine.

The sun was hot, Bowdrie's lips were cracked and dry, his canteen was empty. A patient buzzard circled overhead and a tiny lizard stared at the Ranger with wide, wondering eyes. It was twenty miles to water unless some remained in the *tinaja* where Mooney was holed up, and twenty miles in the desert can be an immeasurable distance.

Neither man held any illusions about the other. Tensleep Mooney was a fast hand with a six-shooter and an excellent rifle shot. His courage was without question. His feud with the gunslinging Baggs outfit was a legend in Texas. Al Baggs had stolen Mooney's horse. Mooney trailed him down, and in the gun battle that followed, killed him, recovering his horse. The Baggs family were Tennessee feudal stock, and despite the fact that killing a horse thief was considered justifiable homicide, a brother and a cousin came hunting Tensleep. Mooney took two Baggs bullets and survived. The Baggs boys took three of Mooney's slugs and didn't.

From time to time a Baggs or two took a shot at Mooney, and at least two attempts were made to trap him. Others were killed, and the last attempt resulted in a woman being shot. Then Tensleep unlimbered his guns and went to work. Until then he had been rolling with the punches, but now he decided if the Baggs clan wanted war, they should have it.

Gene Baggs, the most noted gunslinger of the outfit, was in San Antonio. One Tuesday night Mooney showed up and gave Gene Baggs his chance. The Variety Theater rang with gunshots and Gene died of acute indigestion caused by absorbing too much lead on an empty stomach.

Killings seven and eight had taken place near Big Spring,

one of them a Baggs, the other an itinerant gunfighting cattleman named Caspar Hanna. Settling disputes with guns was beginning to be frowned on in Texas, so the Rangers got their orders and Bowdrie got his.

Mooney was tricky and adept at covering his trail. Cunning as a wolf, he shook off his trailers, and even lost Bowdrie on two occasions. Irritated, Bowdrie followed him to the Mexican border and kept on going. Out of his bailiwick though it was, the chase had now become a matter of professional and personal pride.

So now they were in the dead heart of Apache country, stalemated until darkness. If Mooney escaped in the dark, Bowdrie was scheduled to walk home, the odds against his survival a thousand to one. If one left out the heat and lack of water, even the miles of walking in boots meant for riding, there were always the Apaches.

"Thirsty, Ranger?" Mooney called.

"I'll drink when I'm ready," Bowdrie replied. "You want to come out with your hands up? You'll get a fair trial."

"I'd never live for the trial. Without my guns in Baggs country? I wouldn't last three days."

"Leave that to the Rangers."

"Much obliged. I'll leave it to Mooney."

Neither man spoke again and the hour dragged on. Bowdrie tried licking dry lips with a dry tongue. The heat where he lay was not less than 120 degrees. Shifting his position drew a quick bullet. Carefully, he began to dig again, trying to get at the rifle scabbard on the underside of his horse.

Bowdrie had nothing but respect for Mooney. Under any circumstances but the present the two might have worked a roundup together. Tensleep was a tough cowhand from the Wyoming country that gave him his name, a man who had started ranching on his own, a man who had been over the cow trails from Montana to Texas, who had fought Indians and rustlers.

Bowdrie continued to dig, finally loosening the girth on the dead horse.

"Somethin' out there." Mooney spoke suddenly, and Chick almost looked up, then cursed himself for a fool. It was a trap.

"Somebody travelin' north." Mooney's voice was just loud enough for Bowdrie to hear.

"In this country? You've got to be crazy."

He lay quiet, thinking. There had been no faking in Mooney's tone, and travelers in this country meant, nine times out of ten, Apaches. They were in the middle of an area controlled by Cochise, with his stronghold just to the north in New Mexico. If those were Apaches out there, they were in trouble.

Silence, and then Mooney spoke again, just loud enough for him to hear. "Somebody out there, all right. Can't quite make 'em out. Three or four riders, an' I'd say one was a woman."

A woman in this country? *Now?* Bowdrie wanted to chance a look, but if he lifted his head, Mooney might kill him.

"Walkin' their horses." Mooney was a trifle higher than Bowdrie and could see better.

Both men were hidden, Bowdrie by cactus and rock, Mooney by a notch of rocks that hid both himself and his horse.

"The man's hurt, got his arm in a sling, bandage on his head. Looks like the woman is holdin' him on his horse."

Bowdrie had dug deep enough to pull the girth loose, and now he pulled the saddle off and got at his Winchester. As he lifted the Winchester clear, it showed above the rocks.

"That won't do you no good, Bowdrie," Mooney said. "You lift your head to shoot an' I'll ventilate it."

"Leave that to me," Bowdrie replied cheerfully. "I'd rather take you in alive, because you'd keep better in this heat, but if I have to, I'll start shootin' at the rocks in back of you. The ricochets will chop you to mincemeat."

That, Mooney realized unhappily, was the plain, unvarnished truth. He rubbed a hand over his leather-brown face and narrowed his blue eyes against the sun's glare. He knew that Ranger out there, knew that behind that Apache-like face was as shrewd a fighting brain as he had ever known. No other man could have followed him this far. He peered through the rocks once more.

"Dust cloud." There was a silence while Bowdrie waited, listening. "Somebody chasin' the first bunch, I reckon. Quite a passel of 'em. The first bunch is comin' right close. Three horses, a man wounded bad, a woman, an' two youngsters. The kids are ridin' double."

After a moment Mooney added, "Horses about all in. They've come fast an' hard."

"Comin' this way?"

"No, they'll pass us up."

A fly buzzed lazily in the hot afternoon sun, and Bowdrie could hear the sound of the approaching horses. Hidden as he and Mooney were, there was not a chance they'd be seen.

"Should be water at Ojo de Monte." The man's voice was ragged with exhaustion. "But that's twenty miles off."

"After that?"

"Los Mosquitos, or the Casa de Madera, another thirty miles as the crow flies. You'll have to keep to low ground. I'll try to hold 'em off from those rocks up ahead."

"No!" The woman's voice was strong. "No, George. If we're going to die, let it be together!"

"Don't be a fool, Hannah! Think of the children! You might get through, you might save them and yourself."

Chick Bowdrie shifted his body in the sand. A cloud of dust meant a good-sized bunch of Apaches. A small bunch would make no dust. And they were sure of their prey, for this was their country, far from any aid.

If they kept on after the man and his family, they would never see Mooney or Bowdrie. Bowdrie was realist enough to realize all they had to do was lie quiet. The Indians would not see their tracks, as they had come in from the north and the Apaches were coming from the west. Moreover, they would be too intent on their prey to look for other tracks.

"Mooney?" He spoke just loud enough for the outlaw to hear. "Are we goin' to stand for this? I say we call off our fight and move into this play."

"Just about to suggest the same thing, Ranger. Call 'em back."

Chick Bowdrie got to his feet. The family were moving away, but within easy hailing distance.

"Hey! Come back here! We'll help you!"

Startled, they drew up and turned to stare. "Come over here! I'm a Texas Ranger! You'd never make it the way you're headin'!"

They rounded their horses and walked them closer. The man's face was haggard, the bandage on his head was bloody. The youngsters, hollow-eyed and frightened, stared at them. The woman, not yet thirty, had a flicker of hope in her eyes.

"What we can offer ain't much better," Bowdrie said, "but two more rifles can help. If he tried to hold 'em off, they'd just cut around him an' have you all with no trouble."

"They'd get you before you could say Sam Houston. You get down an' come into the rocks." Tensleep paused, grinning at Bowdrie. "But not where that in-curvin' rock is." He rolled his quid of chewing tobacco in his wide jaws. "The Ranger tells me that ain't safe."

The dust cloud was nearer now, and the Apaches, aware their quarry had elected to stop, were fanning out. Tensleep spat. "This here's goin' to surprise 'em some. They reckon they're only comin' up on a hurt man an' a woman with kids."

It was cooler in the shade of the big rocks, and a glance at the *tinaja* showed a couple of barrels of water, at least. There was shelter for their horses and it was a good place to make a stand. Trust Tensleep to choose the right spot to fight a battle.

The desert before them was suddenly empty. The dust cloud had settled. The buzzard overhead had been joined by a hopeful relative. The buzzards were neutral. No matter who won down there, they would win. They had but to wait. The lizard had vanished. Bowdrie had dragged his saddle and bridle back into the rocks. He worked himself into a hollow in the sand, found a place for his elbows, and waited.

Nothing.

That was expected. It was when you never saw Apaches that you could worry. They were confident, but did not wish to risk a death to get the four they pursued.

The woman was washing the man's arm now, replacing the bandage. Tensleep rolled his quid in his jaws and spat upon an itinerant scorpion. The scorpion backed off, unhappy at the unexpected deluge of trouble.

"How many would you say?" Bowdrie asked.

Mooney thought it over. "Maybe ten. No less'n that. Could be twice as many."

"Tough."

"Yeah."

Mooney shoved his canteen at Bowdrie. "What are you? A camel? Don't you ever drink?"

"Forgot how." Bowdrie took a mouthful and let it soak the dry tissues, then swallowed.

Both men understood their chances of getting out alive were so slim they weren't worth counting on. The children stared at them, wide-eyed. The girl might have been ten, the boy two or three years younger. Their clothes were ragged but clean as could be expected after a hard ride. Bowdrie dug into his saddlebag and handed each child a piece of jerky. He grinned at them and winked. The girl smiled warily, but the boy was fascinated by Bowdrie's guns. "Can I hold one?" he asked.

"I need 'em, son. Guns are dangerous things. You use 'em when need be, but nobody plays with a gun unless he's a fool." He indicated the area out in front of them. "This is one time they're needed."

Nothing moved out there; there was only sun, sand, and sky, low brush, occasional cactus, and the buzzards who seemed to simply hang in the sky, scarcely moving their wings. A shoulder showed, and Bowdrie held his fire.

Mooney glanced at him. "You're no tenderfoot."

"I grew up with 'em," Bowdrie commented. "Them an' Comanches."

That exposed shoulder had been an invitation, a test to see where they were, and how many. Yet they believed they knew. They had been chasing a man, a woman, and children.

A half-dozen Indians came off the ground at once. It was as if they were born suddenly from the sand. Where they appeared there had been nothing an instant before.

The thunder of suddenly firing rifles smashed echoes against the rocks, and the whine of ricocheting bullets sent shuddering sounds through the clear desert air. An instant, a smell of gunpowder, and they were gone. Heat waves danced in the still air.

An Apache lay on his face not ten feet away. Another was sprawled near a clump of greasewood. As Bowdrie looked, that Indian rolled over and vanished before Bowdrie could bring his rifle to bear. There was blood on the sand where he had fallen.

"How'd you make out?" Tensleep asked.

"One down an' a possible," Bowdrie replied,

"Two down here, an' a possible. What's the matter? Can't you Rangers shoot no better than that?"

"You light a shuck," Bowdrie replied complacently. "I can outshoot you any day and twice on Sunday."

"Huh," Mooney grunted, then glanced at the scorpion, who was getting ready to move again. He spat, deluging it anew. Then suddenly he fired.

"Scratch another redskin," he said.

Bowdrie lay still, watching the desert. They were doing some thinking out there now. The two rifles had surprised them, and an Apache does not like to be surprised. Their attack had seemed so easy. The Apache is an efficient, able fighting man who rarely makes a useless move, and even more rarely miscalculates. This easy attack had now cost them three or four men and some wounds.

The sky was a white-hot bowl above them, the desert a reflector, yet the sun had already started its slide toward the far-off mountains.

An Apache moved suddenly, darting to the right. Bowdrie had his rifle on the spot where he had seen him drop from sight. He was a young warrior, and reckless. As he arose and moved, Bowdrie squeezed off his shot and the warrior stumbled.

Instantly, several more leaped up. Behind him a third rifle bellowed. So the father was back in action now. Bowdrie's second shot was a clean miss as the Indian dropped from sight.

"Got one!" The father spoke proudly. He crept closer and Bowdrie wished he wouldn't. "Name is Westmore. Tried ranchin' down southwest of here. Mighty pretty country. They done burned us out whilst we was from home, so we run for it."

The shadows began to grow, the glare grew less. Bowdrie drank from the canteen. "I'd have had you tied to your saddle by now," he said.

Mooney chuckled. "Why, you track-smellin' softheaded coyote! If these folks hadn't come along, you'd have been buzzard bait by now."

The woman looked surprised and curious. Westmore glanced from one to the other.

"Wished I could have got you without your guns," Bowdrie commented. "You're too good a man to shoot. I'd have been satisfied to take you in with my bare hands."

"You?" Mooney stared at him angrily. "Why, you long-horned maverick! I'd—"

The Apaches tried it again, but this time it was cold turkey. Both men had spotted slight movements in the brush and were ready when they came up. Bowdrie got his before the Indian had his hands off the ground. Mooney fired at a rock behind where his Indian lay, dusting him with fragments.

"They'll wait until dark now," Mooney said. "I figure we've accounted for maybe half of them. We been shot with luck, you know that, don't you?"

"I know," Bowdrie agreed. "They just ran into more'n they were expecting, but they'll have figured it out by now. No wounded man and a woman could be makin' the stand we are."

"Look!" Westmore pointed. Three Apaches were riding off into the distance. "They've quit."

Westmore started to rise, but Bowdrie jerked him down. "It's an old trick," he explained. "Two or three ride off and the rest wait in ambush. When you start movin' around, they kill you."

The sun slid down behind the mountains in the distance and the desert grew cool. It was ever so. There was nothing to hold the heat, and night cooled things off very quickly. Stars came out and a coyote yipped, a coyote with a brown skin and a headband. Bowdrie dug into his saddlebag and brought out a piece of jerky for each. It was dry and tough but it lasted a long time and was nourishing. They chewed in silence.

A faint gray lingered, disappeared, and gave birth to stars. Chick tossed his saddle blanket to the youngsters. Westmore peered from behind the rocks.

"You reckon those that left will come back with more?"

"Could be. In fact, it's more than likely."

"My name's Westmore," the man repeated, looking from one to the other.

"I'm Tensleep Mooney. This here's a Texas Ranger named Bowdrie. He's been on my trail for weeks."

The woman was puzzled. "He wants to arrest you? Why?"

"This gent here," Bowdrie said, "is too handy with a gun. The governor wants more taxpayers and this gent has been thinnin' down the population somethin' awful."

"But you'll let him go now, won't you?"

Mooney chuckled. "This here Sou-wegian ain't got me yet, an' it'll be a cold day in Kansas before he does."

"Soon as we're rid of these Apaches," Chick said, "I'll hog-tie you and take you back. I'll give you about two drinks between here an' Austin." He turned his head toward Westmore and his wife. "You know what this squatty good-for-nothin' did?

"He knows this country better than anybody. Knows ever' water hole. He passes one by, then swings back in the dark, gets him a drink, an' fills his canteen. Then he goes back to where I last saw him, lets me see him again, an' takes off in the dark. I have to follow him or lose him, so I've spent my days drier than a year-old buffalo chip!"

Talk died and they lay listening. There was no sound. Bowdrie turned to Mooney. "I'm goin' out there. There's at least one Apache out there, prob'ly more. I need a horse. When I get me a horse we'll light out. 'Paches don't like night fightin' an' we should make a run for it."

He dropped his gun belts, then thrust one pistol into his waistband along with his bowie knife. He removed his spurs and jacket, then disappeared into the night.

The woman looked at Mooney. "Will he get back? How can he do this?"

"If anybody can do it," Mooney said, "he can. He's more Injun than many Injuns. Anyway, he's got no choice. He surely ain't goin' out of here a-foot."

There was a shallow arroyo nearby, and Bowdrie found it and went down the sandbank to its bottom, then paused to listen.

He started on, paused again, hearing a faint sound he could not place, then went on. He was circling cautiously, feeling his way, when he heard a horse blow. He circled even wider, then dropped to the sand and crept nearer. He found them unexpectedly, six horses picketed in the bottom of the arroyo. Six horses did not necessarily mean six Indians, for some of the riders might already lie among the dead.

Try as he could, he saw no sleeping place, nor did he see

any Indians or evidence of a fire, which they probably would not have anyway.

Just as he was about to move toward the horses, an Indian rose from the ground and went to them. He moved around them, then returned to his bed on the sand a few yards away. When the Indian was quiet, Bowdrie moved to the horses. Selecting the nearest for his own, he drew the picket pins of all the horses, reflecting they must be stolen horses, for it was unlike Apaches to use picket pins, preferring the nearest bush or tree.

He moved to the horse he had chosen and swung to its back. The horse snorted at the unfamiliar smell and instantly there was movement from the Indian.

Slapping his heels to the horse, Bowdrie charged into the night, leading the other horses behind him. He turned at the flash of a gun and fired three quick shots into the flash.

Circling swiftly, he arrived at camp. "Roll out an' mount up!" he said. "We're leavin' out of here!"

He saddled swiftly, and they rode into the night. Three days later they rode into the dusty streets of El Paso. The Westmores turned toward New Mexico and the ranch of a relative. They parted company in the street and Mooney started for his horse. "Far enough, Mooney! Don't forget, you're my prisoner!"

"Your *what*?"

Mooney threw himself sidewise into an arroyo, but Bowdrie did not move. "Won't do you a bit of good. Might as well give up! I've got you!"

"You got nothin'!" Mooney yelled. "Just stick your head around that corner and I'll—!"

"Be mighty dry where you're goin', Mooney. And you without a canteen."

"What? Why, you dirty sidewinder! You stole my canteen!"

"Borrowed it. You killed 'em all in fair fights, Mooney, so's you might as well stand trial. I'll ride herd on you so's you'll be safe whilst the trial's on.

"I've got the water, Mooney, and I have the grub, and the Baggs outfit has more friends here than you do. If you go askin' around, you'll really get your hide stretched. Looks to me like your only way is to come along with me."

There was silence, and then Bowdrie said, "I will give you more than two drinks betwixt here an' Austin, Mooney. I was only makin' a joke about that."

There was no sound, and Bowdrie knew what was happening, "If you're wise," he said loudly, "you'll come in an' surrender. No sense havin' an outlaw's name when you don't deserve it.

"I'll even testify for you. I'll tell 'em you were a miserable coyote not fit to herd sheep but that you're a first-class fightin' man."

Silence. Bowdrie smiled and walked back to his horse. By now Mooney was headed out of town, headed back to the boondocks where he came from, but he'd come in, Bowdrie was sure of it. Just give him time to think it over.

He had warned him about El Paso, and he was too good a man to be in prison. Maybe a day would come when a Ranger couldn't use his own judgment, but Bowdrie had used his and was sure ninety percent of the others would agree. By now Tensleep was on his way to wherever he wanted to go.

Bowdrie walked his horse back down the street from the edge of town. This wasn't a bad horse, not as good as his roan waiting for him back in Laredo, but better than the bay lying dead in Sonora. The spare Indian horses he had given to Westmore. After all, they were going to start over with all too little.

Bowdrie tied his horse to the hitch rail and went inside

to the bar and ordered a cold beer. Taking it, he walked to a table and sat down.

Well, maybe he was wrong. Maybe McNelly wouldn't agree with his turning Mooney loose, but—

"All right, dammit!" Tensleep dropped into the chair opposite. "Take me in, if it makes you feel better. I just ain't up to another chase like that one." He looked at Bowdrie. "Can I keep my guns until I get there?"

"Why not?" Bowdrie looked around. "Bartender, bring the man a beer."

They sat without speaking. Then Tensleep said, "You notice something? Those youngsters back there? Never a whimper out of 'em, an' they must have been scared."

"Sure they were scared. I was scared." Bowdrie glanced at Mooney, a reflective glint in his eye. "You know, Mooney, what you need is a wife. You need a home. Take some of that wildness out of you. Now, I—"

"You go to the devil," Mooney replied cheerfully.

Corazón

∽◦◦∽

by Elizabeth Fackler

Elizabeth Fackler is the author of novels, short stories, and poetry. Her latest mystery is *When Kindness Fails*, published by Five Star. Sunstone Press has recently reissued her classic novel on the Lincoln County War: *Billy the Kid: The Legend of El Chivato*. Western Writers of America called it "a magnificent achievement in historical fiction." She lives with her husband, Michael, and their two dogs, Pecos and Mitchum, in Capitan, New Mexico.

DAWSON MCCUTCHEON RODE south for two days and two nights. His only leads were a widow named Liliana and a cantina called Escondida, which meant hidden. A second-generation Texan, he knew Spanish well enough to hold his own in Mexico. His mission, though, was no more legal than his badge would be, so he kept it *escondida*, poking against his vest from deep within his jacket's pocket. A crude star cut from a silver *real*, the badge wasn't official because Texas Rangers, strictly speaking, weren't police but militia. His foray south of the border was purely personal.

The Rio Grande slapped his sorrel's knees with a ripple followed by a splash, a cadence above the constant rush of white water stretching half a mile east and west before jagging out of sight behind bends in the canyon. Red bluffs farther west, pale plains to the east, ahead a veil of dense mesquite through which the trail led away from the ford.

He let his horse stop and shake while catching its footing in Mexico. The air felt heavier and sultry as a thicket at noon, except it was dusk and the river was coated with a rosy patina like strawberry frosting on riffled, green glass. His horse bobbed its head, chewing sloppily on its bit, making him drag his eyes off the far bank that was Texas. He nudged his spurs into the animal's flanks, and it moved without hesitation on the trail through the brambled forest.

Varmints skittered through the underbrush, crackling the dead leaves of decades of seasons. He was twenty-five, looking for a man ten years his senior who had taught him how to handle killing a man. Dawson had been fifteen then, Ace Garr twenty-five. Contemplating these simple calculations, he avoided the fact of kinship—Ace was his mother's kid brother—and concentrated on his purpose. To casually stroll into the Cantina Escondida and be accepted as belonging, he had to play the part of a drifter who didn't much care what happened next. Any man who did care was at the mercy of those who didn't, and those who didn't picked up on sore spots fast. Ace had taught him that.

Past the church with its walled garden, Corazón was a scattering of adobe hovels, a couple of *tendejons* offering rustic meals at their tables and basic commodities on their shelves, mostly bullets, beans, and coffee. About all a man truly needed, long as he had a reliable gun and a good mount. Dawson swung down in front of the dugout saloon with no sign proclaiming its name. The horses tied to its rail were a higher quality than those in front of the other saloons. Two more, both brightly lit and wide-open with half-walls all around. More than one burro tied at their rails, the men inside pointedly not watching him.

He settled his gun belt and tucked in his shirt as he walked down the two plank steps to the door of the Escondida, then squared his shoulders and pushed through. He was hit with a cloud of smoke that singed his eyes. Scanning the gloom through a blur, he felt hostility wafting from all the faces turned toward him. He blinked and his eyes adjusted to the lack of light, though he still squinted as he made his way toward the bar. He walked slowly, his boot heels quietly thudding on the hard-packed dirt floor, as he listened for any back action.

A brawny Mexican with a pomaded moustache and slicked-back black hair watched him from behind the bar. Dawson dropped a peso on the counter and softly drawled, *"Buenas tardes, amigo. Hay whiskey?"* The keep lifted a bottle and glass from under the bar and set them down, then whisked the coin into his pudgy paw.

Dawson carried them toward an empty corner table for two. Conversations revived with his passing, so by the time he sat down, everyone was attending to their own business again. He poured himself a drink first, knowing that's what Ace would do, then scanned the room. The men all looked familiar, but it was a type, not an individual. Men with conniving eyes, snide mouths, taut postures, fast hands. The most dangerous breed of *lobo* raised on the Rio Grande: human predators. Trying to look like one of a company he despised, he figured his frown was a pretty good cover, though it probably wasn't much different than the one he'd worn asking for leave to start on this mission.

"Bingham was a friend of mine," he'd told his sergeant.

Sieker nodded. "If I'd known he was dead 'fore the outlaws gave up, I would've killed every last one of 'em. But they'd already surrendered."

Dawson had been there and didn't need to hear it, but understood that Sieker needed to say it. Two weeks they'd ridden hard from Fort McKavett to Fort Davis to stop a scavenging bunch who'd drifted over from the Lincoln County War in New Mexico. Slick at their profession, the bandits had sent two men into Keesey's Saloon to buy drinks all around while the others robbed Sender and Siebenborn's mercantile of 920 dollars cash and an arsenal with ammunition. Jesse Evans was their leader, Ace Garr one of his followers. That Ace had sunk so low shocked Dawson, not having seen hide nor hair of his uncle for nigh on three years. Ace had been caught when his horse stumbled galloping out of town and threw him at the feet of the county sheriff, but Dawson didn't have time to visit him in jail before the Rangers rode out. Tracking the gang for eighty miles across the July-blistered prairie, they cornered the bandits in a rocky canyon. The battle had been each man for himself until one of the bandits was killed and the others surrendered. Only after it was over did they discover Bingham had been heart-shot swinging off his horse. Dark falling fast, the Rangers hog-tied the bandits and spent a melancholy night by a meager fire, staring at Bingham's corpse. Buried him and the bandit in the morning, then rode back to Davis to learn Ace had escaped. Dawson tarried only long enough to change horses and secure his superior's leave.

"You've pulled your weight in the time you've been with us," Sieker had said, "but I doubt you're seasoned enough to nab a desperado alone."

"He's my uncle," Dawson said. "This is family business."

"The law's business is what we're paid for," Sieker barked, "and Mexico ain't our jurisdiction."

Dawson quoted the words of John B. Jones himself, commander of the Frontier Battalion: "Sometimes we gotta act in the interest of peace more'n the strict dictates of law."

Sieker had stared at him hard and long before granting his leave with a growled, "Whatever happens down there is 'tween you and God. Don't go dragging the Rangers into it."

So Dawson was on his own, watching a brown beauty slip through the front door of the Cantina Escondida. She wore a full skirt embroidered with colorful flowers and a pale yellow blouse drooping low on her breasts. Suspended above them was a silver crucifix, and a cuff of silver bangles shivered on her wrist. Shining like starlit ebony from her crown to her waist, her hair was pinned back with combs inlaid with mother-of-pearl, so he knew she wasn't poor, this woman entering the cantina alone to stand in a sliver of shadow and assess the evening's selection.

LILIANA STUDIED THE man alone in the far corner with a bottle bought at the bar. A young gringo, he had watched her come in, and now, each time his gaze scanned the cantina, his pale eyes met hers across the dim, smoky room. From what she could see, he was tall and slender, his clothes loose with a decorum she liked. His light hair fell straight over the collar of his jacket, and his face, though shuttered so as not to reveal anything from within, was receptive to what swirled around him. In that way, it was open and pleasing, a boyish face with a stubble of blond whiskers on cheeks as yet unmarred by evil. The next time his eyes met hers, a small smile graced his mouth.

Swishing her brightly flowered skirt to make its embroidery shine in the lamplight, she approached him. Closer now, she read in his eyes that he wanted what she did, and was about to flounce her skirt down beside him when a commotion turned her around.

Two men had lurched to their feet and the table had been batted from between them, by which man she didn't know, so intent had she been on the gringo. Now as she

watched, one of the men pulled a knife and lunged, tearing
the other's shirt. That man backed away, raising his hands
in a placating gesture as enough blood seeped through to
make the cloth cling. The man with the knife snarled threats
to do worse, but the other kept backing up, his hands away
from his gun.

If the fighters hadn't been between her and the door,
Liliana might have run out and all the way home, so mean
was the mood now filling the cantina. Just then, against the
very tips of her fingers, she felt a soothing touch. She
looked down to see the gringo caressing her fingertips with
his own. She met his eyes, and by his smile knew she was
safe. When she sat down, he rested his arm on the back of
her chair, barely touching her but announcing she was under his protection. They both watched the fighters as the
cut one backed out the door and disappeared in the dark.
The other resheathed his knife and set his table straight,
then bellowed for the keep to bring more tequila.

Liliana looked again at the man she had chosen. When
he spoke, his words lingered crossing his tongue: *"Quieres
un trago?"*

She nodded, knowing it was necessary to spend time
with a man before taking him home. He refilled his glass
and raised it in a toast. *"Salud."* He sipped the whiskey and
handed her the glass half full.

"Salud," she echoed, sipped, and handed it back with a
sliver of liquor still in its bottom. "I am called Liliana. By
what name do you go by?"

A slow smile welcomed her English. "Dawson Mc-
Cutcheon," he said. "It's the name my folks gave me, and I
ain't yet felt the need of a new one."

"You are from Texas."

He nodded.

"I, from Zacatecas. I came here because the house where

I live has been in my husband's family for three generations, but I am the only one left to claim it."

He poured himself another drink, watching the whiskey tumble from the bottle into the glass. "What happened to your husband?"

"He died when the mine he was working collapsed. Living without him, Señor McCutcheon, I am often hungry for the gentle touch of a lover."

Again he smiled before saying, "Call me Dawson."

She smiled too, feeling almost enough had been said. "If you come home with me, we will have to be quiet so as not to wake my son."

Dawson was watching the room. "How old is he?"

"Five years."

He stood up. "Reckon I can handle that."

She saw his gun belt slicing a diagonal below his vest, and noted he lifted the bottle with his left hand. All eyes watched them leave. Walking beside him beneath the dark starry sky, his horse tagging behind at the end of its reins, she worried about what she was doing, knowing from experience that a man who moved with power among men wasn't always gentle with women. But when she remembered his touch on her fingers inside the cantina, she knew he would be a gentleman.

IN THE MORNING, Dawson listened to her stoke the fire in the kitchen, then leave the *casita,* perhaps for more wood. He lay back and stared at the *latillas* above the *vigas* of her ceiling, wondering if she was the right Liliana. Nothing she'd said had hinted of any connection to Ace, but he didn't guess it would be a woman's habit to discuss one lover with another. Hearing timid footsteps approach the bedroom door, he turned on his side and watched a boy stop on the threshold. A sprout in a nightshirt, his black hair was mussed, his dark eyes guarded, his complexion as white as creamy whipped chocolate.

"Buenos dias," Dawson said, trying to disarm the boy with a smile. *"Me llamo Dawson McCutcheon, un amigo de su madre. Tu eres Robertito, no?"*

The boy smiled shyly, showing small baby teeth.

Liliana entered the kitchen with her armload of wood. After dropping it in the box by the stove, she called from that distance, *"Andale, m'hijo."*

The child returned to his room and quietly closed the door.

Dawson watched her come in. She smiled but stayed away from the bed, though the room was so small he could have pulled her back in without getting up. When she lifted her nightgown off over her head, her nude body stirred his desire. She hastily eclipsed temptation beneath homespun drawers and a white cotton dress, confined the wild rampage of her hair in a single braid, and left him alone. He found his clothes and was tugging on his boots when Robertito came to stand in the doorway wearing short, tattered trousers and a dirty smock shirt.

"Vayase afuera," she called from the kitchen. *"No molestes al señor."*

Robertito went as the far as the *portal* beyond the open front door.

"He's not bothering me," Dawson said, coming out of the bedroom dressed except for his jacket.

She noted he was wearing his gun, but hadn't needed to see that he put it on fresh from bed to guess he was a *pistolero*. No other caliber of man patronized La Cantina Escondida. She worriedly glanced at Robertito watching from the *portal*, knowing he was always curious about the men who suddenly emerged from her bedroom into his life.

"Vayase afuera," she told him again, then said to

Dawson, "Sit down," as she lifted the coffeepot off the fire. When she set a full cup in front of him, he pulled her into his lap.

Wondering if she had a job in town, he asked, "You always get up so early?"

"Robertito does," she answered, smiling at her son still in the door.

Dawson turned to look at the boy, who crept a few steps closer. "Did he make his own breakfast?"

She laughed. "Do you think he can cook?"

Dawson shrugged. "Then you oughta let him eat with us."

She tried to get up, but he kept her in his lap, so she said from there, *"Ven acá, Robertito. El hombre desea que tu comas también."*

Dawson watched the boy cross the room and sit at the table. "He doesn't speak English?"

"Someday soon I will teach him."

"Where'd you learn it?"

"My father was over the men at the mine. The American superintendent allowed me to go to school with his children, so I learned from when I was small."

Dawson reached around her to lift his cup. Holding her close with his hand on her waist, he sipped at the boiled black coffee, and set his cup back down. "Why aren't you still there, living with your father?"

"It was he who sent my husband into that mine shaft knowing it was dangerous." She sighed unhappily. "I cannot forgive him. Do you think I am wrong?"

Dawson shook his head.

"Andale pues," she said, dismissing her melancholy with a clap of her hands. "How you like your eggs?"

"Over real easy."

She laughed. "That is something you say last night.

'Over real easy,' you whisper, and I try to turn however you want." She leaned a little away from him. "Did I do good?"

He nodded, hoping he could linger long enough to savor her sweetness at least once more.

While she cooked at the stove, she listened to them talk at the table, Dawson's Spanish softened by his drawl, . Robertito preening beneath the Texan's attention. They spoke of fish in the river and quail in the *bosque,* planning how to catch some for supper. She felt pleased that Dawson would stay another night, knowing her son missed having a father. But after breakfast Dawson rode into town, and she doubted his promise to return. Watching her son play with pebbles in the yard, she felt sad for him. To lighten her mood, she sang a happy song as she walked out to feed her hens.

Sprinkling the grain wide so they wouldn't squabble, she saw Ace sitting his horse at the edge of her yard. She gave him no smile of welcome, merely continued to scatter the feed as she listened to his horse's hooves coming closer. When they stopped, she glanced at her son, so occupied in his game that he hadn't noticed their visitor; then she met the man's dark eyes and whispered fiercely, "Go away!"

"Why?" he asked, his voice rough as gravel in a sluice. "Ain't you glad to see me?"

"Do I look glad? You no come for months and think you can ride in when you please? Is not true. I don't want you here now."

His gaze searched her yard, sliding over the boy as if he were no more than a rock. "Where's that horse was here earlier?"

"What horse?" she said, though her breath was ragged with fear.

"You in the habit of corralling horses, Liliana? Did you

start taking 'em in for board, is that what you're doing?" His tone told her he was teasing, but she knew how fast his fun could turn mean.

Propping the basket of grain against her hip, she shaded her eyes with her other hand as she looked up at him on his horse. "What I do is no business of yours."

Finally, he looked at his son. "The boy's growing right smart, ain't he?"

"*Por favor,* go before he sees you!"

"In case you ain't noticed," Ace said, "he likes seeing me."

"Is no good for him, the way you come and go. I don't want you here."

"I'll go now," he conceded, gathering his reins, "if you promise to give me a proper welcome in the cantina later on."

Her nostrils flared with repugnance, but she said, "I will come."

"I'll look for you 'long about dusk," he said, turning his horse.

She watched until he had disappeared in the *bosque* toward town. Then she dumped the remnants of feed and returned to her kitchen banging the dust from her basket.

DAWSON SAT AT the same table in the cantina he had occupied the night before, savoring a mug of rich Mexican beer as he surveyed the same hardcases idling away another afternoon. Though any one of these men might know Ace, their sort were wary of questions. If Liliana was the widow Ace had mentioned to Cousin Rob, Dawson figured his best bet was to simply ask her about his uncle's whereabouts, but that would mean admitting he wasn't on the up-and-up. Riding down here, he hadn't meant to seduce the widow, but had fallen in step when she invited him home.

Now he had not only her regret to dread, but a good chance jealousy would muddy the play. None of this was how he'd planned it, and Robertito was the final trick in the deal. If the boy turned out to be kin, no matter how the cards fell, Dawson would be in a pinch. When he'd told his sergeant this was family business, he hadn't reckoned on how many folks that might include.

He finished his beer and sat over his empty mug a while longer. But nobody seemed inclined to make his acquaintance, and he suddenly found himself hoping Ace was nowhere in his vicinity. Back in the sun, he decided his brain had been addled to think he could accomplish anything here. He swung into his saddle and turned his horse toward the thickets leading to the ford. In their humid shade he stopped sharp. Going home now would prove nothing except that he'd quit. In his estimation, that was about the worst a man could do, so he turned his horse around and ambled back past the cantina, never suspecting Ace had walked in while he was gone.

LILIANA SMILED AT Dawson through her open front door as he tethered his horse to a post of her *portal*.

He slung his jacket over the back of a chair in the shade. "Where's the boy?"

"Asleep," she said. "Are you hungry?"

"In a bit," he said, untying his cinch.

She watched him shift his saddle to the floor of her *portal*, then lead his horse to the river. As the sorrel drank, Dawson stared at the sandy white beach of Texas across the green flowing water. She wondered if he had come to Mexico fleeing something bad. Suddenly cold in the afternoon sun, she returned to the warmth of her stove and began rolling tortillas. After kneading and slapping the dough, she laid the thin cakes on the griddle to sizzle, then puff when she turned them, their toasted fragrance tickling her nose with pleasure. As she stirred the pot of beans she kept simmering on the back of her stove, she sang softly, wishing her life could always be filled with such simple joys while her son napped and her man tended his horse.

Robertito slid from his bed and stood a moment, watching his mother cook. Rubbing his eyes, he walked barefoot to the front door, then squinted through the slanting sunbeams of late afternoon at Dawson with his horse by the river. Robertito looked down at the man's saddle under the *portal,* the rifle butt poking out of its scabbard, then at the jacket draped on the back of a chair. He sat in the chair, idly kicking his feet against its legs as he watched the red horse lift its head from the river, water falling like coins from its mouth. He leaned back and felt something prick him through the jacket's lining. Slipping his hand into a pocket, he touched metal, cool and hard. He glanced at his mother's back before peeking at what he'd found: a silver star with a clasp! Rubbing the shiny points with his thumb, he looked at the man, then again at his mother. Neither of them were watching, so he pulled out the chain holding his crucifix, clipped the star beside it, and dropped them both to fall against his chest inside his shirt. Laughing, he ran toward the river.

Liliana heard his laughter and running feet. She turned and watched Dawson lift her son onto the horse's back. Robertito grabbed the mane and kicked his bare heels into the horse's belly, but the sorrel only moved lazily to graze on the lush grass of the floodplain. Dawson sat on a rock, lifted his hat to let the sunset breeze ruffle his hair, then settled the brim low above his eyes as he stared across the river at Texas. Liliana sighed, knowing whatever drew his thoughts to that far shore would one day take him back, maybe not tomorrow but a day not too distant. Impatiently, she grabbed her rebozo and hurried from the yard, intending to put her visit to the cantina behind her so she could enjoy Dawson's company as long as he was hers.

Dawson watched her almost running from the yard. He figured she was in a hurry to buy something from town before the stores closed for the night, and wondered why she hadn't asked him to fetch whatever she needed. He led his horse with the boy astride its bare back into the corral, pulled off the bridle, and lifted the boy down. "Think your mama left some coffee on the stove?" When the boy gave him a troubled look, Dawson laughed. *"Piensas qué hay café?"*

"Sí," Robertito said with a smile.

ACE PAID GUAPO Gonzalez to wait in the cantina for Liliana and keep her there while he rode out to see what brushpopper had taken his place in her bed. The sorrel in her corral told him he'd timed his play right. After tethering his horse in the chaparral surrounding her yard, he sneaked up on the house. The saddle with its empty scabbard on the floor of her *portal* was a Texas cowpuncher's rig. That didn't surprise him, knowing Liliana had a fondness for gringos. He pulled his Colt and filled the door, ready for anything but the face of his nephew looking up from a game of checkers with his son.

They were using a deck of cards for pieces and a yellow-and-green plaid cloth for the board, something that tickled Ace in its own right. He raised his pistol flat in his hand to signal a truce as he watched Dawson react to his sudden appearance.

Dawson had been leaning back in his chair, waiting for Robertito's next move. It was easy to slyly slip the keeper strap off his pistol as he slowly stood up. "Ace," he said dryly.

Ace laughed. "What'cha doing here, Dawson?"

Dawson glanced at the gun Ace held, glad he'd moved his Winchester to Liliana's bedroom. "Just came down to say howdy."

"Did you now?" Lean and weathered from living outside the law, Ace surveyed the kitchen's dark corners with the heed of the hunted.

"Want some coffee?" Dawson asked sadly.

"That's hospitable of you," Ace drawled, "being as this is my house. You did know this is mine?"

"Why else would I be here?"

"I can't figure it 'less you followed the owl hoot trail to the Escondida and Liliana offered you a place to lie low. Is that how it happened?"

"Sorta."

"What part ain't exactly right?"

"I ain't hiding."

Looking at Robertito, who hadn't moved, Ace finally holstered his gun. *"Qué tal, hijo?"*

"Nada," the boy whispered.

"Nada? Looks to me like you're playing checkers!" He came closer and lifted the boy high in his arms. "My, but you're getting big. *Un poco hombre, no?"*

"Sí," Robertito answered with a smile more shy than any he'd given Dawson.

Dawson slid the coffeepot over the fire without taking his eyes off his uncle. Ace sat down with the boy on his lap and studied the board, then grinned up at Dawson. "Throwing the game his way won't never make a man of him. Didn't I teach you that?"

"Yeah, you did."

"Don't seem like it stuck, or have you gotten soft without me around?"

"I've gotten older."

"Meaning you wouldn't've if I'd been there?"

Dawson shrugged.

Ace narrowed his eyes as the coffee hissed in its pot. "You come down here to try'n get me to mend my ways?"

"If I had, would you do it?"

"Reckon it's too late."

Dawson turned away from the hurt riding those words. Pouring the coffee, he listened to Ace ask the boy, "What'd you buy with the money I sent your mama?" Carrying the cups to the table, he watched Robertito shake his head.

"Qué compraste con el dinero que le di a su mamá?" Ace repeated.

"Cuando?" the boy asked.

Ace thought a minute. *"Hace seis o siete meses."*

Dawson sat down watching the boy try to remember what had happened six or seven months ago. Living as he did, that stretch of time probably passed in a flash for Ace.

Impatient for the boy's answer, Ace asked, *"Qué cosa tu tienes nueva?"*

Dawson sipped his coffee, watching the boy struggle to remember something new. Robertito looked to him as if for an answer, so he smiled.

The boy smiled back and tugged at the chain around his neck. Out from under his shirt came a brass crucifix and a star cut from a silver *real*. Both men stared at the star, then Dawson slowly set his cup on the table.

"De dónde viene esto?" Ace asked.

"Es de él," Robertito said. He unclipped the star and slid it toward Dawson.

The dark fire in Ace's eyes turned cold.

"Qué pasa?" the boy whispered with a quiver of fear.

"That's a Ranger's star, ain't it?"

Dawson nodded.

"Yours?"

"Yeah."

Ace stood up. "I'm gonna put the boy to bed. Then we're gonna wait for his mama to come home so he don't have to see one of us die."

Dawson watched Ace carry the boy into the bedroom. Listening to the soft murmur of their voices drift through the open door, he remembered all Ace had meant to him that summer after his father died, and how Ace had helped him accommodate killing his first man, though it had been a young buck Comanche no older than he was.

Dawson could recall every detail of that day: how the boy's long braids had curved about his head like rivulets of oil escaping from his ears with the blood already thickening in a flat pool on the black loam of the garden. War paint in precise white circles on his cheeks, his open mouth showing the edges of teeth top and bottom, his dull eyes lacking any spark of life. His wiry body clothed only in moccasins and breechclout, stomach collapsed below his ribs, each of them countable beneath the ashen skin.

Dawson had struck the stock of his Henry into the dirt and leaned on the gun with half his weight. His stomach felt wrung like a rag as vomit burned his throat. He swallowed it back down, constricting his chest in a vise of control that crowded his heart. A sob tore from his mouth, and he moaned, leaning over his rifle, hiding his face.

A strong hand settled on his shoulder, gripping him as if from inside, holding him together. "Ain't nothing to be ashamed of," Ace said. "We won!"

Dawson stood up straight and met his uncle's eyes, hot from the thrill of the fight, then let his gaze scan the yard: Two other warriors, both grown men, lay sprawled near the raw log fence. A whippoorwill sang from the pasture, horses snorted in the restored quiet, a gentle breeze of peace after battle tickling leaves in the orchard where apples hung heavy like pendants of blood. Dawson met his uncle's eyes again.

Ace smiled. "Let's get shuck of these heathens 'fore the women come home."

One foot in front of the other, Dawson followed Ace to the corral. They set their rifles aside only long enough to saddle two horses and bridle a third, never more than a step and a half from their weapons. Carrying them again, they led the horses to the dead, slung each over the back of the nervous, nickering roan, then swung onto the two bays and rode out the gate. Dawson glanced at his uncle's face, alert with surveillance of the velvet green hills rolling into the distance. Dawson watched them too, thinking, *So this is how it's done: You simply go on, do what's next, and don't let regret weaken your vigilance.*

A creek crowded with willows hugged the edge of the prairie they rode across. Wanting to rein his horse into their cover and ride listening to the horses splash through water, he realized he was thirsty. He asked his uncle why they didn't hide themselves in the trees.

Ace didn't so much as glance from his constant surveillance of the prairie. "'Cause they'd plot our progress and intercept us at our least advantage." He let that settle in, then said, "They're watching us now. From where I'm not sure. But I can feel 'em, can't you?"

Dawson honed his senses for any inkling of company on the vast stretch of grass soughing in the wind. He shook his head.

"They won't attack," Ace said. "We won and they know it."

"What're we doing then?" Dawson managed to mumble.

"Returning their dead. They'll let us be 'cause of it."

The horses were plodding uphill now. Dawson looked back at the three Comanches shifting against each other on the bare back of the roan. Their arms flopped uselessly, their feet stuck out, legs already stiffening. At the top of the hill, Ace swung down and handed Dawson his reins. His horse shifted beneath him as he watched Ace gently lift each Comanche off and lay him down to disappear in the tall grass. The boy was first. Being lightest, he had been loaded on top. As soon as it was done, Ace took his reins and rode back down the hill. Leading the roan, Dawson followed him.

They ambled slowly, aiming at the roof of the house barely peeking above the horizon. "We'll have to scuff the blood and hide it good," Ace said. "No sense scaring your mother and sisters. I doubt this band'll come poking around again anytime soon." He studied Dawson's face. Though Dawson tried to muster a shield of indifference, Ace said, "You gotta remember, kid, they picked a fight and lost. That's all there is to it. Ain't no wrong nowhere in what you done."

"Don't feel good, though," he said gruffly.

"Shouldn't! Them that take pleasure in killing ain't true fighters. Not among white men anyhow. Some things gotta be done is all. When a man's pushing you—and those riding into our yard shooting to kill us surely were—it's his choice, not yours, and his consequence to bear." Ace grinned. "They picked on the wrong two men this time out."

Dawson smiled, proud to be called a man though he was only fifteen. By the time he had reached his majority and owned the legal rights of manhood, he had killed two more Comanches and a white braggart busting up a saloon. He had a reputation as a man not to be messed with, but he also went to church most Sundays, supported his mother and then unmarried sister with his labor on their farm, and had a sweetheart in town. His life had been balanced and predictable before he joined the Rangers.

That happened because after the last Comanches were sent west to the Nations, a new breed of predator moved into Texas. Shootists, thieves, and gamblers invaded the outposts formerly patronized only by hardscrabble farmers. Gaining experience was one of the reasons he'd joined the Rangers, another being a growing weariness of trying to earn a peaceable living while forever dealing with some riffraff or other raising a ruckus. He'd decided the law needed a firm hand to take root, and joined the Rangers to do that as much as earn wages to set aside for his future.

Ace, however, took another track. Not a landowner, he left the family farm after the Comanche threat had fallen to history. He drifted north to Tascosa and fell in with bad company, eddied down a drunken spiral of debauchery, and moseyed south to the border where he developed the habit of taking what he wanted with no never-mind about paying. Dawson heard news of him now and then, his name connected to a robbery or pointless outburst of violence in one hellhole or another, but it was the killing of George Bingham that cut his rope short.

Not that Ace had done it, but he'd ridden with the men who did. Watching him come out of Robertito's room and close the door, Dawson wondered if there was any chance Ace would go home and stand trial. His part in the crime had been a simple robbery that wouldn't net more than a couple of years in Huntsville. Seeing Ace glare at the star on the table, Dawson picked it up and slid it inside his vest pocket.

"You think that changes anything?" Ace asked.

Dawson shook his head.

They both listened to footsteps running toward the house. Then Liliana stopped in the doorway, her rebozo clutched tightly over her heaving bosom. Her gaze flew around the room, looking for Robertito, before she met

Dawson's eyes. "He's asleep," Dawson said, nodding at the closed bedroom door.

She glanced at it, then scowled at Ace. "I told you to no come here."

"Why shouldn't I," he drawled, "when my nephew's visiting?"

She looked at Dawson and whispered, *"Él es tu tío?"*

Dawson nodded, seeing in her eyes the hurt he had dreaded.

She shivered as if to shake ice off her back, then tossed her rebozo aside and stalked toward the stove. "Is nothing to me. Are you hungry?"

"I am," Ace said, sitting back down, watching Dawson.

Dawson pulled out a chair. "Sure. Let's break bread like family."

"That's what we are," Ace said, "though you seem to've forgotten."

"I didn't forget."

Liliana worked at the stove, keeping her back to the men.

"How long you been a Ranger?" Ace asked.

She turned then and stared at Dawson, but he kept his focus on Ace. "'Bout two years."

"You come down here to get me?"

"Take you back, if I can."

"Under arrest?"

Dawson nodded.

"You hear that, Liliana?" Ace said, his gaze locked on Dawson's. "He's here to arrest me!"

"Madre de Dios," she accused. "You place me and Robertito in the middle of that?"

Dawson looked at her then. "I didn't want to. It just happened."

Her shoulders sank, the hard stance of her anger giving way to forgiveness. *"Ah, sí,"* she sighed. "I believe you."

Ace's frown darted back and forth between them. Dawson's hand itched to be nearer his Peacemaker, but he knew if he moved, Ace would jump to the play. Liliana brought plates to the table, went back for silverware, dropped forks and knives to clatter beside the plates, then returned to the stove and lifted a tea towel off a pan of enchiladas she slid into the oven, banging the door.

"Too bad we don't have some whiskey," Ace said.

She went to her bedroom for the half-empty bottle Dawson had brought. Smacking it down in front of Ace, she turned to the cupboard for glasses.

Ace glowered at Dawson. "Drinking in bed, were you?"

Dawson kept quiet, having no honorable answer.

Liliana brought the glasses and turned back toward the stove, but Ace caught and held her beside him. Dawson stood up, his hand loose by his gun.

Ace thumbed the cork off the bottle and sloshed whiskey into the glasses, spilling some on the table.

"See what a pig you are," Liliana muttered.

Ace pushed a glass toward Dawson. "Sit down. We're having a drink 'fore breaking bread."

"What're we drinking to?" Dawson asked, not moving.

Ace lifted a glass. "How 'bout the bonds of kinship?"

Dawson tried to read Ace's intent, gauging the balance between threat and reconciliation. Meeting his hope halfway, he picked up the glass with his gun hand.

Ace emptied his glass, his eyes pinned on Dawson, and quietly set it back down. His steady control fed Dawson's hope.

"To kinship," he said. He sipped the whiskey and slid the glass on the table.

Quick as a rattler, Ace drew his gun and lunged to his feet. Liliana screamed, twisting to escape. He thrust the barrel between her breasts and pulled the trigger. She slumped limp as blood drenched the front of her dress. He dropped her and edged toward the door, his weapon now leveled at Dawson.

Dawson's palm was halfway to his gun, his fingers splayed as his hand hovered in the air. He heard the bedroom door open and felt a shock of horror ricochet from the boy. Ace stepped back off the *portal* and disappeared in the dark. Dawson drew his gun and ran. In the yard he heard Ace's horse gallop away and his sorrel whinny from the corral. Turning toward it, he saw the boy fall to his knees beside Liliana. Her blood seeped onto his nightshirt and rose with his wail like a flower of grief. Dawson took another step toward his horse. Above its restless hooves in the soft dust, he heard the boy cry, and he turned back around.

IN THE FIRST light of dawn, he smoothed the blanket and tossed the saddle on his sorrel, leaned for the cinch and tied it, then stared across the cantle at the boy standing mute beside the fresh grave. Dawson led his horse toward it. Stopping behind the boy, he gently laid his hand on the small, rigid shoulder.

"I'm going after him now," Dawson said. "If I'm not back in two days, I want you to walk into the village and tell the priest what happened. Can you do that?"

The boy nodded.

Dawson squeezed his shoulder. "I'll be back for you."

He swung into his saddle and rode toward Corazón. In front of the Cantina Escondida, only one horse was tied to the rail. A good-quality black gelding, it stood with its head down and a rear hoof cocked, as if it had been there all night. Dawson tied his sorrel beside it and slipped the keeper strap off his pistol as he descended the two steps into the dugout.

Ace was alone in the dim, smoke-stale room, at the same corner table where Dawson had sat. Dawson walked across the hard-packed dirt and stopped a scant stretch away. Ace watched him, not moving behind a nearly empty bottle of whiskey.

"Stand up."

Ace's smile was a crooked reminder of better times. "You gonna arrest me?"

A flicker of hope lit the dark of Dawson's intent. "If you surrender, I'll take you back to Texas for trial."

"On what charge?"

"Robbing Sender and Siebenborn's mercantile."

Ace emptied his bottle into a dirty glass, threw the shot back, and set the glass down. "You come all this way on account of some storekeeps?"

Dawson shook his head. "Friend of mine was killed tracking the scum you rode with."

Ace's dark eyes squirmed with injustice. "Wasn't my doing."

"Would've been, if you'd been there."

"So you took it on yourself to make certain that next time I ain't?"

Dawson nodded. "Told my sergeant it was family business."

"Where I come from," Ace drawled, "family don't turn on each other. Was a time you came from the same place."

"I've just left a kid mourning his mother," Dawson spit out. "That's where I come from."

Ace laid his hands flat on the table. "Remember when we killed them Comanches what come shooting into our yard?"

Dawson nodded.

"Remember what I said 'bout them picking a fight they lost? That's what Liliana done by bedding you."

"Stand up," Dawson said, his throat dry.

"Okay." Ace leaned on his hands and heaved himself out of the chair. "But one thing I gotta say, Dawson."

"What?"

"I ain't going nowhere."

The twisted mockery of Ace's smile dropped Dawson's hand to his gun. Ace flipped the table on edge and drew his Colt in the crash. Dawson fired, his bullet spinning Ace into the corner. Slumped against the wall, he dropped his hand and pulled the trigger, his bullet digging a furrow in the floor that didn't quite reach Dawson's boots.

Still holding his gun, Dawson leaned with his hands on his knees as the stench of gunpowder mingled with the stale smoke in the room. He opened his mouth and gasped the bad air into his lungs, let it out with a moan, then stood up straight and squared his shoulders to muster the weight of another chore of family business.

The black shifted impatiently when he draped the corpse across its saddle. His sorrel nickered in welcome as he untied its reins. Leading the burdened black, he rode back to the *casita*. The boy sat cross-legged by his mother's grave, watching silently as Dawson dug another beside it. He smoothed the mound, then stood a moment leaning on the shovel as the afternoon breeze dried the sweat from his shirt.

Looking at the boy, he asked, "Did you get everything you want from inside?"

Robertito nodded.

Dawson threw his jacket behind his saddle, settled his hat low above his eyes, and lifted the boy onto the black. Swinging onto his sorrel, he reined it toward the river.

The crossing was deep and the horses swam half the way. Gaining the firm ground of Texas, they shook Mexico off their hides before ambling north. Robertito twisted in his saddle to watch the river disappear, then looked at Dawson and asked, "Where will I live now?"

Dawson smiled. "You'll be staying with a lady in town."

"What town?"

"It's called Round Rock."

Robertito mouthed the name under his breath. "Is the lady married?"

"Not quite yet," Dawson said.

To Kill a Ranger

‑‑‑‑‑

by Brendan DuBois

Brendan DuBois is the award-winning author of short stories and novels. His short fiction has appeared in *Playboy*,
Ellery Queen's Mystery Magazine, *Alfred Hitchcock's Mystery
Magazine*, *Mary Higgins Clark Mystery Magazine*, and
numerous anthologies. He has twice received the Shamus
Award from Private Eye Writers of America for his short
stories, and has been nominated three times for an Edgar
Allan Poe Award by the Mystery Writers of America. He
lives in New Hampshire with his wife, Mona. Visit his website at www.BrendanDuBois.com.

NEAR A GROVE of cottonwood trees somewhere in a dusty
section of the Texas panhandle, Henry Hayes squatted
by the early morning fire, eating a piece of gristly bacon
with his fingers, waiting for his idiot cousin Joshua to make
it back from the nearby town. His horse was hobbled near
the grove, trying to find some bits of green for his own
damn breakfast, as Henry waited. He was thirty years old,
a veteran of the War Between the States, and right now, at
this moment, he had a couple of silver dollars to his name,
his gear, and his .44 Colt revolver, and if Joshua came back

with good news, he intended to do something about his lack of money, and right quick.

He chewed the bacon, spat out a piece of pig's hair. The bacon was smoked and salty and old, and he had gotten it about a week ago, at another town called McMurty. He stretched up, rubbed at his bearded face, squinted off to the west. There was a town over there, a town called Denton, and if Joshua had done a good job, he planned to pay that nice little town an ugly little visit later this morning. He shifted some, scratched at his beard again, and then bent down to pour himself some coffee, though the weak brew he had this morning could barely be called coffee at all. More like a chicory-and-acorn-nut mix than anything else, and the bitter taste reminded him of the years with his regiment during the war, marching and fighting and sleeping and fighting some more. He sipped at the hot brew, thought he heard something over the low wind.

He shaded his eyes and there was a horseman approaching. He put the metal cup down and waited, maneuvered himself around so that he could draw quickly if he had to. Nothing left to chance, that's why he had lived so long— all right, if not so well—and he thought the horseman was his cousin was coming back, but wouldn't it be a hell of a thing if it was somebody else and he got his head blown off while bending down to empty the coffee cup?

But as the horseman drew closer, he relaxed some, recognizing the gait of the approaching horse and the sloppy seating of the rider, and he knew Joshua had come back. Joshua drew the horse to a stop by the stream and leapt off, smiling his gap-toothed smile, slapping dust off his pants. Joshua was ten years younger and ten years dumber, and the only reason Henry rode with the boy was because of the company, and because sometimes, he served a purpose, like now, scouting on up ahead in Denton. The lad had a sunburnt and freckled face that made him look like a schoolboy, ready to go out in the yard and play snap-the-whip, and that innocent look made most people either ignore him or try to befriend him. The dumb boy went along with it well, and would come back later to tell Henry where the bank was, or the saloon, or the boardinghouse, or anyplace else that had money or goods to steal.

Joshua ambled over, still grinning. "Get myself a cup, Henry?"

"Sure," he said, handing over his own cup. "Finish it off."

Joshua swallowed, made a face. "Sorry, Henry, that stuff's swill, 'pared to what I had back there in Denton this mornin'. Had myself a nice fair breakfast with—"

"Shut it," Henry said, voice low, and Joshua did just that. Joshua had learned some things well along the trail they had cut through Texas and Arkansas, and one of the first things was to know when to shut up. Joshua would just yap and yap and yap, like some damn lost kitten or something, and it was someplace outside of Nacogdoches when Henry leaned over his saddle and just gave the kid a big slap to the face. Joshua had nearly fallen off off his horse from the blow, and Henry had just said, "You ride with me, you keep your mouth shut most of the time, all right? You talk when spoken to, or when you got somethin' important to say, but Judas Priest, stop talking to me about Betsy Murphy and how you almost got into her bloomers."

So that had been that. But now, after hearing Henry, Joshua nodded and seemed to straighten up, and he said, "Just a little town, Henry. Take you about two minutes to see it all. Saloon, couple of homes, a bank, livery stable—"

"You know what I'm lookin' for," he said. "Is it there?"

Joshua nodded quick, like a little bird, bouncing its head up and down. "Yep. Assay Office is right there, just like we heard over in Poulton."

Henry felt a little bit of satisfaction. That was the way to do things, to take time. Sure, it made for some dry spells when there weren't many good pickings, but better to take the time than to be quick and end up dangling from a rope tossed over a tree limb. There were other outriders out there who raised merry hell from town to town, drinkin' and whorin' and robbin' everything and anything, and in a month or two or three, they were caught. And they usually got a fair trial and then they were hung, and that was that. Henry had gone through the late war without being shot by a Federal soldier to end up dead 'cause he was too eager, too hungry. He did the jobs he could, but he also spent a fair amount of time lookin' and listenin'. And last week, while they were resting up in Poulton, some drunk at a saloon there went on about how the Assay Office in Denton had cheated him because it had used false weights. Seemed the Assay Office took in some of the precious metals from a couple of mines in the county that were close to Denton, and this drunk didn't think it was fair, that there was only one office within a day's riding distance.

Henry didn't particularly care if this drunk had gotten cheated or not. What did interest him was the Assay Office, how big it was, and how well guarded. Which is why he and his cousin had ridden off in the direction of Denton, and why Joshua had gone in there yesterday, to look for work as a stable hand or hotel boy or whatever, but to also learn what things were like in that town. Like the scouts that went ahead in his regiment, poking and prying where the Yankees were encamped, that's what Joshua did for him. Of course, Joshua was no soldier, and would probably wet his drawers at the sound of cannon fire, but he had held up well these past months, not complaining much and sometimes doing gunplay—mostly cover fire—when Henry was making good his escape.

Now he said to Joshua, "What's the office look like? What kind of building?"

So as the two of them stood by the small stream, Joshua talked about the building and how big it was, and how it had one door out front and a smaller one out back— "that wasn't locked, if you can believe it"—and there was a saloon on one side of the Assay Office and a barbershop on the other side, and how the only guard was an old man with a shotgun across his lap, dozing in a chair on the boardwalk outside, and on and on the questions and answers went, as the sun went higher up into the Texas sky.

Then Henry, knowing that he pretty much knew how the town looked like from what Joshua had just told him, kicked the fire dead and bent down and emptied the coffeepot and set to washing the pot and the cup with dry sand. He said, "You done good. This is how it'll go. Just a raid. I'll go in by myself and you stay outside. I'll go into the rear and make it quick, just picking up what I can, and then we'll ride the hell out 'fore anybody knows what's going on."

He licked his dry lips, felt a warm tremor in his belly and in his hands as well. This could be good, a quick raid on the Assay Office that could set him and his stupid cousin up for a while, maybe head down to Louisiana for a while and relax, stop riding so much and sleeping out on the ground. He didn't read much, but he knew how the dime novels made a big deal of robbery and gunfighting, but he had been sleeping on the ground for almost his entire life, from being in the regiment as a youngster to working as a steer hand at a few dusty ranches, and now, sliding into what he knew best: killing men and robbing men of what they had, 'cause that's the man he was. No amount of churchgoing or hymn-singing was ever going to change that, and he was going to—

"Uh, Henry?" his cousin interrupted.

"What?" he snapped, and the young boy stepped back, like he was afraid he was going to get hit or something. "What is it?"

Joshua no longer looked so young, and in fact, he look scared. The boy wiped at his face and said, "There's one other thing I was going to tell you. About the town."

"And what's that?"

"There's an old man, lives in the town. Name's Gus Mc-Cloud. He's a Texas Ranger. Or was 'fore he got too old. And, uh, well, that does change things, don't it?"

Henry got up from his work, picked up the coffeepot and cup and put them way in a leather rucksack, walked over to his horse, still valiantly looking for something green to eat. Joshua stood still for a moment, and then tagged along. "Did you hear me, Henry? What I said back there? That the town's got a Texas Ranger that lives there."

Henry fastened the rucksack to his saddle, turned to his cousin. "So? And I'm sure there's an old man who's a lawman there too. And it don't matter. Old men don't scare me. Hell, Texas Rangers don't scare me none either."

Joshua's face seemed to be paler. "You heard what they did, last year, didn't you? In Brownsville?"

"I reckon you're gonna tell me, so go ahead."

Joshua swallowed. "I read it in a paper, few months ago. There was a rustling ring, working out of Brownsville. The Rangers went in to do a job and there was some gunplay. One of the Rangers got killed. And the other Rangers . . . well, they went out and did what they did, and there was twelve rustlers killed."

Henry kept quiet, tightening up the straps on the saddle, removing the hobble. Joshua said, "And that ain't all. The twelve dead rustlers? The Rangers brought them into the center of town, stacked 'em up like cordwood. Send the people there a message, nice and loud, like a school bell. A hell of a thing, don't you say?"

"I guess."

"Well . . . don't you think we might want to . . . you know, not go into town? I mean, a Texas Ranger and all . . ."

Henry turned, glared at his cousin. "You saddle up, Joshua. Saddle up now. We've got work ahead of us."

Joshua stared at his older cousin for a bit, then looked down at the ground and walked back to his horse.

THEY RODE IN silence for a while, Henry grimacing every now and then as a particular jolt caused his butt to hit the saddle harder. There were a couple of sore boils on his butt cheeks and they hurt something awful, which was something else the dime novels never wrote about.

The ground was relatively flat as they headed to Denton, following the streambed for a while, and then a row of telegraph poles. Joshua kept quiet and Henry suddenly felt sorry for the kid, just asking questions and all, and he said, "Joshua."

"Yessir."

"Look here, and listen well, all right?"

"Yessir."

"There ain't nothing special about a Texas Ranger," Henry said, looking out to the horizon, seeing a smudge that probably meant smoke from Denton. "He puts on his boots one at a time, just like you and me. Understand?"

"I do."

"Now," Henry said, holding the reins tight in his hands.

"A Texas Ranger, part of what he has is that big story behind him, that big legend. How a Texas Ranger eats rattlesnake meat and pisses vinegar, how he can ride a hundred miles without food or sleeping, just to catch some outlaw. That he can shoot the wings off a fly with both eyes closed. That's how a Texas Ranger works. Just a story to scare kids and fools. Nothing else."

"But Henry, I mean, there's been stories about—"

"Look, did I say you could talk? Did I?"

"Nossir."

"All right then. Just listen and tell me what I want to hear. This old man, who told you about this Texas Ranger?"

"The mayor," Joshua said. "Mayor Turner. Old man with a big black hat, long white beard, wears a fancy vest . . . smells like lilac water. He was talking to some of the traders out in front of the hotel. Talking about how proud Denton was to have an old Ranger in town, to keep the peace and protect the people. Said Gus McCloud was an old man but he could still do his job. That's what he said."

Henry nodded, kept looking on ahead. Yep, smoke smudges were getting more clear. They were getting closer.

"That's just fine," Henry said, "Thing is, he's an old man. His eyesight's gone, his hands and arms are trembling, he can't see straight or shoot straight. And he probably can't move quick either. So we're gonna go into town, and as quick as can be, you're gonna be in front of the Assay Office while I go in the back and do my business. And then I'll come out front, ready to shoot anybody who gets in my way, and the two of us will ride out, and by the time they get this Texas Ranger awake from his nap, we'll be over the next rise and nobody'll catch us. Nobody. That's what we'll do, all right?"

He looked over at his younger cousin, who nodded in reply. Henry said, "You got any questions?"

"Nossir, none at all."

"Good."

Henry winced as his rear hit the saddle again, striking a boil. He don't know why it was, but sometimes like this, he wished his cousin would ask him a couple of questions, because sometimes—like now—he felt like he had something to say. And if Joshua asked the question, "Well, Henry, why do you do this?" he knew what the answer was: that ever since the war he had liked killing. There it was, right out in the open, and he wasn't afraid to think it. He liked the feel of a gun in his hands, a rifle or revolver, didn't matter much, but he also liked seeing what happened when he pulled the trigger. That like some magic, he could reach out and make a man fall down, make a man bleed and moan and beg for mercy, and God help him, ever since the early days in the regiment, that's what he liked. Oh, he liked the stealing and spending and drinking and whoring, but killing was what he liked to do, and he had a shiver, thinking of what was ahead of him.

To kill a Texas Ranger.

My Lord, he thought, how pleasurable that might just be. And think of the dime novels that might be written about him, Henry Hayes, for what he had done.

That'd be a hell of a thing.

Ahead, the low buildings of Denton were beginning to reveal themselves.

THERE WAS A rutted and beaten-up road of sorts that led into Denton, chewed up by wagon wheels and horseshoes. He and Joshua paused for a moment, just to catch their breath, see what was there, and a wagon and tired-looking horse rolled by, farmer and wife sitting up forward, couple of kids in the back of the wagon, hanging onto the wooden sides. The farmer was bearded and looked angry, and the woman looked old, face pinched, like the last time she had smiled was when she was twelve. He felt a shiver of thanks that he had never settled down with a woman, and no doubt never would. Only a couple of things women were good for, and Henry had found out that whatever they had that he needed, some coin was all that it took for him to get it. Either a meal in a kitchen or a romp in the bedroom, he knew he'd never depend on a wife. To keep him home, chained to a farm or a ranch or some shack outside of a beaten-up town like Denton?

The hell with that.

He looked over at Joshua. "Okay, boy, let's get a m[...] on."

ENTERING THE TOWN, he felt a tingle of anticipation, thinking of what was ahead for him. It was like he was back in the regiment, that queasy, tingly feeling in your gut when the shouts and yells would erupt, you would hear the pop-pop-pop of the gunfire get louder, sometimes sounding like a roar of thunder, and smelling the gunpowder and the sweat of fear and then seeing the bluebellied bastards ahead of you, knowing that some of them, standing and breathing and thinking right at this moment, would be bleeding out to death, and all because of you.

My, the joy that would bring.

The town was like a half-dozen other towns in this stretch of Texas, except the main street seemed more narrow. There were boardwalks on either side, and the usual cluster of buildings: livery stable, the telegraph office, a bank, a couple of saloons, and a tired-looking building with a sagging roof that grandly proclaimed itself to be the Denton Excelsior Hotel. Horses were lined on either side, bound to hitching rails, and the dusty street was cluttered with horse turds and buzzing clouds of flies. Women with straw baskets over their arms walked across the road, holding up some of their dirty skirts, and a couple of dogs were fighting over a bone near a blacksmith shop.

"There," Joshua said, his voice eager. "Over there, to the right."

"Okay, keep it easy." Henry looked at the building, just like the boy said. Assay Office flanked on one side by another saloon, and by a barbershop. He rubbed at his scratchy beard. There was a thought, to get a nice shave be-
going over to the Assay Office, but that would be stu-
get in and do the job and get the hell out, before
le in the town knew what was going on and old
oud, Texas Ranger, got himself out of bed and
way out to the street.

drew closer to the Assay Office, Henry grinned. What a bit of luck. He said, "I thought you told me that the place had a guard out front. Ain't nobody there now."

Joshua leaned forward in his saddle. "That they do. There was an old man there yesterday, sitting in a chair, shotgun in his lap." Joshua turned to him, grinning. "Old fool's probably sitting in an outhouse somewhere, that's what."

Henry said, "Then it makes everything easier. You just stay out front, you get your gun ready, and shoot anybody that makes a move when I come running out. All right?"

Joshua nodded, licked his lips quick-like. "Sure, Henry. I'll do that."

"Good. You just wait and watch."

Joshua halted in front of the Assay Office, while Henry rode up and dismounted. He threw the reins around the hitching post, not tying them off at all, and then stepped on the boardwalk, gave a quick look in. Waist-high counter, woman and man working there. Maybe husband and wife. Gad, bad enough to be married to a woman, but to have to work all day, standing next to her . . . He pulled at his gun belt as he slipped down a narrow alleyway, filled with trash and bones and more flies, so narrow his shoulders were brushing the sides of each building. Around to the rear and there was a door there, locked now, instead of being unlocked like Joshua had said, and he stood by barrels of trash, looking at a cluster of shacks behind him that were probably the homes of some of the people here. What a place. He tried the door again, still locked, and remembered a horseman in the regiment had served for a with a general named Nathan Bedford Forrest. The h man said the general was a crazy old man who was the b general ever, and one of the general's favorite sayings was, "Get there fustest with the mostest," or something like that.

Well, Henry was here, and it was time to get there fustest. He took out his revolver and placed it against the doorknob, closed his eyes, and fired.

The *boom!* sounded pretty goddamn loud in the rear of the building, which was fine. He shouldered the door open and went through a narrow hallway, and sure enough, he was in the rear of the office, with desks and ledgers and, glory be, an open safe. The man and woman had come through, dressed in their trading-clothes-finest, to see what the noise and fuss was all about, and he kept his gun up and said, "This'll be quick, and I'm gonna take what I want, and you're gonna let me, and nobody needs to get hurt. You savvy?"

The woman and man said nothing, but the woman was looking at him with pure hate and spite, and he just tried to ignore her while he went to the safe. He knew he didn't have time to examine the canvas bags, so he grabbed as many as he could, tying off a sling so he could put them over his shoulders, and damn it all to hell, what happened then was that the man stepped out of the office, just for a moment, and while Henry said, "Don't do it, fool," the man came back with a shotgun.

Henry didn't hesitate, knowing what a scattergun like that could to his insides at this range. He fired again, the *boom!* louder still in this room, and it looked like the bullet struck the man's shoulder, making him spin, and the damn woman started screeching like a harpy, and now it was just move, move, get the hell out before the whole town came over to see what the hell was going on.

went around the counter, out to the front door, open-
and stepping outside in the hot air, not believing
he had been, and how good it was going, and—

hell?

goddamn hell?

Joshua was gone.

His cousin and his horse weren't there, not at all.

And the street seemed empty.

Damn it.

He went over to his horse, undid the reins, dumped the canvas bags over the saddle, and then got up, moved away from the Assay Office and the screaming woman inside. He turned around, saw that the street that he and his cousin had just come through was now blocked by some wagons.

Not good.

He wheeled around, to head out of town through the other end, and that way was blocked as well.

By a tall man, standing alone.

Henry held the reins with one hand and his Colt revolver with the other, and started riding out and riding hard. He got closer to the man, saw him standing stock-still, like he was rooted to the place, and the old man's hand was on his holstered gun, and Henry got closer, saw the sun glinting off the Texas Ranger badge pinned to his shirt, and Henry didn't hesitate at all, he fired off shot after shot, aiming right for the damn Ranger's chest, and damn it to hell, the old man just stood there, didn't move, just stood there, and Henry was shifting his gun, ready to blow the old fool's head off, and then—

A blow, right to his chest.

Another to his belly, which flipped him off the horse.

And he slammed to the ground, on his back, by the old man's feet. He couldn't breathe, couldn't speak. All he could do was look. And what he saw was wood, can you believe, thin planks that looked like they were holding up that Ranger, and he looked up at the leathery man's quiet face, and he closed his eyes.

HE WOKE UP to the shouting. A familiar voice. He blinked his eyes and Joshua was leaning over him, yelping the same thing, over and over again: "They caught me good, Henry! Right after you went down the alleyway! I couldn't do nothing! Henry, they're gonna hang me! Henry, you gotta do something!"

He coughed, his chest aching something fierce, and, oh, God, his belly . . . not his belly. He had seen bad belly wounds during the war, where soldiers would moan and shout and scream as they slowly died, for there was hardly anything a surgeon could do for a belly wound, and God, it hurt so much. . . .

A voice, from a man he couldn't see. "Let's get him in the shade at least. We should do that."

Strong hands picked him up, put him down on a board or a plank, and he was brought up to a boardwalk, and he couldn't help it, he was crying from the pain. Some kind soul wiped at his face with a cool washcloth and he whispered, "Thank you . . . thank you . . ."

Then a man came into view, with a black hat and long white beard and vest, and from somewhere, Henry remembered what Joshua had said earlier that day, a lifetime ago. This man was the town's mayor.

The mayor nodded and said, "Figured you was gonna get away with robbin' the Assay Store and shooting Frank Perkins, am I right?"

"Yeah . . ."

The mayor was smiling. "Bet you didn't figure on running into a Texas Ranger on your way, out, though."

Henry coughed, felt the burning spread in his belly. His fingers and arms could move, but he was too scared to touch the wetness on his chest and belly. "What . . . what happened?"

More voices around him, but he could only hear the mayor. The mayor said, "What happened is, we didn't like the looks of your boy, comin' in yesterday, and when he came back today, with somebody as rough-lookin' as you, me and a few volunteers decided to see what was gonna happen. Saw you sneak through the alleyway, figured you wasn't going there to piss or something, so we grabbed the boy. Figured best to have him out of the way. And then we got Gus McCloud out to where he'd do us the most good, and we got the street blocked. So all you had to do was head towards Gus."

"But . . . who shot me . . ."

"Oh, a couple of the boys up on the roof of the hotel. But know this, boy, they fired only after you started shootin' first at our Texas Ranger. . . ."

Henry groaned and tried to speak, and the mayor drew closer. "What's that, boy? What did you say?"

Henry groaned again. "But the Ranger . . . he's already dead. . . ."

That caused some laughter, and the mayor kept on smiling. "Surely is, for more than a year now. Poor Gus got confused last winter, when we got a fierce snowstorm through here. Wandered away from his room and died out there, and froze to death. And it was like the luck of God himself, he stayed out there, when the sun dried him out. Like the doc said, old Gus was so tough and ornery, no varmint dared chew on him. So we brought him back and we got a nice wake goin' on for him, and don't know how it happened, but it just did. You see, boy, having a Texas Ranger in town, even a retired one, meant trouble went somewhere else. And we didn't want word gettin' out that Gus was dead. So we stored him in a nice, cool root cellar, and maybe every few months or so, we have to bring 'em out and prop 'em up, just like today. Course, poor Gus can't shoot that well nowadays, so we give 'em so help."

That caused some laughter from the other men, and Henry raised his weak voice. "But . . . it'll be known. . . ."

"By who? You? Or that boy of yours, who's gonna be dancin' at the end of a rope 'fore the day's out?"

"But the damn Ranger is dead!" Henry said, groaning again from the exertion.

The mayor grinned, revealing tobacco-stained teeth. "Don't you know, boy, you can kill a man, you can kill him dead, but there ain't no way you can kill a Ranger."

Henry couldn't help himself. He groaned, groaned real loud, as the pain just grew in his belly. The mayor leaned forward. "The doc, he's busy with Frank Perkins, working on his shoulder, so he can't be here with you, though there's nothing he can do. Our preacher, though, he's comin' over here, but I don't think he's gonna make it in time. You got any last words to say, boy, now's the time to say 'em."

He looked up, everything hazy, and he said, as clear as he could, "You go to hell, old man."

The mayor cackled. "I might just rightly do that, son, but I guarantee, you're gonna get there first."

Avenger

by Juanita Coulson

A native Hoosier who now resides in Ohio, Juanita
Coulson began writing professionally in 1963. To date she
has published seventeen novels and an assortment of short
stories and nonfiction—SF, fantasy, historical novels, mysteries, a comic-book history, media-related nonfiction, and
others. She is also a singer and composer, with several
recordings in print.

HE STARED AT the ruins. Everything he treasured was
gone. Some of the rancho's pillaged and burned struc-
tures still smoldered, the smoke drifting lazily in the autumn wind. Here and there lay the bodies—men and boys
cut down ruthlessly as they had fought to defend the property. His kinsmen and their loyal employees—all of them
slain without mercy.

The livestock was gone, of course, along with everything else of value on the property. The *bandidos* had been
very thorough. After they'd killed the defenders, they'd
looted. And what they'd found not worth the taking, they'd
put to the torch. Nothing remained to suggest this had once
been a prospering homestead.

His companions were speaking to him, commiserating,

sharing his grief and rage. But their voices barely penetrated the terrible darkness gripping his soul. Despite the others' presence, he felt utterly alone.

I am the sole survivor. What I worked so hard to help build is ashes.

Then one word of the surrounding conversation stabbed through the black wall of his despair. A friend was examining signs left by the raiders. Signs all too well known of late throughout this region. Studding his discovery with loud curses, the man spat a name: Matarife.

So! It was Matarife who had murdered family and servants, stolen the stock, burned the rancho. Matarife, the infamous *bandido* leader, the one who called himself "Slaughterman."

The survivor had a target now. His grief was channeled into a burning desire for vengeance. He had to kill Matarife. That was debt owed to his dead, and it was the only medicine that might ease his sorrow and hate.

He thought hard, planning more carefully than he ever had—hot anger being forged into cold calculation.

By now, the *bandidos* no doubt were long gone. And if the survivor and his companions tracked them, the signs inevitably would lead to the river—and across. Into forbidden territory. When Matarife struck, that yellow coward always retreated to his hideout over the border. There he could enjoy his ill-gotten gains, brag of his conquests, and decide where to raid next. That had been the outlaw's pattern for months. No reason to think he was going to change.

The survivor glanced at his friends. Good men, all of them. But each had family and obligations elsewhere. He had none. Not now. Matarife had taken away all of it. As a result, he alone was free to act. No duties to tend to, and no one to care what happened to him.

And yet . . .

How to get the job done? There was no way he could bring down Matarife by himself. The Slaughterman had too many followers, alleged to be dead shots, every one. No lone assassin had a prayer of reaching their leader. Any such attempt would be committing suicide to no purpose.

He had to face facts: Matarife was too well guarded for one man to take.

A dedicated *group,* however—*that* should do the trick. The survivor nodded, satisfied with the train of his thoughts, making his decision.

Captain McKenzie's Rangers. The troop was currently on patrol in this area. He'd join up with them. By all reports, McKenzie was already sniffing out Matarife's trail. The survivor could bring fresh news of the murderer's most recent attack, and then add his weapons and skills to those of the captain's other men.

It wouldn't be easy. Captain McKenzie might not want or need him. He might have to do some hard talking to convince the officer to let him be part of the hunting team. Whatever it took, whatever argument or promise, he'd make it.

He'd see Matarife dead, no matter the cost.

WILL BRIGGS SHIFTED his weight, easing muscles strained by the effort of sitting motionless so long. He couldn't allow himself to stiffen up. If anything happened, he had to be able to act fast. There'd be no time then to work kinks out of his joints. He took a deep breath and focused on the darkened prairie to the south. A half-moon, though almost covered by cloud, still gave enough light for a sharp-eyed youngster to see remarkably well. During Will's sixteen years he'd kept lookout over his family's little holding on more occasions than he cared to count.

Until the last occasion, when he'd been away fetching supplies and returned to find . . .

He shifted his position again minutely. Though he was dedicated to carrying out his assignment, it felt like he'd been sitting here for hours. This sort of enforced rigidity took its toll. Smothering a sigh, the boy consoled himself by remembering that his watch would be over soon. Maybe he'd have a chance to grab at least a bit of sleep before the troop moved out again.

Will tensed, all his senses suddenly drawn taut. There was movement out there in the black landscape, a barely detectable stirring, far less than that of a breeze ruffling the sagebrush. But hard-learned lessons had taught the boy how to detect the difference between natural surroundings and an intrusion.

Smoothly, soundlessly, he brought his rifle to bear on the site of that faint disturbance, waiting.

The next time it moved, he'd bring it down, *if* his eyes confirmed that it was indeed what he'd first glimpsed—human.

A gloved hand closed around the rifle barrel, forcing it down and off target. Startled, momentarily forgetting the need for quiet, Will snarled, "What d'you think you're . . . ?"

The rest of his words stuck in his throat. Captain McKenzie was kneeling beside him, whispering, "Don't shoot, son. That's one of my scouts, coming in to report."

Will's anger died as quickly as it had risen. He nodded, grateful he'd been spared from making an embarrassing mistake. Cutting down a Ranger scout sure wouldn't gain him any friends here. He was still too new to the troop, on a sort of probation. He had to mind his manners closely if he hoped to fit in and accomplish his goal.

The captain transferred his hand from the rifle to Will's

shoulder, pressing firmly. The two eased back down from the sandy knoll serving as a lookout post. Man and boy didn't risk standing until they were well shielded below the small rise. Then McKenzie hurriedly led the way back to their campsite.

Reese, his second in command, had already roused the troop. Men were rolling up blankets, gathering gear, and checking weapons, anticipating action. Their captain looked southward, waiting patiently.

When the figure finally emerged from the darkness, Will's hands tightened anew on his rifle. Without conscious thought, he swung the muzzle toward the approaching scout. McKenzie's growl stopped him and, reluctantly, Will lowered his gun. Moving a step closer to the officer, he muttered, "He's a Mex, Cap'n. He's one o' them that we're huntin'."

"No, Will. Not one of them. One of mine."

"Those filthy raiders killed my folks. Told y'that's why I wanted to join up with you, to run 'em down and pay 'em for what they done. . . ."

McKenzie motioned for quiet. His voice low and calm, he said, "I know. We all do. Not a man here doesn't nourish a hate for Matarife and his *bandidos*. But you'll follow orders, Will, if you want to ride with us. Trust me on this. We'll catch that gang of cutthroats, and soon. Just have some patience, son."

For a moment, Will bridled, then bit his lip and fell quiet. Captain McKenzie wasn't all that much older than Briggs. At least not in years. In know-how, though, and confident savvy, he was a hardened veteran. The boy had heard plenty of tales to confirm that. And if he needed further proof, he had only to watch the way the officer's men reacted to his commanding presence and hastened to obey his words. Whatever his doubts, Will knew he had best hold his tongue. He very much wanted to remain a member of this troop. No Ranger captain brought more border raiders to ruin than McKenzie. That was exactly the sort of man Will Briggs had vowed would be his leader on this quest. In the end, that would bring him to his much-sought goal.

The Mexican moved like a cat—smoothly and noiselessly. He was little more than a man-sized silent shape, barely visible in the pale light.

"Paco," McKenzie murmured in greeting.

"Fire okay," the man replied gruffly. "No *bandido* close by. They will not see."

Nodding, the captain said, "Stir the coals a bit, boys. Let's have some coffee and breakfast before we ride." As they set about that task, their officer and the Mexican hunkered. Paco set aside the shotgun he carried and began to scratch at the dusty ground. When the campfire glowed to renewed life, Will saw that the scout was drawing a crude map. Along with others, he bent closer, trying to see, listening intently.

"They come along these arroyos. Matarife men . . ."

"Scouts," McKenzie speculated, thoughtfully stroking his mustache. He frowned, considering strategy. "How many?"

"*Tres.* Here, here, here." Paco indicated traces from the river northward on his rough chart. Will imagined three stealthy *bandidos* making their way along dry runs and other sheltered paths. They'd be checking to see which settlements were less well defended and ripe for the plucking. They'd be checking too for signs of any lawmen about. The invaders wanted to avoid contact with gunfighters who might be their equal. Rangers definitely qualified.

But . . . could the Rangers believe this scout's report?

The boy eyed Paco sidelong, wondering and suspicious. The captain trusted his man, and had told Will to trust him too. And yet . . . That dark face, the accented speech brought to mind images of the swarthy, murderous men who had raided Will's home.

There also was a certain coldness about the Mexican, a quality that made hair rise on the boy's nape. He couldn't quite pin down what bothered him so about the fellow. Paco looked to be in his thirties or forties, and the cut of his features suggested a well-bred background. Why was such a man scouting for the Rangers? That didn't seem to make sense.

"Could go here, here, here," Paco was saying, pointing to the three different scout tracks. "We move to this place, Capitán, and wait. Then it is easy get them all, one by one by one."

"You're sure there are no more?" McKenzie asked. "We don't want a loose tongue warning Matarife where we are."

"*Seguro, Capitán.* We capture one and make him talk. They know where Matarife is. This way we take them all." Paco didn't sound eager or excited at the prospect of capturing the notorious *bandido.* Instead, he seemed abnormally reserved and precise. Something in his manner made Will feel as though a lump of ice had formed in his guts.

McKenzie accepted the scout's words with another curt nod. "Looks like it'll be some hard riding today, boys." He stabbed a finger at the rough map. "We'll split up and see if we can't round 'em all up. Jarrett, you and Reese, this one. Andy, Nathaniel, this one."

"Want 'em alive, Cap'n?" Jarrett inquired.

The officer turned to Paco again, as if seeking the scout's advice. For some reason, that action angered Will. Listen to a scout's report, sure. But the captain ought not to behave as though the Mexican knew more than he did.

"Only need one alive," Paco said in a shiver-causing flat tone.

"You heard. Make sure Matarife's boys never get back across the river. Clear?" There was a murmur of agreement, and some evidence that the four men given those orders would be happy to carry them out to the letter.

"Will, you, I, and Paco will take the third man. He's going to be our telegraph to Matarife's plans."

The boy opened his mouth, then thought better of what he was going to say. He was in no good position to be asking fool questions. And whatever he'd been about to ask would likely qualify as foolish to the captain's ears. The better course was to buckle down and tend to business as he was commanded. He'd pray that there'd be time enough ahead to fulfill all his hopes.

Matarife was within striking distance now—if the Mexican scout could be believed. And Will desperately *did* want to believe that their quarry was almost within grasp.

IT HAD BEEN not just a hard day's ride, but two hard ones. They'd pushed their ponies far past kindness and themselves just as much. Will had been reassured that, once they were on their way, it became apparent that McKenzie knew this territory intimately. The officer plainly didn't need Paco's guidance for the journey. The Mexican had drawn a mount from the troop's *caballado,* and trailed along silently after his commander and the boy, seemingly disinterested in where they were going.

The man's attitude puzzled Will so much that he dared ask McKenzie about it. "He don't appear to care if we catch this *bandido* or not, sir."

"He cares," McKenzie said, not taking his eyes from the steady course they were cutting through brush and gully. In the heat of the day, Jim McKenzie looked both fierce and weary. His blue eyes were unnaturally bright, hinting at the ailment that would someday, no doubt, bring him to the grave. But his energies never flagged. They never had since the first time Will met him.

For long minutes, there was no further talk between them. The two rode along side by side, their ponies trudging across the dusty prairie. Finally, McKenzie said, "Believe me, Paco cares. He just has other things on his mind at the moment. Every man who joins the Rangers has a story, Will. Some of them terrible stories. We don't inquire too deeply as to a man's motives—as I didn't into yours," he reminded the boy. "All I can say is, don't judge. One never knows what you may have to do or what choices you may be forced to make, until you're up against the wall." A crooked smile split the officer's face. "We just hope it won't be a 'dobe wall, eh?"

Rattled, Will forced a soft laugh and nodded his understanding. "If we catch 'em this side of the river, there won't be any executions by firing squad, I guess."

His comment sobered the older man. McKenzie heaved a sigh and said in an odd voice, "No, no firing squads. I think I can promise that."

It was late in the day when they reached their destination. McKenzie ordered a cold camp, and the three settled down to wait. During the night first Jarrett and Reese, and then Andy Immler and Nathaniel, rode in to join the early arrivals. It was obvious his regulars, like the captain, were very familiar with this rendezvous spot. They had probably used it before on similar operations. Will tucked away this bit of information in the back of his mind. Right now, he had no real plans beyond his goal of paying back Matarife. But if he survived that encounter, he just might decide to remain with the Rangers. Learning their habits, their campsites, and their style of operation would be useful, in that case. He couldn't afford to waste such opportunities.

They staked their ponies out in a nearby patch of graze and sat down to wait. Will shivered from the cold, and so did the others. Except for Paco. The man didn't seem conscious of night chill. Nor had he seemed to feel the heat of the day during the long ride to this camp. He squatted like a heathen statue, his shotgun cradled in the crook of his arm.

False dawn loomed before Paco finally moved. He bent close to McKenzie, whispering in the captain's ear. The officer nodded and assigned each of his men with a touch on the shoulder or a barely audible murmur of instruction. They spread out and took up their posts, waiting tensely.

Matarife's scouts had not survived so long by being over-reckless. Once, during the *bandido*'s slow, cautious approach toward the ambush point, the outlaw's pony snorted uneasily. Had the brute caught the scent of the troop's horses, even though they were picketed downwind? For a long moment, the Rangers held their breath, afraid they'd be forced to strike sooner than McKenzie had planned. Fortunately, the bandit's mount quieted and didn't react again. After a brief hesitation, the scout continued his course down a long slope thick with brush and scrub. As he reached the bottom of the rise, the Rangers rose all around him.

A pistol was drawn, and then quickly dragged out of the bandit's grasp before the man had a chance to fire. In a moment, he was sprawling on the ground, helplessly pinned.

In the east, a few wispy clouds were coloring with sunrise, which gave the lawmen more than enough light to see clearly what they'd brought down.

"Qué paso? Me llama José Gutierrez. Amigo, amigo . . ."

Paco spat a harsh string of Spanish at the prisoner. Then he told McKenzie, "I know this one. In the *cantinas* south of the border, he boasts of how he . . . he uses the *mujeres* and *muchachas* in the all places they have raided. He *boasts* of this, Capitán. This one is lower than any animal."

The outburst startled Will. Paco's words and tone hinted at a background of education and good breeding. Despite filth and ragged garb, he spoke like gentleman, expressing his contempt for a fellow countryman.

No, far more than contempt. A bitter hate. Loathing of the deepest degree.

Paco bent over the captive and seized the man's hair, dragging him half upright. Still pinned by the other Rangers, José couldn't resist. He gazed at the scout with sudden dread, and his tormentor smiled.

That smile, now visible to the entire troop, thanks to the first rays of the rising sun, was terrible. Will might have been looking at a ravenous, grinning wolf. Although Paco had his hands full, pinioning José's right arm, the boy did his best to shrink away from Paco's frightening expression.

"Matarife ven cuando? Por qué camino?" The scout yanked the captive's hair hard, making José cry out in pain. Then the *bandido* steeled himself and pressed his lips tightly together, shaking his head in stubborn determination.

"He musta sworn one o' them heathen oaths, Captain," Reese volunteered. "I heard Matarife makes 'em all promise on their mothers' graves never to talk if they should get caught. I don't think we're gonna get much outta him. We sure didn't out of the others. . . ."

Will had already heard passing references to the fates of Matarife's other two scouts. Though he himself had sworn to exact a bloody vengeance for his losses, the brief accounts had left him feeling a bit sick. He hadn't dealt with such cruelty until now. The *bandidos* certainly deserved death, but he'd supposed he and his comrades would either dispatch the outlaws cleanly with a shot apiece, or take them alive and drag them before a magistrate. He'd seen men swing for their crimes. Will wouldn't mind seeing Matarife and the scum that served him die the same way. But . . .

"I will make this one talk," Paco promised. He hurried over to the saddles and fetched a couple of ropes. As he was returning to the prisoner, the scout drew his knife. For a moment, Paco waited, looking at McKenzie. The young officer's eyes glittered unnaturally in the early morning light. Finally, with obvious reluctance, he nodded.

The Rangers bound José's hands and hauled him to his feet. Dragging him bodily, they hauled him beneath a cottonwood. By the time they got there, Paco had the second rope slung over a stout limb and was tying off a noose. He dropped that over the prisoner's head. Tightening the hemp, he said, "We talk, *bandido*. *Much* talk." The scout drew his knife down along José's cheek. Delicately. Drawing only a little blood. A promise of more, as it were.

He shifted to the opposite cheek, repeating the stroke. Paco pricked with the point at the edge of the captive's right eye, then at his left. "Just a bit to start, *bueno*? Just a bit. You talk, it goes *muy rapido*. . . ."

McKenzie turned and gestured violently, ordering the rest of his men away from the scene. "Saddle up. We're riding southeast. Paco told me he's pretty sure Matarife's coming in from that direction. We'll get ahead of him and set a trap."

"Captain," Will protested, jerking a thumb over his shoulder, "we can't just ride away. Not with *that* goin' on. It's downright uncivilized, unchristian! Something

Apaches or Comanches would do to a prisoner, not white
men . . . !"

"Leave it be, son," McKenzie commanded. His manner
was firm, warning the boy that he would hear no further ar-
guments. "If you want to remain part of this troop, you will
do as I say and leave be things that you don't understand."
The officer took a deep breath and went on in a calmer
tone. "Paco will join us later—after he gets the information
we need."

"But how can we be sure he will do that?"

McKenzie's face was haunted. "He always does. Now,
get your pony ready to ride. That's an order."

Subdued and deeply troubled, Will obeyed. Somehow,
he forced himself not to look back toward the cottonwood.
He mounted up with the rest and rode out, McKenzie leading the way. They went at a walk, Jarrett and Immler scouting ahead, just in case.

Once, when they were but a short distance away from
the stand of cottonwoods, Will thought he heard a sound. It
might have been a scream—or an attempt at a scream. Perhaps it was only a varmint, falling prey to some predator
and crying out in its death throes.

The Rangers were a little over a mile out when Paco
overtook them, coming on at an easy lope. He resembled a
man who'd enjoyed a finely prepared meal and topped that
off with some *vino* and sport with a lovely and willing
señorita. Will scowled in disgust, deliberately turning his
back on the man.

But he couldn't help overhearing a hasty conversation
between the scout and his captain. Paco indeed had the information they sought: Matarife would be bringing his outlaws along the dry scrub creek bed five miles away.

"I know that area," McKenzie said. "There's a good spot
with plenty of cover right beyond he'll likely be coming

across. We'll be waiting for him. Did . . . did you find out what time he'll be moving?"

"Tonight, Capitán. He creeps through the dark, to hide his ugly face from daylight."

The officer grunted his understanding and raised an arm. "Let's ride, boys. There's a watering hole along the way. We'll give our horses a breather and then get set up long before Señor Matarife knows we're in place."

Will was torn. Anticipation made his blood race. Matarife! They were finally going to catch him—and his gang! They'd make that whole bunch of devils pay for all that they'd done to him and so many others.

If Paco was to be trusted.

Plainly, McKenzie trusted him, and must have done so often. But Will wasn't sure that was sufficient assurance for him.

And the way that Mexican looked when he'd ridden in to join them! The man was positively gloating. It didn't take too much imagination to know what had happened to the hapless José. Paco had tortured a prisoner to death, and no one had stopped him. Not McKenzie. Not any of the Rangers, including Will himself.

Dared they call themselves Christians?

Yet . . . Paco didn't talk like a heathen. Underneath the dirt and that accent, he sounded very much like a learned, cultured man. What was his story? And what could have turned him into the brutal executioner he had become?

Everything went as the scout had promised and as McKenzie had planned. Their horses refreshed, the Rangers made the ambush site well before darkness. The captain assigned them to well-shielded positions. Every man made certain of his ammunition and weapon, getting ready for any kind of dustup that might come their way.

They waited. Will mulled his doubts and hopes and

remembered his murdered kindred. He clung to that awful memory, letting it feed his courage. This was his chance to avenge them. He must make the most of it.

While they waited, a variety of worries plagued the Rangers. What if clouds came in, covering the moon? What if the *bandidos* decided to take a different route at the last moment? What if some unknown spy warned them off and they never came this way at all? Each man lurked alone, shaking off the cold, hoping their hands would stay steady on rifle and pistol when the critical moment arrived.

They worried for nothing. The sky stayed clear. And as if following a schedule, Matarife and his men rode north from the big river when twilight was just beginning to brighten the eastern hills. The bandits came in straight along the draw—perfect targets.

Paco hadn't lied. All of his information was proved true. There had been no other outlaw scouts ahead of Matarife's main party. Nor had an unsuspected spy eluded detection and raced back to warn the *bandidos* of this ambush. Matarife and his men rode into the trap as jauntily as if they paraded down a pueblo street, hailed as heroes.

Following McKenzie's prior orders, everyone in the troop held fire until their quarry had reached the spot where the outlaws were covered on all sides.

It was then that the captain stood and shouted, "Matarife! *Renuncia!*"

A lightning bolt might have struck in the midst of the raiders. They froze in their saddles for a heartbeat, then sawed frantically at their reins.

Too late!

Matarife and the rest drew weapons, and the night exploded, shattered with the exchange of pistol and rifle fire.

The Rangers, prepared and well shielded, wreaked havoc among the invaders. A few *bandidos'* rounds chipped

stone from boulders or chunks from trees protecting their
adversaries. But for the most part, it was no real contest.
The outcome was never in doubt, and the men from across
the big river began to go down.

Everything was happening so fast Will had little space
to think. He fired his rifle again and again, each time paus-
ing only long enough to make sure of his aim. He'd done a
lot of hunting in his sixteen years, keeping the cook pot
filled, and that sharpshooter's skill now served him very
well. With each body that staggered and dropped, he
seemed to hear the spirits of his murdered kin cheering
him on.

And then it was over.

Someone lit a small pile of greasewood, giving the troop
ample light to examine what they had wrought. McKenzie
moved among friend and foe, counting, assessing, totally in
command. "Boys? Anyone hit?" A chorus of noes answered
him. The single complaint came from Jarrett, a burly and
experienced older Ranger. He'd suffered a bullet crease on
the tip of one ear, and bitched mightily about that pinking.
The other Rangers taunted him mercilessly for making a
fuss over nothing.

Will let their bantering exchanges wash past him. He focused on one thing: Where was Matarife? Had they got
him? Or had he escaped in the confusion?

Frustrated at the unsteady greasewood light and general
confusion, the boy demanded, "Where is that murdering
bastard? Did he get away?"

"No, Señor Briggs. He did not get away."

Will turned toward that deep voice. Paco, his expression
smugly satisfied, hunkered beside a writhing form. "He is
here," and the scout gestured grandly, an artist exhibiting
his handiwork.

Drawing closer, Will stared a moment, then swung away,

choking down vomit. The creature squirming in agony made no coherent sound because the *bandido*'s mouth was full of blood. So was his belly, a hideous, gaping open wound, plainly the result of a point-blank shotgun blast.

McKenzie came up beside the boy and took in the grisly scene. "I should have expected this," the officer muttered. "Well, what's done is done."

Appalled, Will cried, "Captain! He's been gut-shot. And his tongue's been . . ."

"Yes, I know." Something in McKenzie's tone made the younger man shrivel inside. He no longer envisioned his dead kindred congratulating him on his courage. Instead, he was sure they were turning away from him and his comrades, horrified at the vengeance wreaked here for their sakes.

Heaving a tired sigh, McKenzie went on. "You aren't the only one who had a score to settle with Matarife, Will. And some scores were much, much bigger than yours."

With that, the officer moved off, briskly directing his men as they tended to the necessary aftermath of the battle. Several *bandidos* were still alive, though in bad shape, and—if they lived—they'd meet justice before the nearest magistrate. Rangers began putting together travois to transport the wounded. Some horses were crippled and had to be shot. McKenzie bustled about, calm and in charge, supervising everything.

Will sensed the officer found a sort of escape from black thoughts by that route, occupying himself with this tidying up. For the youngest Ranger, though, there was no escape. He turned again toward Paco, still hunkering beside the dying bandit leader. The scout no longer seemed gleeful at his foe's defeat. Rather, he looked solemn, waiting patiently for what must come.

"Put him out of his misery!" Will snapped. "If you don't, I will. . . ."

Paco rose and stepped between the boy and that living corpse thrashing about in the dust. "No, you will not, Señor Briggs. Do not make me prevent you from doing so. I do not want to cause you any harm. You are one of us. You have suffered at his hands. Do you not rejoice that he is at last repaid for his evil acts?"

"Repaid? Yes, but . . . not like *this*. It should have been . . ."

"You mean he should have died quickly and cleanly?" The Mexican's speech was now pure and crisp, his English excellent, with only the slightest accent. "He did not deserve to die so neatly. Not after all he has done to so many innocent souls. Not for what he did to *me*." That last word came out as hard and cold as ice, making Will recoil in sudden fear.

"Wh . . . what he did to you? But you're . . ."

"I am a Texan, A true citizen. I was born in Texas and have lived here all my life. I am Francisco de las Vegas, at your service. I once owned one of the finest ranchos you ever will see. . . ." Vegas broke off, and a telltale wetness filled his eyes. Then he went on. "But no more. It was destroyed by Matarife. I . . . I was away, selling some of my prize stock in the county seat, and when I returned . . . gone. Everything gone." His voice softened as he added with sympathy, "Just like you, William. Just like you. He took everything from both of us." After a long pause, he asked tentatively, "Your mother? Was she at your rancho when . . .?"

Will, beginning to feel numb and ashamed, shook his head. "My ma died when I was ten."

"Ah, *qué lastima!* Had you a sister perhaps?"

Again the boy shook his head.

Paco laid a hand on Will's shoulder. "Then in a way, you were fortunate. Yes, to lose your kinsmen and all you had known, that was terrible. For me . . . ah! For me it was . . . different. You see, he did not *kill* everyone at my rancho."

Behind him, that writhing figure made horrible, muffled strangling sounds. A man half choking on his own blood and, without a tongue, unable to express his agony in any other way. Will had been told that a man so wounded could take a long time to die. A very long time.

Francisco de las Vegas spoke now in a fatherly manner, for the first time revealing his years. Under the grime necessary for his recent work, there was the Texan equivalent of a grandee, a man possessing all the pride and dignity of that rank. His pride shone forth now, and with it a pain that explained a great deal to the boy facing him.

"My wife, Maria, and my beloved daughter, Antonia . . . he left them alive. But . . . he forced himself upon . . ." Vegas stopped, momentarily covering his eyes, shuddering at the awful memory. When he straightened, he said faintly, "They . . . they have retired to the convent. They will remain there the rest of their days, never to come forth again. Life, all earthly life, is finished for them. Forever. For me as well. I have only one life left to me—to seek out and punish those like Matarife and all the rest of his kind. Oh, yes," the man said, nodding, madness a mask now dominating his features. He repeated, "Oh, yes! There are others. And I will find them all. I will never rest until they all end just as he has. Until they all pay. Until I have avenged . . . everything."

"But . . . that could take . . ." Will's protest trailed away into silence. Pity gripped him, and horror, for he heard his own oath coming from the proud Texan's lips.

"On the grave of my sainted mother, I swear I will punish them. To the last man! No matter the cost. No matter how long it takes." Once more, the former grandee peered down at Matarife's barely living remains, and he smiled a death's-head grin at his foe's sufferings. "*Sí!* I will find them all, and I will have vengeance."

The End of Autumn

∽◦◦∽

by Russell Davis

Russell Davis currently lives in New Mexico with his wife, Monica, and their three children. His short fiction has appeared in numerous anthologies, including *Sol's Children*, *Single White Vampire Seeks Same*, *Villains Victorious*, and *Little Red Riding Hood in the Big Bad City*. His most recent novel, *Twilight Zone: A Gathering of Shadows*, is available from ibooks. In addition to writing, Russell is an editor for Five Star Publishing, running their romance and women's fiction line as well as supervising their speculative fiction series. He's currently hard at work on several novel projects.

For G. G. Boyer

THE OLD MAN stepped out onto the porch in the first dim light of the day. The air was crisp with frost, and steam rose in river-fog swirls from the cup of coffee he set with deliberate care on the porch rail. He filled and lit his pipe, and watched the quiet sun rise over the valley, listening to the birds in the cottonwoods and the two horses in the corral. A broad-shouldered, weather-beaten man with a shock of white hair and steady brown eyes, he began every morning this way, sipping his coffee and smoking his pipe while the valley woke up.

Most days, there was little else for him to do. Today would be different.

He finished his pipe, knocking the remains of the burnt tobacco into the dirt, and downed the last of his coffee. Stepping back inside the simple split-log home, he put his cup in the sink and belted on his gun. It rode comfortable and low on his right hip, the leather holster worn smooth from long years of use. He put on his hat, a broad-brimmed Stetson the color of tree bark, and grabbed his bedroll and gear from the kitchen table. Outside, as though sensing a change, the horses nickered loudly, and the old man smiled. Glancing fondly around at the simple home that had been his for the last eleven years, he shook his head and stepped back outside.

The birds were singing their autumn songs as he crossed the dirt yard to the corral. At the gate, he whistled once, softly, and the horses perked up their ears and ambled over. He thought briefly about taking the Paint, but decided against it. The Paint was a lovely horse, but had no sense. Today, he'd need a horse with sense.

"Come here, Taproot," he said softly. "Come on." He lowered a bridle over the big gray's nose and pulled him out of the corral, leaving the gate open. The Paint would head for the pasture behind the house with little encouragement.

Leading the horse to the small shed where he kept his tack, he saddled Taproot and loaded his bedroll and other supplies, putting his Winchester into the boot and securing it with a leather thong. He glanced back at the corral. Sure enough, the Paint was heading out back. Good horse, he thought. That damn Paint was pretty enough to make a picture.

He eased into the saddle, remembering days when it felt a whole lot easier climbing on, let alone riding. Still, he sat comfortably enough—a man who had spent many long hours on the back of a horse. He nudged the horse with his heels. "Come on, Taproot," he said, "let's head out."

The horse obeyed, shaking his mane as if to say it seemed a good idea to him. Heading across the valley, the old man thought about looking back, but decided not to. That was all he'd done for eleven years. Looked back. Smoked his pipe, drunk his coffee, run his few horses, and looked back. Today would be different. Today he'd look forward—for a little while, at least.

As they crossed the small stream at the edge of his property, the birds singing in the yellow-gold leaves of the cottonwoods, he smiled to himself.

Grant O'Keefe, Texas Ranger, was riding again.

SPLIT OAKS, TEXAS, wasn't much of a town. It was situated northeast of Houston, and the best thing going for it was the water supply of a large lake and the Trinity River, which ran all the way to the Gulf. Because it was quite a ways off the beaten track, it drew in characters of questionable repute—men running from their past, women looking for work as whores, and the occasional criminal hoping to hide out in relative comfort. There was only one saloon in Split Oaks, a two-story built by an enterprising woman who called herself Georgia, and named her saloon The Shady Lady. It was, Grant thought as he rode in around lunchtime, probably the second-best thing Split Oaks had going for it.

He tied Taproot to the hitching post and stepped inside. Georgia herself was behind the bar and when she saw him, her green eyes lit up like emerald fire. "Grant O'Keefe?

Great good Lord, I haven't seen you in an age! Where you been keeping yourself?"

Grant smiled. He'd always liked Georgia. She was phony as hell, with her Southern accent and her put-on manners, but the woman ran a clean place and kept her eyes and ears open. When he'd been a working lawman, she'd tipped him about the comings and goings of more than one outlaw. Besides that, she was damn pretty—even though she was getting a little long in the tooth herself. "Hello, Georgia," Grant said, walking up to the bar, where she met him and enveloped him in a hug. "You're as beautiful as always."

Georgia could blush on cue and she did. "You always were a charmer, Grant. But don't lie to me. I know I'm not young anymore."

Grant grinned. "Who says?"

Geogria blushed prettily again, and then shooed him to a bar stool. "Sit down, sit down. Tell me what I can get for you and we'll talk about old times."

Grant seated himself and ordered a beer and the hot lunch plate: roast beef, potatoes and gravy, carrots, and corn bread. Georgia told the cook in the back what to make, and brought him his beer, then took up a seat next to him. The lunch crowd was usually pretty sparse at The Shady Lady, and today was no exception.

"So, Grant, tell me where you've been hiding. It's been, what, five or six years since you've been in here?"

"More like seven, Georgia. How is it that I've gotten old and you still look like you did when you rode into this town and smell just as good?"

"You're not old yet, Grant. I'm willing to bet there's still iron in your pistol," she said, laughing and placing a familiar hand on this thigh.

Grant laughed with her, and sipped his beer. The woman

was still as fresh as a spring daisy, which was one of the things Grant liked about her. "Well," he allowed, "maybe a bit of iron left." They laughed some more and the cook brought his plate out.

They talked about nothing important while he ate, and Grant watched the mirror behind the bar. He told her of his little spread and spending his days in the quiet valley. She talked about times changing, but men were still the same, coming into The Shady Lady for food and booze and a woman, then riding on to the next place.

After he finished, she looked at him for a long moment, then said, "So, what brings you to town, Grant?"

He grinned. "You always were direct when you wanted to be, Georgia."

She nodded. "You have to be in my line of work. What brings you in?"

"Oh, mostly curiosity, I reckon. A fellow rode by the house about ten days ago, stopped to ask for a cup of coffee and to sit a spell. Said he'd just come from out this way. I asked about you and how the folks around town were doing and he started out saying a whole lot of nothing. I finally pried out of him that there's a bit of trouble in Split Oaks."

Georgia shook her head. "That's an understatement if there ever was one."

"So I gathered," Grant said, "when he told me that people were being run off their homesteads and losing cattle . . . or worse."

She looked carefully into the mirror at the tables behind her, then said, "It's often worse, Grant. People have been killed when they resisted."

"Resisted who?" Grant asked.

"A Mex fellow who showed up here a few months back with half an army with him. Calls himself El Corazón del Diablo. The Devil's Heart."

Grant felt his eyes widen a bit, then shook his head. "He's trouble all right, has been since he chewed his way out of his mother's womb."

"You know him?" Georgia asked.

Grant nodded. "Ever since I shot him and hauled him off to Houston about fifteen years ago. Cattle rustler, among other things. Figures he's not in prison any longer." He took a long swallow of beer. "His real name is Pablo Castillo—which he hates—and a meaner Mexican never lived."

Georgia clutched his arm. "Oh, Jesus, Grant! You've got to get out of here right now. He comes into town all the time and never alone. He'll shoot you for sure."

Grant chuckled. "I suppose he might at that, Georgia. But I'm not going anywhere."

"Grant, you have to. You're not a lawman anymore. We've sent for a marshal. Please!" she said.

"You know as well as I do, Georgia, that it could be weeks or longer before a marshal gets here, and the Rangers are spread so thin they'll be lucky to hear about it after it's over." He sighed. "No, I figure I'm the closest thing you're going to get for a long while. I've still got enough lawman in me to know that I can't just ride away. Once a Ranger, always a Ranger."

Georgia shook her head sadly. "That's what I was afraid of, Grant."

They sat quiet for a long while, not saying a word, and eventually, went upstairs together to give comfort to each other the only way they could.

GRANT WAS SITTING at the bar when he heard them ride in on the other end of the street. Yelling and cursing, Mexican *bandidos* loved to make a spectacle of themselves. Once, a shot rang out and a dog yelped and then was still. Stupid fools, Grant thought. They've gotten so used to having their way with the folks around here that the idea that there might be a lawman around—even a retired old man like himself—never crossed their minds.

The last time Grant had seen Pablo, he'd been headed for prison, swearing in Mexican for all he was worth. Pablo had been little more than a kid back then, rabid-dog mean but with little sense. Grant doubted that prison life had improved him all that much. He downed the last of his whiskey and nodded to Georgia. "Guess I'd better go handle this foolishness," he said, laying a double eagle on the bar.

"You don't have to, Grant," she said, so soft he could barely hear her. "Sit this one out."

Grant smiled, remembering how they'd made love that afternoon. How sweet she smelled, with the autumn wind blowing in through the window and the smell of lilac perfume mixing with the last leaves of the year. Turned out she was right—there was still a little iron left in his pistol. "I guess not, Georgia. Wouldn't be right."

"I know," she said. "Be careful."

He nodded. "Always am," he said, then turned and walked out of the door. The Mexicans were still down the street a ways, and Grant figured he'd have a better chance on horseback. From here, he could see the last people scattering and hear the sound of shutters being slammed shut. The horses they rode were of good quality, which meant they were probably stolen.

Grant unhitched Taproot and swung on. "Come on, old boy," he said, turning the horse with a gentle tug on the reins. "Let's go put a stop to this."

Out by the lake, the wind stirred again and leaves flew upward and out over the water in a swirl of chaotic yellows and golds. For a long moment, he watched this and thought about turning the horse around and riding out of town. What was he doing? He wasn't young anymore, wasn't a Ranger anymore. He was an old man who hadn't done a thing except smoke his pipe, drink his coffee, and watch his horses graze in years. Still, right was right. He couldn't stop upholding the law now simply because he was old any more than he could stop the wind from blowing the last of the leaves off the cottonwoods.

He moved Taproot to the center of the street and walked him easy toward where the Mexicans tried to hold their skittish horses around Pablo. They saw him in a moment and Grant saw Pablo, The Devil's Heart, hold up a hand for his riders to stop. A quick count of hats told Grant that there were six riders with him. My luck, he thought, is that there's always one more outlaw than I have bullets in my gun.

Pablo gestured again—he always did have a good nose for danger—and the riders moved out in a string to either side of him. Grant let Taproot walk toward them, stopping him when the distance was close enough to read eyes. The street was quiet except for the wind, and the air had the cold bite of first winter in it.

Grant stared hard at Pablo, seeing how the years had hardened him, made him even more dangerous than he'd been. He was wearing a black linen shirt with bone buttons and faded and patched denim pants. But his eyes, black like magnesium, were flat and lifeless. Finally, Grant spoke. "Well, Pablo, I see you survived prison. A shame. I was hoping someone would put you out of your misery while you were there."

The Mexican grinned. "I am The Devil's Heart," he said, hitting himself in the chest. "Nothing can break me." He spit, never taking his eyes off Grant, then nodded. "I thought it was you, *Ranger* O'Keefe. You got old, didn't you?"

"Happens to everyone eventually," Grant said. " 'Cept maybe those who get in the way of a bullet or the hangman at a young age."

"You're too old, *jefe*," Pablo said. He had called Grant that the first time they'd met. It meant "chief," but apparently sarcasm wasn't lost on the Mexican. Pablo was saying, "I heard you retired, couldn't shoot straight anymore." His riders laughed.

"I did retire, Pablo," Grant said with a tight grin. "But I don't reckon it had anything to do with how straight I can shoot. Still walking with a limp?"

The outlaw's smile faded. "*Si,*" he said. "It still hurts when the rains come." He spit again, and remembered pain crossed his face. "I still owe you for that."

"I hope it hurts like hell," Grant said. He gestured to the riders and the street around them. "From what I hear and see, it looks like I should've gut-shot you when I had the chance."

"You got no chance now, *jefe*," Pablo said. "This time, I'm gonna kill you."

Grant stared hard at the Mexican, then his men. "You, Pablo," he asked, "or these cowardly dogs you've got sniffing around you?" Grant knew the time for talk was almost over, could feel it in his guts.

"Does it matter, old man? You die just the same."

Grant took one more look at the men surrounding him. The one on his extreme right was by far the most dangerous. He hadn't even cracked a smile when Pablo insulted Grant, just stared, his hand hovering over his gun. Grant inched his own hand closer to his six-shooter.

"I'll give you one chance, *Pablo*," he said, stressing the hated name. "Leave Split Oaks, or better still, leave Texas entirely, and I won't shoot you like the mangy scoundrel you are." Brave words, he thought, for a man who hasn't fired a gun at anything more threatening than a deer in the last eleven years.

The Mexican laughed. "*One* of us is leaving, *señor*," he

said. Quick as a snake he went for his pistol and yelled, "Kill him!"

Grant had an instant to be thankful for Taproot, who wouldn't spook at the sound of gunfire. In his vision, everything slowed to a crawl, though he knew things were happening with incredible speed. Drawing his own weapon, he turned and fired at the nameless Mexican at the end of the line, hoping that Pablo's own skittish horse might throw off his aim. He saw the Mexican's gun go off at the same moment the man was hit. Grant felt the slug burn past his ear, saw the man fall of his horse with a red hole in his chest. The horse shied, and slammed into the horse next in line, causing that outlaw to drop his pistol and clutch for the reins.

Bullets flew and the sound of the gunfire was enormous. Something shoved him in the left shoulder, and Grant knew he'd been hit. Taproot sidestepped and turned slightly, and Grant's next shot went low, hitting the horse instead of the outlaw. The horse screamed, fell, and landed on top of his rider, who was pinned beneath.

Another slug burned him in the leg at the same time Grant fired again, this time hitting the outlaw now directly in front of him and just to Pablo's left in the forehead. A surprised look crossed the face of the man before he dropped dead from his horse.

Between the shouting of the Mexicans, the screaming and whirling of the horses, and the gunfire, the street was a chaotic haze of smoke and dust. Grant tried to spot Pablo, whose horse had crow-hopped backwards, couldn't see him, and fired instead at another nameless outlaw who'd spurred his horse forward in the line. Grant's slug took him in the belly and the man pitched forward onto his horse before rolling off to lie motionless in the street.

Suddenly, a giant-sized fist slammed into his chest, and

caused Grant to double over in his saddle. He coughed weakly and saw the telltale red stain spreading on his shirt. Three of the outlaws were dead, and one, based on Grant's sketchy knowledge of Mexican, was lying underneath his horse with a broken leg or worse. That left two, plus Pablo. One more than he had bullets in his gun, and probably three more than he had the strength to finish. He coughed again, feeling the blood in his throat.

Grant tried to lift his pistol, which seemed so much heavier than it had before. He knew if he could finish Pablo, the other two would most likely leave the people of Split Oaks alone—at least until they found a new leader. By then, Grant suspected, he'd be past caring. He'd finally managed to raise his pistol when two blasts from a shotgun went off behind him.

Taproot turned in that direction, guided by Grant's knee signals, and there in the street were the last two Mexicans. Dead as his last hatband. Behind them stood Georgia, looking flushed and beautiful and not a bit scared. My God, he thought, that's a wonderful woman. She looked so perfect, holding that shotgun with smoke rising out of the barrels, while behind her the cottonwoods on the lake stirred in the wind. It was the prettiest thing he'd ever seen, even better than his horses.

When her eyes widened with shock, for a long second, Grant thought she'd seen how he'd been shot, then she screamed, "Behind you!"

From behind, Grant almost felt the words, "Now you die, *jefe*!"

The Devil's Heart had gotten his horse under control and in turning toward Georgia, seeing how she looked there in the street, Grant had completely forgotten the last Mexican.

With the last of his strength, he yanked on Taproot's

reins, and the sensible horse knew what he meant, reared back, and spun around. The slug took the horse in the head, and Grant fell clear as Taproot fell dead. What little breath he had in him rushed out of him when he hit the ground, and Grant saw stars whirling in his vision.

Somehow he managed to get his gun up just as Pablo was bearing down on him. Grant fired once, then again. With a crazed smile still on his face, The Devil's Heart cracked and, finally, broke. He fell from his horse, caught a foot in the stirrup, and was dragged, bouncing like some kind of crazy doll, down the street before his boot came loose and left his dead body in the dirt.

Grant heard people come running, and knew they could handle the remaining Mexican with the broken leg. Georgia peered down at him, her face backlit by the last of the day's good sunlight. "Oh, my God," she whispered, staring at his wounds.

"Would you believe," he said, trying not to cough and failing, "that sonofabitch shot old Taproot?" Then he passed out.

A WINDOW CAME into focus, and beyond it, in a grayish wash of daylight, the first snowfall of the year. That will take care of the leaves, Grant thought. He coughed, and remembered how things had ended on the street.

From the foot of his bed, he heard Georgia stir, and then she moved to the side. "Grant?" she said. "You rest easy now."

Seeing her, Grant wondered why he'd never asked her to leave The Shady Lady and come be with him. She was damn pretty. "You just rest," she was saying.

"I reckon I'll be getting all the rest I need soon enough," he spit out, then was overcome by another bout of coughing.

Georgia was quiet for a long minute. Then she put a cool

hand on his forehead and took his left hand in hers. "Yes, Grant," she said. "That's what the doc says."

"How long?" he wheezed.

"Not long at all, I suppose," Georgia said. Her voice was soft and low. "As long as it takes."

"That's all right then," Grant said, drifting again. "It's not all that bad."

"You were a great lawman, Grant," she whispered. "One of the very best."

"All things end," he whispered, staring out the window again. "Even autumn."

Outside, the snow was coming down in long sheets. Georgia watched it with him until he finally slept, and then watched him until he drifted away into the dark.

Dancing on Air

∽◦∾

by Robert J. Randisi

Robert J. Randisi's Western novels include *The Ham Reporter, Targett, Legend, The Ghost With Blue Eyes,* and *Miracle of the Jacal.* His most recent Western novel, *Lancaster's Orphans,* was published in January 2004. In 2004, *The Funeral of Tanner Moody*—part anthology, part collaborative novel—will be published by Leisure Books. Its authors include John Jakes, Elmer Kelton, Kerry Newcomb, Jory Sherman, and James Reasoner. Randisi is the editor of the Western anthologies *Tin Star, Boot Hill, White Hats,* and *Black Hats.* Also in 2004, the first novel in a series called *The Widowmaker, Invitation to a Hanging,* will appear from Pocket Books. As J. R. Roberts, he created and writes the long-running Western series *The Gunsmith.*

"{The Man} *had formed a connection with the limb of a tree, as he was found suspended by the neck . . .*"

—An excerpt from Jacob Hand's report

1

SERGEANT JACOB HAND looked up at the man hanging from the tree and wondered how he was going to put this in his report.

Hand was a sergeant in the Frontier Battalion, which to most folks—despite what Governor Richard Coke's new bill said—was still the Texas Rangers.

For years the responsibility of the Texas Rangers was primarily Indian fighting, but thanks to Coke being elected governor in 1874, they now received assignments that also sent them after Mexicans and other criminals including rustlers.

Hand had been dispatched to Laredo, Texas, by Major John B. Jones to track down and bring to justice a notorious "cow thief." What he found, even before reaching town, was a man hanging from the limb of a tree. Grabbing his Book of Knaves from his saddlebag—also called the Bible II, or simply the Black Book, and carried by most Rangers—he compared the description of Manny Fernandez to the hanging man and found that they matched. The clincher was the huge brown mole on the man's right cheek.

"HE SHOULD BE easy to identify," Jones had told Hand before dispatching him from San Antonio.

"Mole on the cheek," Hand read from his book.

"It should say 'huge brown mole,'" Jones pointed out.

"I'll make a note," Hand said.

At forty-two Jones was twelve years older than Hand, who had been a Ranger for two years now. Although Major Jones was not an impressive physical specimen—barely five-seven, 125 with his boots on—he had earned the respect of his men by being smart, courteous, humorless, and serious about what he wanted from his Rangers. He touched his mustache, which dropped from beneath deep-set, penetrating eyes.

"I'm sending you alone because we're shorthanded here."

Hand shrugged and said, "There's only one rustler, right?"

"Actually, I don't know how many there are, but Manuel Fernandez is certainly the brains behind the operation. The way to bust the operation is to put him away."

"I understand."

"Arrest him, bring him in," Jones said. "That's your assignment."

"No problem."

"There's only one potential problem."

"What's that?"

"Vigilantes," Jones said. "Some of the townspeople or ranchers might want to take the law into their own hands."

"I'll keep that in mind." Hand realized since his boss had no sense of humor, he probably never saw the potential for it in the statement.

"They've already lynched two men in that area," Jones said. "I don't want it to happen again. I want you to go down there and resolve the situation one way or another."

"Yes, sir."

MANNY FERNANDEZ SWUNG in the breeze as Hand stared up at him. The man's tongue was protruding, his feet had not been tied, and his neck wasn't broken, so it was obvious he'd died dancing on air. There'd been nothing humane about his execution.

Hand walked around the area, studying the ground for a telltale something, and was finally rewarded. He found a hoofprint among many. But this one had a curious star-shaped indentation in it. Something had left this mark imprinted on the hoof, which would make the horse easy to identify. Hopefully, the horse belonged to someone and had not simply been used to hang Fernandez. Worse, it might even turn out to belong to Fernandez.

Hand returned the Black Book to his saddlebag and then considered his assignment. Technically, it was over. Fernandez's rustling days were over, and Hand was free to return to San Antonio, but he decided not to. He'd seen vigilante justice before, he didn't like it then, and he didn't like it now. He intended to ride into Laredo and see what he could find out. Whoever was responsible for lynching Manny Fernandez had charges to stand up to, and Hand was going to see that those charges were preferred. . . .

2

Hand had to leave Fernandez where he was. He had only his own horse, and he couldn't very well tie the body to it and then walk into Laredo. He'd have to return with another animal to use to transport the body. In order to keep the body safe from scavengers—the kind that crawled or walked anyway—he left it hanging from the tree. There was nothing he could do to keep the buzzards from it, but maybe he could return before they did too much damage.

Laredo was right on the Mexican border, and had a sister town across the Rio Grande called Nueva Laredo. As Hand rode down the main street, he knew his identity was no secret. All of the men involved in lynching the cow thief Fernandez would have been waiting for his arrival—perhaps even the arrival of more than one Ranger. What they got was a single man with a strong sense of justice that caused him to be offended whenever a person or persons took the law into their own hands. He knew that was the reason Major

Jones had sent him down there. He'd warned Hand about the vigilantes and he knew his young Ranger would take whatever steps were necessary to resolve the situation in south Texas. Either bring in the rustlers, or the vigilantes who killed them. That was his job, and yet for young Ranger Jacob Hand it was much more than that. . . .

HAND REINED IN his horse in front of the sheriff's office and dismounted. He decided to lay the retrieval of the body at the feet of the local law and let him deal with it. That would leave him free to do his job—or more to the point, his duty.

When he entered, the sheriff was coming out of the cell block carrying a broom. He was a well-fed-looking fifty or so, with gray hair and tired-looking eyes. When he saw Hand, his shoulders slumped.

"I been waitin' for you, Ranger."

"Then you know?"

"About the hangin'?" the man asked. "Yeah."

"Why didn't you stop it?"

"I'm only one man."

"With a badge."

The sheriff laughed shortly. "You're a young man. I hope you didn't decide to wear a badge because it would give you some kind of special power."

"I decided to wear it to uphold justice."

"Very noble." The lawman walked to his desk and sat down. "I'm Sheriff Frank Noble. What can I do for you?"

"Do you know who hanged Fernandez?"

"No," Noble said. "Oh, it was the vigilantes for sure, but they wore masks. I couldn't identify any of them."

"Would you if you could?"

"Probably not," Noble said. "I gotta live in this town, Ranger."

"You're supposed to be serving the needs of this town, Sheriff."

"You got to live someplace to know what its needs are . . . Ranger."

Hand decided not to argue the point. The man was obviously ill-suited for his office.

"Well, maybe you can get somebody to go out there and cut him down and bring him back?" Hand asked. "Take him over to the undertaker's?"

"Sure, Ranger," Noble said. "I can do that for you. You gonna take him with you?"

"Yes."

"Should be able to have you on the trail in no time."

"Oh, I'm not leaving yet, Sheriff," Hand said. "I've still got a job to do."

"I thought your job was to bring in Fernandez for rustling."

"My job is to uphold the law," Hand said. "Manny Fernandez was murdered, and I'm going to find out by who."

Noble firmed his jaw. "I'm not gonna help you, Ranger. There won't be any help here for you."

"That's okay," Hand said. "I've got my badge."

"I tol' you," Noble said, "a badge don't give you no special powers. Ain't no badge that can stop a bullet."

"I'll take my chances," Hand said.

3

Ranger Jacob Hand left the sheriff's office and walked his horse across the street to the saloon. He needed a beer to wash the dust out of his throat, and also figured that showing up in the saloon at midday would announce his arrival to anyone who had not seen him ride in.

He tied his horse off outside and entered the saloon, proceeding directly to the bar.

"Beer."

"Sure, Ranger," the young bartender said. "You lookin' for somebody?" the man asked as he set the mug in front of Hand.

"Why?" Hand asked. "You know of somebody I should be looking for?"

The man shrugged and moved away. He busied himself wiping an already clean section of the bar with a rag.

Hand turned, leaned against the bar, and looked around. His aim was to give everybody a good look at the Ranger badge. The badge had been assigned to him, but everything else he possessed he'd had to pay for himself, including the Peacemaker and bowie knife he wore on his hip and the Winchester '73 rifle in his scabbard outside on his horse— not to mention his horse and saddle.

"Found a man hanging from a tree just outside of town," Hand called out. "Fella named Manny Fernandez. Anybody know anything about it?"

The place was about half full, and all he got for his question was a lot of blank stares, until a man sitting in the back spoke up.

"Heard he was a cattle rustler. That right?"

"That's correct, he was," Hand said.

"Seems to me he deserved to get strung up then," the man said, " 'specially in south Texas."

"That may be," Hand said, "but it's not for a vigilante committee to say. That would be for the law to say."

"Sometimes," the man said, "the law moves too slow, Ranger."

Hand placed his beer down on the bar and squinted to get a better look at the man.

"Can I ask your name, sir?"

"Callahan," the man said. "Dillon Callahan."

"And do you work for one of the ranches around here, sir?"

"I ramrod the Double L spread," Callahan said. "Everybody here knows me."

Hand had acquainted himself with the top spreads in the area, and the Double L was the largest.

"You work for Mr. Lawrence Lacy, is that right?"

"That's right," Callahan said, "Larry Lacy. Best boss in the business."

"I'd like to talk to him," Hand said. "Can you tell me where I might find him?"

"You might find him at home," Callahan said. He was sitting with two other men, who seemed amused by what he was saying. Probably Double L hands. "Then again, you might not. Guess you'll have to ride out there to find out."

"Guess I will." He turned and finished his beer, said to the bartender, "Thanks," then turned and walked outside. He was untying his horse when the Double L ramrod and the two men came out.

"Hey, Ranger," Callahan said.

"Yes?"

"Why you wanna be botherin' Mr. Lacy?"

"Well, cattle rustler was hanged by a bunch of vigilantes," Hand said. "Your boss is the biggest cattle man in the area. You figure it out."

Callahan stepped down off the boardwalk, followed by the other two men.

"What's it matter if a cow thief got strung up?" the foreman asked.

"Like I said inside," Hand repeated, "it's for the law to decide who hangs and who doesn't."

"You sayin' you think our boss was the leader of them vigilantes?" one of the other men asked.

"I don't know," Hand said. "Is that what I'm saying?"

"Why you wanna cause trouble—" the man started, but the foreman quieted him down.

"Shut up, Wade. The Ranger's just doin' his job, right, Ranger?"

"That's right, Mr. Callahan."

"I got some advice for you, though."

"What's that?"

"You ain't gonna make too many friends around here if you try to cause trouble for Mr. Lacy."

"I'll keep that in mind."

"See," Callahan said, "I got a lot of respect for Mr. Lacy, so I wouldn't take it kindly if you was to cause him trouble."

"If I didn't know better," Hand said, "I'd think you were threatening a Texas Ranger, Callahan."

"I guess I'm threatenin' a man," Callahan said, "who happens to be a Texas Ranger."

With that, the ramrod turned and walked away. The two hands each gave the Ranger a hard look and then followed their boss. Hand figured that if Larry Lacy wanted his men to join him in a vigilante group, they'd do it without hesitation. The big question was, would they hang a man from a tree on his say-so?

4

Getting directions to the Double L was not a difficult thing to do, but before riding out there Hand went to the livery to talk to the local blacksmith. The smithy in any town, over a period of time, probably shoed almost every local horse, and then some. Hand figured he was the man to question about the star-shaped indentation he'd found.

He approached the livery on foot, trailing his horse. He'd taken the time to loosen one of the horse's shoes first. As he walked into the livery, a man turned to face him. He was short, in his forties, and he wore his shirt with the sleeves cut off to reveal bulging arms. From the waist up he could have been six-four, but if to make up for the bulging arms and deep chest, God had given him short, bandy legs. The man was barely five-foot-six.

"Can I help you, Ranger?"

"Looks like my horse threw a shoe," Hand said.

"Lemme take a look."

The smithy took the reins and walked the horse around to where he wanted him. He moved oddly, as if his legs were stiff, or as if they had been broken once and improperly set.

"Shoe's loose, all right," the man said.

"I thought so—"

The man straightened and looked at him.

"Looks like it was pried off."

"Really?"

"Maybe somebody wanted to keep you here for a while."

"Maybe. Can you fix it now?"

"Won't take long," the man said. "You can wait, if you want."

Hand looked down at the ground, which was peppered with hoofprints. He didn't see the star shoe he was looking for, though.

The smithy got a new shoe, hammer and nails, lifted the horse's hoof between his legs, and went to work. Watching him, Hand realized what small feet the man also had.

"You got somethin' you want to ask me?" he said while he worked. He spoke around the nails he held in his mouth.

"How do you mean?"

"You're lookin' at the ground like a tracker," the smithy said.

"You're observant."

"What're you lookin for?" The smithy hammered in a nail.

"A hoofprint," Hand said. "It's got a star shape in it, like the animal stepped on something."

"A star shape?" Another nail.

"Like this."

Hand leaned over and drew a crude star shape inside one of the old hoofprints on the ground. The smith hammered in the last nail, allowed the horse's hoof to hit the ground, then turned and took a look.

"Have you ever seen anything like that?"

The man stared at it for a few moments—maybe too long—then shook his head and said, "No."

"You never shoed a horse with that mark in its hoof?"

The smithy looked at Hand. "I think I'd remember."

"Yeah," Hand said, "you'd think. What do I owe you?"

"Nothin'," the man said. "Pleased to help the law get back on the trail. Headin' out?"

"Why would I?"

"You was here for the cow thief, wasn't you?" the man asked. "I heard he's over to the undertaker's."

"He should keep there for a while," Hand said. "I'm riding out to the Double L."

"What for?"

"To talk with Mr. Lacy."

"About vigilantes?"

"That's right."

"I'd be careful about bringin' up that subject up if I was you."

"Why's that?"

"Mr. Lacy, he hates vigilantes."

"Is that so?"

"Yep."

Hand wondered why the man's foreman hadn't told him that.

5

"I hate vigilantes!" Larry Lacy said.

Hand was in Lacy's office in the man's two-story ranch house. The rancher was tall, white-haired, and at the moment, angry.

"Don't talk to me about vigilantes!" Lacy was standing behind his desk while he raved.

"Mr. Lacy," Hand said, "it's my job to find out who the vigilantes are and arrest them."

"For what?" Lacy asked. "For hanging that cow thief?"

"You yourself said that vigilantes are cowards."

"I did say that," Lacy said, "but there are worse things than vigilantes."

"Like what?"

"Like horse thieves," Lacy said, "and cow thieves."

Apparently, as much as Lacy hated vigilantes, they were third on his list.

At that moment Mrs. Lacy entered the room. She was a handsome woman in her forties—probably twenty years younger than her husband—and at the moment she was scowling at Jacob Hand.

"Ranger, I did not let you into my house to upset my husband."

"I'm sorry, ma'am."

"Lawrence?"

"It's all right, Alicia," Lacy said. "You can leave us."

"I'm not leaving until you sit back down and calm down," she said forcefully.

"Very well, Alicia," Lacy said. He sat down behind his desk. "There."

"Please, Ranger . . ." she said to Hand.

"I'll try not to upset him, ma'am."

She gave him another harsh look and left.

"I'm sorry," Lacy said. "My wife used to be a school-teacher."

"That explains why I feel like a scolded child," Hand said. "Mr. Lacy, I'd like to look at all the saddle stock on your ranch."

"Why?"

"Because I'm looking for something."

"What?"

"A star-shaped indentation on a horse's hoof."

Lacy leaned back in his chair. "You found such a track at the site of the hanging?"

"Yes."

"But if you find the horse it belongs to, you find only one of the vigilantes."

"That's all right," Hand said. "If I find one he'll give up the rest."

"How do you know?"

"Vigilantes are cowards," Hand said. "That's why they act in groups. If I can separate them, they'll turn on one another rather than take the fall themselves."

"So you think one or more of my men were with the vigilante group that hanged that cow thief?"

"It's possible," Hand said. "I'm just following up some possibilities."

"It was my understanding," Lacy said, "from a telegram I received from the governor, that you were sent here to stop the rustling."

"That's correct."

"With the thief dead," Lacy said, "isn't your job done?"

"No, sir," Hand said. "The assignment I was given might be done, but not my job."

"I see," Lacy said. He had calmed down considerably. "You're something of a zealot, Ranger Hand."

"I'm not sure I know what that means, sir."

"It means that you sometimes take your responsibilities to the extreme," Lacy explained.

"If that means that I intend to see justice done," Hand said, "then I guess I am . . . what you said I am."

"A zealot."

"Yes."

Lacy got up from behind his desk. "You know, we've been losing a lot of cows to rustlers of late, but we're not the only ones," he said. "There are other spreads who have been getting hit."

"I realize that, sir," Hand said. "I'll be checking in with them as well. I had to start somewhere, and I thought I'd start with the biggest."

"Let's get it over with then. I'll take you out to the stables."

As they walked from the house to the stable, Hand could feel the gaze of the cowhands on him.

"They're not going to be happy when you start checking their horses," Lacy said.

"Maybe I should start with yours then," Hand said. "Might take the sting out."

Lacy turned his head quickly without breaking his stride and said, "You've got nerve, I'll give you that."

They entered the stable, the largest Hand had ever seen.

"My horse is over here," Lacy said, leading the young Ranger to a stall.

Hand took a moment to study the ground, but there were so many tracks that one with the star would have been obliterated. He opened the stall and stepped inside. Lacy's horse was a black gelding who stood about sixteen hands, with three white stockings. He spoke to the animal in low tones while lifting each leg in turn and checking the bottom of the hoof.

"Satisfied?" Lacy asked.

"Yes." Satisfied that if Lacy was one of the vigilantes who hanged Manny Fernandez, he wasn't riding the star-printed horse at the time.

Hand spent the better part of an hour checking the other horses in the stable, and to Lacy's credit he stood right there with him.

"That's it," Lacy said finally. "That's everybody's horse."

"What about your foreman?"

"Callahan? What about him?"

"I saw him in town earlier, with two other men," Hand said. "Did they come back?"

"Not that I know of."

"Well, is Callahan's horse here?"

"Now that you mention it," Lacy said, "no."

"Then I still need to check theirs."

"Then you'll have to wait until they get back," the rancher said, "or do it in town. Meanwhile, you've got other ranches to visit. You've got your work cut out for you, Ranger."

"I suppose I do."

They'd started to walk out of the stable when Hand spotted a horse he hadn't looked at.

"Wait," he said, pointing to the stall. "Who's horse is that?"

"Hmm? Oh, that's not a saddle mount. It's my wife's horse she hooks her up to her buggy. Alicia doesn't ride."

"You mind if I check it?"

"What. for?" Lacy asked. "I told you, it's not a saddle mount."

"I know," Hand said, "but I'm here, and I'd like to be thorough."

"Well . . . it's a waste of time, but it's your time," Lacy said. "Come on."

They walked to the stall and Hand opened the door. The horse was a bay mare, on the large side, probably around nine or ten years old. She rolled her eyes at him as he approached her, but stood still while he raised her legs to check her hooves. When he lifted the right forefront and looked underneath, there it was, the star-shaped imprint imbedded in the hoof.

"Mr. Lacy?" Hand called.

"Yes?"

"Would you care to explain this?"

Lacy entered the stall and said, "Explain wha—" then stopped when he saw the hoof. "Jesus. There's got to be some kind of mistake . . . an explanation."

Hand released the hoof and brushed his hands off by rubbing them together.

"Maybe we'd better ask your wife."

6

"I have no idea what you're talking about!" Alicia Lacy exclaimed. She glared at her husband. "How dare you let this man question me this way."

"This man is a Texas Ranger, Alicia," Larry Lacy said, "and he claims your horse was at the site of a lynching."

"From the position of the tracks," Hand offered, "I'd say your horse was the one the man was sitting on, ma'am—the one he was hanged from."

"And from that you infer that I was there?" she demanded.

"I'm just asking questions, ma'am."

They were back in Lacy's office, this time the three of them. On the way back to the house Hand discovered that Alicia Lacy was the second Mrs. Lacy, a woman Lacy had brought back with him from the East after a business trip several years earlier.

"She's still not used to the ways of the West, Ranger," Lacy had explained, "not the way my Lucy was. She and I were married for thirty years before a fever took her."

Hand had assured Lacy he would give the man's wife the benefit of the doubt.

"Ma'am, I need to know if anyone took your horse, or if you loaned it to anyone in the past few days."

"No one uses Betsy but me," she insisted. "I do not loan my horse to anyone."

"Anyone who works here has access to the animal, Ranger," Lacy pointed out. "They could take it and use it, return it, and Alicia would never be the wiser."

"If someone did that," Alicia Lacy said, "I want them fired!"

"Believe me, Mrs. Lacy," Hand said, "when I find out who did it, they will be more than fired."

LACY WALKED HAND out of the house and they stood together on the front porch.

"I'm afraid our sheriff won't be much help to you, Ranger," Lacy said.

"I've already found that out."

"I meant what I said about vigilantes," Lacy said. "I do hate them—but this man was a cattle thief. That was a fact. Why don't you just take his body and leave?"

"I can't do that, Mr. Lacy," Hand said. "I guess I am a— what did you call me?"

"A zealot," Lacy said, "and it's not necessarily a bad thing, Ranger. I just think you're all alone in this. I'd help you if I could. . . ."

"Tell me about your foreman."

"Callahan? He's a good enough man, I guess."

"That's not much of a vote of confidence."

"Well, he sort of became foreman by default," Lacy said. "I had a foreman for a long time, but his horse stepped in a chuck hole and rolled on him, and he died. Stupid accident! Pat Sandler was a good man. Had been my foreman for years. After he died I needed to appoint someone fairly quickly, so I chose Callahan."

Hand had the feeling there was more. When it wasn't forthcoming he said, "And?"

"I'm not at all sure I made the right decision."

"Why's that?"

"Well, you saw Callahan with two men, right?"

"That's right."

"He had friends among the men and I believe he has been showing favoritism. That's not a good thing for a foreman to do."

"I guess not."

"I think I'll have to replace him, but I'm looking to hire someone from outside. Until then . . ."

"He seems devoted to you," Hand said. "He just about threatened me when I said I was coming out here."

"Is that a fact? That surprises me."

"Why?"

"Because we don't exactly see eye to eye on things,"

Lacy said. "Just between you and me, I wouldn't put it past Callahan to be one of the vigilantes. His friends too."

Hand frowned. He wondered if Lacy was pointing his finger at Callahan and his friends to divert Hand's attention away from his wife.

"Will you still be checking with the other ranchers?" Lacy asked.

"No," Hand said. "The only reason I had to do that was to search for the horse with the star mark on its hoof. I found that here."

"So someone from here is with the vigilantes."

"So it would seem."

"Well, I'd be obliged if you'd let me know when you find out," Lacy said.

"I'll let you know," Hand said, "just as soon as I arrest him, Mr. Lacy."

"Good luck then."

Lacy went back inside, and Hand went down the steps to where his horse was tied. He noticed he was being watched by a bunch of men standing by one of the corrals, but he didn't recognize any of them as having been with Callahan—or even as having been in the saloon.

He mounted up and rode toward the front gate, still thinking about Mrs. Lacy and her horse, and wondering how far Lawrence Lacy would go to protect his wife.

7

Hand was about halfway between the Double L and Laredo when he realized two things. One, he was almost to the tree that Manny Fernandez had been hanged from, and two, he was being followed.

He didn't know if the fact that the hanging tree was

halfway between town and the ranch was important, but being followed certainly was. There were enough trees, rocks, dry washes, and creek beds for someone to use as cover while trailing him. He was tempted to kick his gelding into a gallop and see if they came after him, but rather than outrun them, he preferred to find out who was doing the following, and why.

He waited for his chance, and found it when he came to an outcropping rock he could use for cover. He turned the corner, reined his horse in, and turned it. Removing his Peacemaker from his holster, he sat his horse and waited. From the sound of the hooves on the rocks, it sounded like more than one rider approaching. When they came into view he was surprised that one of them was a woman—Alicia Lacy. The other rider was one of the men who had been with the foreman, Callahan, in town.

"Stop right there, please," Hand said, and they both reined in their horses.

"Ranger," Alicia Lacy asked, "are you pointing a gun at me?"

"I'm afraid I am, ma'am," he said. "Please advise your man to remove his gun from his holster slowly and drop it to the ground."

Alicia Lacy turned her head to look at Hand. She was dressed like a man, and sat her horse with confidence. It did not escape Hand's notice that it was the animal with the star-shaped hoofprint.

"Davis, do as he says."

Reluctantly, the man did so.

"And the rifle," Hand said. The man hesitated, as if he was waiting for something to happen, so Hand snapped, "Now!" because he was also waiting for something to happen.

Davis dropped his rifle to the ground, looking distressed.

"Now, Mrs. Lacy, your rifle."

She hesitated, but before he could bark at her he heard what he was waiting for—the scrape of a boot on rock. He'd had the definite impression that there were more than two riders behind him, and when only two appeared—and one of them was one of Callahan's men—he had to wonder where the foreman was.

At the sound of the boot scrape, he turned quickly and fired reflexively. The man sneaking up behind him had his gun drawn, but had no chance to fire it. Hand's bullet hit him square in the chest and knocked him onto his back.

Hand turned back quickly, and saw that Davis had scrambled from his horse to grab for one of his guns, and Alicia Lacy was pulling her rifle from its scabbard.

He hated to do it, but he shot the woman. His bullet struck her in the shoulder and knocked her from her horse. She landed hard and lay still.

Davis had picked up his pistol and was trying to get around his skittish horse. Hand didn't know if either of the wounded people was dead, and still had to wonder where Callahan was. He dropped from his saddle to the ground and went into a crouch just as Davis got out from behind his horse. He fired once, but Davis was moving and the bullet struck his left arm. The man raised his right hand and returned fire. The bullet missed, but struck the rock next to Hand, sending slivers of stone into his face. He felt them bite into his skin, but mercifully, miss his eyes. He scrambled to the side as the man fired a second time, then fired his own return shot, which this time struck home. Davis grunted and fell over backward.

Hand slammed his back against the rock so no one

could get behind him, wondering where Callahan was. He waited listening intently, but all he could hear were the moans of the wounded. Hastily, he ejected spent shells from his gun and replaced then with live ones. Only then did he cautiously move to check on the first man he'd shot. Finding him dead, he then moved to Mrs. Lacy, checking first the rocks above him to make sure Callahan had not take to high ground. Satisfied that he was in no danger, he leaned down over Alicia Lacy. She'd been hit in the shoulder, but it looked as if she had struck her head when she fell, and it was that that had rendered her unconscious. Her breathing was even, so he moved on to check Davis.

The man was lying on his back, trying to breath. The air was not coming easily to him and there were blood bubbles on his lips.

"You're going to die, Davis," Hand told him.

"God . . . no . . ."

"Where's Callahan?"

"Was supposed . . . to back . . . our play." Each hesitation was a vain attempt to capture some air.

And then he was dead.

Hand stood, looked around, and holstered his gun. Apparently, Callahan had run off. There was no better recommendation for the man to have been part of the vigilante group that had hanged Manny Fernandez.

8

When Jacob Hand rode up to the Lacy house for the second time that day—this time with Sheriff Frank Noble in tow—he saw Dillon Callahan run into the house when he saw them.

Hand now knew that Callahan had been Lacy's foreman a lot longer than the rancher had let on. This he'd learned from Sheriff Noble when he'd brought in the two bodies and the wounded woman. He'd left Alicia Lacy at the doctor's, taken the two men to the undertaker's, and then gone to the sheriff's office with his news. . . .

"You SHOT MRS. Lacy?" Noble had asked.

"Before she could shoot me, yes," Hand had said, "and two of her husband's men. Now I have to go back to the ranch to arrest both Dillon Callahan and Lawrence Lacy. You coming?"

IT WAS DURING the ride to the ranch that Hand had heard about Callahan's length of service to Lawrence Lacy. They'd stopped at the doctor's first. Alicia Lacy had gone after Hand to try to protect her husband, but she had been in too much pain to deny what had happened. This had left the sheriff with no choice but to accompany Hand to the Lacy ranch to arrest the richest man in the territory. . . .

NOW THEY REINED in their horses in front of the house and ran up the stairs. In his haste Callahan had left the door open. Hand recalled the way to Lacy's office, and they got there as the man was taking a shotgun down from a wall rack.

"Hold it!"

Lacy froze, but Callahan went for his gun. Hand had no choice but to kill yet another Lacy ranch hand—and probable vigilante.

Lacy looked at Hand with blazing eyes, and the Ranger knew the man was gauging his chances.

"You shot my wife, you sonofabitch!" he said.

"And you can either pull that shotgun off the wall, or leave it there and come to town to see her. Your choice."

He saw Lacy weighing his options, and then the man released the shotgun and backed away from it.

"You should never have told me your wife's horse wasn't a saddle mount, Mr. Lacy. When I saw her riding it I knew you lied, probably about everything. I'm arresting you for the vigilante hanging of Manny Fernandez."

Lacy looked at the sheriff. "You going to let him do this?"

"I got no choice, Mr. Lacy. He's a Texas Ranger!"

"The governor made a big mistake expanding the scope of your authority," Lacy said to Hand. "This charge will never stick."

"Maybe not," Jacob Hand, "but I'm taking you in anyway. . . ."

IN THE GOVERNOR'S Mansion in Austin several days later, Major John B. Jones sat in front of Governor Richard Coke's desk, armed with Jacob Hand's written report.

"John, you knew when you sent this boy to Laredo what would happen, didn't you?" Coke asked.

"Well, sir," Jones replied, "I didn't know he'd end up arresting the richest man in the territory, but I pretty much knew he'd get his man."

"His man being the head of the vigilantes . . . no matter who it was, right?"

"That's correct, sir," Jones said. "The boy didn't give a hoot who it was, he just arrested him."

Coke tapped his desk with his fingers and said, "This arrest may not stick, Major."

"Maybe not, sir," Jones said, "but word'll get around. People will know."

"Read me that last part of the boy's report," Coke said. "About the hanged man." He shook his head and chuckled. "I've got to meet this young sonofagun!"

Major Jones read the last line of Hand's report about Manny Fernandez's hanging.

"... *suppose he intended to avoid the law, and succeeded admirably.*"

The Last of the Ranger Chieftains

⌒◦⌒

by Marthayn Pelegrimas

Marthayn Pelegrimas has written over forty short stories in
the dark fantasy, mystery, and Western genres, appearing in
such anthologies as *Tin Star*, *Boot Hill*, and *Guns of the
West*. Her historical novel, *On the Strength of Wings* (Five
Star), was published in July of 2001.

HE SAT, METHODICALLY wiping the brush back and
forth across a rough cotton rag, then swished the bristles
in a tin of water. The clean liquid swirled with brown, turned
muddy—a dirty shade of ochre. He stroked the brush across
the rag again.

The sun was drifting toward the west, casting his studio
in warmer shades now. Much better, he thought, than the
blazing whiteness that had burned his eyes when he'd
stopped for lunch. The ache pinching his temples was sub-
siding. He sat there for a moment, not moving, barely
breathing, frozen in thought.

Could he paint a masterpiece? he wondered. One that
would somehow work off the guilt?

No. He shook his head back and forth, slowly, sadly, then rested his chin on his chest. Lids fluttered to cover over his watery eyes. Had anyone walked into his studio at that moment, come upon him in that pose, they might have thought the man sat overcome by prayer. Maybe they would have been right. How many times a day since the funeral had he asked for forgiveness?

But Rip had seemed so fit in San Antonio. Frail, true, but quite well for a man in his eighties. When they met for the interview—damn that interview—he had seemed in fine health.

The artist straightened up. Dipping the clean brush into a tiny pool of white, he feathered broad strokes onto the canvas. The pure absence of color reminded him of Rip's bushy beard. Tossing the brush aside, he gave in to the pain that he had fought so diligently all day. Slowly he leaned in to inspect his work, but instead of seeing pigment washed across a canvas, he was remembering. And he was back again in the Menger Hotel.

JOHN SALMON FORD's tall, lean frame loomed over him. Even though the artist had been waiting for Ford, the intrusion startled him.

"Mr. Remington?"

Frederic Remington stood to greet his guest. It was a clear, chilly day but inside, smoke clouds hung over the heads of several men as they leisurely puffed their cigars.

"Mr. Ford, what a tremendous honor it is to at last have the privilege of meeting you."

"Allow me to return the compliment, sir. I've admired your drawings for years. Your style surely seems to have captured the trueness of the land."

After shaking hands, both men hesitated a moment, allowing embarrassment from the compliments to recede.

"Sit . . . please." Remington made a graceful motion toward the armchair opposite his own. The leather was the color of brandy and as Ford rested his hand on the arm, he was aware of the hundreds of fingers before him that had rubbed the hide smooth. The artist offered Ford a cigar and as they lit up, the tobacco fragranced their meeting place, relaxing them.

They exchanged awkward words at first, two strangers struggling to find that common ground on which to meet. After ordering whiskeys, they discussed the weather until the drinks arrived. Then they raised their glasses in a toast.

"To Ben, and his help in arranging this meeting."

"To Ben." Ford clinked his glass against his companion's and they drank.

"So," Ford began, "Ben tells me your interview is to appear in *Harper's* Magazine?"

Remington nodded. "I do pieces for them frequently."

"And now you figure to get the old man before he kicks off, am I correct?" Ford laughed at his own joke.

The artist was reluctant to smile, still unsure how familiar he should get with the old Ranger. "Mr. Ford, I—"

"Rip. My friends call me Rip."

Remington set his glass down on the low, polished mahogany table by his right hand. Pulling a tablet and pencil from the breast pocket of his jacket, he smiled. "I'd like to start my interview with your name . . . Rip. How did that come about?"

"Well, back along the time I was fighting in the Mexican War, under Jack Hays, I was adjutant of the regiment. One of my duties included writing letters to family members when one of their boys was killed." He paused, studied the smoke floating above his head. After more than a few moments, he spoke again.

"I envy you, Mr. Remington, not only being able to

communicate through words, but through your art as well. Words alone hold such restrictions. How could I tell some poor mother or father that all the hopes and plans they were waiting to pin on their son were forever lost?"

Remington didn't answer, but waited. Soon enough, however, he realized Rip was not speaking literally, but waiting for an answer in earnest.

"I can't imagine, Mr. For . . . Rip. I can't begin to imagine."

"What I started to do, solely as a means of conveying my sincerest regrets, hoping to add some sort of warmth, somehow, to the cold facts, was write the sentiment 'Rest in Peace' at the beginning of every such letter. After a while it sort of got shortened to R.I.P. and so did my name."

The interview had officially begun.

Remington was soon to find out how very charming Old Rip could be. He loved elaborating about his years as a doctor, lawyer, editor, publisher, member of Congress, surveyor, Indian fighter, and finally, dwelling on his exciting life as a Texas Ranger. The artist still couldn't believe he was sitting across from one of the most famous men in Texas history.

"Tell me about Antelope Hills," Remington asked after they had ordered a second drink.

"I was wondering when you were going to ask about that one." Old Rip smiled. "Yep, that was something. It was spectacular, reminded me of the days of chivalry, the jousting tournaments of the knights. The feats of horsemanship were splendid. The whole performance was a novel display."

THE ARTIST DIDN'T paint in the figure of Iron Jacket. The Commanche Indian chief was often described as a mystical being. Dressed in his painted coat of mail, which must have been stripped from the body of a dead Spaniard years before, the medicine man was known for blowing at the arrows or bullets racing toward him. It was said the objects would fall at his feet, collecting on the ground in an impotent heap. His display had his warriors convinced they were invincible. No, even though Iron Jacket was a fierce, imposing figure, it was the grandeur of the scene Rip had described that Remington wanted to capture.

He worked on the teepees in the background of the wash, skillfully shading the top of each one. The figure of a solitary, fallen warrior lay in the left corner of the foreground. Remington chose a smaller brush to work on the details of the man's skin tones. When he was satisfied, he picked up a brush already wet with a pale yellow and dabbed at the two feathers lying broken near the brave's head. A wounded bird, Remington thought. With the river visible in the right corner, it was obvious to anyone viewing the painting that the Comanche had tried making it to his camp in the distance. He had just crossed the river to warn his people of the Rangers' attack, but never made it.

At least he could get this painting right, Remington thought. Even if he hadn't gotten it right for *Harper's*. God, how he'd fouled up that article, made Ford look like a doddering old fool. And to send the Ranger an advance copy!

How could he have been so arrogant?

"I KNEW YOU'D want all the glorious details about that one," Old Rip had said when Remington asked about the famous battle. "Let's see, I was forty-three when I led my men into the Comancheria. You probably weren't even born yet."

"No." The artist shook his head. "Three years too soon for me to have even been a twinkle."

Rip threw his head back and Remington waited to hear a hearty laugh, but instead the old man only let out a low sigh.

"My Lord, but I'm ancient. You'll have to admit one thing, however, my friend. I've led the lives of ten men. Why, when I first came to Texas from Tennessee, I was a physician. A respected one at that. And then editor of my own newspaper, got into politics . . ."

"Antelope Hills, Rip. For now let's talk about that."

Ford stuck out his chin, scratched his beard. It seemed he enjoyed making his interviewer wait. Finally he spoke. "It was the day after Governor Runnels signed in the bill. I'll never forget, it was titled: 'An Act for the Better Protection of the Frontier.' The very next day, mind you, the governor summoned me, offered up a commission as Senior Captain. I was in command of the companies already in service and ordered to recruit one hundred more men. One of those men was my own father, bet you didn't know that. Did you?"

Remington nodded. "As a matter of fact, I did."

"Huh. Well, the Indian problem in Texas was real bad then, and I had enough experience under my belt to feel competent, not to mention flattered at the opportunity. But it was a tall order to rid the country of those savages. Especially when dozens of Rangers were close to the end of their terms. It wasn't too long before I was left with not too many more than my hundred men. Thank God for Shapley Ross."

"The Indian agent?"

Rip nodded. "And one of the best Indian fighters I have ever known. He organized more than one hundred Indian auxiliaries: Caddos, Anadarkos, Wacos, Tawakonis, and Towawas. They all joined up because of Ross, knowing he would be riding alongside me. Our orders were to follow all trails of hostile and suspected hostile Indians and inflict punishment. By God, that's just what we did."

"Even if it meant riding into Indian territory?" Remington asked.

"I considered my job was to find the Indians, not to learn geography. I did what I was ordered to do, and I did it the only way I knew how."

REMINGTON STOOD UP, rubbed his knees. Sitting too long caused his joints to stiffen. Walking around his studio, he looked at the many items he had collected throughout the years. A crude pot sat on the floor in a far corner. It had been glazed white. Red the color of Georgia clay had been thickly brushed near the base in a sunburst pattern outlined in black. He held it lovingly with both hands, closed his eyes. Had the native artist responsible for this beautiful object been killed by a Ranger's bullet? he wondered.

Bending to replace the pot, he slowly walked over to the wall adorned with an odd variety of his favorite pieces. Lifting a six-shooter from its rusted hook, Remington grasped the gun tightly in his right hand and walked out of the studio into the golden sunlight. Wind rolled through the high grass, reminding him of the ocean. Why? he asked himself. Why hadn't he paid more attention to the old Ranger?

He stared off into the distance, trying to conjure up something that might somehow ease his mind.

"THOSE INDIANS WERE excellent guides and trackers. You know what I've learned in all my years, Mr. Remington?"

"I wouldn't be so bold as to offer a guess, Rip."

"I've learned to be humble enough to let every man I meet teach me something. Oh, sometimes it's a big something, like how to close a wound—save a life. But most times it's a little something. Like how to look at the ground differently after the rain."

Remington nodded.

"Our scouts found out there were Comanche camps across the Red River; we left Camp Runnels and rode north. I remember the exact date, it was April twenty-second, eighteen fifty-eight. There were one hundred and two of us Rangers and one hundred thirteen Indians commanded by Ross. They rode as much as twenty miles ahead of us. Trackers and flankers, working with some instinct they seemed to be born with.

"We moved northwest, along the base of the Wichita Mountains. It took sixteen days of riding, but we finally came to an abandoned campsite. Our scouts figured there had been close to four hundred Indians on that very spot, just a few days before. And the fact that several hostile points had been left stuck in the side of a buffalo carcass showed us we were on the trail of Comanches. But it wasn't until three days later that we actually spotted one of them hunting. Our scouts followed that man and discovered the location of their camp."

Rip was an excellent storyteller. Remington could almost feel the anticipation those Rangers must have experienced that day. At one point he forgot about note-taking and sat forward in his chair, listening, literally, on the edge of his seat.

"I had to act quickly then. If too much time was wasted trying to lay an elaborate plan, we would have surely been spotted by another Comanche who happened upon us. So I made the decision to leave my father and a couple Rangers behind to guard our wagons and animals. The rest of us made a hasty check of our gear and weapons and then moved out."

Remington remembered to scribble down some of the

facts. When Rip told him how his men took cover while he and Shapley Ross crawled up a hill to have a better look, sharing a spyglass, Remington's hand raced across the paper.

"We spotted what we figured to be at least three hundred Comanche down in the valley. They were oblivious to the Rangers and scouts on their trail, Mr. Remington. Those hostiles showed no signs of panic or fear. Maybe because we had gone deep into Comanche territory and none of them were expecting us to show up anywhere near their camp. So Ross and I ordered the men to stay low and we continued.

"That night we made camp and I told Ross I planned to attack in the morning. Keechi, my chief scout, reported the Comanches were camped on high ground on the other side of the river. At seven A.M. we rode out. The first thing we came upon were five lodges, not the main camp. Our Indians attacked and managed to kill or capture every Comanche except for two braves who got away.

"We rode for three miles, trying to catch up to them. That's when we got our first good look at the main camp."

"Can you describe that sight to me?" And the image Rip described took life inside the artist's imagination. Colors, textures, even the warm breeze sweeping across the prairie grass, rippling the water, gusting along the arms and faces of the Rangers and Indians.

Old Rip nodded. "It was overwhelming. There were dozens of white teepees spread out along the river. Smoke rose from campfires. It was spring and the grass was so very green. We stood back, up on a ridge, and watched those two Indians racing across the river to warn their people. Sad, really, when you think about it. Here they were desperate to help their own, and instead helped us more. Led us right to them. Even showed us the perfect place to cross over to their camp.

"I had our scouts ride ahead and to the right of us. Wanted the Comanches to think they were the enemy and the only people they had to fight were Indians like themselves. Then we moved in."

"That's when you saw Iron Jacket?"

"Yes. While we were waiting for one of our reserves to close in on the village. It was Jim Pockmark. An expert marksman—steady nerves, unerring eye. When their chief fell, it seemed to break the Comanches' spirit. Oh, they would occasionally halt and try to make a stand. However, their efforts were unavailing and they were forced to yield the ground to our men.

"Battle not only assaults the body and spirit, Mr. Remington, but the ears as well. The groans of the dying, cries of frightened women and children, mingled with the reports of our firearms." Rip stopped suddenly, lifting his head as if hearing a ghostly cry. His eyes closed slightly as he continued. "Shouts of men as they rose from hilltop, thicket, and ravine. All that commotion attracted hostiles from another camp several miles upriver and they came down upon us, fighting.

"In the end, seventy-six Comanches died—at least that was the official report, but I believe the number to be much higher."

"Why's that?" Remington asked.

Rip was alert now, apparently more comfortable talking about the battle in historical terms rather than emotional ones. "When you consider the wounded we left behind, a large number must surely have died. Eighteen Indian women and children were captured; I believe one of the young ones was Iron Jacket's son. A prisoner told us, in great detail, how the Comanche had been preparing for a major attack. We also rounded up three hundred horses."

* * *

IT WAS CALLED the Battle of Antelope Hills because the Rangers and auxiliaries had found the Comanches by following the broad trail leading to the Canadian River, opposite the Antelope Hills. It had been a noteworthy battle because it was one of the grandest assaults ever made against the Comanches. Riding into Indian territory had taken courage and bravery seldom seen before. But Remington titled his painting "We Struck Some Boggy Ground," a tribute to Old Rip's descriptions of the terrain that day.

When he was certain the masterpiece was dry to the touch, he wrapped it carefully in brown paper. He wanted to deliver it personally.

KATHRYN FORD ENTERED the sitting room, snapping the artist's calling card between her fingers. "And what have you come for this time, Mr. Remington? To tarnish my father's character with still another article? Wasn't your name in large enough letters on the last one? Always looking for publicity, isn't that right, Mr. Remington?"

Remington stood, leveling his gaze at the angry woman. Her hatred for him made every part of his body feel heavy. While she continued her tirade, he remained still, accepting what he thought was owed him. His arms hung in front of him awkwardly, until his fingers met and gently braided together in a loose clasp.

"Well?" she demanded.

"Please." He motioned toward the settee covered with a worn tapestry. "Can't we sit a moment? Talk like the civilized beings we both are?"

Kathryn Ford was an attractive woman. Her long blond hair had been pulled back and the golden tones of her skin made her green eyes seem even greener. "Insulting my father, holding him up to public ridicule, is that what you think civilized people do to one another?"

"If you'll allow me—I have something for you."

"Too late, Mr. Remington."

The artist started toward the hallway, where he had left the painting. "I've apologized to you quite profusely, Miss Ford," he said as he walked away from her.

"For what precisely? For writing an article which portrayed my father as a senile old fool? For getting facts wrong but attributing the errors to him and not to your own self-indulgent stupidity? Or for the kindness of sending him an advance copy which brought about his stroke? Or could it be, Mr. Remington, that you want to apologize for never visiting my father when he lay paralyzed? Not once! Not one single time in that entire month of agonizingly long days and nights did you inquire as to his health. And then to have the audacity to show up at the Confederate Cemetery during his eulogy. Hoping people would talk? Say my, what a sensitive, caring man the great Frederic Remington is. Why, how sympathetic he is to take time out of his busy life to come all the way to San Antonio for an old man's funeral."

He stood in front of her holding the canvas. "How can you think, Miss Ford, with such absolute certainty that my journalistic inaccuracies in any way caused your father's stroke?"

Before she had a chance to express herself, Remington leaned the large painting against a corner chair. Then turning to face her anger again, he confided, "I might offer you some happiness, however, by confessing the guilt I will forever feel for having done a shoddy job on that infernal article. But let me tell you one last time that I only meant to pay homage to your father."

Kathryn's attention had been drawn to the package Remington stood near. There was really nothing the man could say to make her heart ache less. "What's that?" she asked, pointing.

"It seems I am a more accomplished artist than I am a journalist. The words have always come with more difficulty. No matter how intent I am on forming the perfect sentence, the words always seem to have a life of their own and scatter across the paper without any regard for me. But my paints . . . now they are very cooperative." He could not bear to feel her anger a moment longer. "Please, Miss Ford, allow me to apologize from that deepest place inside my soul that forces me to best express myself through my painting."

Remington didn't wait for her to speak. Carefully, he tore the wrapping paper down the middle. When the entire canvas was exposed, Miss Ford stood silent. Then, out of the corner of his eye, he saw her slump down onto the settee.

He hadn't expected a gush of emotion, but was surprised when the only sound audible in the large room was the creaking of floorboards in a room on the second floor, obviously directly over their heads. He could only assume it was a housekeeper making a bed or dusting.

After a few more moments of awkward anticipation, he turned. "Please accept this, Miss Ford, with my heartfelt regards, and I pray that in time you will think I have honored your father in my own way."

Kathryn Ford still didn't speak. But it was not her intention to insult Remington any further. She was simply and completely overwhelmed at the images the artist had captured. And for the first time in her life, she could feel what it must have been like for her father, riding with the Rangers and his auxiliary scouts. The scene of that morning drew the bystander right into the ranks.

It was the sturdy haunches of the Rangers' horses that first caught the eye, but then one moved upward to the men themselves mounted on top, charging their enemy, six-shooters held high. Teepees lined the horizon, and the realism of the scene made her feel closer to understanding the man who had been her father; briefly she was able to share that day with him. Tears stung her eyes, but they hadn't sprung from emotion, but from the all too real dust stirred up by the stampeding troops. What her father had remembered most about that day was the thunder of the hoofs, the screams of the women, shouts from his own men.

How lonely the Indian brave looked, off in the distance. The panic he must have felt. How he must have fought for his life. The lives of his family. His people. His entire village.

"Well, then, I'll leave you with this and hope when we meet next you'll have a few kind words for me."

Remington waited for her to look at him. When she didn't move, he started for the door.

"Never," she whispered.

He turned back. "Pardon me?"

"Don't you understand, Mr. Remington?" she asked. "This painting is magnificent. You've shown my father and his men in all their glory."

"Thank you. I tried. . . ."

Kathryn Ford pulled herself up from the sofa. Walking toward the artist, she wanted to reach out and strangle him. "Don't you see? This makes everything worse."

He stood dumbounded. "I'm sorry, but I don't understand."

Tossing the calling card at him that she had been clenching since the start of their visit, she glared up at him. "It makes your words seem even more despicable."

She waited for a reaction but he just stood, apparently not comprehending a word she had said. Grabbing his arm, she pulled him back into the parlor.

"Look!" Her hands swept the air in front of the painting. "The magnificence of the battle. One can almost smell the fear mingled with courage and dirt. The tension between

Texans and Comanches. How could you not feel it? You painted it so brilliantly."

"Yes," he said after a moment, "I feel it."

"*Now*. You feel it *now*. But it's too late. Certainly you, the privileged, educated, haughty Frederic Remington, know how true it is about the pen being mightier than the sword."

He nodded.

"And it is your words people will remember, at least in my lifetime. But I am glad for two things, sir."

"And what would they be?"

She smiled. "I am glad for the guilt that will live in your heart for years to come. And lastly, I am glad to have this painting to remember my father by."

She sat in front of the canvas again. When he was certain she was finished with him, he showed himself out.

NOW, SITTING IN his studio, the artist still didn't know if he felt better or more guilty than before his delivery. He tried consoling himself with the fact that he was an artist— charged by God to use his talent to make some sense out of a world in constant upheaval.

He leaned back against the familiar boards in his chair. His back relaxed a bit. The light was going. He'd had enough today.

Wiping his hands on a piece of flannel from an old shirt, he stood back to look at the clay. If he was as honest with himself as Kathryn Ford had been, he'd have to admit he hoped to be remembered for his paintings and statues rather than his writing.

AUTHOR'S NOTE: Frederic Remington did interview John Ford at the Menger Hotel. He did write an article for *Harper's* Magazine. He did botch up the job. All the details concerning the Battle of Antelope Hills are historically accurate. Ford suffered a stroke months before Remington's article was printed.

"We Struck Some Boggy Ground" is in a private collection. Remington made his artistic breakthrough in 1895 when he turned to sculpting. John Salmon Ford was eulogized as "the last of the Ranger Chieftains, whose name for nearly a half century had been a household word in Texas."

Ford did have a daughter, but it is total speculation if Remington ever met her.

McNelly's Avengers

by Ronald Scott Adkins

Ronald Scott Adkins lives in Cedar Rapids, Iowa, with his wife, Renee, and his cat, Jazz. His first Western story, "Balance of Power," was published in 2002 in the anthology *Guns of the West.* He is director of the Noble Pen Writer's Group and an advocate of literature and the arts in eastern Iowa. His latest passion is gardening, especially heirloom plants (which are bound to crop up in future writing projects). He is currently at work expanding "Balance of Power" into a novel.

"Is Capt. McNelly coming? We are in trouble."
—Sheriff John McClure, Nueces County, to
General William Steele, April 18, 1875

THE PRISONER FACED McNelly, grinning at him with a freshly split lip. He spit a tooth at the Ranger's feet. It lay there in a puddle of blood.

I knew the captain wanted to slap that smile off his face, to beat out the rest of those black, rotted teeth. But the captain wasn't a man to do that sort of thing.

Instead, he turned to Casoose Sandoval.

Casoose bent down, picked up the tooth, and put it in his

pocket. Then with a nod from the captain, Sandoval was on that bandit again like a wild hound. He cracked him upside the head with his pistol, lifted him by the shirt, and punched that ugly mouth. "I know this one," he said. "His name's Garcia."

Garcia was the second bandit we'd captured since being called down to the Nueces Strip. Local ranchers were having a hell of a time. Raiders crossed over from Mexico, stole cattle, burned farms, raped, killed, or panicked everyone around. Armed posses patrolled the trails, but they caused nothing but trouble. The Army, what there was of it, couldn't find a trace of the raiders and couldn't keep the vigilantes from adding to the fracas. South Texas became bandit country, lawless territory.

So they called for the captain.

This Garcia, I figured, couldn't—or wouldn't—tell us much more than his *compadre*. The only thing we didn't know for sure was when they planned to move across the border.

"Speak," said the captain.

Nothing came out of Garcia's mouth but a steady stream of blood. Sandoval dropped him to the ground, kicked him twice in the ribs, then bound his hands with pigging string. He grabbed a length of rope and fashioned a noose around that poor bastard's neck. It was a good twenty-five paces to the nearest cottonwood, but Casoose dragged him the whole way, got him to his feet, and swung the rope over a stout branch.

The captain turned to me. "He's your capture, Lieutenant Robertson. Give Sandoval a hand."

I saluted McNelly and joined Casoose at the tree.

"You take the rope," said Sandoval.

I hoisted Garcia up just enough to make him stand on

tiptoe. The noose chafed a swath of raw skin. His head turned red like a ripe apple. He could breathe some, in loud, wailing rasps, but still didn't say a word.

"This one's got his mouth sewed shut," I said. "He don't want to talk to us."

"He talk to me," said Casoose. "He talk to me."

Sandoval had that look on his face again. His eyes, already a sharp, piercing blue, grew even brighter, like they could shoot sparks. The left one started to twitch, which set his whole meaty, jowly face to wiggling. He smiled big and wide every time the prisoner gasped for breath. He took everything slow, savoring it, making it last. Sandoval was spooky on a good day. But when he had a prisoner, someone to play with, I'd swear he was possessed. He looked like the Devil from my Sunday school stories—short, squat, greasy, with a fire-red beard and long, stringy hair. He sure didn't look like any *tejano* I'd ever seen.

Sandoval winked at me and I gave the rope a hard pull. I heard a loud pop from Garcia's neck and thought for sure this interrogation was over. I expected to see him hanging there like a sack of feed, but even then he fought against the twine that cut into his wrists. He wiggled his feet, stretching to find solid earth that wasn't there.

I lowered him down, then yanked him a yard or so off the ground again and let him drop. Another hard pull and he was way up in the branches.

"You got something to tell us now?" Old Casoose asked calmly, almost gently.

Garcia could only gurgle and spit, blood running down the corners of his mouth.

Sandoval took this as a yes. He moved his horse—an ugly, mottled old roan—under the prisoner's feet. "Bring him down, Pudge," he said to me.

I lowered the rope while Casoose guided Garcia's feet onto the horse's rump.

I looked around at the Rangers gathered about the tree. Some were laughing, pointing, ribbing each other. They took pleasure in watching this Mexican bandit stretch. They said he looked like a catfish on the line. Some wore no expression at all. Standing there to watch the interrogation was an expected duty—as much as it was my duty to help wring out information from my capture. And some, like Berry Smith, our youngest recruit, couldn't hide the shock of what they saw. They stood there with their jaws hanging down, their eyes wide.

I looked at Captain McNelly. He watched all this from a distance, just outside the shade of the tree. His thin, pale face was a grim mask. His jaw was set tight on an unlit cigar. To my dying breath I'll never understand that man. Such a thin, frail little fellow, he looked more like a preacher than a captain of the Rangers. But he'd fought for Texas against Indians, against the Union, against the Reconstructionists. He'd done it all in the name of justice. And now he was ordered to bring justice to the Nueces Strip, to end the Mexican raids on our good Texas cattle.

The captain stepped up to the prisoner, and without taking the cold cigar from his mouth, asked, "When does your party move?"

Garcia said nothing.

McNelly clamped down on that cigar. He stared into Garcia's eyes with a look that would have melted candle wax. Garcia didn't flinch once. I gave him that much. It took quite a will to stare down the captain.

Sandoval handed McNelly a good-sized length of tree branch. The captain held it in his hands, judging its heft. Then, all of a sudden, he reared back and took a swing at

Garcia's kneecaps. Garcia swayed like a drunk, trying to keep standing on the back of that horse.

The captain hauled off and hit him again, this time on the back of the legs. Then, speaking clear and slow, to make sure Garcia could understand his English, McNelly said, "You're stealing Texas beef. When do you move them to Mexico?"

Sandoval stepped between Garcia and the captain. Looking up at the prisoner with a big wide grin, he took the stick from the captain's hands and beat Garcia soundly about the privates. Then he said, "You talk, this will stop."

Garcia said something in Mexican I didn't understand. But I was sure it meant something like "bullshit," or "my ass." Whatever it was, it made Casoose laugh out loud.

All this time, the prisoner worried so much about where his feet were that he must have forgot about the noose around his neck. He sure didn't notice when Sandoval winked for me to give the rope considerable slack.

"I'll not ask again," said the captain.

"You'll never catch them," Garcia said as McNelly turned and walked away.

I've seen the captain interrupt a wedding to arrest the groom. I've seen him stare down a pack of vigilantes, sending them home unarmed and quaking. I've seen him cut a murderer's throat for boasting. But I've never seen him hang a man. He left that for Sandoval.

Old Casoose knew his job. He signaled for me to tie off the rope and join the other Rangers around the tree.

Most men will tell you they don't fear death. But what they'll never confess is how much they fear the pain of dying. Every time I fired my pistol as a Ranger, I knew there was someone who fired back. Odds were always even that my bullet might go wide, while my enemy's might strike true. I wondered what that would feel like, feared it in some way. I dreamed sometimes that a hot slug pierced my heart, that the agony was unbearable, and that I prayed for death. I woke up cold and sweating.

Like the way Garcia was sweating now, watching Mc-Nelly walk away, and seeing the glint in Sandoval's eyes grow brighter. The prisoner's whole countenance began to quiver. Then, standing straight as he could, he turned his head to the sky and started mumbling something in Mexican. I took it to be praying. The only one he was going to talk to was his maker.

Sandoval nudged his leg to get his attention. Garcia spit blood in his face.

Casoose cursed him.

Garcia prayed louder and faster, his voice rising in pitch until he was shouting like a little boy, and crying like a young girl.

Sandoval swatted his roan on the flank and it took off like the devil was scorching his tail.

Garcia let out a scream I'll never forget as his foothold ran free.

The sharp crack of his neck was like dry branches broken over the knee. I turned my head, wincing, and saw many of my comrades do the same. Young Berry stood there, frozen, eyes wide and mouth gaping. He fought back the gorge rising in his throat until he could hold it no longer. He retched the whole time Sandoval untied the rope and let the dead man crumple to the ground. Then Berry watched, as I did, as Sandoval looked into Garcia's lifeless eyes for a moment, then took an ankle in each hand. He dragged the corpse over to a small sand hill where he would bury it in an unmarked grave.

*   *   *

GARCIA'S ONLY WORDS to McNelly, "You'll never catch them," were all we needed to know. The raiders were driving south and it would be a footrace to the Rio Grande.

The captain ordered us to break camp and mount up.

First in the saddle was young Berry Smith. I'd never seen a boy so wide-eyed and eager. The day he turned sixteen he badgered his daddy, our company cook, to take him to meet Captain McNelly. The captain looked him up and down, had him fire off a few shots at some old whiskey bottles, then signed him up.

"You think we should bring on someone so green?" I asked McNelly.

"Why not?" the captain shot back. "His heart is strong and eager. And he comes from good stock. Old Man Smith serves the Rangers well."

"But he's never been in a fight. He could slow us down, get in the way."

McNelly pulled a fresh cigar from his coat pocket, gave it a good long approving sniff, then put it cold between his teeth. "Then, Lieutenant Robertson," he said, putting a hand on my shoulder, "it will be your responsibility to see he's adequately prepared. Consider him under your direct command."

And that was it. Berry Smith was now my charge, my Ranger. I had to tame a wild side I'd never expected. That first day, we took target practice together. He was a crack shot standing up or hunkered behind cover. He could hit anything, so long as he, or it, wasn't moving. On horseback, though, he'd come charging in hell-bent and never once hit the mark.

Six times he did this, until his cartridge ration was gone. "Be right back," he said to me.

"Where're you going?" I said, sounding like a lieutenant.

"I need more ammunition," he said, kind of timid.

I stepped in front of him. "You've wasted enough. A Ranger doesn't squander his ammunition. Someday the enemy may have one more shot than you, and that's enough to get you killed." I let that sink in for a second. "How much money you got on you?"

Berry looked at me puzzled.

"How much?" I asked again.

He fished in his pockets and came up with a nickel.

"All right then," I said, taking it from his hand. "For the rest of the day, every round costs you five cents and you got enough for one shot." I handed him one of my cartridges and pocketed the nickel. "Load up, mount up. And make it count."

I'd pay cash money for a picture of his face when he loaded that one round. But he did it, rode back about fifty yards, and again came charging in like his ass was on fire. This time, instead of spraying the bushes, he waited until he was closer. He steadied himself, took aim before he fired. His one shot hit the target. We took practice like this—one cartridge at a time—for a week. By Sunday supper I'd have put money on him against any Ranger in camp.

He had the heart of a Ranger, the skills to be one of the best, but only time and combat would tell if he had the stomach for blood. He couldn't answer that one great question— did he have what it took to kill a man—until he sighted his adversary down a rifle and pulled that trigger. This I knew for certain: Berry would answer that question here in the Nueces Strip.

The first settlers called this place the Desert of the Dead. Nothing grew here but cattle and wild mustangs. What wasn't sand, blowing and shifting into ever-changing hills, was waste-high grassland. There was no water, no trees to speak of save for some oak mottes, a mesquite, or huisache tree here and there. Further south, great clumps of Spanish dagger dotted the open fields, and salt grass circled lakes of foul black water. And everywhere the air was thick and hot and hard to breathe. When I thought of Hell, I thought of the Nueces Strip.

And when I thought of Satan, I thought of Casoose Sandoval. How fitting that he made this land his home. He knew every trail, every crossing, every town in this wasteland, and every soul who crossed his path. His reputation preceded him when he first met Captain McNelly. The captain knew of the soulless pleasure Sandoval took in draining the life from men, but still didn't hesitate to make him a Ranger. This was brutal country, McNelly told me once, and sometimes brutality was needed to bring order. It wasn't long before Sandoval was the captain's keen eyes and ears, his good strong arm, and trusted avenger.

They rode point together as we headed south toward the Rio Grande. They made quite a pair to look at. McNelly was so slight and pale, you were worried a stiff wind might blow him off his mount. Sandoval hunkered down in his saddle, short, squat, with that bright red hair catching the wind and fanning out like flames. The captain rarely spoke above a soft mumble, but Casoose had a voice that could rumble down a canyon like thunder. Both held a fire that glowed in their eyes, burned you to the core if you stared too deeply. Stoking that fire was each's own unspoken passion that drove them together, drove them south to battle.

The high sun scorched our backs, drowned us in our own sweat as we rode on. The blowing sand was so white I had to squint or go blind. There were no landmarks to guide our way.

Berry rode up beside me. "Hey, Pudge?" he asked.

I saw the captain cock his ear my way. He was quick to laugh with his men, share meals with them, and join in on our poker games when not on duty. But when called to action, he expected everyone to remember he was a Ranger and act accordingly.

"Is that how you address an officer, Smith?" I shot back, loud enough for the captain to hear.

Berry straightened his back and lowered his voice. "Excuse me, sir. Lieutenant Robertson, may I ask a question?"

"You may," I said. I slowed up some so the captain would fall out of earshot. Once I thought we were safe enough back, I grinned at Berry. "What's on your mind?"

"That Garcia man, he didn't say nothing. How do we know where we're going?"

"Old Casoose knows where we're going."

"That Sandoval scares me some," said Berry.

"Tell the truth," I said low, "he scares me sometimes too."

"I think he scares a lot of people. But the captain seems to trust him."

"More than you know, Berry."

"And what'll we do when we get there?"

"What the captain tells us to do. You know that."

Berry's green youth was showing on his face. He knew only the growing legend of Ranger McNelly. He'd never fought alongside him before, never seen what he could do.

"You see," I said, "the captain's like a chicken hawk. He doesn't sit around and ponder like the hoot owl, thinking this and thinking that before he flies off to hunt. Captain knows there's prey out there. All he's got to do is find it. And when he does, look out. He swoops down"—I clapped my hands together and Berry's eyes grew wide—"and strikes with razor-sharp claws."

"And Sandoval?" asked Berry. "What's he?"

"I guess he's like the owl. He's always got his eyes and

ears open, judging the lay of the land, getting to know all the critters that burrow and scurry in the tall grass. He knows all their hiding places, all the little trails they run on. He doesn't swoop down out of the sky unless he knows what might be waiting for him. But when he does strike, you can bet for sure he'll come up with his kill."

Berry grinned. "Owls and chicken hawks. What's that make you?"

"I'm more like that possum your daddy shoots and serves us for supper." I laughed, patting the belly that bulged some over my belt buckle.

"That why they call you Pudge?"

"That's a story for another time," I said.

I saw McNelly shade his eyes as he looked out over the flatlands, following Sandoval's hand as it swept across the horizon. The captain nodded agreement to something said, then Sandoval rode off.

The captain waved me forward. "Lieutenant Robertson."

I rode up to join him.

"There's an oak motte two miles southwest. Take the company and make dry camp." He paused to pull the unlit cigar from his mouth, took a deep breath, and let out a string of loud, raspy coughs. I held his arm for fear he'd double up and fall off his mount. The effort of it all brought some color to his cheeks and left him winded. "Standard patrols," he said quietly. "I'll join you directly." With that, he spurred his horse and rode off in the direction of Sandoval.

IT TOOK AN hour's ride to reach the oak stand, and it wasn't much better than the sand hills. At least out on open land the wind cooled you some while it threw dirt in your face. Strategically, though, it was a perfect place to camp. We were high enough up a rise to see out over the plains, and the thick stand of scrub oak kept us hidden from view.

I posted the guard, then found a shady spot where I could sit, peel off my shirt, and wring out the sweat.

Berry Smith helped his father dole out hard tack and cold coffee to the men. Even under cover, we didn't risk a cook fire. Besides, the captain believed men fought harder on an empty stomach. He expected every horse and Ranger under his command to go thirty-six hours without rations, if need be. And he lived by his own code. I never heard him give an order he wasn't willing to carry out himself. Except for executing prisoners. That he left for Sandoval.

Berry handed me a cup of coffee, then sat beside me to gnaw on his piece of hard tack. "Lieutenant?" he asked.

"Captain's not here," I said. "Call me Pudge."

Berry took a swig of coffee. He grimaced, forcing himself to swallow. "I still haven't learned how to like this brew." He handed the rest to me. "Can I ask you a question?"

"What is it?" I took a long swallow. I liked the way Old Man Smith made the coffee.

"Was that the first time you had to help with a hanging?"

I swirled the leavings around in the bottom of my cup. "No."

"You seemed all right by it. I mean, I saw some of the other men and they looked about to faint. But you looked like you were . . ."

"Enjoying it? I'll never enjoy hanging men the way Sandoval does."

"But you stepped right up. You pitched in."

"I was ordered to. It was my job, my capture. My duty. You do things sometimes because you're told to. If you can, you put on a face for others and get by. And try not to lose your grub behind the hanging tree."

Berry looked at me with a question he couldn't put to words.

"It's like your daddy's coffee," I said, pitching the dregs out onto the ground. "When I first signed on, I couldn't stand it. My first swallow about killed me. I tossed the whole cupful into the dirt and nearly got whupped for it. The captain himself came over and scolded me something fierce for wasting good rations. He said, 'If you've been given more than you need, Robertson, then you won't miss half of them for the rest of the week.' I learned to love your daddy's coffee from then on."

Just then, Old Man Smith came over to refill my cup. "You listen to this one," he said to Berry. "You can learn a lot from Pudge. He reads books."

"I read a book once," said Berry. "*Uncle Tom's Cabin.*"

"And what did you learn?" I asked.

"Not much, I don't think. It left me confused."

"Books will do that sometimes. Just keep reading."

Old Man Smith tapped Berry on the shoulder, a grin on his face and a wink in his eye. "He tell you yet why he's called Pudge?"

Berry leaned closer. "Tell me. You promised."

For some reason, I always rested my hands on my belly when I told this story. "There's this cantina in Banquette that cooks up the best tamales in Texas. I finished off a good dozen once when Corporal Sullivan bet me I couldn't eat two dozen more. I've never backed away from a challenge, you know. I gobbled up those two dozen and another dozen for good measure. Your dad here pats me on the stomach so hard I think I'm about to explode. And he says, 'You must've packed them all in that pudge of yours for the lean winter.' And the name stuck."

I heard an approaching horse. The sentry raised his rifle.

The captain rode up fast and dismounted, returning the sentry's quick salute. He took a seat under a tree near me and Berry. He pulled a fresh cigar from his coat pocket and stuck it in his mouth. Behind that cigar was the hint of a smile. He only smiled like that when plans were made.

"You find them, Captain?" I asked.

"Not yet, but soon," he said.

Nothing to do but wait.

NIGHT FELL AND I took my turn at watch. It was good to keep moving. Bodies at rest are susceptible to the creeping fear that catches you unawares. I ordered Berry to stand guard with me. I didn't want him sitting alone in the dark, pondering all the spooks and spectres that haunt young minds when danger is near. He needed to stay sharp, alert. He needed to remember he wasn't a boy anymore, but a Ranger.

A half-moon cast soft shadows from the trees. Berry and I stood under cover of those shadows and looked out over the open field stretching south to the Rio Grande. Pitch-black earth met the slate-gray sky at the horizon. Everything in sight was an unbroken line, save for dark clumps of dagger grass.

Berry whispered, "Pudge?"

"Yeah?"

"Why doesn't the captain ever light those cigars?"

"He's consumpt, boy. Smoking would only kill him quicker."

"Shouldn't he be home, or in hospital?"

A dark spot on the field had moved since I last looked. It took a second, but I found it again, a little bigger, a little closer.

"Pudge?" asked Berry, waiting for my answer.

"He has a job to do."

"But he's going to die."

"We'll all die, Berry, in our time."

"Are you afraid to die?" he asked.

"Everybody is. Now, quiet. Look out there. Tell me what you see." That shadow was closer still.

"I don't see nothing."

"Look. There. A sharp pair of eyes is what keeps a Ranger alive sometimes."

Berry leaned forward, following where I was now pointing. He studied the land for the longest time, then found it. "Something's moving," he said, almost shouting.

"And what would be moving this time of night?"

"An animal?" asked Berry.

"Maybe . . ." I said.

Berry pondered a moment. "Or a man on horseback?"

"Most likely."

"Who do you supposed it is?"

"We've only got one man out—and that's Sandoval. So it's him or a bandit-spy coming to catch us in our bedrolls."

I heard Berry slip his pistol from its holster. "What do we do?" His voice was tight, the excitement of danger catching in his throat.

"Nothing," I said, "for now. We're on watch, so we watch. Replace that firearm, Ranger. Draw your weapon when you need it."

"Yes, sir."

We stood quiet for a while, until Berry started fidgeting.

"Speak your peace, Berry."

"You think that's Sandoval?"

"We'll know soon enough."

The shadow grew larger, grew closer.

Quiet again, but only for a minute.

"Pudge?"

"Now what?"

"You think Sandoval is afraid of dying?" Berry asked.

"Of course he is."

"But he kills so easy, you'd think he and death were *compadres.*"

"Sandoval fears death like you or me," I said. "He's just gotten used to killing."

"That why he's a Ranger—to kill badmen?"

"Near enough."

The shadow now took the shape of a lone rider. And that lone rider, whoever he was, spurred on his mount like the Devil was only half a mile behind. "Your daddy never told you about Casoose?" I asked.

"Just that he's been a Ranger for some time."

"Sandoval has no place to go. You know what *la venganza* means?"

"Blood oath," said Berry.

"Something like that. Some bandits tried stealing Sandoval's herd. They beat him half to death, then made him watch as they killed his wife and daughter. I'll bet that was when he first got that look in his eyes. Seeing your kin die like that would change any man, give him the strength to do some amazing things."

"He killed those bandits, didn't he?"

"Well, one of them got away. But the other four, Sandoval beat with his bare hands until there wasn't much more than a spark of life left in any of them. By the time that fifth bastard got back with help, his four *compadres* were hanging from the same tree and Sandoval was gone. That was ten years ago."

Berry was quiet for a time, then said softly, "So the captain signed on a murderer?"

"These are lawless times, boy. You use what weapons you can. Besides, it wasn't really murder. It was vengeance—*la venganza*. McNelly told Sandoval that the best way to find that fifth man was to join the Rangers. Sooner or later, they'd meet up and Casoose could send him off to the other four, his blood oath fulfilled."

The lone rider cast a spark of light that flared for a second, then dulled to the glow of a smoldering ember. "Only Casoose is that crazy," I said, "to signal his approach in bandit country by lighting a cigar."

Sandoval rode into camp smelling of sweat and stink and whiskey. He greeted the captain without saluting, and they talked for a couple of minutes while Casoose fed and watered his horse.

The raiders were driving the herd straight south, like our prisoner Garcia had hinted. They'd make the Rio Grande and Mexico by noon.

"Give me twenty volunteers," said the captain, rousting the men from their bedrolls. "We can catch them if we mount now and ride hard."

Young Berry was the first to step forward.

"Oh, dear," said his father, standing beside me.

The captain heard Old Man Smith and walked up to him. "You have something to say?"

"Captain, sir," said Smith, his voice timid and low. "I would be beholden if you allowed Berry to stay in camp."

McNelly pulled a fresh cigar from his shirt pocket, bit off the tip, and spat it onto the ground. "He volunteered like any good Ranger."

"Yes," said Smith, "but he's never been in a fight and he's an only child. It would break his mother's heart if he should get killed. Simply break her heart. She only let him sign on because I promised to take care of him."

The captain rolled his cigar between his thumb and

finger, pondering. "Request granted," he said. "Berry will stay behind and . . ."

"Sir," said Berry, standing at attention and saluting, "how can I fight for Texas if I never fight? I'm a good shot and a strong rider. And I'm not afraid."

You should be, I thought.

McNelly looked straight into Berry's eyes, looked over at Old Man Smith, glanced down my way. Then he returned Berry's salute and said, "Saddle up. We ride out in ten minutes."

"Oh, dear," Smith said again.

"I'll keep an eye out for him," I said as Smith headed for the supply wagon.

Smith spoke with his back to me, his voice sounding tight, full of worry. "He looks up to you, Pudge. He'll listen to you."

THE CAPTAIN ORDERED silent riding, which was hard for me at night. I'm not a superstitious man, but I spent enough time in south Texas to hear all kinds of wild tales and ghost stories. You ride in the dark long enough and every rock, every yucca stand looks like a spectre. Some things just give me the whim-whams. Talk, even answering Berry's fool questions, would have made the hours pass quicker.

Dawn broke pink and orange on the eastern horizon when McNelly ordered us to stop. "Rest a moment," he said, his breath coming harder and harder the longer he pushed himself in the close, musty air of south Texas. "Take water. Give some to your horse. This may be the last chance for quite a while." He commandeered the white shirt off a Ranger's back and ordered it torn into long strips. He rode down the line, handing us each a swath. "Tie this around your arm. I want no confusion as to who the enemy is today." We Rangers wore no uniform or badge. Some of us were as brown-skinned as the Mexican bandits we pursued. The battle might break out in a dozen places, and no one wanted to die at the hands of his comrade.

I made sure my emblem rode high and tight on my arm, and I made sure Berry's did the same. "Check your weapon," I said to him, "and make sure you're cinched up good."

"I'm ready," Berry said.

No, you're not, I thought.

Rested, we spurred on and rode harder than before.

The sand hills eroded into hardpan prairie, salt flats, and marsh grass. We weren't too far off from Brownsville and the sea. I smelled salt water on the wind, but couldn't tell if it was from the ocean or the black water marshes up ahead.

The sun just cleared the horizon when we caught sight of the herd. We charged on, keeping low, but about three miles off the bandits saw us coming up fast. They fired into the air to get the herd running. They drove the cattle hard, straight for the bogs of Laguna Madre.

We gained considerable ground, but the bandits had the herd across the water before we could engage them. We stopped at the shore and watched the raiders form a defensive line behind a rise.

The captain rode up beside me, his eyes sharp and fierce.

"This don't make much sense," I said. "If they drove hard, they'd be halfway to Mexico by the time we crossed."

McNelly studied their position, his eyes sharp and fierce. "Idiots," he said with a chuckle. "They're digging in, bracing for battle." He turned to face his company of Rangers. "Men, across this *resaca* are some outlaws who claim they're bigger than the law—bigger than Washington law, bigger than Texas law. This won't be a standoff or a dog-fall. We'll either win completely, or we'll lose completely. Now, line up shoulder-to-shoulder."

I don't know how we looked to those bandits across the lake—a straight line of men twenty-two across—but I felt both emboldened and terrified at the same time. Brave, because there was a trusted Ranger on either side of me. Afraid, because nothing stood between me and a hail of bullets from Mexican rifles.

The captain ordered us in. "Take your time," he said as we waded into the marsh. "Don't hobble your mount in this mire. Let them wait for us. Don't fire. Don't even draw your weapon."

No sooner had we broken the water than the raiders began firing. Shot after shot rang out, none of them coming anywhere near.

I turned to Berry, who rode beside me, bolt upright in the saddle, his jaw set firm but his eyes confessing the fear of death that shook him inside. I put on a big, wide grin and poked him in the ribs. "See what happens when you squander your ammunition?"

Berry chuckled, relieved to let off some steam.

"Today, you'll have more shots than the enemy," I said, and clapped him on the shoulder. "Pretty soon, the only thing stinging us will be these blackflies."

Every step forward raised another cloud of flies and mosquitoes. We brushed them away with our hats, which must have looked like we were brushing away their bullets. *Arrogant gringos,* I'll bet they cursed.

We crept forward, step by step, and that rattled some of the bandits. A couple abandoned their position and took off running. Truth was, we couldn't gait much more than a walk. Our horses found it hard to do even that through the two feet of water and soft, muddy bottom.

We neared the other side. Casoose Sandoval was the first to draw his weapon.

"Wait until I give the order," said the captain, "then shoot straight ahead. Don't shoot to the left or right. And don't shoot until you've got your man good in your sights." The confidence in his voice gave me courage. "Don't walk up on a wounded man. Pay no attention to a white flag."

"That's a mean trick they play on green hands and young Rangers," I said, and the whole line, including the captain and Sandoval, grinned.

We reached the dry land, and no sooner had we put our front hooves on shore than the whole lot of Mexicans skinned out for the flatland.

The captain raised his right hand, then pointed to the scattering enemy. "Form up in twos." I moved up alongside Berry. "Choose your targets, men, and get after them." With that, he spurred on and charged.

"Go for them, boys," I shouted.

The bandits abandoned the herd. They broke off, each going his own way but each still pointed roughly toward the Rio Grande. They all remembered the way home.

I saw McNelly flag down two Rangers. He pointed westward and they followed him.

"Where are they going?" asked Berry.

"They're going to flank them. Push them back and force a stand."

The captain soon had a group of raiders cut off. The cowards suddenly got brave, turned right around, and charged toward McNelly. The captain killed his target straight off. Another Ranger knocked one bandit off his horse, while the rest turned tail. McNelly rode up fast on the wounded bandit, raised his pistol, and killed him before he could get off a shot.

The men near me were itching to fight. "Fire," I shouted, pointing straight at the lead bandits.

Sandoval rode up beside me. He stood in the saddle, took aim, and knocked his target forward, clear over the head of his mount. I rode up to finish what Casoose had started. The bandit leaned on one elbow, blood pouring from his chest. He still held his carbine in his shaking hands. He raised to fire, but Sandoval cut in front of me and shot him in the throat.

"Mine," said Sandoval, giving me the Devil's grin. He dismounted beside the dead man, took his rifle and cartridge belt, and as an afterthought, picked up the sombrero that lay beside the body. This he tossed to me. "Yours," he said, and with that he was off to rejoin the battle.

McNelly's flanking maneuver didn't work as planned. The raiders broke in every direction. "Single man from here on," I shouted.

I could hear gunshots clear across the hardpan. I lost track of many Rangers. Our field of battle must have spread out for miles. There were clouds of dust fanned out everywhere. Each cloud of dust was a bandit at a dead run and a Ranger hard on his tail.

One bandit I encountered, though, showed real backbone, and it almost got me killed. He lay facedown in the dirt, his blood turning the dust to mud. As I rode past, I spied his hand going for a pistol. He had me sighted before I could turn. The bullet buzzed by my arm, slicing my shirt. I took a breath and finished his life.

Berry rode past me. He was fifty yards ahead and gaining ground on his quarry. I saw him shoot and watched the raider fall from his horse.

"I got him!" Berry hollered.

The raider took one in the shoulder, but didn't look too bad off. Blood pouring down his arm, he got to his feet and ducked into a sizable stand of dagger grass. I was still some ways off when Berry jumped off his horse and charged in after him.

"Ranger!" I yelled. "Get out of there!"

I heard three shots fired and prayed Berry was a faster draw. Another shot, and I heard the gurgled cry of a young man dying.

"Son of a bitch," I said aloud, jumping off my horse and running for the thicket. "Son of a bitch."

I didn't hear Sandoval ride up behind me.

I cocked my pistol.

Sandoval cut in front of me. "The fight is there." He pointed to two raiders making a break across the open field.

I ignored him and headed toward the dagger grass.

Again, Sandoval came around and faced me. "No," he said quietly, taking aim at my chest.

I cursed him, but mounted up and rode with him.

Seeing us approach, the bandits fired quick and wide. Still full of rage, still seeing Berry lying dead in that thicket, I shot one bandit more times than needed to kill him.

"Good," said Sandoval, raising his rifle in salute. "Good."

Casoose's shot missed the target, knocking the enemy's horse out from under him. The bandit got to his feet and raised his pistol. Seeing Rangers come at him from all sides, he twisted and turned like a cornered animal. There was no place to go but a patch of yucca. He dove for cover and was gone.

McNelly must have seen everything as he rode up from the west. He dismounted before we could reach him and stood by the edge of the thicket.

"Captain," I said.

McNelly put a finger to his lips to shush me. "Lieutenant,"

he said, loud enough for anyone to hear, "bring me some cartridges. My pistol is empty."

The bandit jumped out from his hiding place with a
bowie knife in his hand. The only one not shocked was Mc-
Nelly. Cool and calm, the captain squeezed the trigger. The
raider fell to the ground, surprise forever on his lifeless face.

The sun was burning down from high noon before the
sounds of battle faded. Those raiders not dead were across
the Rio Grande.

"Our mounts can't stand another hard chase," said the
captain, pulling a cigar from his pocket. "We'll take this
victory."

Five Rangers, cattlemen before they signed on, were ordered to move the herd to Brownsville where they could be
sorted out. Everyone else paired up to find what horses and
supplies we could salvage.

Casoose and I rode back to the dagger grass where
Berry had fallen. Berry's horse stood side by side with the
mount of the bandit.

"He's not far," Sandoval whispered.

Pistols drawn, we walked slowly into the thicket. We
found Berry a few paces inside. His face wore the grimace
of death agony, and his finger still squeezed the trigger of
his pistol.

A steady trail of blood led to a patch of marsh water and
cattails. I threw stones into every clump of reeds until I hit
something solid. Then I fired once. The cry of pain told me
exactly where to aim. I fired again, and again, and again.
Every shot was met with a cry of pain, until there was silence.

The bandit's body floated from behind the cattails. I
hauled it onto dry land and dropped it at Sandoval's feet.
"Mine," I said to him.

Many raiders would never see Mexico again. One

young Ranger would never see his mother and father again.

"What do I tell his daddy?" I asked the captain.

"That he died bravely, like a good Ranger. He died doing his duty."

I laid Berry's body over the back of his horse and headed off toward Brownsville. Sandoval rode to fetch the rest of the men.

The captain rode up and down our line, looking each one of us in the eye. "When we reach town, you will touch nothing. I want every man sober. The people will see how we honor our fallen."

We must have looked like some grim parade we when rode in. People stood in the street and watched us go by. Some saluted us. Some turned their heads at the sight of us. We were sweaty and greasy, hungry and tired.

The captain shook hands with the Brownsville sheriff, who ordered his deputies to collect the dead bandits.

The undertaker took care of Berry. He placed his coffin in the courthouse, where it would lie in state until morning. Townspeople filed in to place flowers around it. I stood in the corner, a haggard guard lurking in the shadows.

Old Man Smith stood for a long time with a hand on the casket. His body shook.

"I'm sorry," was all I could say.

"You did your best," he said without looking at me.

I placed a hand on his shoulder. "He died a Ranger."

"He died young."

I left him to grieve.

Outside, the setting sun did nothing to cool the evening air.

The deputies had returned with the bandit corpses. McNelly ordered them stacked like cordwood in the town square overnight. "A message to all outlaws in the Nueces Strip," he proclaimed.

Before all light was gone, I watched Casoose Sandoval walk to the pile of dead. Slowly, with great purpose, he lifted each bandit's head and studied the face. Disappointed, he walked away cursing.

The fifth man was not among them.

A Ranger's Acquaintance

by Mike Stotter

Mike Stotter has worked at various jobs in publishing, including helping best-selling author George G. Gilman (whose *Edge* and *Steele* books were set in the mythical West) produce a fanzine. Stotter has written his own well-reviewed Westerns, including *McKinney's Revenge* and *Tombstone Showdown*. His short stories have appeared in various anthologies including *The Best of the American West Vol. 1 & Vol. II, Desperadoes, Future Crimes*, and *The Fatal Frontier*. Stotter's children's nonfiction titles, *The Best Ever Book of the Wild West* and *Step into the World of the North American Indians*, are used in elementary schools as teaching aids. He continues to be involved in the British crime scene and runs a website devoted to the genre, www.shotsmag.co.uk.

San Antonio
Texas
January 2003

TO THE EDITOR OF THE SAN ANTONIO STAR

Dear Sir,

I came across the enclosed papers when searching
through my great-great-grandfather's belongings. I had no
idea that he spent his early days fighting for Texas as one
of the elite band of Rangers. Indeed, I had always under-
stood that he was a ranch hand. As to whether the details
are historically correct I cannot certify. From my limited
knowledge I do know that the dates tally, the people de-
scribed and discussed actually lived and were Texas
Rangers. John Duval wrote an account of one Ranger in a
*book called **The Adventures of Bigfoot Wallace, the***
***Texas Ranger and Hunter**, and my great-great-*
grandfather mentions him several times in this account.
These memoirs form part of a larger collection which he
may have been writing with a view to being published, I
can't rightly say. You may wish to run it in your paper as it
may be of some interest to your readers.

Yours truly,

Mr. Cameron Hale

DECEMBER 1875, SAN ANTONIO, TEXAS.
A sketch of my involvement with the Meir Expedition
by Private Edward Hale, Texas Ranger

I have read varied accounts of what has became known
as the Meir Expedition, some outrageous in their lies, some

misrepresenting the Facts. During this time I became Acquainted with Big Foot Wallace, a Texas Ranger who now is famous in his latter years by recounting his adventures. The idea of writing down what I can recall is for my benefit and those generations to follow. I'll tell you quickly about myself—I wass born and raised in Mercer County, Kentucky and led an uneventful life until I wass of age and left my parents and siblings and headed westwards. Not much after my twentieth Birthday I became a Texas Ranger. I wass riding round Bexar County when I herd that the Rangers needed men to fight against Mexico. I knew it wass for me. I rode into their camp on the Rio Grande with four other like-minded men Equipped with a horse, a single-shot rifle and a Bowie knife. I'd herd that this is all wee need to provide to enlist. After proving I could ride and shot from horseback, Captain Green made me swear the Texas Ranger's Oath of Allegiance and slapped me on the shoulder.

"You can ride and shoot," says he. "And you're a Ranger."

In early December of 1842 wee were camped on the west side of the Neuces. Wallace wass not in a cheerful mood when he came up to our fire. When I asked what wass bothering him he said that he had been told that General Somervell had been ordered by Sam Houston to break up the men. At that time wee wass over seven hundred men strong. Somervell had been the brigadier general of the militia and had already broken down the Texan force from twelve hundred men. Now he wanted to weaken our strength further. I had been led to understand that Somervell was in charge of a retaliatory raid into Mexico to pay General Woll back for what he did to Texans along the border. Wallace sat down and laid his rifle across his knees and spoke softly. He said that if

Somervell carried out that order then he would mutineer
and take anyone with him across the border into Mexico
and fight the Enemy. This wass to be kept a secret from the
men but within minutes word wass spreading on what
Somervell wass planning and the men gathered around Big
Foot and gave him their support. I will give you a slight
Idea about Big Foot Wallace. He wass twenty-five years
old, loud and a rowdy giant of a man over six feet in moc-
casined feet. Buckskin clad, shaggy haired, he reminded
me of a Mountain Man. When his brother and cousin (who
had served under Fannin) were killed at Goliad, he joined
up to exact Vengeance on the Mexicans. He hailed from
Virginia but his accent marked him as a Scotsman and he
often boasted that his forebears descended from Scottish
Highlanders William Wallace and Robert Bruce. This was
one story he always stuck to, others he repeated and Exag-
gerated but he was a likeable roguish person. And he wass
the best shot of the company. Whilst I consider General
Alexander Somervell the most spineless and gutless
Ranger if ever one existed, Wallace wass the opposite and
a canny soldier. He didn't oppose the General and kept
his council secret from the officer and wee followed the
order to march towards Laredo. Wee lost some men on
the way who had enough of marching around and not seeing any action and the General made it difficult for us:
making camp without water or supper and parading the
troops. Well, wee wass camped outside of San Antonio
when the General gathered the troops and asked that all in
favour of crossing the Rio Grande to step to the right,
those who wanted to go home to step to the left. Wee
didn't care for orders to return home, wanting to exact
Revenge and plunder Mexican towns, so wee cheerfully
walked to the right. Here some two hundred men left our
company to return. Them that were left voted that

Somervell lead us against the Mexicans. The plan was simple, to capture Mexican prisoners so we could exchange them for our boys still in the hands of the Mexican Army in San Antonio.

ON THE TENTH of December wee began to march down toward Mexico on the east side of the river. Wee changed directions so many times that wee were as bewildered as the Mexicans. It took five days to get to Guerrero. Wee were tired, hungry, and angry at Somervell for such a waste of time marching us around the country instead of striking into Mexico. I didn't elect for Somervell to be my leader, and others began agreeing with me, including Wallace. Wee all had a hard time of it as wee waited for fresh food. First Lieutenant Ben McCulloch had gone into Guerrero to ask the *alcalde* to facilitate rations for the men; he wass told that everything would be ready by nightfall. But that night the weather turned nasty. A heavy rainfall soaked us to the skin, and wee rode about a mile away from the town and were ordered to wait. Why wee sat out there in such an exposed position I couldnt begin to fathom. The General told us to wait in the open, and when the *alcalde* delivered the rations I saw old Somervell's face fall: dirty blankets, a few beeves, a quart of corn for each horse, and tatty hats. Iffen the *alcalde* wanted to insult us, he couldnt have done more.

The next morning wee wass ordered to about-turn to get back to the river crossing. Here the General took a half-dozen boats to recross the river, and soon wee were back on the Texas side of the river. On the nineteenth of December there wass a big powwow of the staff, and at the end of it Somervell started off home taking some two hundred men with him. I wass glad to see the back of him and his half-assed military tactics.

So that left around three hundred Rangers to do the fighting. Wee made camp along the Rio Grande and made William Fisher our commander. Big Foot Wallace wass all for riding across the river straight off, but the big man wass held fast by Fisher. He wanted a stronger force before crossing. Wee knew that a small group of Rangers were on the west bank further upstream; wee needed to combine our forces. Finally wee had some 350 Texans chomping at the bit to get at the Mexicans.

Wee camped opposite the town called Meir. Ten miles out of town Ben McCulloch, who wass in charge of the spy company, told Fisher that there were too many Mexicans on the other side of the river. Fisher did not heed the advice, and called on Big Foot Wallace to take a small company and reconnoitre the town. Wallace picked me out to be part of his company; he said I wass suitable because I could ride and shoot at the same time.

On the morning of the twenty-third of December wee rode into the town of Meir. Wee were to collect supplies, which the *alcalde* provided by late afternoon, but not the transport. It was clear that the Mex would not keep his end of the bargain. Well, wee just took him with us. Wee remained on our side of the Rio for two days.

In the morning of the twenty-fifth of December, Wallace captured a lone Mexican who wass a citizen of Meir. He told Wallace that there wass a large force of Mexican troops commanded by General Ampudia garrisoned in the town. Just how many he wasn't sure, but guessed around a thousand. Ampudia was stopping the supplies from getting through. Wallace said wee could take them by surprise, and a fellow Scotsman named Cameron agreed. Wee had the better weapons and were better soldiers. Once it wass decided, wee rode into Meir, not caring that there were so many enemy in the neighborhood.

Before mid-afternoon wee entered the town by one of its streets. Wee were met by the Mexican cavalry, who outnumbered us at least five to one, and it wasnt testing for them to have us surrounded. Wallace wass quick to remark that it wasnt safe for us to be there and ordered us to run for it. As the Mex cavalrymen tried to round us up, wee opened fire for all wee were worth. I believe it to be our advantage against the Mex cavalry that we were better trained and the best shots. The cavalry turned on us, but wee broke out as one, punching a gap in the Mex horsemen, and shot our way out. But Sam Walker and others were captured and taken prisoner.

Riding like the Devil Himself wass on our tails, we rode straight to Fisher's advancing column. They turned us back to face the Mexicans again. Each man wass up to facing the Enemy and get Sam Walker released. Well, wee reentered the town but Cannons had been set up in the plaza and commanded the town's two streets. The Cannoneers opened up and raked our ranks with grapeshot. Mex Soldiers poured a withering fire upon us from every rooftop. There wass no order to withdraw, and I took my lead from Big Foot Wallace and took cover in an abandoned adobe house. Wee returned fire at the Cannons and Soldiers.

"Buckos, wee need to silence them there Cannons," Big Foot said. There were ten of us in the adobe and wee were all in agreement. Looking out of the window, we saw a house in the plaza with windows overlooking the Cannons. That wass our objective, but wee had two cannons and five hundred soldiers between us and it.

"Wee gonna have to move closer a little by little. From adobe to adobe," Cameron added.

Wee were at the first adobe for an hour before wee could break out and get entry to the next. Our greater-quality marksmanship wass an advantage. Big Foot used his rifle that he called Sweet Lips to deadly affect. I figured he killed one man for every shot he fired. Two other Rangers were almost his equal. Wee broke into the next adobe and some men continued to lay down a barrage, and us others reloaded and caught a minute or two rest. Three more Rangers joined us, and as the door wass closing, a musket ball hit the 'dobe wall and sent splinters into my face and I wass cut above the eye. Big Foot looked around when I yelled out and said, "Dont worry, *amigo,* you've another eye." I didn't find it funny, but Wallace found it amusing. I took it out on the Mexicans. My first shot took a cavalryman plumb out of the saddle.

The opening of the melee was fierce. Lots of gunpowder filled the air from both sides. At times the noise was so loud I couldnt hear Wallaces orders. Let me tell you, I have seen awful sights from gunfire before, and I can't say it is a pretty sight. Men were lying all around. Some shot by muskets other by grapeshot. But a great number of them, I am happy to say, were Mexicans. Wee escaped the worst of the gunfire being protected by the thick adobe walls. Others were not so lucky. I saw a Ranger shot five times and as he lay dead, the Soldiers on the rooftops still shot at him, laughing and jeering as each bullet struck. At times wee were pinned down by determined fire by these troops of General Ampudia. One time I got to thinking that wee couldnt get any further. But just when my spirits were low, Wallace would do something special or say something that would liven me and the other men; rousing us to fight harder.

For the rest of the day and night wee went from adobe to adobe. When night had fallen, the Mexicans still continued to fight. They had the plaza lit by beacons, and more Mexican Reinforcements seemed to pour in on us. GA (a Ranger whose name I cant recall) had the idea that if he could try to knock out the fires, the men could get to the 'dobe opposite the cannons. I said I would go with him. He flung the door open and rushed out. No sooner as I got one foot outside, I was on my backside on the ground inside the adobe. I can't rightly recall if I ever heard the bullet, but it struck the wall inches from me. Wallace still had me by the jacket collar. "Maybe they want your other eye," he said. GA never made it a half-dozen steps. This made us more determined.

The fighting went on during the night, but the fierceness had dampened. As I fought back the exhaustion, I got to thinking about if we would ever escape. The others around me looked done in. Even Wallaces countenance was etched with tiredness, but he remained on his feet most of the time taking potshots at the shadows.

On the dawn of the next morning, things did not look any better. The General used the cover of night to move in more soldiers. The Mex Cannons opened fire at anything that moved. In the growing light, the 'dobe opposite the plaza, I saw, wass just feet away. Wallace ordered five men to open fire with all they had; the others were to make a break for it. It was the Darnedest order I had ever heard, but we carried it out and each one of us made it into that little 'dobe unharmed. Well, wee were tired, hungry, and thirsty, but as soon as wee got inside the adobe Wallace stood by the window and opened fire on the artillerymen. I copied another Ranger by using our knives to cut out holes in the adobe big enough to get our guns through and see a little ground, but small enough to give us shelter.

Soon our sharpshooting gave the Mex Canonneers a barrage that made them keep their heads down. The shooting went on for hours, and suddenly the Mexicans gave up their positions and withdrew. What a sight that wass. The Rangers had the better of them, and every time some soldiers tried to get back to the Cannons, wee hit them hard. Ampudia never gave them Cannons up; he must have sent a hundred men or more to get them back, but each time wee held them at bay. There were plenty of dead Mexicans in the street, which kept our spirits high. The arrival of a couple more Rangers in our fortified adobe helped. By mid-morning of the twenty-sixth of December we held that position, and I thought nothing could take that from our grasp.

That afternoon everything changed. Dr. Sinnickson, one of the men who had been captured when the spy detachment was cut off, suddenly appeared in the plaza with a white flag. The Mexicans ceased fire, and soon our Texans guns stopped. Sinnickson was taken to the adobe where Colonel Fisher was held up. Shortly after, Big Foot Wallace and Ewen Cameron left the adobe to discover what wass happening. I wass not party to the meeting, but Wallace was fixing to bust a gut when he came back. I cant rightly remember his exact wording, but it went something like this:

"Buckos, the Mex general wants us to surrender. Colonel Fisher is shot up pretty bad and he dont want us to carry on the fight. Theres Texan dead and wounded to take care of. The Colonel reckons ammunition is low and the men are exhausted; he cant see the reason to carry on. Ampudia says he has seventeen hundred men ready to carry on the war, but if we surrender we will be treated with respect. The hell with that, I say! I dont believe a word any Mex General says. The Colonel and Sinnickson want to surrender, I say let them. I aint going to give up. Those who want to go, better get their hides out there now. The rest stay here and we will regroup."

Wee looked to Wallace as our leader now. He had that attitude of confidence about him, an ability to draw people towards him. He was the one you looked to, wanted to copy. You wanted to please him. Wanted to be him. With the guns silenced, we could hear a lot of raised voices from the Texans in other buildings. There was a lot of cussing going round. As wee took stock, I looked out one of the windows and saw Colonel Fisher being carried out of the adobe on a stretcher. Dr. Sinnickson walked alongside him, the white flag of truce held high above his head. They were surrounded by Mexican cavalry. Then a few Texans began leaving the adobes and walking out into the streets and handing over their weapons to the Mexican soldiers. These men were marched out of the plaza and out of my view.

For moren a hour or so more Texans gave up and others came over to us. When it was clear that anyone who was giving up had been taken away, I counted fifty men holed up in this one adobe. Wee started out to fight the Mexicans and by God wee were going to carry on. Several times I heard Wallace tell Cameron that his brothers memory wasn't going to die without being liberated. He called upon his ancestors clan to protect him and his namesake whilst he cleaned his rifle. Wee emptied out our ammunition pouches onto the tabletop, and divided it up equally between us. There wasn't much to go around.

I can tell you that for the time it took to use up that powder wee gave them Mexicans plenty to think about. As they advanced a yard, wee shot them and they went backward two yards. The fighting went on for another hour or two until wee had used up the last of our powder. We had reached the point when wee could fight no more. Then it struck me that Christmas had come and gone and not a word said.

The General sent word for us to surrender, and lined his Soldiers up in front of the adobe and rolled one Cannon into the plaza, and wee watched it being loaded with grapeshot. Ewen Cameron looked at us, and suddenly all the fight was out of him. "Follow me, men," he said, and led us outside.

I lingered behind thinking that it all had been a cruel waste of time and that we'd be all 'dobe-walled for certain.

Wallace pushed me out in front of him. He looked old and bloodless. I couldn't tell what wass going on in his head, but there wass still a hot fire burning in his eyes. He wanted to show defiance and be the last to leave the adobe. "Show 'em some steel, *amigo,*" he said, and shoved me forward.

When I looked over my shoulder, he was surrounded by Mex Soldiers who took his rifle and Bowie knife from him, bantering that he should fight them to get his weapons back. "Dont trust a Mexicans word, buckeroos!" he yelled.

The Outsider

by Robert Morrish

Robert Morrish is the editor of *Cemetery Dance* magazine and co-editor of the anthologies *October Dreams* and *Quick Chills II.* His short fiction has appeared in anthologies such as *Horrors!, The UFO Files, Octoberland, Shivers,* and *Stones;* a collection is forthcoming from Subterranean Press. He's had nonfiction work appear in periodicals such as *Publishers Weekly, The San Francisco Chronicle, The San Jose Mercury News,* and *Rod Serling's Twilight Zone Magazine.* Born and raised in Michigan, Morrish now lives in the Santa Cruz Mountains of California, with his lovely wife, Kayalucia, four dogs, two horses, and a black cat.

WACO STUDIED THE ground at his feet. His body was rooted to the spot as his gaze roamed ahead, scanning the trail. Weeds and small branches were bent. Hoofprints disturbed the dirt. The man he was pursuing had come this way, there was no doubt about it.

Waco looked up, squinting into the setting sun, searching for any further signs of the man's passage. He raised a hand to shield his eyes from the sun's prying fingers, waiting for his vision to adjust. It was then he heard the noise behind him.

How could he have been so careless?

He crouched and wheeled around, hand dropping from forehead to holster in a smooth, lightning-quick motion. But as he sought to grasp his pistol, his fingers fumbled over the grip, still not accustomed to its feel even though he'd been working with it for weeks now. The thought that his lack of skill with his new weapon might just cost him his life danced across his mind like a windblown tumbleweed.

He still had the gun only halfway out of its holster when he saw who it was that had snuck up behind him. The man stood, halfway behind a scraggly oak, not thirty feet distant.

"Durham." Waco relaxed, started to rise from his crouch. "I did not hear you coming. What are you—"

"Don't move, Injun," answered Durham, raising his gun until it was pointing at Waco's head.

A second later, he pulled the trigger.

ALMOST EXACTLY A month earlier, Waco and Leroy Durham had laid eyes on each for the first time. Neither one particularly liked what he saw.

Waco kept his first impression to himself, but Durham made his feelings known by letting loose a stream of tobacco juice that landed inches from Waco's feet, spattering the toes of his boots with the spray. No matter how cantankerous Durham might be, one had to respect his accuracy, with both spittle and guns, as Waco would discover in the months that followed.

A lesser man might have lost his head in response to Durham's act. But not Waco. He knew pride, knew it as well as any man, but he also knew foolishness. This was neither the time nor place for fighting. He just eyed his short, angry adversary, taking stock of the man. Durham seemed little more than grizzle and gristle, his body worn and weathered like jerky that had been left out in the sun. His clothes—soiled, faded, and torn, showing none of the signs of respect that the informal uniform deserved, and received, from the other Rangers—seemed to say much.

Waco stared on, willing his eyes to burn a hole through the man. He felt a hand on his shoulder.

It was Baker, the one who had brought him here.

"Come on, now," he said. "None of that." He tugged lightly at Waco, leading him away.

"Don't let old Leroy bother you," said Baker once they were a few steps away. "He's ornerier than a sack of copperheads. Ain't nothing personal. He's just had himself a bad patch."

"What is a 'bad patch'?"

"Sorry," answered Baker with a small smile. "Just a sayin'. Means a run of bad luck, I guess you'd say. For Durham, it was losin' his wife and son to yellow fever a couple years back. He ain't never really been the same since."

After that, Baker continued leading the newcomer around the post, introducing him to the other Rangers. Most of the company of forty men, including Captain Kinney, were out on patrol, so the introductions didn't take long. None of the other men were as overtly hostile as Durham had been, but none of them exactly embraced the new man with open arms. A couple wary comments of "Welcome aboard" were the best he got, with a grunt and a nod being the norm.

"Why they call you Waco anyway," asked Baker once he'd finished the introductions.

"When I signed on, they could not pronounce my Indian name. They said it sounded like Waco, so that would be my name."

Baker laughed. "That sounds about right. We had a couple

Mexicans join up last year—one of them's still with us,
but he's out on patrol right now—and I recall their names
got twisted around pretty good. There ain't no Juans here,
just Johns, if you know what I mean."

"I believe I do." Waco was silent for a moment, weighing his thoughts.

"Baker," he said suddenly. "Why did they put you with
me? Did you, what is the saying, 'draw the short straw'?"

Baker was looking back toward the corral, where Jones,
one of the men he'd just introduced to Waco, was saddling
up to head out on patrol. After a long moment, Baker turned
back and said, "Probably because I get along a little better
with Indians than most of the men here. When I was
growin' up, my ma and pa were on pretty good terms with
the local tribe.

"Lipan Apaches," he added. "Same as you."

"I thought it would be something like that." Waco smiled
for the first time that day. "I am grateful for your help. I know
it will not be easy for me here."

"Aww, most of the men are all right. They'll warm up to
you once you drink with 'em. There's only a couple bad apples." He paused, the July sun bearing down on the two men,
etching their shadows in the dust. "Have to ask you, though,
if you don't mind—what made you decide to sign up anyhow? We don't get many of your . . . too many Indians."

"This I know." Waco was well aware of the lonely path
down which he walked. But he also knew that he was not
the first to take the path. There had been several Indians in
the Rangers before him, as far back as five or six years ago.
But none had stayed in for longer than three months. Why
exactly they had left so quickly, he did not know.

"My story is much like yours," he said. Baker looked at
him quizzically.

"You help me because of things that happened when

you were a boy," Waco explained. "I wish to join because of what happened when I was a boy. One day, my father was out hunting when the Comanche came. There was only my mother, my little brother, and me. A Ranger who was scouting the Comanche saw us. He did not have to help us, but he did. He knew what the Comanche would do to us if they found us, so he led us away. I have wanted to be a Ranger ever since."

Baker whistled. "I'll be darned. Sounds like you got yourself a good reason."

Waco allowed another small smile. There was more to it than what he had said, but nothing he wished to speak of.

There was the new weapon that the Rangers had, the pistol that kept firing. He had heard stories about how they had used the weapon to wipe out a band of Comanche near San Antonio the year before. And Waco had heard Texas would soon become part of the white man's Union. Add it up and it was clear that Texas would belong to the white man. Waco figured it only made good sense to align himself with the winning side.

And finally, there was the matter of Waco's blood. Despite what Baker had said, Waco was not pure Apache. His mother was indeed Lipan, but his father was of the Tonkawa, another of the prairie tribes. Against all custom, his parents had lain together. As a result, Waco was a man with no tribe, an outcast. Joining forces with the white man could hardly be any worse than the solitary life he had lived so far.

"I reckon we oughta quit jawin'," said Baker, "and get busy teachin' you a few things, don't you figure?"

"Yes," agreed Waco, "let us start."

THREE WEEKS LATER, Waco felt as if he knew the ways of the Ranger almost as well as he knew the ways of the Indian.

Not that the two were completely different—he had found, to his surprise, that the Rangers had learned and even adopted some Indian techniques of riding and fighting, in order to better combat their enemy.

He was spending his first month working side by side with Baker, before he would patrol on his own. He had learned to use the five-shot revolver, the weapon he had heard so much about, and he had been taught about the Rangers' ways of spying on their enemies, how they followed the North Star when riding at night, and how they rode into battle.

Through it all, Red Wing had been at his side, a rock in Waco's time of need. A nine-year-old chestnut gelding, Red Wing was Waco's heart and soul. Without him, he would be nothing. Together, they were one.

"If you would've joined up a few years ago, there wouldn't have been no trainin'," Baker told Waco one day. "Men didn't join up for no longer than three- or six-month hitches then, and there wasn't no time for trainin'. That's all changed now. Major Hays got us more men, and enough money to keep everybody paid."

"I have heard much about this Major Hays. I hope I meet him someday."

"You stay around long enough, you just might." Baker smiled, which he did a lot. And every time he did so, his lips would curl up and the hairs on his long, droopy mustache would completely cover the mouth beneath. Waco had asked him once how he could stand the hairs always getting in his food and drink. Baker had told him that you just got used to it, like anything else. Waco had smiled in return, although he thought there might be some things that one never got used to.

During those first few weeks, Waco's relationship with the other men in the company gradually improved. He didn't see them all that much, as he was usually out on patrol with

Baker, and when they did get back to the post, the others were usually gone. But when he did see them, most now would look him in the eye and speak to him. It clearly didn't hurt matters when he drank with some of them one night, as Baker had suggested. Most had seemed to welcome his presence that night, although a few kept asking him to say "firewater," as if it were some big joke.

Even Durham had spoken to him once, a few days before, although only to ask him, "Got any tobacco?" Waco wasn't sure if that was supposed to be a joke or not.

The *other* joke Waco had been forced to put up with came in the form of Baker's frequent remarks about Waco's tracking ability, or lack thereof. "Everyone knows that Indians are supposed to be great trackers," Baker would say. "What happened to you?"

"I know it is not one of my greatest skills," was Waco's general response, but usually Baker was laughing before Waco could even get all the words out of his mouth. Although Waco did not particularly enjoy being the butt of Baker's jokes, he knew that it also signaled a certain level of acceptance, and he knew that was a good thing.

One night, as they were setting up camp, Baker asked, "Did it surprise you at all that they let you in, you bein' Indian and all?"

"Some, yes," said Waco. "but I had men—white men—who spoke for me. And I have a good horse." He paused, stroking Red Wing's neck. "The captain spent a long time looking at my horse, longer than he spent looking at me, before he agreed to take me."

"That don't surprise me none. We got a sayin' here—'A Ranger ain't no better than his horse'—and it's surely true. Don't matter if you're the toughest, best-shootin' man in all of Texas. If you don't have a good horse, you'll be dead soon enough, that's for sure."

"It is good then," said Waco, "that I have the best of horses." As if in answer, Red Wing dipped his head, rubbing his nose against Waco's hand.

"I'm pretty fond of Rascal here myself," answered Baker.

Indeed, he was. So fond that it almost cost him his life a few days later.

THE DAY THAT Baker almost died broke clear and cloudless, spring finally starting to give way to summer despite its stubborn attempts to hang on for just a bit longer. As the morning birds sang, the two men feasted on *panoln* and salted rabbit, girding themselves for the journey ahead. Sated, they rolled up their blankets, packed their rations, and saddled up Red Wing and Rascal.

"If we're lucky today," said Baker, "maybe nobody'll accuse us of stealing any of their livestock."

They had passed through a settlement on the Nueces River the day before, a day's ride out of Corpus Christi, where they'd been greeted by one particular settler who was none too glad to see them. The man came charging out from his ramshackle log cabin, shouting and waving his arms. Baker and Waco had slowed, thinking the man was seeking their help, but instead found that he only wanted to keep shouting at them.

"You ain't nothin' but pig-stealers and spies. Maybe we ain't got as many problems with Injuns no more, since you started comin' round, but we got a big problem with you stealin' our pigs! And now it looks like you done joined up with the Injuns."

He went on like that. Once it became clear the man wasn't going to stop, they had simply ridden off, leaving his shouts in their wake.

"You get some people like that," Baker said. "Can't

nothin' make 'em happy. As far as they're concerned, we're never around when they need us. Or like that fella back there, we're to blame for whatever ails 'em."

"Is there truth in what he says?" asked Waco.

Baker didn't answer right away. "Might be," he said finally. "A lot of different Rangers pass through here. Some of 'em like to drink and carouse. And it's easy enough to get hungry out here. I wouldn't put pig-stealin' past some of 'em."

Baker made a joke about it after that, and then quickly changed the subject. Clearly, though, it had bothered him, for it was still on his mind that next morning.

But before Waco could think of a response, Baker mounted Rascal and looked back expectantly. They were headed to a settlement further downriver, to look into rumors of stolen horses, and Baker seemed eager to get going.

"Don't forget your hat," added Baker as Waco climbed on Red Wing. It was a frequent remark. Waco had never before worn a hat, and had a hard time getting used to the feel of it. But it was part of the uniform, so he pushed it down over his hair and tried not to think about the way it squeezed his head.

They rode for the better part of an hour, following the river, until reaching a tributary that ran across their path. They followed this river another half mile upstream before Baker motioned to stop.

"We'll cross here, "he said. "This is about as good a spot as we'll find this far south."

Waco nodded. "Let me cross first this time."

"You sure? It's still running pretty fast and high here. I could go—"

"Do not worry. I have done this many times."

"All right, then. You're the boss," said Baker with a smile. "Let's get to it."

Waco eyed the river for a moment, gauging the best spot to cross. He dismounted and led Red Wing a short ways upstream, then paused and stroked the horse between his ears as he whispered to him, reassuring him.

"Let's go," he said finally, leading Red Wing into the water.

The river was close to a hundred feet wide at that point, and the going was slow. Waco waded through the rushing waters, carefully choosing his footing on the slippery rocks littering the river bottom. The water rose higher than Waco had expected, to his shoulders and even a bit above. He struggled to keep his left hand, holding his rifle and holstered pistol, above his head, while he kept his other hand on Red Wing's flank. Finally, just as Waco thought he would have to start swimming, the river bottom began rising again as they approached the far bank. A few long moments later, he and Red Wing were emerging from the water, shaking off the clinging wetness.

Waco looked back. Baker was well into the river, nearing the midpoint. Alongside, Rascal followed faithfully, but he was clearly nervous, rearing his head every few steps as the water continued to rise.

They passed the middle of the river, the water swirling around Baker's upper chest as he struggled against the current. Suddenly, he lurched to one side, a foot slipping on a submerged rock. His head disappeared beneath the surface.

A moment later he reemerged, spluttering, pulling himself upright with the aid of Rascal's reins.

Still recovering from his misstep, Baker didn't see what happened next.

Waco saw it coming moments before it happened, but his shouted warnings were drowned out by the water's din.

He could only watch helplessly as an uprooted tree,

carried swiftly by the current, slammed into Baker and Rascal.

The unexpected blow knocked both off their feet, catching Rascal more squarely and sending the horse careening downriver.

Baker managed to recover after being carried no more than twenty or thirty feet. In a deeper part of the river now, he was treading water, successfully fighting the current. If he had simply swum for the bank at that point, he would have been fine.

But then he saw Rascal, still struggling to right himself as he was swept helplessly along. Further downstream, directly in his path, lay an outcropping of jagged rocks. Forsaking the shore, Baker started swimming with the current, trying to catch up with his horse. There seemed little he could do, but that clearly wasn't going to stop him from trying.

Waco took a step into the water, but then stopped. He stood there, watching the scene unfold, unsure what to do.

Baker swam on as Rascal fought. He drew up alongside his horse some twenty feet before the rocks threatened. Baker tried pushing Rascal toward the riverbank, but his efforts to shoulder the twelve-hundred-pound beast seemed fruitless. Panicked, the horse fought against the current, against Baker, against everything.

But then, suddenly, he seemed to calm down long enough to realize it was Baker who was pushing him. Long enough to trust.

And then, miraculously, the two began to veer toward the bank. Slowly, they angled toward safety, the angry current refusing to yield. Waco started running along the bank, yelling, encouraging them, even though he knew they couldn't hear him.

It looked as if they were going to make it. Waco could

see only a single rock in their path now, on the outer fringes of the river.

Paddling furiously, they were carried closer to the rock. Closer.

Rascal, on the outside, cleared the rock. Baker, on the inside, did not.

He slammed hard into the rock and then hung there, his clothes snagged on the craggy surface.

Without hesitation, Waco charged back into the river, water splashing as he struggled to reach his friend. He dove into the deeper water, powerful strokes carrying him quickly along. Waco may not have been a good tracker, but he was an excellent swimmer.

When he reached Baker, the man was still unmoving, his face hanging submerged in the water. Holding onto the rock, Waco pulled Baker's head up with his other hand, shook him, yelled at him. There was no response.

He put one arm around Baker, braced himself against the rock, and pushed off, heading toward the bank.

He struggled mightily, the current unforgiving. Finding a strength born of desperation, he fought on, somehow making progress.

Sometime later, he had no idea how long, Waco crawled from the river, dragging Baker onto the bank, and collapsed, gasping for air. He wanted nothing more than to just lay there, drawing breath into his lungs, until his strength returned. But there was no time for that.

He forced himself to his knees and turned to Baker, who lay unmoving on his side. He was empty; no breath filled him, no life. Waco knew his friend's spirit was hovering, preparing to depart this world. It was up to him to force it to return.

He turned Baker over on his stomach, so the water could escape, placed his hands between his shoulder blades, and began rhythmically pushing, trying to force the water from him.

Waco kept at it for what seemed like many long minutes, but he could get no sign that Baker's spirit had returned. Gasping anew, he paused to catch his breath.

But he could not let himself rest. There was no time.

His heart threatening to burst with sadness, he threw himself at Baker's unmoving form again, his hands thrusting.

Finally, as Waco was about to give up all hope, Baker's body jerked and stiffened. He gagged, then vomited river water, his breath coming at last in shuddering heaves. Waco fell back, relieved but exhausted.

When he strength had returned, he stood and took a look around. Red Wing was standing with Rascal on the bank, a little further downriver, munching weeds, Rascal seemingly none the worse for wear.

Waco hefted Baker up and half-carried, half-dragged him to the horses. After some struggle, he managed to get Baker up into the saddle. Waco secured the half-unconscious man as best he could and then mounted Red Wing. With Rascal's reins in hand, he set off in what he believed to be the direction of the settlement.

That day was a week ago now. Waco had had found the settlement and left Baker there to be cared for, setting off alone on the trail of a horse thief who, Waco discovered, had resorted to murder. . . .

WHEN WACO SAW Durham raise his gun until it was pointing at him, he froze, mired in a moment in which the world seemed purely and utterly silent.

He flinched when the first shot rang out.

Again, when the second shot came.

And again for the third.

But no feeling followed, no sensation of impact or pain, or blood flowing wetly across his skin.

After a moment, he realized there were sounds coming from behind him—a cry, a gurgling sound, and then a dull *thump*.

Durham lowered his gun, but otherwise didn't move or say a word.

Waco turned slowly around, as if he were moving underwater. Everything, *everything,* seemed to be moving at about one-tenth its normal speed.

A man lay crumpled on the ground, not far from where Waco stood, no farther from him than Durham in the opposite direction. Waco felt a vague sense of shame; he'd had no idea the man was so close. The body was still twitching. Behind it, the sun was tugging at the horizon, threatening to pull the body over the edge with it as it sank.

Waco glanced back at Durham, then walked slowly over to the body. The injured man stopped moving before Waco got to him, but blood was still trickling from his wounds, swallowed up quickly by the parched earth.

It was Jiminez, the man Waco had been following for the last week. A dead ringer for the "Wanted" posters. Waco nudged him with one foot, but the man didn't respond. If he wasn't dead already, he soon would be.

Waco heard footsteps stirring the dust behind him. A stream of tobacco juice shot past him and hit Jiminez in the face. He still didn't stir.

"I hear this fella killed himself at least three people." Another spurt. "He don't look so tough now."

"Shouldn't you have warned him—?"

"He was about to put a bullet in you, boy. Weren't no time to ask him to give himself up."

Waco turned to face the other man. "Why are you here, Durham? I did not expect you."

"I know that." Durham squinted his eyes a little tighter. "But I bet you're glad I'm here now, ain't ya?"

"Of course. But why? Why would you help me? I did not think—"

"I heard 'bout what you did for Baker," Durham said, interrupting. "Everybody did. You're a Ranger now. Somebody's gotta make sure you don't get yerself killed. Might as well be me."

Waco shook his head. There was much he did not yet understand. "How did you find me?"

"Wasn't hard. Knew you started followin' this fella from the Marsh settlement. Knew which way you were headed. This fella leavin' a trail of bodies helped. And there's some white men can track just as good as Injuns, you know. Or better."

"Thank you, Durham. I am in your debt."

"You don't owe me nothin'. 'Cept to watch my back if you ever get the chance. Now give me a hand with this fella." Durham grabbed the dead man's feet, offered up another throat-clearing spit. It came out mostly clear this time.

He looked back up at Waco. "You got any tobacco?"

No Luck at All

❦

by Rod Miller

Rod Miller's poems and stories about cowboys and the West have appeared in several periodicals and anthologies. He has also published nonfiction and humorous essays. He is a member of Western Writers of America, and his story "The Darkness of the Deep" appears in the collection *Westward: A Fictional History of the American West*, published in honor of that organization's fiftieth anniversary.

"GET THEM BOOTS."

Responding to the mumbled command, one of the dismounted killers tugged the boots off the body while the other piled loot—a rifle, a brace of pistols, odds and ends of clothing and camp gear—onto the pack mule.

The leader sat astride his pale horse above the bloody destruction and studied the worn badge in his hand. With the ball of his thumb he rubbed off a fine layer of dust and read the words TEXAS RANGER before tucking it into a vest pocket.

As the corpse cooled in the desert heat, the plunderers turned their attention to stripping the tack off the dead horse. Less than a week had passed since the horse and rider came into the country, sent to exterminate this swarm of locusts who picked clean everything in their path.

"NEAR AS WE can tell, there's just three of them. But they don't leave anything in the way of witnesses," the sheriff told the Ranger. "By the time they ride off, there's hardly a thing left for the coyotes and vultures, let alone anything in the way of explanation. We don't know who they are. Or where they came from.

"There's a lot of empty land around here and folks is spread so far and wide that no one ever sees them, only what they've done—and then not until it's too late to do any good. But they've been killing and robbing on both sides of the border since springtime. Now and then, some of their plunder turns up in shops down in the border towns, usually brought in by Indians for barter. But nobody believes these killers is Indians—too savage, even for them. Most likely they themselves got the stuff in trade from the thieves."

The Ranger sat quiet, letting the sheriff lay out his tale. He suspected the man was more interested in talking about the bandits than tracking them down. A hotel dining-room table separated the two. It was hard to say whose jaws were working harder—the Ranger, enjoying his first hot meal in days, or the lawman, talking.

A pounding on the door in the middle of one night is how the sheriff's story began. A scared muleskinner had left his teams and freight wagons in the street to report a bloody mess on the trail into town. The sheriff gathered a posse and got there in the early morning, but it was clear they were about a day late to do the family any good.

The Mexican family, it appeared, were on the way to market to trade loads in a donkey cart when set upon.

Dried chilies were trampled in the dust and beans and corn were strewn about.

The people had fared no better than their goods. The man and his wife were tangled together in a bloody heap, stripped of their clothing with throats cut. Each was punctured with numerous stab wounds, and from the mutilation of the young woman, the sickened posse imagined the unspeakable atrocities she must have suffered before being dumped in a pile with her husband.

But their greatest horror was for the child.

Little more than a baby, and of a sex now indeterminable, it was tied to the wheel of the cart—hung there as a target for knife-throwing practice. They could imagine the steel spinning toward its mark; almost hear the blades repeatedly striking home. What they could not imagine was the why. A mere child. A baby. Of an age and innocence that could not possibly have given offense. What manner of men were these?

The only shot fired there had been the one that blew a hind leg off the donkey. Still harnessed to the cart, it appeared to have bled slowly to death, hobbling in circles hauling its grisly load until falling dead in the shafts.

Coyotes had visited in the night, and the destructive work of flies was well on its way. Buzzards wheeled overhead, patiently waiting their turn. The sheriff and his helpers hoped to end the desecration by burying the family in a common grave deep enough to discourage scavengers; the donkey's carcass was left where it lay as a distraction.

Meanwhile, the best tracker from the posse cast about for a trail to follow, but any trace of the killers was indecipherable, as they looked to have come and gone along the same road as their victims, the freighters, and any number of others since rain had last washed the road clean.

"There's no telling even which way they went, Sheriff," the tracker reported. "But it looks as if there were three of them, from the footprints around the bodies. I'd guess they had three, maybe four horses. And a mule for sure."

"Pack animal," suggested another posse rider. "For hauling off their plunder. Who knows what they stole from these Mexicans farmers. Probably everything they'd been able to scratch out of the dirt all this year."

"Hmmmph," the sheriff grunted. "Wouldn't be none too difficult to find somebody more worth robbing than these poor souls were."

"They did this just for sport," someone suggested as the posse started the slow ride home.

"I'VE GOT TO be honest with you," the sheriff told the Ranger, bringing his tale to an end. "I'm not entirely sorry we couldn't find a trail to follow. I'm not sure I'd want to meet up with that bunch."

The sheriff told the Ranger other stories of the destruction the killers had spread across the land, stories other lawmen had told him and reports he'd heard through the grapevine: of a ranch hand shot and stripped and tied to his horse's tail to drag for days; a family of homesteaders stewing in a stock tank, their shack burned and animals slaughtered; the town marshal who went hunting them and ended up dead and dangling with his hide peeled, hung head-down from a cottonwood tree in a river bottom; the old Indian staked out naked to die slow in the sun; the two Mexican soldiers found hacked to pieces and impaled to scrub trees on their own swords. . . .

There were others. The marauders cared not who their victims were. It seemed no one who crossed their path survived the encounter. As a result, they were not concerned with stealth or subterfuge. They rode where and when they pleased and killed at will. The only consistency was the thievery.

"Like I said, where that stuff ends up is anybody's guess. Little bits of it shows up now and again amongst traders and shopkeepers, but the trail that it took to get there is a tangled one—a swap here, some barter there, and it's changed hands a time or two 'fore anyone recognizes it for what it is. It seems most of it comes through the Indians, but they won't say how or when or even if they laid hands on it.

"My guess is these bandits steal for the hell of it, carrying off anything they think they can get shed of easy. Then they burn or ruin what they don't want, destroying it for entertainment. But if you was to ask me, I'd say it's the lives they're after. Leastways, they've yet to not take one when they had the chance, far as I can learn."

That thought lay there on the table between them for a quiet moment until the sheriff spoke again.

"Well, sir, I sure am glad they saw fit to send a Ranger out here to deal with this. If there's anything more I can do to help—anything at all—don't hesitate to call on me. It's getting late and I guess I better be making my rounds. And I suppose you're wanting to hit the hay so as you can get an early start hunting those varmints down," the sheriff said as he rose from his seat. "Finding them out there in all that empty ain't going to be easy, but maybe you'll get lucky."

Later, up in his room, the Ranger allowed to himself that luck would have little to do with it. Leastways, that was his experience. It was more a matter of work, and now was as good a time as any to get to it. He retrieved his saddlebags from where they hung over the back of a chair, and found in them a stub of a pencil and a folded piece of foolscap, which he smoothed out and studied.

On the paper was a hand-drawn map of the country thereabouts, one he had sketched from memories of earlier visits. He had no illusions about its accuracy for scale or detail, but was confident that the relationships among major features—mountains, canyons, passes, streams, roads, main trails, and such—were essentially correct.

Sprinkled around the map were a number of Xs where, according to the reports he had been given when he took on this assignment, the men he was after had committed their foul deeds. Next to each X was scribbled the approximate date the incident had occurred. He pored over the map, dragged the pencil lead across his tongue thoughtfully, and added a couple more Xs and dates based on what the sheriff had told him.

The marks on the map appeared to be distributed pretty much at random. The only obvious pattern the Ranger could see was that the gang avoided the scattered towns and villages, attacking only in out-of-the-way places. Thinking he could link some of the incidents by time, he drew lines connecting the sites according to proximate dates. Although widely separated by both distance and time, the crime scenes did tie together somewhat as a result of the exercise.

He learned that the killers tended to zigzag through the country, wandering across low mountain ranges or onto neighboring drainages between strikes, always working more or less toward the Indian lands and the border. This seemed sensible for the bandits, he thought, keeping them several steps ahead of detection and allowing them to increase their load of loot as they neared the tribes and the border traders where they could market the goods.

But he believed, as the sheriff did, that the money derived from the thievery was but a sideline for this bunch. There were easier ways, quicker too, to load up on plunder for profit. No, it wasn't money that drove them. It was blood lust, pure and simple. Something in these men was twisted like discarded fence wire to where they took satisfaction, pleasure even, in cruelty and killing.

The loose pattern he discerned in the scratches on the map suggested that if he headed west and a little south and over the mountains toward the river on the next broad plain, he would be closer to his quarry.

Just how close, he could not know.

AFTER A FEW hours of restless sleep and a tasteless breakfast, the Ranger headed for the livery stable.

"Morning to you," said the hostler. "Yours must be that white gelding that came in late yesterday. My partner said you'd be along early. Well, your horse is fed and watered. I gave his feet a look-see. Whoever tacked on those new shoes did a fine job. He's ready and waiting for the saddle in that third stall there. A man's lucky to have a horse like that."

As the Ranger rode out of town, the day was starting on a small ranch some forty miles west of there. The place was tucked into a bend of the river where the extra moisture supported enough acres of grass to keep a small herd of scrub cattle alive. Away from the water, feed was scarce, so the nearest neighbors were about five miles away up- and downstream. Only the man and his wife were left to work the ranch—their children grown and gone—and in fact, the two of them were about all the place could sustain.

Watching the sun rise over the far horizon, the woman made her way to the small barn, milk bucket in hand, while her husband of forty-three years walked toward the pasture to check his bunch of spindly cows.

From the lows bluffs above, three mounted men looked on.

"Damn!" said the one on the black horse through a snaggle-toothed grin. "Them folks down there, their luck has plumb run out. But us—well, boys, we're in luck."

Silence returned as they studied the layout. Then the leader of the band offered his opinion.

"Luck ain't got nothing to do with it," he said. "Any man that puts his trust in luck is a fool." With a cluck of his tongue and a lazy poke of spurred heels into his mount's belly, he started down the trail toward the ramshackle homestead.

Luck, he thought. Do these dolts believe luck has anything to do with keeping them living high instead of swinging from the end of a rope? He hacked a gob of yesterday's trail dust from his throat, leaned out over the horse's shoulder, and spit on the ground figuring that if these idiots that had thrown in their lot with his supposed luck, they were dumber than he thought.

Slowly, even casually, the horsemen made their way down to the river bottom and rode into the trampled hardpan yard among the few tumbledown buildings.

"Go get him," the leader muttered, lifting his chin in the direction of the rancher walking the pasture. The rider on the big sorrel turned and rode off on the errand. The third man dismounted, tied his black and the pack mule to a fence rail, and walked to the barn.

Inside, unaware, the woman leaned her forehead into the cow's flank squeezing streams of milk into the pail, lulled by the rhythmic squirts.

The marauder grabbed her by the shoulder and flung her across the milking stall and into the wall. She did not even have time to scream before his booted foot landed in her ribs, forcing her breath away. With a smile, he picked up the pail, stuck his face inside, tipped it back, and drank deeply of the warm, foamy milk.

Outside, the other rider drove her husband back toward the yard, urging him along with a stock whip as he stumbled along sucking wind and struggling to keep his feet. They stopped near the waiting leader, still sitting his horse so calm and quiet you could imagine him dozing off.

The rancher, worried and frightened, fought for air as he asked, "What do you want? Where's my woman?"

The man who had driven him in laughed maniacally and popped the back of the old man's head yet again with the stinging lash of the whip.

The leader did not respond or even react.

"What is it? What do you want?" the rancher cried, nearing hysteria.

This time, the leader answered: From beneath his black duster he raised a shotgun and let go with a blast to the man's belly. The load of shot crashed the old nester into the corral fence. Tangled in the rails, he hung there helpless and witnessed the wasting of his life's work as he slowly, slowly bled out.

Meantime, having drunk his fill, the raider in the barn swung the bucket by its bail until it stopped suddenly against the woman's head. He slit the cow's throat, watched the hot blood spill and puddle onto the packed dirt floor. As the cow weakened and dropped to its knees, he dragged the woman outside. Dropping her in the dust and landing another kick in the ribs for good measure, he made his way to the house.

As he threw pots, pans, trunks, boxes, clothing, and anything else he laid his hand to out through the door and windows, his partner with the stock whip entertained himself chasing chickens and popping off their heads with a snap of the lash.

After amusing themselves for more than an hour with plunder, torture, and eventually, the murder of the old woman, the three piled their pick of the spoils atop the laden mule.

Figuring the smoke plumes would soon enough bring neighbors nosing around, the killers rode out of the haze and stink of the ruined ranch, splashing through the shallow water of the slow river, across the floodplain, up the eroded escarpment, and onto the empty desert.

With the riders on the sorrel and black horses behind, and the pack mule bringing up the rear, the man in the black duster set a course a little south of east.

He figured to top the low range of distant mountains and follow an easy, narrow canyon he knew of down the other side. By the middle of the morning, he reckoned, they'd take to ground somewhere in the hills off the canyon while he mulled over where to strike next, after which they would call this trip good and ride southwest again, back into the Indian country and no-man's-land along the border to relax for a spell.

If things got too boring, he could always slaughter himself a savage or two.

THE RANGER CHEWED over his situation along with a hunk of jerky. After the day's ride, he had camped on a rise, just out of sight of a trail he had followed up a ravine that had become a canyon as the hills rose around it. Soon, he'd ride the rest of the way up that canyon. Soon. But not just yet.

That sheriff back there wasn't a coward, he decided—nor were his cohorts in the towns roundabout. He—and the others—did a passable job dealing with criminals and lawbreakers. But fighting evil like this was something else again. The perpetrators of this reckless thievery, this wanton destruction, this wholesale slaughter were beyond understanding, let alone facing. Even *he* had not wanted the job. When the assignment came down, he told the captain he could not do it, that it was too much for one man.

"You're right," the captain answered. "But we ain't sending a man. We're sending a Ranger."

Still, the Ranger tried to beg off, claiming he was not up to it. But the captain was having none of it.

"Look, you're the best Ranger I've got. You were the best I had when we started this outfit, and you're still the best," he said. "Not to mention lucky."

But the Ranger didn't believe in luck. Nor did he view his performance as a Ranger as anything out of the ordinary. He had backed down his share of badmen over the years, sure, and rid the country of assorted vermin from time to time. In the process he had attracted a few admirers among the folk he worked for and with, even though he had never sought glory for himself.

Facing danger was part of a Ranger's job, and so was risking your life to save lives—but the wickedness he was expected to overcome this time was more than he cared to deal with. At his age, he figured his Rangering years were about used up. And his luck—if there was such a thing—was likely about used up too.

"You're nowhere near used up," the captain argued. "Even if you was, these thieves and butchers don't know it. They're likely to quit the country soon as they know you're after them. And they wouldn't be the first badmen to do just that."

In the end the Ranger agreed, if reluctantly, to take on the task. Still, he could not help thinking these were not ordinary badmen he was sent to overcome. Ordinary men—bad or otherwise—would not—could not—do what these scapegraces did with seeming abandon. He feared there was not enough blood in the three of these murderers to atone for all the innocent blood they had shed. Even his own blood might be shed—should it come to that—in payment for their sins. And though he accepted that risk as part and parcel of being a Ranger, he did not relish the thought.

As he sat mulling it all over and watching the sun rise, he heard someone coming long before he could see them.

There was a faint, curious tinkling and clanking of metal coming down the trail he meant to go up. He smothered the small fire and crept to a place where he could watch unseen.

The three horsemen he saw looked ordinary enough, if dirty and disheveled and run-down. But the pack mule in tow, the source of all the noise, was something to see. More than anything, it reminded him of a walking medicine show. As the parade drew nearer, the colorful banners and clanging bells that made up the mule's precarious load became bundles of clothing and boxes and bags and pots and pans dangling at all angles from the packsaddle. Rifles sprouted from the pile like bagpipes.

The Ranger knew he had found what he'd come looking for.

THE KILLERS WERE well down the canyon when dawn broke. The leader rubbed the itch out of his eyes with balled fists, an itch that grew worse with the climbing sun. He knew the other men had been asleep more than they had been awake for more than a few miles, and even the horses stumbled with fatigue now and then. But he fought to keep his eyes open, wanting to make a few more miles before hiding out for the day.

Had he not been so determined to stay alert, he would not have noticed the hoofprints on the dusty trail where there hadn't been any before. That meant a lone rider on the way up the canyon had left the trail not far from here. A shod horse, so it was no Indian—a white man probably, Mexican maybe. Whoever it was didn't want to be seen any more than *they* did. He'd have to pay attention to the back trail now, in case whoever was out there took a notion to follow them rather than continue up the canyon.

Soon enough, the hairs in the small of his back started tingling, and he knew they were being followed.

He liked to have worn out his neck craning around trying to get a glimpse of whoever was back there, but whoever it was was no fool. The man trailing them never revealed himself, hanging back around every turn until he could ride on unobserved. Well, the man in the black duster thought, he's up to something. Hatching a plan.

Well, we'll just see if his plan works out.

ALLOWING THE HORSEMEN to get a good ways down the trail, the Ranger drank the dregs of his bitter morning coffee, bundled up the last of his camp, and rode off in slow pursuit formulating a plan of attack. He stayed nearby but out of sight for an hour or more, relying on the noise of the jangly pack mule to cover his hoofbeats.

Then, edging around an outcrop, he saw only two riders ahead—mounted on the sorrel and the black—and knew he would never carry out his plan. He felt the tremor from the bullet that hit his horse at the same instant he heard the thwack of lead pounding flesh, followed instantly by a rifle's report. As the horse buckled beneath him, he swung from the saddle and felt the scorpion sting of the bullet that killed him.

THE TWO SCAVENGERS picked the horse clean, pilfering the saddle bags and bedroll, adding even the saddle to the spoils atop the mule. Noting that the horse was recently shod, one asked the mounted leader if he should pry the new shoes loose to add to the plunder.

"Nah," he mumbled. "It's bad luck to pull the shoes off a dead horse."

The Blood Beneath When the World Draws Back

∽◦∾

by Tom Piccirilli

Tom Piccirilli is the author of eleven novels, including *The Night Class*, *A Choir of Ill Children*, *A Lower Deep*, *Hexes*, *Coffin Blues*, and *Grave Men*. He's published over 130 stories in the mystery, fantasy, and Western fiction fields. Tom's been a final nominee for the World Fantasy Award, and he's a three-time winner of the Bram Stoker Award, in the categories of Novel, Short Story, and Poetry. Learn more about him at his official website: www.tompiccirilli.com.

SMOKE FOUND THE dying child in the rocks about midday, gave her water and shade for the two hours she lasted, and buried her beneath a red plum bush.

Another nine miles on, he discovered the girl's mother where they'd set up camp, eaten beans, and taken turns at her. Chuka lay dead nearby with his feet bare. Smoke read the signs in the sand the way he'd been taught, traced their movements, the scene coming to life before him. His father told him it got spooky sometimes, when the shadows filled in and you could even hear voices, see every movement second by second as if you were actually there.

The woman had been smart and didn't resist much, though she must've been near-insane after what they'd done to her daughter. Patient, yet writhing inside as she chewed off the tip of her tongue in anticipation, swallowing her own blood in the dust-choked heat. She waited until all three hundred pounds of Chuka was about to clamber on top of her, slobbering and laughing, his britches unbuckled and almost to his knees, while the others looked away and drank another bottle of tequila.

Smoke leaned over and spoke as if Chuka could hear him. "You goddamn bastard, you got a surprise coming."

Eyes watering from the stink of Chuka's filthy body, the woman reached down and grabbed hold of his blade and tugged it from the sheath, yanked her hand back, and stabbed him in the neck. When he reared up to shout, she slashed his throat.

She knew how to handle a knife, and might've had a chance against the other two, drunk as they were, if Chuka hadn't flopped forward and pinned her. He thrashed for a while bleeding and making gurgling wet sounds, but Willets and Reed, realizing they had nothing to fear, just guffawed and handed the bottle back and forth, watching.

Smoke could feel Chuka's overwhelming fear in his last seconds, trying to drag himself to his feet but unable to do so with his pants undone. She stabbed him twice more in the shoulder hoping to drive him aside, but he was too weak, mewling for help and suddenly praying for God to forgive him, Baby Jesus to save him. He died quick and trapped her in a bear hug. Not enough blood on the ground to have done it, his heart must've given out.

Then Willets and Reed took renewed interest in the woman, breaking three of her fingers to get the knife loose and hauling Chuka into a patch of scrub, pulling off his battered boots in the process, and tossing them aside. The smell of death aroused them again until they were having plenty more fun. It lasted a while, one of them vomiting up the liquor, until somebody put the pistol in her mouth and ended it.

Smoke took some satisfaction in leaving Chuka's body to rot where it lay while burying the woman.

The next afternoon, at a sign formed by weathered planks reading LAST CHANCE IN 33 MILES, he came across the preacher drinking mescal, lying in the shade beneath a honey mesquite shrub. A burro stood ten feet away looking vaguely puzzled. A faded red wagon sat off at the edge of a dry wash, but hadn't gone all the way over. On its side was cracked and worn lettering that Smoke couldn't make out.

The burro's bridle and harness had been improperly tied, and snapped loose when the wagon's back wheel crossed over the ledge of the arroyo. The axles hadn't cracked, but the jolt must've sent the preacher flying.

Pawing his chin, Smoke considered how he'd seen more people in the last twenty hours than the whole month before, and all of them were dead or dying. His father would have paused to ponder on that—try to figure out what it might mean, if anything, and maybe write a song about it on his banjo. Smoke tried not to let himself be distracted by his father's voice as he swung off his sorrel and went to the preacher's side.

"You any good with that knife on your belt?" the man asked.

"Yes, but it won't be easy for what you got in mind."

"Headstrong, obstinate animal. The moon came up and he just decided to quit walking. Knocked me out of my seat and I landed wrong. He swaggered off and had me crawling around all mornin', and now he's shown up again wantin' to be friends. Gimme your gun so I can kill him, would you?"

"You swung towards an arroyo in the dark," Smoke said. "If not for your donkey stopping when he did, you would've gone over and broken your neck."

The preacher had a naturally round face that had loosened up further with age and hard drinking. His neck had slackened into pink double chins, but he had an easy smile despite his suffering. Coils of silver hair ebbed over his ears and around his collar. "Well, then, good thing I held onto my jug. A man shouldn't die without a last indulgence, a bit of charity."

The preacher's left leg was swollen to double its normal size. Gangrene had set in. He still wore his frock coat, but was barely sweating after a full day in the sun. Smoke knew the man would die of dehydration before infection if he didn't get some water immediately.

There was half a canteen left. Smoke slid it from his saddlebag and handed it to the preacher. "Here, you need water now."

"You want me to sober up for surgery?"

"Just drink. Let me help you off with your coat."

"I've got chills."

Smoke's father stopped singing, draped his arm over the banjo, and said *Not a good sign*. "I'll put it over you like a blanket."

Considering the liquor, heat, and pain, the preacher held his own pretty well and still had his wits. He studied Smoke for a minute. "How old are you, son?"

"Nineteen."

"You're hardly a man at all."

Smoke grinned and said, "If it bothers you, I'll head into town and send the doc back. I hear tell he's pushing eighty. You want I should go?"

"Well, don't get all choleric."

Smoke had never been to Last Chance, and didn't know how old the doctor might be or if there even was one. But the preacher wasn't going to last another day. No way to get him to town fast enough as the western sky began to darken to purple, starlight already beginning to seep in across the horizon. Smoke got his bedroll and lariat down and began to unknot the rope.

"Think you can save everything above the knee?" the man asked.

"It's where I'll cut."

"If I die, my name's Tilson. Reverend Dudlow Phinneas Tilson. Born December 12, 1829. Died . . . this Monday or Tuesday?"

"I was about to ask you if it was still July," Smoke said.

"Anyways, died on or near abouts August 4, 1879. *May God welcome his tormented soul into Paradise and allow him eternal peace in the loving arms of a choir of beautiful, tender angels.*"

"You want that carved in stone or will the side of a barn do?"

Tilson frowned, and the sagging folds of his stubbled, ample face fell in on themselves. "Christ, you sure are cantankerous for someone who ain't even got chest hair yet. Can't you just let a dying man talk on?"

Smoke grabbed the jug and handed it back to Tilson. "Drink up."

"Now you give it to me, after my tongue's been fouled with that river water."

"Here, lay back on my bedroll."

"I got a softer one."

"I'll get it."

"How do you sleep on this?"

"After you're loaded, I'll do what I can. In the morning, I'll pack you in your wagon and get us into town."

"Don't forget that marker."

Tilson's face filled with alarm, confusion, and a genuine dread that his life might be coming to an end before he'd discovered so much as a small purpose to it all. Smoke recognized the expression. His father had died with it carved into his features four years ago at Big Spring, a Comanche lance in his back, just a few weeks before the decimated tribe made peace with the U.S. Government after the Buffalo War massacres.

Smoke gathered wood, made a fire, and plunged his blade into the center of it. Panic filled the preacher's eyes as he eagerly sucked at the mescal, watching the knife heat up in the flames.

TILSON AWOKE IN the back of his wagon, suffering on the trail, and begged Smoke to stop and make a noon camp. Smoke was hesitant—he'd done a fair job of taking the man's leg off, cauterizing and binding the wound, but he felt anxious to get Tilson to a doctor. They were only a few hours outside of Last Chance now and he wanted to make the final push for it, get on with his own business, but the preacher sounded frightened, in need of talk, and maybe even confession.

The preacher eased his pain by talking, asking questions and keeping his mind off himself. "Heard tell that you Rangers cut your own badges out of coins. That true?"

"No," Smoke said. "A watchmaker in Santa Fe made this one for me from melted-down pesos."

"That official?"

"More so than the marshals that order theirs out of mail catalogues. Most Rangers don't wear badges."

"Why's that?"

"Got enough troubles without putting a bull's-eye on their shirts."

"Still, it's a sign of your authority," Tilson said. He was trying desperately not to look at the space where his lower left leg used to be.

"Doesn't count for as much as you might think. Only causes friction with the local sheriffs who don't want to share command with outside lawmen."

"How you get any respect?" the reverend asked.

"I earn it."

"I mean, without a badge, how do you prove you're a lawman?"

"They gave us papers," Smoke said, realizing how laughable it sounded.

"Now what's this?"

"The Adjutant General of Texas issued documents. Some Rangers keep them in folds in their pockets. Proof that they are who they say they are. You want backing from a town marshal or need to gather a posse, you're supposed to pull the papers out and show them off. I burned mine this past winter down in Mud Flats. They helped keep me warm on a December night when I would've froze to death otherwise. So I got no real cause to complain about the Adjutant and his foolish ways."

Reverend Dudlow Phinneas Tilson grew quiet then. The jug was empty and the water almost gone. They had to get moving again, but Smoke found himself enjoying the agreeable calm between them.

"I ain't had a woman in a long, long time," the preacher said. "Years, in fact. Think it was back in '68. Someplace in the Oklahoma panhandle. She was lacking in front teeth."

"Consider it a value to your soul."

"Hell with that. Wish I'd had one more pretty gal on my arm, walkin' in the moonlight. Shoulda danced more too. And visited the ocean. You know, I ain't ever seen the ocean, not even the Gulf of Mexico. Was a time I dreamed of being a whaler. Do what you love. Listen to me when I tell you to take the time to enjoy yourself some. I can tell you're aiming to be dead 'fore you see your twenty-first birthday."

Smoke had finally been able to piece together the chipped and faded words on Tilson's wagon: TO FORGIVE THE SINS OF MAN THEY MUST FIRST BE UNDERSTOOD. BE KIND TO ONE ANOTHER. YOUR FATHER IS WATCHING.

Maybe there was something to it, maybe not.

"Where were you headed?" Smoke asked.

The question seemed to surprise Tilson, and he took his time in answering. At last, he tried to smile, but could only bare his teeth. "Nowhere," he whispered, saddened by the revelation.

"Don't feel bad. I haven't met a man in six hundred miles who owns a roof any more sturdy than a canvas tent." Smoke was surprised that his words sounded so bitter, and before he knew it, the rage was on him. Something twisted inside his chest and a quiet, heavy grunt worked loose.

"Ain't never seen one like you before," the reverend said.

Smoke glanced up.

"Never knew anybody who could keep their hate so under wraps, close to their hearts. I see it works free in you every so often, and you snatch it back out of the air and stick it back down inside you. All that hate you got reserved for just one man or more?"

"Two," Smoke said, standing and packing up the gear, suddenly in a rush to get on the prod again. "Let's go, Reverend. We'll be in sight of pretty girls again in no time.

Then you can sit in all the moonbeams you fancy for as long as you like."

LAST CHANCE, TEXAS, didn't appear to have many opportunities at all—if any—but there was a doctor's small house right out on Main Street, and a light burned in the back window. He wasn't quite as old as eighty, but he had a hobbled walk and a bent back, a well-trimmed gray beard, and bifocals. His arms were wiry and strong, though, and he helped Smoke carry Tilson into the office, where he inspected the preacher's amputation.

The doc raised his spectacles and took a long look at Smoke. "You did this?"

"Yesterday. About thirty miles east of here."

"What'd you use?

Smoke held up his knife.

"Goddamn, son! You've got a lot of sand to even make the attempt. You did a nice job cauterizing the stump too. Not much more I can do for him now but give him something for the pain and put on clean bandages."

"My burro needs to be put up," Tilson said.

"I'll take care of it," Smoke told him.

"Don't let anybody try to groom him. He hates that."

"Don't worry yourself."

"Thanks. My life might not have been worth saving, but I appreciate it all the same."

"Just take care," Smoke said. "You already understand enough about the sin of drinking. Go learn about some of the others, if need be."

Smiling, Tilson leaned forward, shook Smoke's hand. "I'm gonna say something to you I haven't said in twenty years."

"This got something to do with your lack of toothy women or wanting to hunt whales?"

"No."

"Let's hear it then."

"I'll pray for you," the preacher said.

HE VISITED THE livery and left the burro and his sorrel, then walked towards the sheriff's office and saw that the door was open, light streaming out across the boardwalk. Someone shouted, "You rotten cheat! You black liar!"

The tall, rangy sheriff sat in his chair, feet up on the desk, playing cards with his two deputies. He glowered and barked at Smoke, "Who the hell are you and what do you want?"

Smoke didn't respond. He looked into the man's face, studied it for a moment, and moved off. He tried the hotel first and then the two whorehouses around the block, but came up empty. It took only five minutes of asking men in the street before he learned that a saloon on the north side of town rented rooms and girls on their top floor.

That might really be his last chance to find Willets and Reed before heading back onto the trail. Smoke stopped into a restaurant and had a modest meal, thinking of Willets and Reed and men like them. They always wanted noise and action after being out on the desert, a way to come back to the world. Smoke, though, always needed extra time to fit into society after living on the range for weeks.

He wondered if he should get some rest, find them in the morning when they might be exhausted after carousing. But he was three days behind now—if not for Tilson's mishap, Smoke would've caught up with Willets and Reed the first night in town, when they would've been at their most relaxed, drunkest, and weakest.

He cleaned his Colt .45's at the table, and nobody said a word to him. He paid his tab and headed up the street.

The saloon had no name, but was already shaking sawdust into the road, three stories high, well-lit, and busy. There was plenty of music, stomping, singing, and squealing ladies. The wind had shifted, and the fiery breeze brought on the stink of sex.

Smoke walked inside. The action, the foul odor of the room, and the mobbing bodies stunned him for a second until his senses managed to fit everything in. His eyes watered and his throat started to close. The forty-foot bar stood packed with drinkers, and the people kept moving up and down the wide staircase in a constant procession. The gaming tables were crammed with well-dressed and well-heeled gamblers, crowding rannies just in off the desert.

Scanning the room, Smoke searched for two men he'd never seen face to face. He'd gotten into the hunt with four other Rangers at Eagle Pass, where Chuka and his friends had raided a couple of mining camps. The regional law was having a hard time, but nobody had been killed yet. The other Rangers felt more needed in Del Rio, where a band of cattle-rustling night riders had been leaving murdered vaqueros along the San Felipe canals. Smoke went on alone. He had a feeling that the trio of Chuka, Willets, and Reed would turn out to be worse than first expected, and along the way he'd bitterly discovered he'd been right.

The music started thrashing into another tune, and a couple of the dancing girls wafted over. Smoke glanced toward the end of the bar and saw the stock of a ten-gauge shotgun angled out from beneath. That might come in handy if he needed it. He ordered a beer and stood sipping it, walking among the crowd and asking an occasional question. He could almost see himself from up above, circling the room and getting closer.

He described Willets to the madam who ran the girls upstairs, and she said, "He had an hour with Lucy this evening, about seven. Always smells nice. He's been here a few days with that stumpy-legged friend of his. Vicious little bastard, that one. He likes to mark the girls."

"You let him?"

"He's willing to pay extra to do it."

"And the girls?"

"That got no say."

The muscles in Smoke's back tensed and his face tightened. "You think they're still here?"

She gave a quick look around and said, "Not likely that their kind got any business elsewhere. I don't see 'em, but my eyes ain't so good anymore." She openly appraised him, shook her head, and gave a sniff. "If you got a quarrel with them, you'd better go upstairs and get your knobby wet 'fore they kill you, son. I'll only charge you half the usual, seeing as how it's bound to be your first and last time."

Smoke turned his back, took up position at the bar near the doors again. He might have to wait a few hours before the place thinned out enough for him to recognize the pair, but it would happen. It took him a while to find his calm again, but once he had it he vowed not to lose it again.

He ordered a shot of tequila, and the barman stared at him like he'd just spit on the flag of Texas. Smoke changed up to double whiskey and drank it slowly, the way his father and grandfather used to do. He'd never acquired a taste for the stuff. The liquor burned and unsettled his stomach, but the flood of warmth in his chest helped him to focus. He kept eyeing the room.

A rannie with a rough face crowded with pox scars elbowed him aside and said, "Better you should have tipped a glass of goat's milk, Ranger. Leave the hard drinking to men."

That stopped him. Smoke said nothing, but he stepped away and tried for an amiable grin. His smile felt as if it had been seared on with a branding iron. He hadn't counted on anybody recognizing him as a lawman. "Me?"

"I know a Ranger when I see one. You all got that same hard-ass way about you, like you're so much better than the rest of us. Goddamn, boy, you gotta be the most baby-faced Ranger I ever seen!"

Smoke thought about it. "There's one other in my company, fella name'a Roy Calhoun. He hasn't started to shave yet."

"And you?"

"I need to scrape my chin near every other week."

"Haw! You ride under Jones or McNelly?"

"Captain Leander McNelly."

"What they call the Special Forces, eh?" the rannie said, and pulled a disgusted expression. "You do anything besides handle open-range feuds and toothless Comanches?"

"On occasion."

"Not often, I'll bet."

He understood the man's stance now, the hard way he held himself, uncomfortable and tangled, jittery in a fashion as if hating everything about his own life. Smoke saw the signs and read the man's life: how he'd tried to be marshal or soldier or Ranger and failed, and now respected but reviled them, angry at himself for not being able to live up to the harsh standards but realizing he'd been turned away for good reason. His inner conflict was gnawing at him strand by strand, and had been doing so for years.

"Worst problem you got is the Mexs."

"Worst is lawless Texans," Smoke said.

"There's still a few hostiles out there. Them Kiowa women probably give you a hard time. You hide out up on the Okie rez much, watching 'em do that sun dance of theirs?"

"No. Spent a lot of time down on the Nueces Strip, chasing bandits."

"Ever catch a real one, sonny?"

Smoke ignored him. If a play had to be made, Smoke might as well use it to his benefit. Everyone in the area hushed up some, interested in seeing a fight. "They range back and forth across the border, killing citizens and stealing livestock," Smoke said.

"That ain't a bandit. That's just a ranch hand out havin' a good time!" The rannie was almost yelling, as if he was talking to a group of friends, but he was alone. Everybody he was showing off to was inside his head.

"Maybe so. But somebody's got to end the border violations and rustling."

"You got the devil's eyes, boy. You a breed?"

"No."

"I think you might be lyin'."

"Raised on the salt fork of the Brazos—born just outside Fort Belknap."

"Texas ain't for half-pints."

"You got that right."

"You act as if you don't like me much, son," the rannie said, packing all his large and small frustrations down into his voice so that it became lower, colder. "You look as though you might even want to draw on me. That the case? And you gonna do something about it?"

"My business isn't with you."

"No?"

"No."

"And what if I say different?"

Strange how Smoke felt nothing but compassion and high regard for the man, thinking he'd be good to have alongside him in a fight. "It's been fine listening to you. You've cooled my sweat."

Smoke turned away, knowing the man would never jump him. He didn't have the brass to face up to his worst fears, and somehow he'd tied Smoke into them all.

He took another sip of whiskey and felt Willets and Reed staring at him now, the heavy pressure of their ugliness settled squarely on his back. His father started singing another song, and this time there were female voices accompanying him, maybe the girl and her mother. He tried to make out the words, but there was too much noise in the saloon, and he almost spun around to tell everybody to shut up so he could listen. His father was watching.

The itchiness between his shoulder blades finally began to burn so badly that Smoke gave in and looked behind him. It took only a few seconds before he made eye contact with Willets, who actually winked. Beside him sat Reed, who was making a hell of an effort to appear disinterested and downright bored. A half-finished bottle of whiskey rested between them on the table. Smoke finished his drink, set his back teeth, and walked over.

They appeared content, well-rested, satisfied with themselves, but ready to start a ruckus. Smoke's father had warned him there were men who could only sleep well after a long day of blood.

Willets, the charmer, with a smug smile and a hard sort of polish about him, but capable-looking. His shirts would always be clean and starched when he wasn't running from the law. Good with the ladies, polite to whores, kissing hands and offering flowers. He was freshly shaved, bathed, and sprinkled with powder and toilet water.

Reed, stubby and thick-bodied, with squat fingers and a wreath of overgrown hair knotted with barbs and thistles. He remained cushy in his ignorance and brutality, using it as a way to prop up his tiny spirit. His loathing for women was obvious, eyeing them with open rancor, and when he bedded one, he wasn't satisfied unless he left her weeping with at least a split lip and a ring of bite marks on her belly and breasts.

Smoke stepped in close and Willets said, "You the troublesome twerp that's been dogging us the past couple weeks?"

"I've been following."

"Thought you were right up on us, but then you trailed off. Been waiting a few days to give you a chance to catch up."

"Is that so?"

"Sure."

It was a lukewarm lie, but it proved Willets was the smarter of the two. He'd grown edgy sitting around town while Reed continued to romp and look for trouble. Now, seeing Smoke, Willets almost appeared ashamed that he'd been worried at all. Reed spit on the floor and barely glanced at Smoke, poured himself another drink and tossed it back, then had another.

"You got no reason for living, boy?" Reed said. "You tired of life already?" His voice was oddly high-pitched, almost feminine. He probably didn't talk much when a gathering of men were around. "You ain't even had a woman yet, have you? You wanna go to the grave unsullied, that it?" He let loose with a repulsive titter that sounded girlish and silly. "So you're lily-pure when you shake hands with St. Peter."

"It's his job to keep people safe," Willets said.

"Yeah?"

"They say the Rangers are the toughest law in Texas."

Reed spit again, on Smoke's boot. "That right?"

"Yep. He travels far and near, high and low to bring law and order to this great state. He saves cattle, horses, and women without even breathin' hard."

"Uh-huh." Reed let out that ugly chuckle again, pulling it up from way down low, the same way he drew his guns. "But he ain't been much good at it lately, now has he?"

Smoke took a breath and read the men, all that was around them and inside them. He saw the blood beneath the world as it drew back to reveal the truth that lay below. Different colors flowed through from below, and he watched the signs take structure and weight. Is this how it happened with the Comanches and other tribes?

He'd been tracking them for weeks and had learned much about Willets and Reed—what pistols they used, how much they weighed, the stink of their food and their spoor, their weaknesses, how much they paid for their tequila when they could get it, the size of their feet and how many bunions each had, who had a bad back tooth and couldn't crack the bones of a jackrabbit's leg, and most importantly, how much they hated, and just what forms that hatred would take.

He saw how Reed and Willets would rise at the same time, already moving in opposite directions using other patrons as cover. Willets was leaner, with longer legs, and kicked out to turn the table over. Anything to cause distraction. Grinning because he was back in the action, while Reed growled and threw his squat body forward, barreling past the dancing girls. Even as he ran, he'd stare at the women's skirts and knees, and the killing frenzy would fill him and he'd want to grab hold and squeeze until the squeals turned into screams and set his blood to boiling.

Both of them turning now to catch Smoke in the crossfire, Willets drawing his Colt Peacemaker while Reed drew a Remington .44 from the small of his back, where he kept the pistol stuck inside a holster stolen from a leather craftsman in Nuevo Leon. Smoke would try to dodge, but saw that he couldn't leap out of the way fast enough before Reed drew down on him. Smoke swung around to face Reed, brought up his gun, fired once, and saw Reed fly backward with his chest spewing. But Willets was behind him, letting out his own sick laughter, and Smoke wouldn't have time to wheel around before—

He thought of the dying girl in the rocks, the terrified woman stabbing Chuka in the neck but unable to get loose, and said, "Your father taught you nothing but anger."

It hit Willets like a backhand across the face. His eyes clouded and the smirk fell an inch. He cocked his head a touch. "What'd you say about my pa?"

"He the one that broke your right ankle? The limp is slight, but it's been with you since you were a boy. Must hurt something fierce on winter nights. No wonder you tend to keep south."

Black veins in Willets's forehead stood out and started crawling. "What'd you say about my pa?"

"I'd guess he's the kind of man who'd chase his family around the wood shed carrying an ax handle."

"Hey—"

"You got sisters?"

Now they were out of position, Reed leaning in and hoping to appear relaxed with his hand hovering near his pistol. A little surprised to see Willets so uneasy, the grin gone, so much heat in his face.

"Your ma limp too?" Smoke asked with genuine concern in his voice. "She still alive? Or did you have to bury her on your own? While your old man haunted his favorite whorehouse, too drunk to make it home in time?"

"You shut yer trap now, boy!"

Smoke found it odd that a man like this would murder a woman and child for no offense at all, but here Smoke could go on and on about Willets's family and he'd listen and whine and never go for his gun.

With a low growl of confusion easing from his throat, Reed slid closer. The dancing girls had finished their latest number and were taking a break, moving to the far corners of the bar and easing into seats near the door, welcoming more farmers and cattle punchers inside.

Smoke knew the next part would sound ludicrous, but his father had taught him to always try and bring them in alive if he could.

"Put up your guns. I'm handing you over to the local sheriff."

"You go straight to a fiery hell, son," Reed said, and started things off.

He hadn't finished sliding the .44 from his belt when Smoke drew and shot him in the face. Reed spun out of his chair and toppled sideways almost directly into Willets's arms. Smoke lunged forward and aimed his Colt at Willets's chest.

"Don't."

Shouts and giddy shrieks exploded, but most folks just kept sitting, drinking, playing cards, and watching. A show was a show. The madam leaned against the railing up top with a surprised expression. A couple of girls frowned, wondering what it might do to business tonight.

Reed was already dead but continued trying to talk, his ears spilling blood as his mouth worked aimlessly. Willets dumped him on the floor and said to Smoke, "You think you're slick, don't you?"

"Nope."

"Slicker than crow shit, that's you!" he shouted, and went for the Peacemaker. Smoke pulled the trigger and watched Willets's chest blossom red. The man kept on grinning, still trying to raise his pistol, giving it everything he had. Smoke stared at him, a peculiar sadness overcoming him, not getting any of the gratification he'd been hoping for. Willets groaned and showed his teeth, his arm almost straight, and Smoke shot him again.

A few people actually applauded, like this was nothing more than another stage number, as if two men weren't laid out across the sawdust-strewn floor. The madam called down, "Damn, son, if I'd'a bet against you I woulda lost my nickel."

A hollowness in his stomach seemed to sweep over him. Smoke had a sudden and intense desire to get back on the range. He turned toward the door, and the bartender said, "You just gonna leave 'em there?"

"I'll get the sheriff."

"I'll haul 'em out back in the alley."

This somehow wasn't over yet. Smoke thought about his own hatred and the fact that Reed and the madam had both been right, Smoke had never been with a woman yet. He thought of the preacher, who could stroll with a pretty girl only when he got handy with crutches. That look of dazed bewilderment on the face of his father at the end.

Smoke marched toward the street, and one of the dancing girls shrugged away from him until she was pressed back to the bar. He could smell juniper and mountain cedar and wild bluebonnets drift inside.

"What's your name?" he asked.

"Sandy."

He held his hand out to her and eventually, cautiously, she took it. He brought it to his lips and said, "Miss Sandy, things ought to be normal enough around here by tomorrow night. Save a dance for me, will you?"

She promised she would, and he left listening to the faint music of a banjo, imagining the lithe and graceful steps he would take.

"With Nothing but My Naked Knife!"

by James Reasoner

James Reasoner is the author of *Under Outlaw Flags* and co-author of *Cossack Three Ponies*, both published by Berkley Books and nominated for the Spur Award. A professional writer for more than twenty-five years, he has written everything from mysteries to science fiction and fantasy. He lives in a small town with his wife, Livia, also known as the novelist L. J. Washburn, and their two daughters.

"THE *CAPITÁN* WAS on a fine horse and I on but a pony, but still we were side by side—*parajitos*—all the time during the fight. I fired my cartridges and then went into them with my knife!"

Don Francisco de la Garza Falcon leaned forward intently toward the campfire, and his hands fairly flew through the air as he described his actions during the battle earlier that day with a band of Comanches. The young Rangers gathered around him listened, their faces bearing expressions that combined skepticism and admiration. Most of them had been involved in the skirmish as well, but having been occupied with fighting Indians and staying alive themselves, they didn't know exactly what Don Francisco had done during the clash.

I was aware of the truth myself, having been toward the rear in case my medical services were required, but I kept silent and smiled as I listened to the boasting. A good story has its virtues, whether strictly factual or not.

"You lit into them Comanch' with nothin' but a knife?" one of the Rangers asked dubiously.

"Sí!" Don Francisco said. "With nothing but my naked knife!"

The truth of the matter was, the don had not distinguished himself in the engagement. But then, he seldom did.

The Ranger company of which I was a member, serving as company surgeon, had been patrolling for quite some time in southern Texas, in the brushy country between the Nueces River and the Rio Grande. We were under the command of Captain John Salmon Ford, sometimes known as Old Rip. A few days earlier, knowing that a Comanche war party was in the area, Captain Ford had taken the daring step of splitting his forces, sending part of the company to the southeast under Lieutenant Andrew Walker, while Captain Ford himself took the remainder north toward the Nueces. Captain Ford suspected that when the Comanches encountered either group of Rangers, they would flee, but their flight would take them directly into the path of the other group of Rangers.

The plan had worked perfectly. Lieutenant Walker's men engaged the Indians first and drove them northward following a brief, sharp action. In the meantime, Captain Ford's party, including myself, moved along the Nueces River toward a crossing that we knew was favored by the Comanches. Sure enough, we arrived at the crossing at the same time as the Indians.

Captain Ford had ridden forward along with Sergeant Level and our scout, the half-Mexican, half-Comanche Roque Maugricio, to meet the enemy. The rest of our men hung back. The Comanches, seeing only three riders challenging them, attacked with gleeful whoops. Then the rest of our force charged forward, firing as they came.

With the exception of Don Francisco de la Garza Falcon.

Don Francisco was not, technically, a Ranger, though he rode with us and occasionally fought at our side. He was Captain Ford's servant, and claimed to be both an aristocrat and a hero in one of Mexico's past wars. Small, mustachioed, quick-witted, and quicker-tongued, he was prone to boasting and complaining, and Captain Ford, who had a habit of giving appropriate nicknames to his associates, called him "Don Monkey."

In this particular clash, as soon as the reports of the guns began to fill the hot Texas air, Don Francisco turned his horse and galloped toward the rear, getting as far away from the action as he could. Arriving there, he practically ran into young Matt Nolan, the company bugler, who went barefoot and was little more than a boy. Matt, seeing Don Francisco fleeing from the battle, began to harangue him. With Matt's words lashing him, Don Francisco gulped, turned his horse around, and raced back toward the front.

But when he got there and found himself in the middle of a tumult of shouted curses and roaring gunshots and choking clouds of powder smoke, his instinct for self-preservation asserted itself again, and round he went, heading for the rear again.

Before he could get there, more Rangers waved their revolvers at him and urged him back into the fight. I was watching the engagement with great interest, and if any of our men had fallen, I was ready to race to their side and render aid. But even so, I took note of the frantic galloping back and forth by "Don Monkey" as he sought to evade danger but found himself stymied at every turn.

The outcome of the battle was success for our side. Several of the Comanches were killed or wounded, and we captured a good number of their horses. That night we returned to our camp at San Antonio Viejo, an abandoned ranch that lay in ruins, where Lieutenant Walker's men rejoined us. The ranch's owner had given it up because of the danger of Indian raids, a danger that the Rangers were attempting to dispel. It was the Year of Our Lord 1850, and Texas had been a sovereign state in the Union for five years. It was time that civilization and progress and safety came to the region, but I feared that it was going to be a long struggle to fully implement those things.

Don Francisco continued his boasting until Captain Ford came over to the campfire and told him to unpack his store of coffee so that it could be divvied up among the men. We were on short rations and running low on most things, including coffee.

With a surprised, horrified expression on his face, Don Francisco looked up at Captain Ford. "Capitán, is it possible you intend to divide *our* coffee among the men?"

Captain Ford was a fine figure of a man, tall and lean, with very alert eyes, white hair, and a short white beard. He was one of the Old Rock, an early settler of Texas when it still belonged to the Mexicans. In reply to Don Francisco's question, he nodded and said, "Yes, sir, that is just what I intend to do."

"My God, who can expect me to fight Indians the way I have been doing without coffee!"

Doc Sullivan, one of the hell-for-leather young Texans who made up our company, chuckled and thumbed his hat back on his fair hair. "We'll just tell the Comanch' to hold off raidin' for a while, until we can get back to Corpus Christi and get some more supplies."

Don Francisco nodded solemnly and said, "*Gracias*. That is an excellent idea."

While the rest of the Rangers laughed, Captain Ford smiled and said, "Go ahead and break out that coffee, Falcon."

Don Francisco just sighed. "*Sí, Capitán.*"

DESPITE THE SHORT rations, we continued patrolling the area, moving out in wide circles from San Antonio Viejo. We finally managed to pay a visit to Fort Merrill, an Army post on the Nueces River, where we replenished our supplies from the Army's stores. Captain Ford rode on down to Corpus Christi while we were there, to seek medical attention for a vexing problem. During one of our skirmishes with the Indians, the captain had received a scratch on his hand from a Comanche arrowhead. When it occurred, the injury seemed minor, but as time passed the wound began to fester and stiffness set into the hand. I told Captain Ford it was likely the arrowhead had been coated with rattlesnake venom and advised him that the condition was beyond my capacity to treat in the field.

Unfortunately, the treatment he received from doctors in Corpus Christi was not successful, and the stiffness continued to plague Captain Ford the rest of his days, though it seldom prevented him from doing whatever he wanted to do.

When he rejoined us, we returned to San Antonio Viejo to resume our patrols. Some of the company had been sent to Laredo with Lieutenant Walker to guard the border crossing there, so our numbers were not as large as they had been. Still, we were Rangers, so we were confident we could deal with whatever situations might arise.

Soon we received word from Lieutenant Walker that he

had engaged and defeated a sizable band of Indians. One of the Comanches, though mortally wounded, had taken some time in dying, and during this interval he boasted of a large war party gathering below the border with the intent of launching a major raid that would wipe out Laredo and penetrate far into Texas.

Of course, Captain Ford could not allow this to take place. At that time we had approximately eighty men at San Antonio Viejo. The captain took sixty of them and headed for Laredo at a hard gallop to reinforce Lieutenant Walker. That left twenty men under the command of Lieutenant Malcijah Highsmith to "hold the fort," so to speak, although there was no fort at our camp, only some tumbled-down stone walls, a few trees, and some tents. About half a mile away were some springs that furnished water for the camp.

I was left behind when Captain Ford went to Laredo because a debilitating illness—probably caused by some spoiled meat—had befallen me and left me unfit for a long, hard ride. I knew that I would be fine in a short time, perhaps as little as twenty-four hours, but with the looming specter of a major Comanche raid, the captain could not afford to wait.

Nor was I the only one left behind who usually traveled with Captain Ford. A few days earlier, Don Francisco had announced that he was going on strike. As Captain Ford's servant, he was paid only ten dollars per month. Since he rode with the Rangers and—at least in theory—fought with the Rangers, he declared that he should receive the same wages as a Ranger, which at that time amounted to twenty-three dollars and fifty cents per month.

This strike by Don Francisco had been short-lived and unsuccessful, and perhaps in a bit of anger, Captain Ford decreed that the don would not accompany the force that went to Laredo. Or perhaps, anticipating a major battle, the captain was simply trying to keep Don Francisco out of danger. This is certainly possible, since Captain Ford was quite fond of Don Francisco, despite his sometimes annoying behavior.

At any rate, we were left at San Antonio Viejo with Lieutenant Highsmith and some eighteen other men. No one expected any real trouble, since to the best of our knowledge the Comanches were massing below the border, a good distance away.

After spending a restless night in my tent, I awoke the next morning feeling much better, as I expected. It was too late to go after Captain Ford, though, so I resigned myself to spending an uneventful week or so at San Antonio Viejo. As I emerged from my tent, I saw Don Francisco walking by. He greeted me with a smile. While his pride was somewhat damaged by being left behind, I suspect he was secretly relieved by Captain Ford's decision.

The don carried a rifle in his hand. He said to me, "*Buenos dias,* Doctor. You feel better today?"

"Much better, thank you," I told him. I gestured toward the gun. "Going hunting, are you?"

He nodded. "*Sí.* A short time ago I heard a bull bellowing over by the springs. I think I will shoot him and make a nice soup from the marrow of his bones. Would you like to go with me?"

A good number of wild, rangy, longhorned cattle roamed the brush country, and they could be dangerous, especially the bulls. I decided that Don Francisco didn't need to be hunting them alone. Besides, I wanted a drink, and even though our water barrels had been filled the previous evening, the cool, clear water direct from the springs would taste even better.

"Yes, I'll go," I said, and we set out at a brisk walk for the springs.

I made one mistake, however: Being taken somewhat by surprise by the don's invitation to accompany him, I left my rifle and my pistol back in the tent.

It was a fine morning, with a hint of coolness lingering in the air that gave no hint of the heat that would build up later in the day. A few birds flitted and sang among the mesquite trees and the live oaks. The sky overhead was blue and streaked here and there by bands of high clouds that rolled in from the Gulf of Mexico. At moments such as that, I was always convinced that there was no finer place on earth than Texas . . . a conviction I still hold.

Don Francisco chattered away in a fashion worthy of the nickname given to him by Captain Ford. "The *capitán* never should have left me here," he said. "Without me at his side to offer him the wisdom of my counsel, he shall not know what to do."

Since I had never known Captain Ford to depend on Don Francisco for counsel, wise or not, I highly doubted that, but I kept the thought to myself. The captain was the sort of man who always instinctively knew what to do in almost any situation. That was one quality that made him such an able leader.

"But I can see why he wanted me to remain," Don Francisco went on. "He knew that a man so young and inexperienced as Lieutenant Highsmith might require my presence so that I can advise him, just in case of trouble."

"I'm sure that was it," I said.

Don Francisco seemed not to hear the dry wit in my voice. "I hope the *capitán* is all right," he said as we tramped along toward the springs, climbing a low, rolling hill dotted with brush. He seemed to be genuinely worried about Captain Ford. Then he added, "I have not yet been paid this month."

We topped the rise and started down toward the springs,

which were surrounded by trees. I looked for the bull Don Francisco claimed to have heard bellowing, but I didn't see it, or any other longhorned cattle. The beasts might have moved on, in which case we wouldn't have that marrow soup the don wanted to make.

I saw something else, though, and stopped to touch Don Francisco's arm. "Look," I said, pointing.

A large cloud of dust rose in the morning sky on the far side of the springs.

There was only one explanation for such a sight, and both of us knew it instantly. A party of at least two hundred riders would be required to raise that much dust, and there weren't two hundred Texans anywhere this side of Laredo.

The Comanche war party wasn't gathering below the border after all. That dying prisoner had either been mistaken or had misled his captors intentionally. The war party was already gathered, and it was right here, closing in rapidly on the small Ranger camp at San Antonio Viejo.

"Madre de Dios!" Don Francisco breathed as he crossed himself. "We must warn the Rangers!"

That thought was already in my mind. I would have turned and broken into a run toward the camp, but this time Don Francisco stopped me by grabbing my arm.

He pointed with the barrel of the rifle, and I saw two Comanche warriors on sturdy ponies working their way along the side of the rise that separated us from the camp. Moving slowly so as not to attract attention, we crouched behind some nearby brush and parted the branches to watch the Indians.

"Scouts," Don Francisco whispered. "They come to make sure the Rangers are camped at the old ruins."

"We have to get back," I said, my voice taut with urgency and, yes, a little fear.

"If we run, they will ride us down." He turned his head

to look back at the dust cloud. "It will be a short time before the rest of the war party is here. They are in no hurry. But if their scouts report that they are discovered, the rest of the band will attack quickly, to preserve as much as they can of the element of surprise."

This thoughtful consideration of the logistics of the situation was a side of Don Francisco I had never seen before. As he tried to figure out our best course of action, I could almost believe that he really had been a war hero.

"Take this," he said suddenly as he pressed the rifle into my hands.

"I can't take your gun—" I started to protest.

"You have no other weapon. I have this." He reached to his waist and withdrew his knife from its sheath.

I remembered his boast of attacking the Indians with nothing but a naked knife. Before this morning was over, he might have a chance to make that boast come true.

"We will split up," he went on. "You will circle around that way—" His hands made their usual eloquent gestures. "While I follow a route in that direction."

"That will take you awfully close to those Indians," I warned.

"I will, how do you say, lie low. Do not worry about me, Doctor. Am I not always the coward, seeking to preserve my own miserable hide?"

"I never said that about you," I told him.

With a little shake of his head, he moved on with his instructions. "Move silent but fast, fast but silent. If you are about to be killed or captured, use the rifle. The shot will alert our *compadres* in camp. But it will alert the rest of the Comanches too, so be swift in reaching the walls."

I thought for a second about those walls. True, they had crumbled in places, but where they still stood, they were thick and would stop arrows, even bullets. If the Rangers took shelter inside the ruins, at least they would be able to make a stand.

"All right," I told Don Francisco. "But be careful."

"Always, amigo," he replied with a broad smile.

We set off in different directions, and the last I saw of him then as I cast a final glance over my shoulder, he was slipping through the brush with the knife clutched in his hand.

I could still see the Indians making their stealthy way toward the camp. I tried to wait until they were looking in the other direction before I moved each time. Slowly, I covered fifty yards, then seventy-five, then a hundred. I couldn't see Don Francisco at all anymore.

Then, as I hurried from a clump of live oaks across a short stretch of open ground toward some more trees, one of the Comanches abruptly jerked around and stared at me. He put his heels to his pony and sent it leaping toward me. He guided the animal with his knees while he raised his bow. I knew he would want to kill me quietly so as not to alert the other Rangers.

Before I could even lift the rifle, there was an unexpected flurry of motion. Don Francisco de la Garza Falcon leaped from some chaparral as the Comanche warrior galloped past. The don reached up, grabbed the startled Indian, and hauled him down off the back of the pony. Both men went rolling to the ground, stirring up a small cloud of dust.

Even through that dust, I saw the morning sun flash on steel as Don Francisco's knife rose and fell with blinding speed. The Comanche went limp beneath him and stopped struggling. But there was a second Indian, and his pony was almost on top of the don.

Once again Don Francisco lived up to his nickname, but

not by chattering this time. Instead, he sprang agilely aside to avoid the slashing blow of a war ax that would have split his skull. The Comanche wheeled his mount and struck again, and again Don Francisco darted aside. I was so amazed by this unexpected display of speed and skill that I forgot to fire, though I probably wouldn't have been able to hit the Comanche anyway, at that range and given the way he was jumping his horse back and forth as he attempted to dash out Don Francisco's brains.

Don Francisco's arm went back and then flashed forward, and I saw the Comanche topple off his pony with the don's knife buried in his chest. Don Francisco hurried over to his fallen foe, pulled the blade free, and slashed it across the Indian's throat just to make sure of him. More than one Ranger had been wounded or killed by an enemy that had appeared to be dead.

Clutching his bloody knife, Don Francisco came up running toward the camp. I did the same, stretching my legs for all they were worth. He was closer than I was and arrived there first, shouting a warning as he came pelting in.

I threw a look over my shoulder as I ran. The Comanche war party was much closer now. I could make out the riders through the trees and brush. They would fall upon the camp within minutes.

But Don Francisco had arrived in time. Already most of the men were hurrying into the shelter of the stone walls. A few of them had rushed out in an attempt to get the horses into the ruins. As I came up, I joined this effort, grabbing the bridles of a couple of animals and tugging them along with me. I'm uncertain whether anyone even noticed that I hadn't been there all along.

Whooping and shouting, the Indians came into view. There was so much dust it was difficult to determine their number, but I remain convinced there were at least two hundred of them, perhaps more. And twenty of us to oppose them.

But some of the Rangers were already in position behind the walls and opened fire. Rifle bullets whined through the air. Those of us engaged in moving the horses hustled the animals into the ruins and hunted some cover of our own.

I dropped down beside a young Ranger who was firing as fast as he could load and reload. "Howdy, Doctor," he said to me. "There sure is a passel of 'em out there, ain't there?"

I nodded and said, "Yes. A passel."

"It's dang lucky ol' Don Monkey spotted 'em and raised a ruckus about it. They might've overrun us before we could get in here if he hadn't."

I didn't argue with the man or point out that I had been with Don Francisco. I knew it was quite likely the two Comanche scouts would have killed me if not for his timely intervention and his unexpected fighting ability.

None of which was on display at the moment. I looked across the ruins and saw him firing at the onrushing Indians with a pistol someone had given him. He thrust the weapon out at arm's length, turning his head away and squeezing his eyes tightly shut each time he pulled the trigger. "Did I get one?" I heard him shout, even though the bullet had gone harmlessly into the ground just on the other side of the stone wall. Then he repeated the process, much to the amusement of the men around him, who laughed even though they were in the middle of a fight for their lives. When the pistol was empty and had done absolutely no harm to the Indians, Don Francisco shook it and cursed it voluminously for its inability to fire straight.

Though we were outnumbered by at least ten to one, none of us panicked. All of the Rangers remained cool-headed throughout the short battle, no doubt due in part to their amusement at the way Don Francisco carried on. We had plenty of ammunition, so the bullets he fired into the ground were not needed.

When it became obvious to the Comanches that they were facing stiffer resistance than they had expected, they pulled back a short distance, out of rifle range. The Rangers took stock and found that they had no injuries. There was no medical work for me to do, so I walked over to Don Francisco and said, "Thank you."

He shook his head and waved his hands. "No, no, do not thank me, Doctor. I did nothing."

"But those two Comanches," I protested. "And you with nothing but a knife . . ."

His dark eyes twinkled. In a quiet voice, he said, "Please, Doctor, say nothing. These men"—and he looked around at the Rangers—"they think of me in one way, and most of the time, that is the way I am. I am a vain little man full of boasts and fear."

"But this morning—"

"This morning it was necessary that I be something else for a time," he said with a shrug. "It is best to say nothing more about it."

I thought then about the Rangers and how their small force, spread over hundreds of miles of rugged terrain, stood between the bastions of civilization and the untamed frontier. Behind that thin line of men, good people struggled to make lives for themselves. The Rangers could not let them down, could not afford to let themselves dwell on the awesome burden that lay on their shoulders. So they rode like devils, fought like devils, and even laughed like devils, sometimes at the antics of the man called Don Monkey.

"I understand," I told him as I nodded. "Nothing more will be said."

"*Bueno,* my friend." He pointed toward the Comanches. "Now, I think our friends are about to attack again. Where is that gun, worthless thing though it is!"

THE COMANCHES HAD a great deal of respect for our rifles and for the Rangers' accuracy with them. Even though we were vastly outnumbered, we turned back every charge the Indians made over the next two days. After several of them were wounded in each attempt on the ruins, they stopped charging and were content to surround us.

But we had water, food, and ammunition and were in fine shape to withstand a siege. I have no idea how long we could have held them off, because at the end of two days, Captain Ford and the rest of the company came galloping into sight, and the Comanches, as we say in Texas, took off for the tall and uncut.

When the captain came riding into the ruins, we discovered that word of our plight had reached him while his force was still on its way to Laredo. Evidently someone had witnessed the initial attack and had gone in search of the captain, telling him that we had all been wiped out. Considering the size of the war party compared to the number of defenders, that was a reasonable, if incorrect, assumption to make.

Lieutenant Highsmith told Captain Ford about how Don Francisco had warned the camp about the impending raid. "It's a good thing he's such a nervous little fella," the lieutenant concluded. "He came running back here in an almighty hurry."

"Yes, I expect he did," Captain Ford agreed. He looked at Don Francisco, and I was never sure if a look of awareness passed between them at that moment or not. All I know is that Captain Ford was a very astute leader and was capable of making good use of all the forces at his command.

Then Don Francisco brandished the pistol he had used during the battle and complained, "Capitán, you got to get us some new guns. These don't shoot straight!"

After the Great War

∽∘∾

by Gary Lovisi

Gary Lovisi has been writing stories and collecting paper-back books all his life. He is the publisher of *Paperback Parade* and *Hardboiled* magazines, and under his Gryphon Books imprint publishes books about the pulps and genre fiction, and nonfiction. A big fan of classic Western books and films, he has been writing short stories successfully in that genre for years and has just completed and sold a Western novel. You can find out more about him and Gryphon Books, or make contact, via his website: www.gryphonbooks.com.

GRANDPA TOLD ME that the West was dying just like he was. I was too young to understand what he was saying back then, but now I know. Grandpa was sad about that turn of affairs. All his old-timer friends were dead and gone now, and he was left alone with just his memories, and me. He shared those memories with me, and I grew and learned them and took them to heart. See, Grandpa had been a Ranger, a Texas Ranger, and that meant something back then, still does today. Back then, Rangers was tough and ornery, they fought Indians and outlaws, and they was my ▮es growing up.

Grandpa filled my head with stories of those Ranger heroes. Stories of Sam Houston's original call for six hundred Rangers to defend Texas, legends like John Coffee "Jack" Hays, W.A.A. "Bigfoot" Wallace, and many others all enshrined in the hearts of Texans. The Rangers were a small corps of flint-hard professionals, organized back in 1835 to fight the Comanche menace on the frontier. Grandpa told me, "A Texas Ranger can ride like a Mexican, track like a Comanche, shoot like a Kentuckian, and fight like the devil. They are Texans to the core."

Right after Grandpa passed, I was drafted to fight in France against the Kaiser and his Hun troops. I was only eighteen, but I acquitted myself well in the trenches. When I came back to Texas with a war buddy in 1919, I had become a man.

In my absence there had been many changes. The old world of my grandpa was long gone, and the new world of what was then being called "modern times" was unknown and strange to me. Automobiles, which had been a laughingstock and called horseless carriages before I left for the war, were now commonplace in many cities. Women dressed differently, and some even agitated for the vote. The towns across the state was wide-open and wild back then. Gambling, whoring, drinking. There was no rule or law. Oil money was everywhere and they was killing men for as little as five dollars in them days.

Being a newly returned doughboy with no matrimonial prospects, I liked the free-wheeling ways and excitement, but when my best buddy Irv was shot in the back in a sporting house outside Waco, the loss was too much. Irv and I had went through a lot during the war together and were like brothers. Now he was dead.

Since it was I who'd brought Irv to Texas, I knew I had to do something about what had happened to him.

Irv, or Irving Goldstein, was a New York Jewboy I'd met
in France. I never met one of them before. I knew there
was none quite like him afterwards. He wore coke-rimmed
spectacles and read a lot of books. From him I started reading books too. Not just schoolbooks, but novels, history, bi-
ographies, even a book about the Texas Rangers. Irv even
taught me to talk French. He told me that, for an ignorant
Texas country boy, I had some real brains in that damn
head of mine. I told him that, for a New York city boy, he
had a right fine knowledge of guns. He was the one taught
me to shoot straight and true.

Irv was a good egg, there was none better. I learned
most of my bad habits from him in France. My first inti-
mate experience of a woman was from a Paris mademoi-
selle he introduced me to. I even began smoking cigarettes
to pass the time in the war. Coffin nails, we called them in
the trenches then.

Irv and I always stuck together, we always talked about
New York and Texas, kidded each other about whose home
was best. So after the war I invited him to come see God's
own Texas country. I knew he couldn't refuse.

Now I felt responsible for what had happened to Irv. He
never knew what hit him, and me just a stupid kid that
should have been watching his back and should have
known better. Well, it growed me up real fast, I can sure
tell you. I was more serious after Irv was gone, and I was
all alone too.

And that's kinda how I became a Texas Ranger. My war
record and medals with my grandpa's good name pushed
forward my application and I was quickly accepted. The
general turmoil of the times made them set me to work
right away dealing with killers and rustlers and other mis-
~ts. My old grandpa would have been proud, but my
:alling was to find the killer of Irv and bring him to

justice. What I found in the end is more than I ever bargained for, but less than I ever expected, and here's that story as best as I can tell it.

My name is William "Jack" Grady. Irv just called me Big Jack. Captain J.L. Blackwood liked what he saw in my six-foot, two-inch, 190-pound size and my accomplishments as an Army sniper in the Great War. Irv knew fancy New York club shooting, and we'd worked that into a job as two of the best men in our outfit with guns. We became sharpshooters and then snipers. It was dirty work, but it kept us alive through the trench warfare. It was funny that a Texan country boy would learn to be such a dead shot from a New York city boy who wore spectacles, but that's the way it was. Grandpa and his stories taught me to love the Rangers, but Irv taught me the skills I'd need to be one.

I really missed that son of a bitch. Now that I was a Texas Ranger, I decided I was going to do all I could to bring my friend's cowardly murderer to justice.

I REMEMBER HOW it all happened. A year ago I'd been seeking female companionship in Room Ten of Belle's sporting house, and Irv had been in Room Eleven right across the hall. It seemed so long ago now. Just harmless fun.

I even remember hearing what must have been the killing shot, but being involved as I was at the moment, and the fact that shots rang out in that section of town every time of night, it didn't alarm me particularly. But the screaming and cries out in the hallway got my attention. When Irv's girl burst into my room all blustery and scared saying, "Mister, your friend has been shot!" I grabbed my drawers and gun and ran into Room Eleven ready for hell or damnation.

What I saw was Irv laying on the floor in a small pool of blood, choking, dying fast.

"Jack," he sputtered, "I am never going to have the chance to show you New York now!"

He died then. And a part of me died too. Nothing will bring men closer to being brothers than going through war together.

AT THE TIME I looked all over for the killer. Didn't see no one. A Waco sheriff's deputy came in and asked me and the girl, Beulah, some questions, but I hadn't seen anything and the girl wasn't talking. She was scared to death all right. She just stared at that big deputy with wide eyes, shaking, and the more he asked her, the more she insisted she didn't know anything and hadn't seen anything either.

"He just stood up, took off his shirt, when the bullet came in through the opened window," she sputtered nervously. That was all anyone seemed to know.

Irv's murder was ruled an unknown shooting and soon forgotten. It wasn't all that unusual back then.

WHAT I DIDN'T know then, but I know now being a Ranger and all, is that Beulah wasn't terrified at Irv's death; she was terrified of that sheriff's deputy who was asking her the questions. She'd been making real damn sure she answered just the way she'd been told to answer. So the case would be dropped. And it was.

That sheriff's deputy was Tom Bull. He was big like a bull, scary, mean, and bad. I'd been learning a few things about him since I'd got my own badge. The city sheriff was honest but old, and didn't have a handle on things; the city deputies were a crooked lot at best. Tom Bull was one of the worst of them all.

ogitating on these facts as I lay back in a barber ce's SHAVES & HAIRCUTS—TWO BITS. I relaxed with el softening up my whiskers as Ace cut my unruly mop of hair into something respectable. I'd been ranging the last three months out in the country, after cattle rustlers and other miscreants, and now was back in town making myself more civilized presentable before I took a long-deserved furlough and resumed my quest for Irv's killer.

That was when Deputy Tom Bull and a pair of his boys entered Ace's establishment. They sat down, waiting on Ace, chewing the fat among themselves. They was a boldly talkative lot. Tom and the boys didn't cotton to Negroes at all and made their notions well known, talking big about keeping them down like they was doing God's own work. It was the usual talk from that segment of people I'd grown up with but did not appreciate. Grandpa Grady taught me different and I honored his ways. "A man's a man," he used to tell me. "You respect him until he proves different. Color don't mean nothing compared to what's in a man's heart."

That's how I got to be friends with Irv. Lotta guys, even Yankees, didn't cotton to Jews. Funny thing was, Irv told me, lotta Jews didn't cotton to non-Jews either. Irv and I used to laugh about that. I knew my grandpa would have liked to meet Irv. Maybe they was meeting now, in heaven.

I sighed and put those thoughts out of my head as I listened in on Tom Bull's remarks. He was going on and on about how to treat Negroes coming back from the war, and that in particular there was this young buck name of Samson Jones who didn't seem to know his rightful place. I knew what that meant.

Then one of Bull's fellow deputies spoke up, and his words surely got my attention. He said, "You might just have to teach that boy a lesson, you know, Bull, like you did with that New York Jew."

I did not move a muscle.

Ace brushed me off, said, "Okay, Ranger, you done. You want that shave now?"

I said no, slowly took off the towel, and wiped my face. I flipped Ace a fifty-cent piece and got up to leave.

One of Bull's boys caught my eye and said, "Howdy, Ranger."

I nodded, looked over at the deputy who had spoken about Bull killing Irv so I'd remember him, said, "Howdy, boys."

Then I went on my way. Calm. Deliberate. My hand shaking to get at my gun, but my mind telling me there'd be time enough for that.

DEPUTY WILLIS P. Stark spilled all he knew when I was able to get him alone and brace him hard.

"I'm a damn city deputy!" he yelled at first, being all obstinate and demanding. How could I do this to him! But once I softened him up a bit, he was all talk after that.

"I don't know! I don't know! Bull just said he'd kilt hisself one of them Jews once a while back." Stark said.

I tightened the noose around his throat.

I pointed to the chair I had him standing upon. It was a rickety old wooden chair. I moved it a bit with my forefinger and it swayed deviously.

The sweat poured off Stark's brows. His eyes glowed like saucers.

"What do you want from me!" he shouted now. "What the damn hell you want from me?"

"Tell me. What exactly did you hear about the Jew?" I asked.

Stark sputtered nervously, "I don't know. Stuff. That he was trouble. They got lots of money. He was cutting into Bull's action, gonna taint his favorite whore forever. Bull just made sure that didn't happen!"

I thought about all that, and I thought about Irv being

dead and this miserable excuse for a sheriff deputy being alive—and it just didn't seem to make much sense.

All that rickety old chair needed was a gentle nudge to set things right.

I could have helped things along, but then I thought of my grandpa, and the kind of Ranger he would want me to be.

I sighed, cut Stark down, put him in irons, and brought him to Captain Blackwood for holding.

I SAW SAMSON Jones later that day. He was a young, good-looking black man with a natural smile that dissolved once he saw me. He had a small dirt farm out of town with a wife, grandmama, and a bunch of youngins. Initially he was not happy to see me ride up to his place, being as I was a white man. I showed him my Ranger badge, and that made him downright nervous.

I said, "It's okay, Mr. Jones. I'm a Texas Ranger, Jack Grady, not a sheriff's deputy."

He just shook his head, said, "It's all the same to me in this county."

I knew what he meant, but I wasn't out there to change the world. I was out there to talk to him about Bull, and Irv's murder, so I changed my tack.

"I hear you're a veteran of the Great War?" I asked.

He nodded.

"I was over there in France, even saw some action. I always have a lot of respect for anyone who fights for his country."

"I was there. Saw it all. Don't want to see no more," he said curtly.

"I know what you mean. How long you been back?"

"Not long. Few months is all. Nothin' change around

here. I wouldn't even be back if it wasn't for my woman and childrens." He looked over at them, smiled.

I nodded. "You know Sheriff Deputy Tom Bull?"

"I knowed him before the war, he just got worse and meaner since then."

"You watch yourself with him," I warned.

"I watch myself. Now what you want?"

"I'm investigating a murder. Irving Goldstein, shot in the back and killed a year ago in Belle's sporting house." It was even hard for me to say it. "You know or hear tell anything about it? Maybe about Tom Bull being involved somehow?"

"I heard about that. That's the New York Jew, ain't it?" he said.

"Yeah."

Jones looked at me closely. "You knew him?"

"He was my friend. We went through the war together." I looked away.

Jones was silent for a while, then he said, "Ranger Grady, there's been talk, that's all. Seems Deputy Bull didn't cotton to his Beulah doing the dirty deed with no Jew. I got the feeling these Jews is definitely somewhere down there with us Negroes on Bull's all-time list. Even though they's white."

I nodded.

"Figure that," he said. His smile was ironic at best.

I thanked him, said, "You watch out for Deputy Bull, and if you run into any trouble or need help, let me know."

He looked at me hard then, said, "What are you saying?"

"I know it ain't easy here, but we're both veterans of the Great War. My grandpa used to tell me that nothing will bring men closer to being brothers than going through the same war together. I believe that to be true because that's how Irv and I was friends. So I wish you and your family well and maybe, some day, we will sit down and tell a few war stories. I got some doozies you might like to hear, and I'm sure you do too."

I mounted and stared to ride off. Jones watched me ride away down the dirt path.

THE SPORTING LIFE hadn't been kind to Beulah over the last year. She'd been trounced out of Belle's after Irv's murder. Seems the whores always got the blame for any trouble with customers. I found her working out of a small adobe shack outside town. She was young and bitter, fallen on hard times and taken to drink. I figured she'd be all used up by Deputy Bull and he'd moved on to greener pastures. I figured wrong. It's like my grandpa always used to say, evil just never sleeps.

"I know you!" she said when I went in to talk with her. "You're a Ranger now? But you was the friend of that boy from outta New York."

I nodded. "I want you to tell me what really happened that night in Room Number Eleven. What you didn't tell, because Deputy Bull told you not to."

"You'll get me killed for sure," she cried. "You don't know what he's like. What he's capable of."

"Tell me!" I barked. "An innocent man was murdered!"

"It was a year ago now, can't you just let it be?"

"Someone murdered my best friend and I aim to find out who and why."

Beulah was silent for a while, thinking, stewing, trapped. I looked at the hovel she was living in and saw she was trapped in more ways than one.

"Come on, girl, I haven't got all day."

"He's jealous, he thinks he owns me. He set me up here after I got thrown out of Belle's so he could use me as his

own private whore like he always wanted. When he heard I
was with a customer during his usual time for us to be together—we had a 'regular' every Monday night—he came
upstairs spoiling for a fight. He busted in the door and saw
your friend taking his shirt off. I don't think he was going
to kill him at first, he was just going to come in and rough
him up, maybe arrest him, give him trouble. You know?
But Tom saw something in my mirror when your friend
took off his shirt."

I shook my head. I didn't get what she was talking
about, but then she walked to a chest of drawers, reached
down deep, and pulled out something. She placed it in my
hand.

"Here. He was a good boy. I liked him," Beulah said
sadly. "I think he liked me too. He didn't deserve to die."

I opened my hand. Inside was Irv's neck chain with the
Star of David medal he always wore attached to it.

"Tom saw that reflected in my mirror off his neck and
he went wild, he pulled his gun and shot your friend in the
back. Then he panicked and covered it up. He told me what
to say and what to do and that if I ever let the truth out he'd
be back for me and do me the same way."

"That's right, Beulah, my love!" a heavy voice called
from behind me. I heard the unmistakable sound of a revolver being cocked. I froze. "Now, Ranger, drop your gun
belt and put your hands up and move against that wall or
I'll drill you where you stand."

I did as he told me, my anger forcing my hand to close
like a vise on Irv's Star of David so tight that the metal cut
into my flesh.

"You little nothing whore!" Deputy Tom Bull roared at
Beulah. "I warned you! Now it appears we gots ourselves a
whore-killing Ranger that's got to be put down by the law
in a rightful and heroic manner."

I knew what that meant. Neither Beulah nor I were getting out of this alive.

Deputy Bull moved farther into the small room.

Beulah started to cry and shake in terror as he approached.

"Won't do you any good to bawl, bitch! And you! Ranger! Move back to that wall now!" Bull barked.

I took a hesitant step backward.

Beulah stopped crying, suddenly straightened up, forcing a smile at Bull, pouring on the sweetness. "Come on, baby, I didn't tell him nothing. You can just get rid of him and we can still have our good thing. You know I like to make you feel good. Where you gonna find another whore who can make you feel the way I do?"

I didn't think it was gonna work, but when Bull looked over at Beulah, I saw my chance. I rushed Bull straight on, and when he turned to look my way and get off a shot, I let loose with Irv's Star of David and chain that hit him right in the eyes.

His shot went off wild and high as my fist rammed into his chin. Bull was out before he hit the ground. Then I put him in irons and told Beulah I was taking her in as a witness and if she knew what was good for her she'd tell all the damn truth she knew about Irv's murder.

I WAS SITTING at a table with Samson Jones talking old war stories again. We had told some fine tall tales, maybe stretched 'em a bit. They did seem to improve with age and the tellin'. A spot of rum in our coffee helped. Sam really liked the ones I told about Irv and me and our adventures in Paris with them mademoiselles. I also told him more about my grandpa and what it meant to him and me to be a Texas Ranger. It was a special thing and still is. Sam understood that.

Sam's wife, Yolanda, asked, "Jack, would you like another cup of that special coffee?"

I smiled, "Nah, Yo, I gotta get going." I lifted up their
little one off my lap and gave him back to his ma. "It was
nice seeing you all again."

"Don't be a stranger, Jack," Sam said. "I knows you
busy and all making Texas safe for the people, and you
have an appointment you gotta keep, but just remember,
I'm saving my best war stories that you ain't never heard
before."

"Ah, holding out on me?" I laughed, and Sam laughed
too.

Then he winked at me, saying in a conspiratorial whisper, "Course, I can't tell you them with Yo and the little
ones here."

"And you better not tell them, Samson Jones!" his wife
chided.

I smiled and said I'd be back soon as I was able. We
shook hands and I rode off.

I HAD THAT appointment to keep. Tom Bull was being
hung today. I stood right in front of the crowd at the penitentiary and watched as the hangman set the noose around
Bull's neck. I took out Irv's Star of David and chain and set
it around my own neck. I did it so that Bull could see it
plain as day. It was the last thing Tom Bull saw before the
trap opened and eternity took him.

I'd like to think that Irv would have enjoyed the irony,
from above or below, or wherever he was watching it from.

Top o' The Hill

∽◦∽

by L. J. Washburn

L. J. Washburn, a lifelong Texan, is co-author of the Spur
Award–nominated novel *Cossack Three Ponies*, and has
authored many novels ranging from sagas of the American
West to mysteries. Washburn's debut mystery novel, *Wild
Night*, which introduced her popular cowboy character
Lucas Hallam, won both the Private Eye Writers of America
Award and the American Mystery Award. She lives in Texas
with her husband, writer James Reasoner, and their two
daughters.

"CAPTAIN! CAPTAIN, WAIT up!" I called after the tall,
erect figure in white Stetson, khaki uniform, and high-
heeled boots striding down a corridor in the Dallas County
Courthouse. He kept going, so I said, "Hey, Lone Wolf!"

Captain Manuel Trazazas Gonzaullas of the Texas
Rangers stopped and turned around to look at me with a
frown on his lean, weathered face. I swallowed my ner-
vousness and trotted down the hall after him, pad in one
hand, pencil in the other.

"What do you want, Casey?" His voice wasn't angry,
but it was brisk and all business.

"How about a comment on the Rawlings case?"

"I said what I had to say in the courtroom. Then the jury had their say. That's all there is to it."

I thumbed my fedora to the back of my head. "Yeah, but—"

"That's all there is to it," he repeated. He turned and started to walk away again.

I thought about following him, but I knew it wouldn't do any good. The Lone Wolf had spoken.

A commotion behind me made me look around. Albert Rawlings was being led out of the courtroom under heavy guard. He would be taken from the courthouse back to the county jail and from there would be transferred to the state penitentiary in Huntsville, where he would serve a life sentence for murder. The jury had taken less than an hour to convict him, largely on the basis of evidence gathered by the men of Company B of the Texas Rangers, under the command of Captain M.T. Gonzaullas.

Rawlings looked in my direction, and his eyes were like ice picks jabbing into my brain. Then I realized he wasn't looking at me at all; his gaze was directed past me toward the back of Captain Gonzaullas. At that moment, I knew that Rawlings blamed the captain for his conviction, and somewhere, somehow he would try to even the score. If I had been Gonzaullas, I would have been scared out of my boots.

But I figured that after more than a quarter of a century as a Ranger, the Lone Wolf didn't scare too easy.

NOT LONG AFTER I'd started covering the courthouse beat, I'd looked him up in the morgue at the paper. Gonzaullas had joined the Rangers in 1920 and had been assigned to border patrol duties in the Rio Grande Valley. It was his job to stop smugglers, and he did such a good job of it that crooks up and down the river quickly grew to hate and fear him. They were the ones who gave him the nickname El Lobo Solo, because of his habit of working alone.

From there he had been transferred to the rough, booming oil fields in northwest Texas, and had brought law and order to them as well, shutting down numerous bootlegging rings. For over a decade, he had been one of the top Rangers working in the field.

Then in 1933, Texas Governor Miriam "Ma" Ferguson fired Gonzaullas and a bunch of other Rangers who had openly supported her opponent in the last election. That pretty much gutted the Ranger organization, so the state legislature formed the Department of Public Safety as a companion statewide law enforcement agency, and Gonzaullas and many of the other dismissed Rangers went to work for it.

Eventually, Ma was gone from office, and the Rangers became part of the DPS, although they were still pretty much an autonomous entity. While working for the DPS, Gonzaullas had become head of their Bureau of Intelligence and had founded their crime lab. But his roots were in the Rangers, and so he went back to them in 1940, taking over command of Company B, headquartered in Dallas. He had been there for the seven years since, taking on all the tough cases.

None of them had been any tougher, though, than the case of Albert Rawlings, bank robber and cold-blooded killer. Now Rawlings had been brought to justice, but several members of his gang were still out there somewhere, on the loose.

As I headed back to the newspaper office, I wondered if Rawlings would try to reach out from behind prison walls to take his vengeance on the Lone Wolf.

"Get that quote for the sidebar?" the city editor asked me as I came into the newsroom. I had called in the lead to rewrite as soon as the jury came back with its verdict.

I dumped my hat on my desk next to the battered old Underwood. "No comment."

"Is that what you're tellin' me, Casey, or is that what Gonzaullas said?"

"That's what Gonzaullas said."

"And you let him get away with it?" The chief shook his head. "I don't know about you, Casey. I don't know if you're going to make a reporter or not."

I didn't know either. I'd been banging my head on journalistic walls since not long after V-J Day. You'd think any guy who could survive Iwo Jima and Saipan would be gutsy enough to make it in the newspaper game, but I'd found it to be tough sledding. I'd begun to wonder if I was cut out for this racket.

My dad had had printer's ink in his veins, though, and I was determined not to let the old man down. I reached for my hat and said, "Why don't I go over to Ranger headquarters and try again?"

"Why don't you do that," the chief said.

The Rangers knew how to live up to their Old West image. The headquarters of Company B was located in a long, low building made out of logs, with big stone chimneys at both ends. The place looked like somehow it had been transported magically from the frontier past and plopped down in Fair Park, the huge compound south of downtown Dallas where the State Fair was held every year.

A sergeant at the main desk stopped me when I walked in and asked me what I wanted. When I told him I wanted to see Captain Gonzaullas, he thumbed an intercom button and said, "Pete Casey's out here, Captain."

I had no trouble hearing Gonzaullas's answer. "What does *he* want?"

"I don't know, Captain."

"Well, send him back." I heard the mixture of resignation and annoyance in Gonzaullas's tone.

When I walked into the captain's office, he was pulling down a map of Texas on the wall. Several other Rangers stood around in their khaki uniforms, though they didn't have their hats on. "Remember, ten o'clock. That's all, boys," Gonzaullas told them, and they filed out. When they were gone, he turned to me, put his hands on his hips, and said, "I don't have any more to say now than I did when you asked me at the courthouse, Casey."

He hadn't been armed while he was testifying, but now he had his guns strapped on again, a pair of pearl-handled Colt revolvers in black leather holsters. I knew he had used those guns more than once in the pursuit of justice. Texas wasn't the wild and woolly state it had once been, but it still had the bark on in places, as the old-timers say. Early on in his Ranger career, Gonzaullas had gotten in the habit of cutting off the front part of the trigger guard on the guns he used, thinking that it might give him a split-second's edge sometime. And he might need that split second to save his life. . . .

"Captain, you didn't see the look Rawlings gave you when they took him out of the courtroom," I said. "He's going to try to get back at you somehow."

Gonzaullas shrugged. "He'll have a hard time doing it from behind bars."

"Not necessarily. Some of his gang are still loose. They could come after you. Rawlings might have even set it all up beforehand."

"There are a lot of people in the world who wouldn't mind killing me," Gonzaullas said dryly. "That doesn't stop me from coming to work in the morning."

I went for my pad and pencil. "Can I quote you on that, Captain?"

For a second I thought he was going to get mad and throw me out of his office. But then he kind of smiled a little, waved a hand, and said, "Why not? Anything else I can do for you?"

I scribbled down the quote. "No, that'll do it. Thanks, Captain. My city editor will be glad I came over here."

"Anything to help the press."

He was being sarcastic, but in the time I had known the captain, I got the feeling that a part of him did enjoy the notoriety. After all, he had been called the Lone Wolf for a long time, and as far as I knew, he had never tried to stop anybody from using the nickname.

I put the pad away, tucked the pencil behind my ear, and left the office. I was able to keep from grinning with excitement until after I'd left the building. I had come to Company B headquarters to get a quote, but I had gotten a lot more than that. I just didn't want any of the Rangers to know it.

When Captain Gonzaullas had pulled that map of Texas down, he had covered up what was underneath it. Not fast enough to keep me from catching a glimpse of it, though. It was another map, more of a diagram really, showing some streets and a large house. A mansion, in fact, and I knew where and what it was.

Top o' The Hill.

HALFWAY BETWEEN DALLAS and Fort Worth was the town of Arlington, once a sleepy little country village that was now growing fast in this era of post-war boom. Highway 80 was called Division Street where it ran through Arlington, and just north of Division Street on the west side of town was a heavily wooded hill. Back in the twenties, some of the trees had been cleared off the top of the hill, and a guy named Fred Browning had built himself a big house up there.

Browning was a gambler, and along with his partner Benny Binion, he had turned the house—known as Top o' The Hill Terrace—into the biggest, fanciest, most notorious casino west of the Mississippi. From the expensive rugs on the floor to the brilliant crystal chandeliers that hung from the ceiling, everything at Top o' The Hill was first-class, including the gambling equipment. Not only that, but the place had a reputation for being on the straight. Browning and Binion didn't need crooked games in order to rake in a fortune. All they needed for that was human nature.

High rollers from all over the country came to the Top o' The Hill to gamble. Celebrities showed up there too. Howard Hughes brought Jane Russell and her famous cantilevered bra. Joe Louis, the Brown Bomber, brought his whole entourage. Fred Astaire did a soft-shoe to entertain his friends. I'd even heard rumors that Bonnie and Clyde visited there back in the thirties.

Of course, even though everybody had heard the rumors, nobody could prove that any of it was true, especially the law. Fred Browning guaranteed anonymity to his guests. He had heavily armed guards all around the outside of the mansion, and visitors had to pass through several checkpoints before they reached the gambling rooms. All the tables and the other equipment were built so that if a guard outside pushed an alarm button, it would all roll out of sight into hidden compartments closed off by sliding doors. An escape tunnel for especially shy guests led to a hidden opening on the west side of the hill. From there, stone steps led up to an elegant little tea garden. If the cops ever busted in, they wouldn't find anything to convict anybody.

Yeah, the authorities knew all this stuff, even though they couldn't prove it, and so did most of the reporters in town. I'd never been in the Top o' The Hill myself, but I had heard plenty about it. I knew too that the fact Browning and Binion were operating a gambling house so blatantly had to be a burr under the saddle of Captain M.T. "Lone Wolf" Gonzaullas.

From what I had seen in the captain's office, Gonzaullas was going to try to do something about it. He had been briefing those other Rangers when I came into the office, and he had said, "Remember, ten o'clock." That sounded to me like the time when something big was going to start.

And when it did, I planned to be there.

I WENT HOME, put on my best suit, cleaned my glasses, and slicked down my hair. Then I waited until dark, which in Texas in the summer was about eight-thirty in the evening, got in my old Packard, and drove out Highway 80 to Arlington.

There were lights on top of the hill where the mansion was located, but not a lot of them. It might be a little gaudy inside, but the outside of the place was pretty sedate, as if it was the home of a rich guy who'd made his money from a legitimate business. For all I knew, Browning and Binion considered themselves legitimate businessmen. They provided a service that the people definitely wanted, and they did it in a fair, classy manner. They were about as much on the up-and-up as big-time gangsters could be.

The driveway wound up the hill to an arched, gated entrance between two huge pillars made of red sandstone. A couple of cars that were a lot newer and a lot nicer than mine sat in line there, waiting to get in. A couple of guards who openly toted shotguns spoke to the people inside the vehicles and then waved them on through. Obviously, they knew the open sesame. I didn't, but I was hoping the angle I had worked out would get me in.

The driver's-side window was already rolled down,

since it was a hot night. As one of the guards came up, I showed him my press card and said, "Hi, I'm Pete Casey. I'm here to see Mr. Browning."

The guard, who was big but not dumb, said, "Is Mr. Browning expecting you?"

"No, but I just need a few minutes of his time. I'm working on a story—"

The guy started shaking his head. "No dice, pal. The boss doesn't need any publicity."

"But the story's not really about him," I said quickly. "It's about Royal Ford."

The guard raised up a little, and I knew he was looking across the roof of the Packard at the other guard. "What about Royal Ford?" he asked me.

"We're going to do a series about great racehorses, and we're going to lead off with Royal Ford."

Now, Royal Ford couldn't be considered a great racehorse. He was no Seabiscuit, let me tell you. But back in the thirties, Fred Browning had spent over a hundred grand to buy him from the old Texas oilman W.T. Waggoner, who had owned Arlington Downs Racetrack at the time. Browning loved that horse, and had run him in races all over the country for several years.

By this time, Royal Ford had gone to that big glue factory in the sky, but I hoped Browning was still sentimental enough about the nag so that the idea of somebody writing a newspaper story about him would get me into the place. Once I was there, all I wanted to do was hang around until ten o'clock. I was convinced that was when Captain Gonzaullas and the Rangers intended to raid the Top o' The Hill Terrace.

"Wait here," the guard said, and I considered that a victory of sorts because he hadn't sent me packing. He went over to a little shack. I figured he was on the phone inside, talking to someone in the house, maybe Browning himself.

When he came back, he said, "Mr. Browning will see you, but only for a few minutes."

"A few minutes is fine," I said. I figured I could stall for a while if I had to.

The gates opened and I drove through. There was a slight climb to the parking area. I left the car and went to the front door of the house, where another big, smart guy in a good suit waited for me.

He took me inside, and I saw that the place was as fancy as it was rumored to be. The foyer had nice paintings on the walls, and a whole suit of armor stood in one corner. The guard patted me down and took me up a curving flight of stairs once he was satisfied that I wasn't carrying a gun.

On the second floor, he opened one of a set of double doors and ushered me into a book-lined room with a big desk in it. Fred Browning sat behind the desk. He was a decent-looking middle-aged guy with a mustache. Other than the fact that he was mostly bald, he reminded me a little of pictures I'd seen of Howard Hughes.

He stood up, reached across the desk, and shook hands with me. "Hello, Casey," he said. "I don't believe we've met, but I've read your stuff in the paper."

"So you're the one," I said with a grin, but he looked like he didn't get the joke.

A second later, I knew there was nothing funny about what was going on, because I felt a gun barrel dig into the small of my back.

"What are you doing here, Casey?" Browning asked. He stuck his hands in his pockets, relaxed and casual despite the fact that his goon had a gun in my back. Or maybe because of that.

"I . . . I . . . Like I told the guys outside, Mr. Browning, I'm going to write a story about Royal Ford—"

"Bull. You're no sportswriter. You cover the courthouse beat."

I tried to put a crestfallen look on my face. Believe me, it wasn't hard.

"I got pulled off that beat and put on sports," I said. "The city editor doesn't like me. I figure it'll be flower shows next if I don't do a good job on this horse-racing series."

"Flower shows, eh?" Browning laughed. "You were a Marine, weren't you?"

"Yes, sir, I was."

"South Pacific?"

"That's right."

"I guess it would be quite a comedown, then, if you got stuck covering the flower shows." Browning flapped a hand at the guard. "It's all right, Jake."

The gun went away from my back. I breathed a little easier, but not much.

Browning sat down and motioned for me to do likewise. I reached into my coat and got my pad and pencil—being careful to do the reaching slow and easy, not wanting to spook the guard even though I'd been patted down and they knew I didn't have a gun. All I had to do was ask Browning to tell me about Royal Ford and his racing experiences, and then I had my hands full taking notes for the next half hour. Browning had promised me only a few minutes, but he seemed to have forgotten about that. He really loved that horse.

I snuck an occasional glance at the clock on the wall of the office. The hands crawled around past nine-thirty. I started to hope that Browning would talk all the way until ten o'clock. But about nine-forty, he said, "I guess that's all."

"This is great stuff, Mr. Browning," I said. "It's going to make a great article. But surely there's more you can tell me."

He shook his head. "No, I'm afraid not. That's all."

He stood up. I tried to keep my seat, but Jake stepped up behind me and put a hand on my shoulder. I weighed close to two hundred pounds then, but when he closed his fingers and hauled up, I went with him. It was that or have bones wrenched out of their sockets.

"I'll walk you out," Browning offered. Always the good host, despite the guns and the goons.

When we reached the front door, I said desperately, "Mr. Browning, just one more favor, please."

"What is it?"

I plastered a sappy grin on my face and said, "Can I, uh, take a look around? I've heard so much about the place, I mean, it's famous and all, and I'd really like to see it. Not to write about it, you understand," I added quickly. "Just to satisfy my curiosity."

Browning never stopped smiling. He just shook his head and said, "No."

And just like that, I was out, and it was still a quarter of an hour until ten.

Oh, I cursed my luck as I walked toward my car. Jake went with me, no doubt on Browning's orders. Nobody was allowed to wander around Top o' The Hill unescorted. When we got to my Packard, Jake pulled the door open for me and said, "Good night."

I was about to get in the car when Jake suddenly turned and called out, "Hey, who are—"

I heard what sounded like a cough from the darkness, and Jake's head jerked to the side. He stumbled and fell against me, knocking me down. Something hot and wet gushed over my hand when I put it out toward him.

Something else plinked off the Packard.

I shoved Jake away and crawled under the car. A frantic voice in the back of my head screamed *Oh, my God!* over and over. I knew Jake had been shot in the head, and whoever had killed him had taken a shot at me too. I'd heard the bullet hit the car.

My first thought was of the Rangers, but I threw out that idea in a hurry. That coughing sound had been a silenced gun. I didn't know if the Rangers ever used silencers on their weapons, but I was pretty darned sure they didn't ambush people like Jake had been ambushed. Somebody else was loose on the grounds, somebody who was a killer.

Feet crunched on gravel somewhere close by. If the killer had been able to see well enough to put a slug in Jake's head, he would have been able to see that someone was with the guard. Me, in fact. And now he was searching the parking area, looking for me so that he could tie up a big fat loose end. I stayed where I was, in the darkness underneath the Packard, trying not to breathe.

Then an engine rumbled, and headlights swept across the graveled lot. More footsteps sounded, but this time they were going away in a hurry. More guests were arriving, and the killer didn't want to be seen poking around the parking area with a gun.

I guess he figured I didn't matter. He thought he could finish the job that had brought him here before I could interfere with him.

My mouth was dry and my head was pounding and I felt a little sick to my stomach, but my brain still worked just fine. And as I lay there for a moment, I remembered that this was hardly the first time somebody had taken a shot at me. Back in the South Pacific, I'd had a whole bunch of somebodies shooting at me. Just like that, I calmed down, and I started to think even faster than before.

Nobody would be dumb enough to try to rob the casino, so that was out. That meant the killer had come here with a specific target in mind, and the only person I could think of was Captain Gonzaullas.

Albert Rawlings was vicious enough to have set it all up beforehand. If he was convicted and sent to prison, a hired killer would go after the man Rawlings blamed for his plight: Captain Gonzaullas. The assassin could have trailed Gonzaullas out here to Arlington tonight, and once he realized that the Rangers were about to raid the Top o' The Hill, what better place to kill the captain? Browning and Binion might even get the blame for the murder. It was a perfect setup.

Except for the fact that I was still alive and had an idea what was going on.

The captain and I didn't always get along, but I liked and respected the guy. It was said of the old-time Rangers that they would charge hell with a bucket of water, and you could believe that of Gonzaullas too. I had to warn him that he had more to worry about than the regular guards.

Trying not to make too much noise, I crawled out from under the car and got up in a crouch. I didn't like doing it, but I checked to make sure Jake was dead. He was. I slipped my hand inside his coat and found his gun. It was a short-barreled .38.

I made my way to the edge of the parking area, staying low the whole time. The car that had driven in a few minutes earlier had disgorged its passengers, who were even now being welcomed into the house. The other guards didn't seem to miss Jake yet.

I knew Gonzaullas was smart. He had to be aware that he would never get the goods on Browning and Binion by going in the front door. That left the escape tunnel. I had an idea where it was, so I started circling the hill toward the hidden entrance. I moved as quietly as I could, sort of like creeping through a jungle on some godforsaken island. . . .

For a second, those memories came flooding in on me and I got the shakes, but I forced them away. As I approached the entrance to the tunnel, I saw a shape suddenly dart out of the shadows, and there was a flurry of action. Then as my eyes got more accustomed to the darkness, I was able to pick out the uniformed figure kneeling on the back of a guy on the ground. I heard the clinking of metal and knew Captain Gonzaullas had just handcuffed the guard posted at the tunnel. He had corralled the guy with a minimum of fuss and commotion.

A branch cracked to my left, really close. Without thinking about what I was doing, I charged in that direction and slammed into somebody in the darkness. I tried to slap the .38 against the side of his head, but I missed. Then something jabbed me hard in the belly. I couldn't help but double over in pain. A foot kicked my legs out from under me, and I went down hard.

I looked up, saw a figure looming over me, and I waited for the cough that would herald the silenced gun blowing my brains out. Instead there was a thud, and for the second time tonight, somebody fell on me.

This one was just out cold, though, not dead. After a second the weight was hauled off of me, and Captain Gonzaullas said, "What's going on here?"

I could see he had one of those pearl-handled revolvers in his hand, and I figured he had just used it to clout the other guy over the head. "Don't shoot, Captain!" I said. "It's me, Pete Casey!"

"Casey!" Gonzaullas reached down with his free hand and pulled me to my feet. "What are you doing out here?"

It was a long story, and I didn't think there was time to tell all of it. So I settled for, "That guy you just knocked out is a hired killer, Captain. Rawlings sent him after you. He murdered one of Browning's guards around at the front of the house a little while ago, and he tried to kill me."

Gonzaullas took it all in, and must have decided he

could get the details later, because he nodded and holstered his revolver. He took another pair of handcuffs from his belt, rolled the guy over, and snapped the bracelets on him. For good measure, he pulled the killer's belt off and used it to tie his ankles together too.

"Where are the rest of the Rangers, Captain?" I asked.

"What Rangers?"

My eyes widened. "You mean you're going in there by yourself?"

He chuckled. "The boys are waiting to move in the front at my signal. But I'm going up the tunnel alone."

The last ride of the Lone Wolf, I thought. But he wouldn't be completely alone.

"I'm coming too."

"Casey—"

"Not to put too fine a point on it, Captain, but if I hadn't jumped this guy, he might have killed you."

"It looked to me like he was about to kill you."

"Yeah, but if I hadn't made a racket so that you'd know something was going on—"

He held up a hand to stop me. "All right, all right. You can come with me, but stay out of the way. And you'll have to look after your own hide, because I'll be too busy to do it."

"Don't worry about me, Captain," I assured him. "I won't be any trouble."

Gonzaullas led the way. He pushed the vines and creepers aside and moved into the tunnel. I was right behind him. The tunnel had cement walls and was dimly lit by some tiny lightbulbs. It was about four feet wide and maybe ten feet tall, and angled up through the heart of the hill. At the far end was a door that let out into one of the rooms where the gambling equipment could be hidden. There were no guards there, so we were able to move across to another door and step into the main gaming room itself. The air was full of talk and laughter, the click of the roulette wheels, the rattle of dice.

It all came to a sudden stop when the Lone Wolf pulled those pearl-handled Colts and called out in a loud, clear voice, "In the name of the State of Texas, you're all under arrest!"

IF YOU'RE EXPECTING some big shoot-out, there wasn't one. There wasn't even a little shoot-out. Gambling was only a misdemeanor, after all, and most of the people in the place were rich. Oh, some of them were embarrassed, sure, but that was about the extent of it. They didn't even have to pay their own fines. As a gesture of goodwill, Fred Browning did that. Above all else, he was a businessman who took care of his customers.

More Rangers came in and took axes to the tables and slot machines and roulette wheels, but that was all they busted up. Gonzaullas was a straight arrow and not about to allow his men to indulge in any wanton destruction. So as it turned out, the Top o' The Hill was shut down for only a few days before Browning managed to replace everything and start up all over again.

In the end, though, Captain Gonzaullas had accomplished his real aim. The Top o' The Hill was supposed to be impervious to the forces of law and order, and Gonzaullas had demonstrated in dramatic fashion that it wasn't. Business declined, and a couple of years later Benny Binion bailed out, taking his share of the profits and heading west to a little town in Nevada called Las Vegas. He hadn't been there long before he opened up the Horseshoe Casino.

Browning hung on a little longer in Arlington, but by 1950, the casino was closed down and the property was for sale. When it was sold, the fancy old mansion was torn down to make way for some buildings put up by the new owner . . . the Bible Baptist Seminary.

The whole thing with the killer hired by Albert Rawlings was kept pretty quiet. The guy cracked and implicated Rawlings, who wasn't going to be getting out of prison in the first place, and now sure as heck wasn't. Captain Gonzaullas asked me not to write too much about it, and I went along with him. By then I'd figured out that I wasn't cut out for newspapering anyway, and started writing books instead.

Captain Gonzaullas retired in 1951 after more than thirty years of service and went out to Hollywood, where he worked as a consultant on movies and television shows about the Texas Rangers. He was a fine spokesman for the Rangers too.

Oh, I said the mansion was torn down, and it was, but those big gateposts are still there. So are the tunnel, the tea garden, and some of the underground rooms. It's some sort of historical monument now, as well it should be, since it was there that the Lone Wolf howled for the last time.

Between a Bank and a Hard Place

~◦∞◦~

by John Helfers and Kerrie Hughes

"Between a Bank and a Hard Place" is Pinkerton Agent
Nancy Smith's second appearance in the American West;
her first was in the critically lauded anthology *Boot Hill*,
edited by Robert J. Randisi. Her creators, John Helfers and
Kerrie Hughes, liked the collaborative process so much that
they ended up getting hitched. They live in Green Bay,
Wisconsin, a far cry from the frontier, but that doesn't prevent them from plotting further adventures for the intrep-
id Agent Smith.

JARED BROTHERTON NUDGED his trotting horse alongside his companions, all of them looking like just one
more group of trail-weary cowboys passing through town.
Pulling his Stetson lower on his brow, he kept his eyes
moving, trying to divide his attention between his four fellow riders and the townspeople passing by on both sides of
the street. The mounted quartet next to him was all doing
the same thing, noting the layout of the streets, the main
roads through town, and other ways in and out.

And the last two were something Houston had a lot of.

After the capital of Texas had moved to Austin in 1839, the city had redoubled its efforts in business, and the resulting traffic boom at nearby Buffalo Bayou had swelled the town threefold over the past four decades. In the distance Jared spotted a few slender columns of smoke from the newer steamships that plied the waterways. They held no real interest for him, however, nor did the crowded sidewalks, except for an occasional glance for patrolling lawmen. It seemed everyone was out and about today; from parasol-wielding society matrons and gentlemen strolling along with their canes to frontier families clad in rough home-spun shopping for supplies to take back to their distant homes. But nowhere did he see the golden gleam of a sheriff's star, or a mounted and armed deputy watching the streets, a fact that made Jared more apprehensive than confident.

A piercing whistle made him look up from his scan of the street to see Baird Tanner, the leader of his group, wave him over. Riding around a buckboard loaded to the gunwales, he reined his horse in next to Tanner's stallion, which blew foam and clicked its teeth at the ear of Jared's roan.

"He doesn't like your horse," Tanner said with a wry smile, not looking at Jared but keeping his eyes roving over the crowd.

Jared had only joined Tanner's boys two weeks ago, and he knew where he stood in the pecking order. He was good enough with his fists, but even better with a pistol, and hadn't had to prove anything to anybody else in the group. Yet. For his part, Jared hoped it wouldn't come to that, since he was after bigger game, so to speak.

"I reckon he ain't too fond of yours either," he replied, looking both ways at an intersection as they rode through it. "But you didn't call me over here to socialize. What's on your mind?"

"I like a man who gets down to business," Tanner replied, a hint of Alabama drawl coloring his speech. Baird Tanner was bold and canny, and held his band together by his strength of will alone. Jared suspected he was educated, as he certainly didn't sound like a rough-and-ready cowpuncher or hard prairie farmer. In another life, he could have respected Tanner, maybe even liked him. But not here, not now.

"We're moving the job up. It's happenin' today," Tanner said.

Jared let his eyes drop as if mulling over what he had just heard. He noticed that the other three had hung back a bit, leaving Tanner and him by themselves. When he raised them again, he found himself staring into Tanner's hazel gaze. "You're the boss. D'ya mind if I ask why?"

"I think we got Sam Bass's problem."

Even though he knew what Tanner was talking about, as the Texas desperado had been captured three months ago when one of his own gang had turned informant, Jared frowned. "I don't follow."

"One of the group is working for the law," Tanner replied, his eyes never leaving Jared's face.

"You got any idea who?" he asked, pushing his hat back to wipe away the sweat on his brow.

"Not yet," Tanner replied. "But it's a safe bet that whoever it is has a nice reception set up for us at the Mercantile tomorrow. So we're gonna rob it today."

"You all decided this in the morning, while I was scouting ahead?" Jared said.

Tanner nodded. He didn't have to say anything more. Jared heard the unspoken words as plain as day. The fact that the rest had decided to move up the job while he was out didn't mean anything right now. Tanner was going to be watching all of them, looking for any sign that any one of 'em had sold the rest out. From what Jared knew of the bandit leader, if he had been under suspicion, he would have already been dead. The fact that the robbery was happening today wasn't going to make Jared's job any easier either.

The young Texas Ranger had ridden north a few months earlier to investigate rumors of a quick-striking, well-prepared gang that had been moving around the state, hitting small-town banks and leaving a trail of mystery behind them. No one had even seen their faces, although one of the men had been shot and killed during a heist in Waco. Even though Jared had just joined the Rangers nine months ago, his boss felt he was the perfect man for the job.

"Since you're still wet behind the ears, no one knows about you; and you're from that backwater town on the Trinity—Dallas, ain't it?" Bobby Clay had asked him. "Well, get back up there and see what you can find out."

Which was how Jared came to be riding into Houston this morning. He wished he could have said that dogged investigative work had gotten him here, but in fact he had just struck up a conversation with a tired-looking man at a saloon in Nacogdoches, which Jared had figured would be their next target. He had been dropping hints in the towns he had passed through that he was a small-time cattle rustler looking for something bigger, hoping to draw the bandits to him if possible. The man he had talked to was Baird Tanner. After hearing a few stories about cutting herds of longhorns from cattle drives and running them across the Rio Grande, Baird had invited him to ride with him, even mentioned a job down south he and his men could use an extra hand on.

Since then they had been heading steadily toward the Gulf of Mexico, but Tanner hadn't taken them near any town with a bank of any size, which was just as good, since Jared wasn't crazy enough to think he could arrest the entire gang by himself. That old saw of "one riot, one Ranger" was a great slogan, but Jared considered himself a realist, and one man against four was undertaker's odds. The other three outlaws all knew their way around a pistol, and one of them, a steel-eyed devil named Robert MacKinnon, Jared wasn't sure he could take on his best day.

There was also the slight problem of not having a shred of evidence to arrest the gang on. Although some Rangers had no problems with dealing justice from the barrel of a gun, this was Jared's first lone assignment, and he wanted to do it right. But Tanner's boys weren't making it easy for him. Unlike other outlaw groups such as the Wild Bunch and the James-Younger Gang, these men kept their names out of the newspapers. None of the people robbed could describe any of them, and they switched horses as easily as breathing.

Also, Tanner himself was too cagey to go without a fuss. He had spilled the beans about Houston only two days ago and had the gang change direction toward the city. In Lynchburg, Jared had snuck away just long enough to cable his boss. A reply had come back early the next morning:

NO RANGERS IN AREA STOP BANK HIRED PINKERTON TO
HELP WITH CAPTURE STOP WILL POSE AS TELLER STOP

Although the idea of outside assistance, especially from up north, rankled a bit, Jared knew he'd need all the help he could get. He'd still have preferred another Ranger, though, especially now that his plans were shot to hell.

He was just going to let the sheriff know when they'd be there so the entire gang could be rounded up as they got to the bank. They'd go inside, start the holdup, then deputies inside and outside the building would have the whole bunch dead to rights. At least, that's how it was supposed to happen.

This cowflops my idea but good, he thought. There was no way the Pinkerton or anyone else would be ready when Tanner's boys pulled the job this morning. All he could do now was hope that the man on the inside had a cool head and a fast hand, because it was very likely he'd need both to see the next morning.

NANCY SMITH LOOKED at the clock on the bank wall for what must have been five times in as many minutes, the same thought on her mind with each glance.

Where is he?

Her new partner, Thomas Goodman, was late for their meeting. Mr. Russell Liberty, the Houston Mercantile Bank's general manager, sat behind his desk across from her, looking over a sheaf of papers. It was a one-page introduction with a contract attached for potential services from the Pinkerton Agency in Chicago to the Houston bank.

Nancy had been working as an agent for four years, and was now a senior agent on remote security projects. She was one of the first female agents Allan Pinkerton had hired, and it was partially due to her exemplary performance that he was hiring more. At twenty-eight years old, she was still young and quite pretty, but did not want a life of children and dishpans, nor did she care to sit at home and live off her parents' money. Nancy loved matching her wits and skills against criminals of all kinds, at had yet to be disappointed in her adventures across the West and in

Chicago. She had foiled stagecoach gangs and train robbers, and was now handling the growing spate of bank robberies across the nation.

Today, however, Nancy had an entirely different problem on her hands. Thomas had been assigned to remain at the bank after Nancy had finished her job, but being late for their initial meeting was not going to reflect well on the company at all.

Mr. Liberty cleared his throat and looked at her over his half-moon glasses. "Miss Smith, I believe in being honest, and while I must say my confidence in Mr. Pinkerton's judgment is high and your own credentials are also excellent, I am worried about this decision to send a woman and an untried young man"—he consulted his gold pocket watch—"who cannot even be on time for this meeting, to foil a potential robbery."

Nancy smiled, hiding her disappointment. While waiting for Thomas, she had learned that the bank manager was also originally from Chicago, and had hoped that he would have accepted her at more than face value. "Don't forget that one of the men in the gang is actually a Texas Ranger who will be assisting us, and the sheriff's deputies we'll be meeting with this afternoon will also be on hand for the capture," she replied. "Mr. Liberty, I assure you we will do the job Mr. Pinkerton sent us to do and that every contingency will be handled discreetly and professionally.

"In fact, Mr. Goodman mentioned his need to survey the structure of the outside of your bank before our meeting. He is most likely analyzing the potential for break-in by way of using the businesses on each side of you."

At least I hope that's what he's doing, she thought. With the ink on his Columbia University engineering degree hardly dry before joining the Pinkertons, Thomas had been babbling all morning about the how the bank's architecture could be altered to prevent any kind of break-in or robbery. Thomas was obsessed with the prevention of crime rather than fighting it, a singular focus that, while making him valuable to Allan's company, also hindered him, sometimes to the point of distraction. After breakfast he had told her he wanted to go on ahead to get a look at the alley behind the bank again, and would meet her inside. That had been ten minutes ago, and there was still no sign of him.

Mr. Liberty cleared his throat again. "Miss Smith, how long must we wait for Mr. Goodman?"

"Perhaps we should begin the tour, and we both can fill Thomas in when he arrives," she said. "I would like to meet the tellers and assess the layout of their posts first, if you don't mind."

"Of course," he replied, rising to escort her out of his office and down the stairs to the main floor.

Nancy surveyed the long rectangular room as she descended the new pine staircase, the smell of sawdust redolent around her. Below, she saw three people behind a long high counter that ran the length of the room and contained separate portals for each teller to sit behind. It was typical of the banks she had recently seen further west, and she wondered to herself for the hundredth time how bank owners could think that a teller window, barred or open, was any kind of deterrent for a robber. She preferred the Eastern banks with their solid wood partitions and locking doors. She had seen the plans to build a more secure bank, but that would only happen if she could prevent this one from being robbed. At least the entire building was brick, and the only windows were in the front, which also had bars behind the glass.

The Houston Mercantile Bank was the newest entry in

the city's expanding business district. Although Texas was a relatively new state, its inhabitants had already gained a reputation for willfulness, and no bank here was federally backed yet. *I'm sure they'll change their mind after a few more robberies,* Nancy thought, *and request to have all their banks regulated and protected by the U.S. government.* But not right now, and certainly not in Houston. Mr. Liberty had made it clear that the private bank wanted no interference from the federal government, and chose the Pinkerton Agency to provide limited security, then hire and train new security personnel once Nancy and Thomas had finished with their improvements.

The bank manager introduced her to the three tellers. Mrs. Jane Priebe was a strong-faced widow in her forties with a prim demeanor. The one man on the floor was Mr. Horace Allen, who looked as though a strong wind could knock him over. As he was being introduced, he nearly jumped out of his skin when a team and wagon rushed down the street outside. Last was Miss Samantha McHenry, whose gleaming smile lit up her otherwise plain face.

As Mr. Liberty introduced Miss McHenry, his hand strayed up to make sure his silk ribbon tie was in place, and he smiled for the first time that morning. Nancy would have needed smoked glasses to miss the beaming look on Miss McHenry's face as she gazed back at the balding, bespectacled manager. Nancy stole a quick glance around to see both of the other tellers either looking away or hiding a smile.

Well, I'll be, she thought, her estimation of Mr. Liberty rising a notch. *They're sweet on each other, and everyone else knows it except the two of them. Well, back to business. The two women seem all right, although I'm going to recommend that Mr. Allen not be on duty tomorrow,* she thought, glancing over at him. *He's really too tense to be in this business in the first place. Besides, three women in the cages will probably seem like an easier target.*

"Ahem," Nancy said, breaking the doe-eyed stares of the man and woman before her. "Shall we continue?"

"Ahh—of course, right this way," Mr. Liberty said, flushing.

He escorted Nancy to the vault behind the teller stand. This was also modern, built of solid brick walls with an iron-barred door at the only entrance. The safe was in a re-inforced corner of the vault, behind yet another cage of thick steel bars and a matching door. *This is a bit better,* she thought. *The only way robbers can get at the cash inside is if they strike during the day, when the manager can be coerced into opening the vault.*

"Mr. Liberty, I must say that your physical fortifications are quite impressive, but I haven't seen any armed guards. I am a bit concerned about the human factor involved in the safekeeping of large amounts of money here."

Liberty raised one eyebrow and nodded as he led her back out of the vault. "Due to recent firings, we've had to—modify our security procedures somewhat, but I think you'll find them more than adequate," he said with an odd little smile. "Since we're expecting unpleasant company tomorrow, I will show you where we keep the guns."

Nancy walked beside the manager through the pass-through in the counter to the center of the main floor just as the front door swung open. But instead of a nattily dressed businessman, three men in tan dusters and Stetsons, with kerchiefs over their faces, entered, all of them brandishing pistols.

"Nobody move and nobody gets hurt!" the lead man ordered as the door swung shut behind them.

*   *   *

As THEY ENTERED the bank, Jared was trying to figure out a way to change his original plan, but discarding each new ploy as he came up with it.

Tanner, MacKinnon, and he were supposed to collect the cash inside. The two other men, Joseph Bailey and George Nichols, had split up, one watching the front of the bank, the other keeping the horses ready in front of the hotel across the street, waiting for the rest of the gang to come out. Once they had gotten what they came for and the employees were locked in the vault, Tanner would tell Bailey, who'd signal Nichols to bring the horses to the front of the bank. The five of them would mount up and head out of town, all within five minutes. Until Jared could pick out the Pinkerton, he didn't dare make any kind of move, knowing that Tanner wouldn't hesitate to kill anyone who got in his way.

Jared's .44-40 Remington pistol felt heavy in his hand as he strode through the door behind Tanner, with MacKinnon almost too close behind him. He heard Tanner's first words, followed by, "Everyone put your hands up nice and slow."

Inside, Jared looked around. They had entered into the middle of a large rectangular room, with a counter for the tellers that divided it lengthwise down the middle. Behind that was a barred-off area that he assumed was the vault. On the wall to the left was a banister staircase, and in the middle were five people, all staring at them with various expressions of surprise and dismay on their faces.

The tellers, two women and one man, were all behind the counter, and a lean man in spectacles and a single-breasted suit coat who Jared assumed was the manager was standing next to a well-dressed young woman, her purse dangling from the crook of her elbow as she watched them all intently. From the dark look on her face, Jared got the distinct impression that she was annoyed with something more than the holdup.

Well, he ain't the Pinkerton, that's for sure, Jared thought, dismissing the man next to her. *That leaves the other fella at the counter.* He tried to catch the teller's eye, but everyone was watching Tanner.

"All right, folks, we just need a few minutes of your time, and then we'll be on our way," Tanner said. "You three." He indicated the line of tellers with the muzzle of his .45-caliber Frontier revolver. "Y'all empty those cash drawers into one bag and hand them to my associate here." He nodded toward Jared. "You, the manager-lookin' fella—"

"Just take whatever's there and get out," he said, causing the woman to glance up at him, obviously surprised, her small purse swinging on her arm as she turned.

"Now, now, no need to get testy. You're going to go in the back with me and open that safe. Then, once we've collected what we came for, we'll be out of your hair." Jared could hear the smile in Tanner's voice, but his pistol was rock-steady.

Tanner began walking over to "escort'" the manager, and Jared caught a flash of movement from the man in the first teller cage. The instant Tanner blocked MacKinnon's view of him, the suited teller brought up not a sheaf of bills, but a deadly-looking black pistol.

"Duck, Boss," said MacKinnon, who had taken a half step back toward the door, while bringing a pair of engraved Colt .45 pistols up and drilling the man with two bullets in the heart. As the teller stumbled backward, his own gun barked, and Jared felt a burning pain flare in his upper chest, sending his own revolver spinning out of his hand.

Damn stupid son of a bitch shot me instead, he thought as he fell backward to the floor.

* * *

NANCY FELT LIKE the last thirty seconds had been the start of her own personal nightmare. In all her years as an agent she had never been at such a disadvantage. Her main weapon was stuck in her purse, she didn't know where her partner was, and worse, she didn't know who not to shoot. When Horace tried to shoot the nearest bandit, she saw Samantha and Mrs. Priebe both drop behind their stations, each woman grabbing and cocking a small pistol.

How can I keep this from becoming a bloodbath? she thought. *Which one is the damn Ranger? It can't be the shooter and it certainly isn't the leader. It must the one on the ground. At least I hope it's him. They've probably got lookouts too. Damn it, where the hell is Thomas?*

Nancy knew she had to try to keep the situation under some kind of control. Everyone was armed except Mr. Liberty, but there was absolutely nothing she could do with either of her guns right now.

"Son of a bitch!" the leader swore. "You all right?" he called across the room.

"Yeah . . . dumb bastard just winged me," Nancy heard a pain-filled voice reply. *He's still conscious, thank the stars,* she thought. *Now how can I use that?*

"What the hell's going on?" Another man said as he stuck his face in, a gloved hand concealing his mouth. "Everyone heard those shots. We gotta get out of here!"

"Bring the horses around to the side alley," the leader snapped. "We're getting what we came for and ride out the back. Move!" The other man disappeared.

"All right, godammit!" he said. "Anyone behind the counter's got three seconds to throw your guns out, or I blow the manager's head off." He finished crossing to Liberty and put his pistol to the other man's temple, thumbing back the hammer, the click loud in the sudden silence.

Nancy recognized the empty threat, since no one else could open the safe if Liberty was shot, but she also knew something the leader didn't.

A muffled sob was heard behind the wooden barrier.

"One . . . two . . ."

"All right," a high-pitched voice said. Then a small pistol was tossed over the counter, followed by another. The leader kicked both guns into a far corner behind him.

"Now both of you stand up." The two woman popped up, their hands in the air. Mrs. Priebe was frowning, and bright tears streaked Samantha's face.

"I'm sorry, Russell," she said.

"It'll be all right," he replied with only a slight tremor in his voice.

"Goddamn, everybody's armed around here except you," the leader said to Liberty. He regarded Nancy for a moment. "What about you, missy? You packing a cannon in that dainty purse of yours?"

He's a cool one, I'll say that much, Nancy thought. "No, sir, I just came in to open an account for my husband."

"Well, you sure picked the wrong day," he replied. "All right, you ladies are going to all walk in a line out here over to that wall." The leader pointed to the far wall near where the Ranger was on the floor, a large red stain growing on his shirtfront near the collar. "He'll keep an eye on all of you, and 'Russell' and I will visit the safe."

Nancy could hardly believe her luck. She led the way across the room, the other women right behind her.

"Line up against the wall, and keep those hands up," the other gunman said, his pistols tracking them all the way.

The other man stuck his head in. "Horses are ready. One minute!"

The leader shoved Liberty through the doorway behind the counter. "Let's go."

It's now or never, Nancy thought, looking down at the injured man a few feet away. "Your man's hurt pretty bad. Looks like a broken collarbone."

"He'll ride if he wants to live," the man replied.

"I could help him with that wound, bind it so he could move," she said.

"What, you a nurse or something?" he asked.

"As a matter of fact I am," Nancy replied. "My husband is a doctor, just moved to town. I can help him."

"Why would you do that?" he asked, suspicion darkening his features.

"To get you all out of here, why do you think?" Mrs. Priebe snapped.

The man's pistol swung over to point at her head, and for a moment Nancy thought the older woman had pushed the killer too far, but he nodded slowly. "All right," he said, edging closer to the door and lifting up a window shade to look outside. "Make it quick, and no talking."

"Don't worry," the injured man said, reaching for his pistol with his other hand, "I'll cover her."

"No, you won't," the outlaw said, one of his guns moving to cover both of them. "Just 'cause the boss trusts you don't mean I do. You just set there and let her work, boy."

Nancy bent down next to the man, who was frowning and breathing rapidly, and set her purse down between the two of them. "Hold still—" she began.

"I said no talking!" the gunman said.

Nancy frowned. *Now how am I going to let him know who I am?* She peeled the shirt back and leaned closer to him, and then the idea hit her. Making sure the man was looking at her, she winked, then she got down on one knee and, taking her skirt in both hands, ripped it up the side.

* * *

JARED WASN'T SURE what had surprised him more, the bullet he had taken, or this slip of a woman who seemed to be making eyes at him.

What kind of game is she playing? He thought. *This ain't the time or the place for—*

His thoughts trailed off when he saw what she had revealed under her skirt. Strapped over her right calf stocking was a four-shot Colt .41 Cloverleaf derringer in a cunning leather holster. She looked at him again, and the message in her eyes was more than clear.

Jared's eyes widened, and he tried not to gasp in pain as she probed his wound. *She's the Pinkerton!* he thought, glancing past her to see what MacKinnon was doing. He was keeping an eye on them and the window. Jared heard Tanner's voice from the back, but couldn't make out what he was saying.

Tearing a strip of cloth off her dress, the woman drew the small pistol and hid it under the cloth, placing the bundle directly on his wound. Wincing with the effort, Jared placed his hand on it, feeling the steel of the gun frame grate against his broken bone. He lifted the cloth a bit, letting the weapon slip down between his left arm and his side. The woman had torn another strip, and held the first wad of cloth in place while she looped the second strip over his shoulder and wrapped it around him. Jared grimaced, but managed to reach across his body to get his hand on the pistol, hiding it in his palm.

"Hurry up over there!" the gunman said.

"I'm almost done," she called over his shoulder.

What about you? he thought, frowning and nodding at her. The woman had finished binding his wound, and she looked at him and actually smiled. Opening her purse, she slipped out a compact full-frame revolver. She made sure the two women standing next to them saw it, then hid it in a fold of her dress as her eyes flicked toward the man at the door.

Jared nodded once, working the derringer into his hand.

A series of shots outside made them all start, and the same man's voice sounded outside. "Come on, the law's coming!"

Just then Tanner's voice from the back of the room. "All right, boys, we got what we came for, let's git!" A second later the manager stumbled through the door, followed by Tanner, two bulging money sacks slung over his shoulder.

The woman clutched the gun to her chest and began to rise. Jared took a deep breath and cocked the pistol by his side, waiting for the right moment.

NANCY'S HEART HAMMERED against her ribs, and her breath quickened in her throat, but otherwise her mind was as calm as could be, given the circumstances. She remembered a piece of advice her mentor Carter Thompson had drilled into her when she was first starting out. . . .

"If you've got a gun, and your opponent doesn't know it, that's good for at least a moment of surprise. Keep calm, aim, and then shoot."

Yeah, but it didn't help poor Horace, she thought. Hearing the commotion of the men returning behind her, she cocked the hammer of her short-barreled Colt Sheriff's Model double-action .45 and rose to her feet.

"Time to go—" she heard the leader call out as she began to turn, hiding the pistol at her side. The leader had come out, pushing Liberty ahead of him. The other gunman had holstered one of his pistols and was reaching for the door.

That was when Nancy took one step forward and brought up her pistol, aiming it at the first gunman. "Pinkerton agent, don't move!"

Both men gaped at her for a second, then the leader snapped, "Jared, shoot her!"

Nancy gritted her teeth, not daring to look down. *God, I hope I made the right choice.* Out of the corner of her eye she saw the man on the floor beside her raise the small pistol she had given him and point it at the bandit near the door. "I can't do that, Baird."

"Shit! Kill 'em all!" the man shouted.

Time seemed to slow to a crawl. Nancy heard the Ranger's pistol roar, and the gunslinger jerked as the bullet hit him. It didn't drop him, however, and he grabbed for his other revolver while steadying his first gun on her. Aiming at his chest, Nancy squeezed the trigger. The .45 flashed, its recoil jolting her arm back, and she saw the bandit's shirt puff where the bullet plowed through him. He stopped dead in his tracks like a run-down clockwork toy, the pistols slipping from his hand to the floor, followed by his lifeless body.

Nancy was already aiming at the leader, but by the time she drew a bead on him he was behind Mr. Liberty, one arm wrapped around the bank manager's throat, the other holding a pistol so tight against his temple Nancy saw a drop of blood well up from the front sight digging into his skin. Above the roaring in her ears, Nancy heard more gunfire from outside, but all of her attention was focused on the man hiding behind the manager. Only a bit of his face was visible behind the other man's head, and the pistol never wavered.

"All right, Baird," she said, trying to keep her voice steady. "Nobody else wants to die today."

"You think I don't know that, Pinkerton?" the man said, pulling Liberty with him toward the door. "Least of all this one I got right here."

"You can't ride out of this, Baird," the man beside her said. "Let him go."

"So I can face Texas justice? No, thanks," the outlaw replied. "No one's crazy enough to take a shot at me now, not when I've got him. We're going to ride out of here, and I'll let him go a few miles outside of town."

"Damn it, it's over! No one's gonna let that happen!" the Ranger said.

"He's got that right," Nancy said, trying to steady her aim on the bandit.

"Lady, you wouldn't dare shoot—" the bandit began as everyone heard the stomp of boots on the bank porch, followed by a figure crashing through the door.

"The sheriff's outside—what the hell—" The lookout's words trailed off as he took in the scene before him.

Nobody moved for a moment. Then Baird's pistol left Liberty's head for a second, swinging toward Nancy. As soon as it did, the bank manager opened his mouth and bit down on the gang leader's forearm. Baird howled in pain, and clubbed his attacker with the butt of his gun, dropping him to the floor.

"Shoot, goddammit!" he yelled.

But his order was too late. The Ranger's pistol barked twice, and the lookout's muslin shirt sprouted two bloody fountains as the bullets hit him in the side. The man fell backward through the doorway, his gun shooting the floor as he dropped.

Off balance, Baird staggered backward, snapping a shot off at Nancy. She kept her head, ducking a bit as the bullet passed by, and lined him up again. Her gun kicked, and the outlaw winced as her shot struck home. Nancy squeezed the trigger again, and heard the roar of the Ranger's gun beside her as they both hit the bandit leader. One of the bullets punched through the bag of money, sending a puff of green paper fragments into the air. The outlaw stumbled against the door, his weight slamming it closed. His bloody fingers fumbled at the knob, then slid down it, leaving a red trail behind him.

"Damn it . . . I thought it might be you . . ." he said. "Keeping you . . . in here wasn't enough, I guess." He laughed once, a trickle of blood dribbling from his mouth, then slumped over, his pistol thudding to the floor.

Keeping her own gun trained on him, Nancy slowly approached the body, staying low so she wouldn't accidentally get shot by the deputies. When she got close enough, she kicked the revolver out of his hand.

"I think he's done for," she said.

"Nancy!" Thomas's voice called from outside. "Are you all right?"

"Yes, I'm fine," she called back, biting off a stronger retort. "There's a hurt Texas Ranger in here, though."

In a moment Thomas was inside, followed by a half-dozen deputies. His normally immaculate suit coat was covered with dust, which also smudged his face, and his voice was a shade higher than usual.

"I was out back when the shooting started; then I saw a man lead five horses into the alleyway," he said. "He had a gun in his hand, so I waited until the right moment and told him to drop his weapon. He turned and pointed it at me and—uh, well, I guess I shot him." He stared down at the pistol still in his hand as if he had never seen it before.

"You had to do what you had to do, it's part of the job. And it's never the easiest part. Are you all right?" she asked, placing her hand on his arm.

"Uh—I think so, I'm not really sure, I mean, it all happened so fast," Thomas said. "I mean, he could have killed somebody."

"Not to mention you," Nancy replied with a wry smile. "But you reacted well, and I think you'll be just fine."

Thomas brightened at her words of encouragement, the

first compliment she had paid him since they had met.

Nancy looked around for a moment. Samantha had made it over to Russell Liberty, and the two were holding each other in the middle of the room, oblivious to everything around them. Mrs. Priebe had shakily taken charge, collecting the various dropped pistols and, wiping tears from her face, directing men to remove Horace's shroud-covered body. A doctor had been summoned and was tending to the Ranger's injury. She walked over to him, suddenly weary as the rush of the fight wore off.

JARED LOOKED UP to see the woman standing over him again. His eyes were a bit dull from the combination of pain and morphine, but he found he could focus on her easily enough.

"Is he going to be all right?" she asked.

"His arm will be bound for several weeks, but he'll be fine," the doctor said. "Did you do this?"

"Yes," she replied.

"It's good work, given the conditions. Saved him from losing more blood."

"She does damn fine work," Jared said, his voice thick. "Ma'am, I owe you an apology."

She frowned. "Why, whatever for?"

"I never in a hundred years figured that the Pinkerton here would be a woman," the Ranger said with a grin. "You proved me wrong."

Nancy smiled in return and nodded. "I believe you did most of the work on this one, Mr. . . ."

"Please, my name's Jared."

"And you can call me Nancy," she replied. "Nice working with you, Jared."

"Ma—Nancy, the pleasure was mine," Jared said, settling back and letting the doctor finish his work. "Any time you need to call on the Rangers again, you just mention my name."

"I'll remember that, Jared," she said. "I'll surely remember that."

The Promotion

〜◦〜

by Larry D. Sweazy

Larry D. Sweazy lives in Noblesville, Indiana, with his wife and dog, a Rhodesian ridgeback. He spent four years in Texas in the San Antonio and Arlington areas before moving back to Indiana to pursue his dream of being a writer. Larry has worked as a restaurant manager, janitor, funeral director's assistant, karate teacher, insurance salesman, and stockbroker along the way, and is currently a freelance indexer, with nearly three hundred back-of-the-book indexes to his credit. His short stories have previously appeared in *Hardboiled*, *Plot Magazine*, and *Kracked Mirror Mysteries*.

THERE WAS THE usual stir at night as Darly carefully slid out of bed. Her steps were light, intentional, and Samuel "Red" Wolfe knew the path his wife of twenty-two years would take. She would ease along the bed and down the hall under the control of a nightmare that would not, could not, go away, to their son's empty room. He would find her at first light, balled up on the floor next to the bed, a shirt or a blanket wrapped tight in her fist.

Red tossed and turned after his wife left their bed, but sleep came more easily for him, even in the days following Jason's death. Holding onto Darly and what remained of their life took all of the energy he had left. And now they were moving back to Lubbock from San Antonio, leaving the house Jason grew up in. Darly had protested at first, but in the end, even she could not deny Red the opportunity to become the Texas Rangers' Assistant Commander of Company C.

"Life goes on," she had said, and then did not speak a word to anyone for a week.

Red awoke a few hours later in bed alone. The house was a maze of cardboard boxes, with the exception of Jason's room. Darly was lying on the bed this time, staring at the ceiling. The room remained just as it was the day Jason died. A shrine to a ten-year-old boy who dreamed of playing football for Texas Tech and becoming a Texas Ranger just like his father had. The walls were red-and-white-striped, a poster of the Masked Rider wearing black riding clothes, mask, bolero hat, and red cape, mounted on a black quarter horse, leading the football team on to the field, hung over the bed. The school fight song, the paper yellowed, hung sideways on a peg just above a row of Pop Warner football trophies on the dresser. Jason had the makings of a great quarterback. Everybody said he was the next gift to Tech from the Wolfe family.

"Hey, baby," Red said. "I have to meet with the moving company and tie up some loose ends at the office. Can you do a few things for me?"

Darly, Darlene to her parents and the church, did not acknowledge Red. There was no sign of the former college cheerleader he once knew and worshiped; she was nothing but a withering yellow rose, her blond hair dull and unkempt, and her blue eyes lifeless as a stagnant pond.

"We can't leave him, Red. I won't."

He had tried arguing, even pleading, to get past her grief, but time was running out. "I'll call Betty. She might be your sister, but she's getting darned tired of helping out. She's done her fair share, Darly."

Darly exhaled, looked over at him and said, "He's alone, Red. All alone. I'm his mother, what am I supposed to do?"

AFTER LEAVING THE movers, Red drove to the headquarters of Company D in San Antonio. In the fields beyond the highway, Indian paintbrush, prairie phlox, with a few bluebonnets and scarlet pimpernels mixed in, were in full bloom. South Texas was unusually colorful and fragrant this year, but Red had barely noticed it was spring.

He had the window down, the radio turned down low. A muffled Guy Clark song droned on about too much to drink and lost love. Two files sat underneath his Stetson. The contract from the movers, and the other, tattered and worn, held all of his notes from the Hardy case.

It was the one case that haunted him, a case Red Wolfe had sworn to solve before he left San Antonio.

Jason was a little over four years old and Red had been at Company D for about a year when he caught the case. Life was good then. Everything was bright and hopeful. Now, it looked like he had failed; even though he was almost certain he knew who the killer was, there was just not enough evidence to bring the case to trial.

Red dug into the glove box and pulled out a pack of Marlboros. He lit a cigarette, chastising himself, but resigned to the fact that his health no longer mattered like it used to. After a couple of long drags, he played the Hardy case over and over in his head, like he'd done a million times before.

THE FIRST THING Red saw was a pool of dried blood in the road, an unusual oil spot that shimmered in the reflection of the setting sun.

July in Government Canyon was as beautiful as it was

miserable. The temperature had peaked at over one hundred degrees for the last seventeen days, but the Edwards Aquifer, the lone source of San Antonio's drinking water, kept the area lush. Oak-juniper-mesquite woodlands peppered the hill country, and it was not unusual to see a feral hog, or hear a bobcat scream at night.

Spanish moss dripped from oak trees just beyond the road that led to the back entrance of the park boundaries that encased most of the canyon, casting a mosaic of shadows on the blood. Red was heartened, excited that the blood might be the first break in the disappearance of Peggy Hardy, a sixteen-year-old high school long-distance track star, who had vanished three days before.

Winslow Trout, the sheriff of Bexar County, sauntered up to Red. A group of deputies were scouring the roadside and the woods beyond.

"You sure this isn't a wild-goose chase, Win? Could be nothing more than roadkill," Red said.

The sheriff chuckled. "Some things never change. You're the biggest damn skeptic in Texas. I figured the same thing when I got the call. Probably a goddamned porcupine. But those skid marks over there, and the fact that this was Peggy Hardy's daily training route, gave me reason to check it out. Trail's getting cold the way it is, so here we are. Where's Skylar? I thought you two were joined at the hip."

Winslow Trout chuckled again; his spare-tire belly shook inside his uniform like a bowl of chocolate pudding. He was a little over fifty years old, and the years of sitting behind a desk and in a police cruiser was taking its toll on the sheriff. Red never doubted Trout's ability, though; he was as smart as a fox and could still run down a bull, or a twenty-year-old punk, if he had to.

"Skylar'll be here, don't worry. He wouldn't want to miss seeing your smiling face."

"Good, I got a couple of new jokes for him."

"Who called?"

"Anonymous. Said we ought to come out and check it out. Skid marks and blood. That's it. Whoever they were they called from a pay phone downtown."

"Figures."

"My sister's kid goes to the same school as the Hardy girl," Trout said. *"This thing's got everybody shook to the bone. Things like this don't happen around here."*

"I know," Red answered, staring at a deputy who was studying something on the ground intently. *"From what I can see, Peggy Hardy had everything going for her. It won't be long before the press gets wind we're out here. They've been camped out at her house like a bunch of damn vultures, holing up the parents inside like prisoners. I sure do feel sorry for them."*

The deputy stood up and shouted, *"I found a running shoe."*

EIGHT YEARS HAD passed since they found Peggy Hardy stuffed in a culvert in Government Canyon, her body broken and battered by the impact of a vehicle. The worst part of it was she had been raped. Forensics pointed to the occurrence of rape before Peggy died. Speculation was she had escaped and her attacker had run her down. But speculation was as far as they got in the investigation. There were no footprints at the crime scene other than the attending officers', which confounded Red to this day. How could the killer not have left any tracks? Two suspects had been cleared. A teenage boy Peggy Hardy had broken off a relationship with a week before was cleared because he was out of town at the time of the disappearance, and Peggy's father was cleared almost immediately.

The only other suspect they could never clear was Junior

Barton, a backyard mechanic who lived just up the road from where they found body. Barton had admitted to talking to Peggy that day. But Red was sure, even after eight years, that Junior wasn't telling him everything he needed to know about his relationship with Peggy Hardy.

After he made his stop at the office, Red's last unofficial act of duty in San Antonio was to give Junior one last visit.

He flipped the cigarette out the window and pushed down on the accelerator. It took him ten minutes to arrive at the cement block building that housed Company D. Traffic buzzed up and down the highway, but all Red could hear was the memory of Peggy Hardy's mother pleading with him to find the killer.

Two months after they buried Peggy, Martha Hardy took a handful of sleeping pills, intent on seeing her daughter sooner rather than later, in the afterlife. She failed, at least immediately. Martha Hardy lay in a coma for eight months and eight days before she finally died. Red had worried that Darly would do the same thing after Jason's death. He was sure he would come home and find her sprawled on the sofa, an empty pill bottle on the floor. The fear had passed after a few years, but recently, he'd seen that same faraway look in Darly's eyes, just like he'd seen in Martha Hardy's.

Ray Hardy, Martha's husband and Peggy's father, was left behind in more pain than any man ought to be able to survive. But Ray hung in there, hoping, praying that someday Peggy's killer would be brought to justice.

"Hey, Red, Skylar's been lookin' for ya," Bess Tildeman, the dispatcher, said. Someone had failed to inform Bess that beehive hair went out in the sixties. Normally, just the sound of her voice made Red smile, but not today. "I think he wants to take us all to Luby's for lunch."

"I won't be here. Tell Skylar I'll be in my office for about ten minutes," Red said.

"You're gonna miss Luby's? Shoot, today is meatloaf day."

The door buzzed open and Red walked past Bess without answering. He could hear her moaning about the meatloaf being just like her momma's until the door slammed shut.

His office was in the same state as his house; nothing but a pile of cardboard boxes ready for transport. Everything was packed away, his desk clear. He needed to call Winslow Trout and make sure Junior Barton was still at home.

Red had asked Win to stake out the Barton place two days earlier just to make sure he wouldn't miss his last chance to catch Junior by surprise. Win felt strongly that Junior was involved in Peggy's death too. But no matter how hard he tried, Red could not make the link to nail Junior down. Junior's story never changed, no matter the threats, or how intensely he was interrogated. Junior said he saw her on her normal run, waved, gave her some water, then went into town and grabbed a beer. The bad thing was that Winslow Trout saw him pull into the bar.

A sealed manila envelope sat squarely on his desk. He knew immediately what the envelope contained.

"You might want to wait to open that until you're on your own," Jane Sewell said as she poked her head in the door.

Red looked up, always glad to see Jane. Today she had a long face and a look in her eye that made him think she'd just done something she didn't want to. Jane was a forensic artist who came to the post in 2000 with the creation of UCIT, the Unsolved Crimes Investigation Unit. Red and Skylar were the lead team, and it was that position that had garnered him the promotion to Lubbock.

"You didn't have to do this," he said.

"You asked." Jane walked in the office and faced Red across the desk.

Jane Sewell was ten years younger than Red, a leggy
A&M grad who had talent seeping from her unpainted fin-
gernails. There were times when he felt a burst of energy between them, and had been tempted on more than occasion to
find out if the attraction was mutual. But he could never
force himself to cross the line. He loved Darly too much to
hurt her like that, and had enough respect for Jane not to
reach out to her from the depths of his own loneliness.

"It was the least I could do," Jane said. "I can't imagine
what it's going to be like around here without you."

"I won't be far."

"Lubbock's a world away."

"True," Red said, gently turning the envelope in his hands.

"Bess is scared to death you're going to miss your
party. . . ."

"Meatloaf is one thing. But I already have lunch plans.
I'll be at the party. Tell her not to worry her fool head off."

Jane smiled. "All right."

"See you there?"

"I wouldn't miss it." Jane turned to leave, but stopped
midway to the door. She started to say something, drew
back, shook her head, and said, "You need to wait, Red.
Don't open it until you're in Lubbock."

"All right." When she was gone from his sight, Red exhaled, restrained his temptation, and put the envelope aside.
He picked up the phone and called Winslow Trout. It was a
quick conversation. Junior Barton was at home putting a
new engine in his truck.

"I was about to put up a missing sign for you," Skylar
Beaumont said as he walked into the office. "We need to go
over some things before you leave."

"I'm going to be gone for a while. Going out to Wayland to have lunch with Winslow Trout."

Red knew Skylar was a little anxious about taking over

the UCIT team, but it sure felt like he was in a hurry to show him the door and make the office his own. It might have been Red's own discomfort, not telling Skylar what he was up to, but the last thing he needed was Skylar tagging along. His visit with Junior wasn't going to be a by-the-book visit.

"Come on, Red, we need to go over schedules and transfers. I still don't have a handle on all this paperwork crap. And passing up Luby's for lunch with Winslow Trout doesn't seem like a fair deal."

"Bess'll help you through the paperwork. Besides, I won't be gone long, Win and I go back a long way, you know that. He really helped me with the lay of the land when I was first starting out here. What the hell did I know about the hill country? I would've been lost without his help."

"You're right," Skylar said. "I guess I'm more nervous than I thought. But any time you sit down with Winslow Trout it turns into an all-day affair."

"Not today. Really, trust me, I'll be back in plenty of time."

"If you say so."

"I do."

Skylar backed away, hands in the air. "I'll see you later then."

Red nodded.

"Tell Winslow a joke for me," Skylar said.

"You know I'm not any good at telling jokes."

"It wouldn't be same and you know it."

"All right, what's the joke?"

"You know what the fish said when it hit a cement wall?"

"Nope," Red answered.

"Dam."

RED COULD DRIVE to Wayland blindfolded. In the days after Peggy Hardy's body was found, he'd made the trip a hundred times. The last couple of years had kept him away, though if he had a chance, he'd stop by and see Ray. Those visits were few and far between, especially after Jason's death. The silence of the Hardy house reminded him too much of his own home. And no matter how hard he tried, every time he was there, he could not keep his eyes off the locked door that led into Peggy's room. He wondered if Ray ever went in there. The last time he had stopped by to see Ray was a week ago. He had been putting off the trip, putting off telling Ray he was leaving for Lubbock. Ray had said something that affirmed his belief that Junior Barton was hiding something. He'd looked at Red and said, "Junior worked on Martha's car a lot. He always was a little sly. Every time she needed a tune-up she went out to see Junior."

It was common knowledge that Junior and Peggy knew each other, in an acquaintance kind of way, but this was the first time Ray had given Red any hint that there might've been something going on between Junior and Martha.

"I never could keep that woman fenced in," Ray had said.

WAYLAND WAS AN old stagecoach town, a heritage that was forgotten as much as it was frowned upon. Mostly, it was a last stop for tourists heading into Government Canyon. A mix of trailer parks, barking dogs, a bait shop, a Stop-n-Go, and a row of broken-down buildings that suggested a moment of prosperity had existed and then evaporated all too quick.

Junior Barton lived in an old house that butted up against Rivell Creek about a mile and a half up the road from where Peggy Hardy's body was found.

Red pulled into Junior's driveway without hesitation.

He could see Junior bent over the front of an old Chevy truck. Two tick-hounds stood up warily and let out a few low-level barks. Red waited for Junior to turn around before he opened the door.

Junior was in his mid-thirties, skinny as a rail, a true nuts-and-bolts genius who had fallen on hard times since the Hardy case had put him in a bad light. Red wasn't sure how Junior made his living these days, nor did he care.

"You better get the hell off my land, Wolfe, unless you got a warrant."

Red stopped at the bumper, arms crossed, his glare shielded by his sunglasses.

"Just a social visit, Junior. Call off the dogs."

"I ought to let them tear you to shreds."

"I'd hate to have to shoot a good dog, Junior."

Junior ran his hands through his scraggly hair and threw a wrench to the ground. "Tiny, Blackie, shut the hell up."

The dogs quit barking, but continued to growl as they skulked to the other side of the porch.

"A social visit? I guess that means I don't need my lawyer, now does it, Wolfe?"

"Can't see why an innocent man would need a lawyer after so many years, Junior. But you're right, you won't be needing a lawyer today."

"That a threat?"

"No threats, Junior. I just have one question for you, and then I'll be on my way."

Junior smiled. "You still think I'm stupid, don't you, Wolfe?" And then the smile faded. "Where's your partner? I thought Rangers always worked in pairs."

"Not today. I told you, this is a social visit."

"Yeah, and I'm the friggin' Easter Bunny," Junior said. "Don't expect no iced tea."

"Just an answer, Junior, and I'll be on my way."

"I already answered every question I've been asked."

"New question."

Junior muttered something under his breath, and then leaned back against the truck. "You're not going to leave, are you?"

"You're going to answer me one way or another, Junior. Just depends on how hard you want to make it."

Junior studied Red for a moment, looked up and down the empty road, and then said, "All right, ask. But I'm tellin' you, I already told you everything I know."

Red uncrossed his arms. "You saw Peggy Hardy every day, waved at her. Even gave her a glass of water a couple of times."

"Yeah, nothing new there."

"Let me finish."

Junior nodded.

"Ray Hardy told me you worked on a Martha's car a couple of times in the months before Peggy disappeared."

"I worked on a lot of cars back then, what of it?"

"Ray kind of insinuated that you worked on Martha's car a little more often than everybody knew about the last time I talked to him."

"Can't rightly say. But Ray Hardy would say just about anything to see me burn."

Red walked toward Junior. "Let me put it this way, Junior. Were you and Martha Hardy having an affair?"

"That's the stupidest question anybody's ever asked me, Wolfe. I knew Martha Hardy ever since she was in high school. I liked her, but not like that, she was too messed up. She came out here a lot, dropped off her car, and disappeared for a while. I can tell you who she was having an affair with, though. . . ."

FARLEY'S DINER SAT at the crossroads of Highway 45 and 51. North would take you straight to the Alamo, south to Mexico, east to Tyler, and west to Lubbock. All Red wanted to do was head north, sweep Darly into his arms, and head for Lubbock. But he knew he couldn't. He had to finish what he'd started.

Right now, he sure wished Skylar was with him.

Winslow Trout's county cruiser was sitting in Farley's parking lot. Two other cars sat at the back of the building.

Red walked in to the smell of chicken-fried steak and the sound of Win laughing, probably at one of his own jokes.

"'Bout time you showed up, I was gonna send the posse out to look for you," Win said.

Seems like a lot of people are looking for me today, Red thought. He was feeling a little nervous, a little uncertain, and that was not a feeling he was used to dealing with.

A waitress in her early forties with too much makeup on backed away from the booth Win was sitting in.

"Can I get you anything, sweetie?" she said to Red.

"A Dr. Pepper'd be just fine."

"Anything else?"

"That'll do."

"Bring him some of those cheese fries, Wanda. I'm goddamned addicted to those things," Win said.

"I'm not hungry."

"Well, bring 'em out anyway, I'll eat 'em."

Wanda headed for the kitchen, shouting, "Another order of fries for the sheriff, Ernie, and put some extra sauce on them. Win likes it hot."

"I sure do, baby," he said with a belly laugh.

Red slid into an orange vinyl booth and lit a cigarette.

"That's going to kill you one of these days, Red."

"Yeah, like those cheese fries are the foundation of the food pyramid."

"Damn, Red, when did you get a sense of humor?"

"Skylar's rubbing off on me."

Win sopped up the last bit of cheese on the plate in front

of him with a limp fry and inhaled it. "How is Skylar?"

"Nervous. He sent a joke for you."

"Good, I haven't had much to laugh at today."

Red stared at Win for minute, studying his face, thinking of all of the time they had spent together. He stubbed out the cigarette and dropped his right hand to his side.

"What do you get when you cross a Texas Ranger with a mechanic?"

Win stopped chewing. "This don't sound like a joke Skylar would tell. I don't know, what do you get?"

"Sooner or later," Red said, "you get the truth."

"How come I'm not laughing?"

"Because I already been out to Junior Barton's place. I always knew he was holding back, but I figured he was guilty. That's what you wanted isn't it, Win?"

"I don't know what the hell you're talking about, Red."

"I made a mistake a long time ago. I was looking at the biggest clue there was in the investigation and I didn't know it."

Win shifted in his seat. His face was drawn tight, flushed, and his eyes were darting around the room, avoiding contact with Red at all costs.

"Now, if you're thinking about doing anything stupid, you ought to know my finger's on the trigger, and I'll blow your balls off before you can say boy howdy."

"Before you start accusin' a man of something, Red, you better know . . ."

Wanda walked to the table with a white china plate full of cheese fries. "Here you go, boys," she said.

Win slid his foot out from underneath the table and tripped the waitress. As she fell, distracting Red, Win jumped up, grabbed Wanda around the neck, and put his gun to her head.

The plate of fries shattered on the table and Wanda

screamed at the top of her lungs. Red reacted out of instinct. He threw his left hand up to deflect the shards of china while he kept a tight grip on his weapon. He raised the Colt revolver, automatically training on the center of Win's forehead.

"Looks like we got us a Mexican standoff, Red. Now lay down your gun, and nothing will happen to sweet Wanda here."

"I never figured you for a man who went after young girls, Win. Junior told me about you and Martha. Ray thought Junior and Martha were running around, but Junior cleared that up for me. It wasn't until he told me about you strong-arming him that I began to wonder whether or not you might have killed Peggy. So, I looked at my notes, at your reports, and damn if there wasn't a few things just a hair out of whack the day we found Peggy. You had about two hours unaccounted for. But why would we question you? Hell, I never even looked at it until today. My guess is it was you that called us out to the canyon, figuring you could throw the trail onto Junior. Your boot prints were everywhere around Peggy's body, but that made sense, didn't it? I never could understand how the killer got away without leaving prints. Now I do. Junior's alibi was tight, other than nobody being around when Peggy ran by. But it was enough, wasn't it, Win? Enough not to send an innocent man to prison and to keep the scent off you. As long as Junior kept his mouth shut about you and Martha, you were never a suspect. And you had that covered, didn't you, affirming Junior's alibi?"

Tears were streaming down Wanda's face.

"I had to do something, Red. The little brat found out about me and her momma. She was gonna tell her daddy."

"And you raped and killed her to keep her quiet? Come on, Win."

Red saw Ernie out of the corner of his eye slowly making his way out of the kitchen with a butcher knife in his hand.

"Things got out of hand," Win said. "I figured she liked it hot, like her momma."

Ernie was about three feet behind the sheriff when a customer walked in the door.

Win jumped at the bell and caught sight of Ernie. He swung Wanda around and shot Ernie in the stomach.

The customer, a weary traveling salesman, ran back out the door.

Red lunged at Win, knocking Wanda into the booth, and rolled onto the floor. He got one shot off as he gained his balance.

Winslow Trout staggered backward as a bloody hole appeared just below his heart. "Damn, Red, that was the worst joke I ever heard," Win said, and then fell to the floor with a resounding thud.

Two hours later, Red was walking out of Ray Hardy's house. He wasn't surprised when he saw Skylar pull into the drive.

"How's Ray?"

"He'll be all right," Red said. "He didn't take it too well when he found out that Martha and Win were having a fling, but he knew she was stepping out with somebody. He just kept saying how all this was his fault. If he would have left when he found out, Peggy would still be alive. I know how he feels. If I wouldn't have let Jason walk home from school that day, he would've never been hit by a car. We can't change the past, I guess, but we'll keep playing it over and over in our heads wishing we could."

Skylar put a hand on Red's shoulder. "It's been a lot of years and that's still a hard one to swallow. It sounds like Ernie and Wanda are going to be all right." he said, waiting a beat before saying anything else. "I don't figure you're going to be up to your party, but I talked to Betty a while ago, and she said Darly would be there."

A slight smile crossed Red's face. "I'll be there."

"All right, then."

Red exhaled. "Funny, but I'm going to miss Win."

Skylar nodded. "Me too," he said, and then drove away.

Red took one last look at the Hardy house, and saw Ray cross the living room and head toward Peggy's room. Red looked away, went to his vehicle, sat down, lit a cigarette, and picked up the envelope that Jane Sewell had given him.

He pulled out a picture of Jason, fully rendered in acrylics. Jane had aged him to the present. All he had asked her to do was give him a head shot, an idea of what his son would look like today if he were still alive. Like always, Jane had gone above and beyond the call of duty and talent.

Jason was dressed in a Texas Tech football uniform, holding the football up in a victorious touchdown stance, smiling to a faceless crowd.

Copyrights and Permissions

ATTACKED. OUTRAGED. AVENEGED.

LYNCHED

A NOVEL OF WESTERN JUSTICE BY
ED GORMAN

WHEN MARSHALL BEN TULLY CAME RIDING BACK INTO
TOWN, THERE WASN'T A SOUL STIRRING.
NOT THE SPRAWLED, BLOODY MAN OUTSIDE HIS DOOR.
NOT THE STRANGER STRUNG UP OUT BACK.
NOT HIS RAVAGED WIFE.

A DIRTY KIND OF JUSTICE TOOK OVER WHILE HE WAS
AWAY, BUT NOW THAT HE'S BACK, NOT A SOUL
RESPONSIBLE WILL STIR FOR MUCH LONGER.

"Ed Gorman writes like a dream."
—Dean Koontz

**"One of the best Western
writers of our time."**
—*Rocky Mountain News*

Available wherever books are sold or at
www.penguin.com

LINGO BARNES IS ON HIS WAY TO DURANGO, COLORADO, WHEN HE STUMBLES UPON THE KIDNAPPING OF EMILY LOU COLTER. NOW HE MUST SAVE THE GIRL AND KEEP HIMSELF OUT OF THE LINE OF FIRE.

JUSTICE HAS A NEW HOME.

HANGING VALLEY

No one knows the American West better than

JACK BALLAS

Author of *West of the River*

0-425-18410-2

BERKLEY